P9-CMF-195

Author's National Edition

THE WRITINGS OF
MARK TWAIN
VOLUME XX

This is the authorized
Uniform Edition of all
my books.

Mark Twain.

Copyright, 1899, by S. L. Clemens
FROM THE PAINTING BY SPIRIDON, 1898

TOM SAWYER ABROAD
TOM SAWYER, DETECTIVE

AND OTHER STORIES, ETC. ETC.

BY

MARK TWAIN

(SAMUEL L. CLEMENS) 1835-1910

ILLUSTRATED

ΛΑΜΠΑΔΙΑ
ΕΧΟΝΤΕΣ
ΔΙΑΔΩ ΣΟΥΣΙΝ
ΑΛ ΛΗΛΟΙΣ

SILLIMAN COLLEGE
LIBRARY

HARPER & BROTHERS PUBLISHERS
NEW YORK AND LONDON

Copyright, 1878, by Slote, Woodman & Co.

Copyright, 1882, 1894, 1906, 1910, by Samuel L. Clemens

Copyright, 1896, by Harper & Brothers

Printed in the United States of America

C-R

PS
1300
.F11
V.20

12.00 (35m.)

1-31-39 Carol Cop

ILLUSTRATIONS

PORTRAIT 1898 . . . . *Spiridon* . *Frontispiece*

"WE CATCHED FISH" . . . *Dan Beard* . . . 84

MAP OF TOM SAWYER'S TRIP. 134

"I RECKON I GOT TO BE EXCUSED" *A. B. Frost* . . . 139

MAP OF PARIS . . . . . . *Mark Twain* . . . 435

35302

CONTENTS

TOM SAWYER ABROAD 7

TOM SAWYER, DETECTIVE 137

THE STOLEN WHITE ELEPHANT 229

SOME RAMBLING NOTES OF AN IDLE EXCURSION . . 254

THE FACTS CONCERNING THE RECENT CARNIVAL OF
    CRIME IN CONNECTICUT 305

ABOUT MAGNANIMOUS-INCIDENT LITERATURE . . . 326

PUNCH, BROTHERS, PUNCH 334

THE GREAT REVOLUTION IN PITCAIRN 341

ON THE DECAY OF THE ART OF LYING 355

THE CANVASSER'S TALE 363

AN ENCOUNTER WITH AN INTERVIEWER 371

PARIS NOTES 377

Contents

LEGEND OF SAGENFELD, IN GERMANY 380

SPEECH ON THE BABIES 388

SPEECH ON THE WEATHER 392

CONCERNING THE AMERICAN LANGUAGE 396

ROGERS 401

THE LOVES OF ALONZO FITZ CLARENCE AND
ROSANNAH ETHELTON 408

MAP OF PARIS 433

LETTER READ AT A DINNER 437

TOM SAWYER ABROAD

TOM SAWYER DETECTIVE
AND
OTHER STORIES

TOM SAWYER ABROAD

CHAPTER I.

TOM SEEKS NEW ADVENTURES

DO you reckon Tom Sawyer was satisfied after all them adventures? I mean the adventures we had down the river, and the time we set the darky Jim free and Tom got shot in the leg. No, he wasn't. It only just p'isoned him for more. That was all the effect it had. You see, when we three came back up the river in glory, as you may say, from that long travel, and the village received us with a torchlight procession and speeches, and everybody hurrah'd and shouted, it made us heroes, and that was what Tom Sawyer had always been hankering to be.

For a while he *was* satisfied. Everybody made much of him, and he tilted up his nose and stepped around the town as though he owned it. Some called him Tom Sawyer the Traveler, and that just swelled him up fit to bust. You see he laid over me and Jim considerable, because we only went down the river on a raft and came back by the steamboat, but Tom went

road a body ever see, and the racket of it was something awful. Nat passed his arms through the loops
and hung on for life and death, but pretty soon the
hack hit a rock and flew up in the air, and the bottom
fell out, and when it come down Nat's feet was on the
ground, and he see he was in the most desperate danger
if he couldn't keep up with the hack. He was horrible
scared, but he laid into his work for all he was worth,
and hung tight to the arm-loops and made his legs
fairly fly. He yelled and shouted to the driver to
stop, and so did the crowds along the street, for they
could see his legs spinning along under the coach, and
his head and shoulders bobbing inside through the
windows, and he was in awful danger; but the more
they all shouted the more the nigger whooped and
yelled and lashed the horses and shouted, "Don't you
fret, I'se gwine to git you dah in time, boss; I's gwine
to do it, sho'!" for you see he thought they were all
hurrying him up, and, of course, he couldn't hear anything for the racket he was making. And so they went
ripping along, and everybody just petrified to see it;
and when they got to the Capitol at last it was the
quickest trip that ever was made, and everybody said
so. The horses laid down, and Nat dropped, all tuckered out, and he was all dust and rags and barefooted;
but he was in time and just in time, and caught the
President and give him the letter, and everything was
all right, and the President give him a free pardon on
the spot, and Nat give the nigger two extra quarters
instead of one, because he could see that if he hadn't

had the hack he wouldn't 'a' got there in time, nor anywhere near it.

It *was* a powerful good adventure, and Tom Sawyer had to work his bullet-wound mighty lively to hold his own against it.

Well, by and by Tom's glory got to paling down gradu'ly, on account of other things turning up for the people to talk about — first a horse-race, and on top of that a house afire, and on top of that the circus, and on top of that the eclipse; and that started a revival, same as it always does, and by that time there wasn't any more talk about Tom, so to speak, and you never see a person so sick and disgusted.

Pretty soon he got to worrying and fretting right along day in and day out, and when I asked him what *was* he in such a state about, he said it 'most broke his heart to think how time was slipping away, and him getting older and older, and no wars breaking out and no way of making a name for himself that he could see. Now that is the way boys is always thinking, but he was the first one I ever heard come out and say it.

So then he set to work to get up a plan to make him celebrated; and pretty soon he struck it, and offered to take me and Jim in. Tom Sawyer was always free and generous that way. There's a-plenty of boys that's mighty good and friendly when *you've* got a good thing, but when a good thing happens to come their way they don't say a word to you, and try to hog it all. That warn't ever Tom Sawyer's way, I can say that for him. There's plenty of boys that will come

"Don't I tell you it hasn't got anything to do with farming? Farming is business, just common low-down business: that's all it is, it's all you can say for it; but this is higher, this is religious, and totally different."

"Religious to go and take the land away from people that owns it?"

"Certainly; it's always been considered so."

Jim he shook his head, and says:

"Mars Tom, I reckon dey's a mistake about it somers — dey mos' sholy is. I's religious myself, en I knows plenty religious people, but I hain't run across none dat acts like dat."

It made Tom hot, and he says:

"Well, it's enough to make a body sick, such mullet-headed ignorance! If either of you'd read anything about history, you'd know that Richard Cur de Loon, and the Pope, and Godfrey de Bulleyn, and lots more of the most noble-hearted and pious people in the world, hacked and hammered at the paynims for more than two hundred years trying to take their land away from them, and swum neck-deep in blood the whole time —and yet here's a couple of sap-headed country yahoos out in the backwoods of Missouri setting themselves up to know more about the rights and wrongs of it than they did! Talk about cheek!"

Well, of course, that put a more different light on it, and me and Jim felt pretty cheap and ignorant, and wished we hadn't been quite so chipper. I couldn't say nothing, and Jim he couldn't for a while; then he says:

"Well, den, I reckon it's all right; beca'se ef dey didn't know, dey ain't no use for po' ignorant folks like us to be trying to know; en so, ef it's our duty, we got to go en tackle it en do de bes' we can. Same time, I feel as sorry for dem paynims as Mars Tom. De hard part gwine to be to kill folks dat a body hain't been 'quainted wid and dat hain't done him no harm. Dat's it, you see. Ef we wuz to go 'mongst 'em, jist we three, en say we's hungry, en ast 'em for a bite to eat, why, maybe dey's jist like yuther people. Don't you reckon dey is? Why, *dey'd* give it, I know dey would, en den —"

"Then what?"

"Well, Mars Tom, my idea is like dis. It ain't no use, we *can't* kill dem po' strangers dat ain't doin' us no harm, till we've had practice — I knows it perfectly well, Mars Tom — 'deed I knows it perfectly well. But ef we takes a' axe or two, jist you en me en Huck, en slips acrost de river to-night arter de moon's gone down, en kills dat sick fam'ly dat's over on the Sny, en burns dey house down, en —"

"Oh, you make me tired!" says Tom. "I don't want to argue any more with people like you and Huck Finn, that's always wandering from the subject, and ain't got any more sense than to try to reason out a thing that's pure theology by the laws that protect real estate!"

Now that's just where Tom Sawyer warn't fair. Jim didn't mean no harm, and I didn't mean no harm. We knowed well enough that he was right and we was

2**

making fun of the man,— a lean pale feller with that
soft kind of moonlight in his eyes, you know,— and
they kept saying it wouldn't go. It made him hot to
hear them, and he would turn on them and shake his
fist and say they was animals and blind, but some day
they would find they had stood face to face with one
of the men that lifts up nations and makes civilizations,
and was too dull to know it; and right here on this
spot their own children and grandchildren would build
a monument to him that would outlast a thousand
years, but his name would outlast the monument.
And then the crowd would burst out in a laugh again,
and yell at him, and ask him what was his name before
he was married, and what he would take to not do it,
and what was his sister's cat's grandmother's name,
and all the things that a crowd says when they've got
hold of a feller that they see they can plague. Well,
some things they said *was* funny,— yes, and mighty
witty too, I ain't denying that,— but all the same it
warn't fair nor brave, all them people pitching on one,
and they so glib and sharp, and him without any gift
of talk to answer back with. But, good land! what
did he want to sass back for? You see, it couldn't do
him no good, and it was just nuts for them. They
had him, you know. But that was his way. I reckon
he couldn't help it; he was made so, I judge. He
was a good enough sort of cretur, and hadn't no harm
in him, and was just a genius, as the papers said, which
wasn't his fault. We can't all be sound: we've got to
be the way we're made. As near as I can make out,

geniuses think they know it all, and so they won't take people's advice, but always go their own way, which makes everybody forsake them and despise them, and that is perfectly natural. If they was humbler, and listened and tried to learn, it would be better for them.

The part the professor was in was like a boat, and was big and roomy, and had water-tight lockers around the inside to keep all sorts of things in, and a body could sit on them, and make beds on them, too. We went aboard, and there was twenty people there, snooping around and examining, and old Nat Parsons was there, too. The professor kept fussing around getting ready, and the people went ashore, drifting out one at a time, and old Nat he was the last. Of course it wouldn't do to let him go out behind *us*. We mustn't budge till he was gone, so we could be last ourselves.

But he was gone now, so it was time for us to follow. I heard a big shout, and turned around — the city was dropping from under us like a shot! It made me sick all through, I was so scared. Jim turned gray and couldn't say a word, and Tom didn't say nothing, but looked excited. The city went on dropping down, and down, and down; but we didn't seem to be doing nothing but just hang in the air and stand still. The houses got smaller and smaller, and the city pulled itself together, closer and closer, and the men and wagons got to looking like ants and bugs crawling around, and the streets like threads and cracks; and then it all kind of melted together, and there wasn't any city any more: it was only a big scar on the earth.

their saying she warn't simple and would be always getting out of order. Get out of order! That graveled him; he said that she couldn't any more get out of order than the solar sister.

He got worse and worse, and I never see a person take on so. It give me the cold shivers to see him, and so it did Jim. By and by he got to yelling and screaming, and then he swore the world shouldn't ever have his secret at all now, it had treated him so mean. He said he would sail his balloon around the globe just to show what he could do, and then he would sink it in the sea, and sink us all along with it, too. Well, it was the awfulest fix to be in, and here was night coming on!

He give us something to eat, and made us go to the other end of the boat, and he laid down on a locker, where he could boss all the works, and put his old pepper-box revolver under his head, and said if anybody come fooling around there trying to land her, he would kill him.

We set scrunched up together, and thought considerable, but didn't say much — only just a word once in a while when a body had to say something or bust, we was *so* scared and worried. The night dragged along slow and lonesome. We was pretty low down, and the moonshine made everything soft and pretty, and the farmhouses looked snug and homeful, and we could hear the farm sounds, and wished we could be down there; but, laws! we just slipped along over them like a ghost, and never left a track.

Away in the night, when all the sounds was late sounds, and the air had a late feel, and a late smell, too — about a two-o'clock feel, as near as I could make out — Tom said the professor was so quiet this time he must be asleep, and we'd better —

"Better what?" I says in a whisper, and feeling sick all over, because I knowed what he was thinking about.

"Better slip back there and tie him, and land the ship," he says.

I says: "No, sir! Don't you budge, Tom Sawyer."

And Jim — well, Jim was kind o' gasping, he was so scared. He says:

"Oh, Mars Tom, *don't!* Ef you teches him, we's gone — we's gone sho'! I ain't gwine anear him, not for nothin' in dis worl'. Mars Tom, he's plumb crazy."

Tom whispers and says: "That's *why* we've got to do something. If he wasn't crazy I wouldn't give shucks to be anywhere but here; you couldn't hire me to get out — now that I've got used to this balloon and over the scare of being cut loose from the solid ground — if he was in his right mind. But it's no good politics, sailing around like this with a person that's out of his head, and says he's going round the world and then drown us all. We've *got* to do something, I tell you, and do it before he wakes up, too, or we mayn't ever get another chance. Come!"

But it made us turn cold and creepy just to think of it, and we said we wouldn't budge. So Tom was for slipping back there by himself to see if he couldn't get at the steering-gear and land the ship. We begged and begged him not to, but it warn't no use; so he got down on his hands and knees, and begun to crawl an inch at a time, we a-holding our breath and watching. After he got to the middle of the boat he crept slower than ever, and it did seem like years to me. But at last we see him get to the professor's head, and sort of raise up soft and look a good spell in his face and listen. Then we see him begin to inch along again toward the professor's feet where the steering-buttons was. Well, he got there all safe, and was reaching slow and steady toward the buttons, but he knocked down something that made a noise, and we see him slump down flat an' soft in the bottom, and lay still. The professor stirred, and says, "What's that?" But everybody kept dead still and quiet, and he begun to mutter and mumble and nestle, like a person that's going to wake up, and I thought I was going to die, I was so worried and scared.

Then a cloud slid over the moon, and I 'most cried, I was so glad. She buried herself deeper and deeper into the cloud, and it got so dark we couldn't see Tom. Then it began to sprinkle rain, and we could hear the professor fussing at his ropes and things and abusing the weather. We was afraid every minute he would touch Tom, and then we would be goners, and no help; but Tom was already on his way back, and when we felt his hands on our knees my breath stopped sudden, and my heart fell down 'mongst my other works, because I couldn't tell in the dark but it might be the professor, which I thought it *was*.

Dear! I was so glad to have him back that I was just as near happy as a person could be that was up in the air that way with a deranged man. You can't land a balloon in the dark, and so I hoped it would keep on raining, for I didn't want Tom to go meddling any more and make us so awful uncomfortable. Well, I got my wish. It drizzled and drizzled along the rest of the night, which wasn't long, though it did seem so; and at daybreak it cleared, and the world looked mighty soft and gray and pretty, and the forests and fields so good to see again, and the horses and cattle standing sober and thinking. Next, the sun come a-blazing up gay and splendid, and then we began to feel rusty and stretchy, and first we knowed we was all asleep.

3 **

CHAPTER III.

TOM EXPLAINS

WE went to sleep about four o'clock, and woke up about eight. The professor was setting back there at his end, looking glum. He pitched us some breakfast, but he told us not to come abaft the midship compass. That was about the middle of the boat. Well, when you are sharp-set, and you eat and satisfy yourself, everything looks pretty different from what it done before. It makes a body feel pretty near comfortable, even when he is up in a balloon with a genius. We got to talking together.

There was one thing that kept bothering me, and by and by I says:

" Tom, didn't we start east?"

" Yes."

" How fast have we been going?"

" Well, you heard what the professor said when he was raging round. Sometimes, he said, we was making fifty miles an hour, sometimes ninety, sometimes a hundred; said that with a gale to help he could make three hundred any time, and said if he wanted the gale, and wanted it blowing the right direction, he only had to go up higher or down lower to find it."

"Well, then, it's just as I reckoned. The professor lied."

"Why?"

"Because if we was going so fast we ought to be past Illinois, oughtn't we?"

"Certainly."

"Well, we ain't."

"What's the reason we ain't?"

"I know by the color. We're right over Illinois yet. And you can see for yourself that Indiana ain't in sight."

"I wonder what's the matter with you, Huck. You know by the *color?*"

"Yes, of course I do."

"What's the color got to do with it?"

"It's got everything to do with it. Illinois is green, Indiana is pink. You show me any pink down here, if you can. No, sir; it's green."

"Indiana *pink?* Why, what a lie!"

"It ain't no lie; I've seen it on the map, and it's pink."

You never see a person so aggravated and disgusted. He says:

"Well, if I was such a numbskull as you, Huck Finn, I would jump over. Seen it on the map! Huck Finn, did you reckon the States was the same color out-of-doors as they are on the map?"

"Tom Sawyer, what's a map for? Ain't it to learn you facts?"

"Of course."

"Well, then, how's it going to do that if it tells **lies**? That's what I want to know."

"Shucks, you muggins! It don't tell lies."

"It don't, don't it?"

"No, it don't."

"All right, then; if it don't, there ain't no two States the same color. You git around *that*, if you can, Tom Sawyer."

He see I had him, and Jim see it too; and I tell you, I felt pretty good, for Tom Sawyer was always a hard person to git ahead of. Jim slapped his leg and says:

"I tell *you!* dat's smart, dat's right down smart. Ain't no use, Mars Tom; he got you *dis* time, sho'!" He slapped his leg again, and says, ' 'My *lan*', but it was smart one!"

I never felt so good in my life; and yet *I* didn't know I was saying anything much till it was out. I was just mooning along, perfectly careless, and not expecting anything was going to happen, and never *thinking* of such a thing at all, when, all of a sudden, out it came. Why, it was just as much a surprise to me as it was to any of them. It was just the same way it is when a person is munching along on a hunk of corn-pone, and not thinking about anything, and all of a sudden bites into a di'mond. Now all that *he* knows first off is that it's some kind of gravel he's bit into; but he don't find out it's a di'mond till he gits it out and brushes off the sand and crumbs and one thing or another, and has a look at it, and then he's surprised

and glad — yes, and proud too; though when you
come to look the thing straight in the eye, he ain't
entitled to as much credit as he would 'a' been if he'd
been *hunting* di'monds. You can see the difference
easy if you think it over. You see, an accident, that
way, ain't fairly as big a thing as a thing that's done
a-purpose. Anybody could find that di'mond in that
corn-pone; but mind you, it's got to be somebody
that's got *that kind of a corn-pone*. That's where that
feller's credit comes in, you see; and that's where
mine comes in. I don't claim no great things — I
don't reckon I could 'a' done it again — but I done it
that time; that's all I claim. And I hadn't no more
idea I could do such a thing, and warn't any more
thinking about it or trying to, than you be this minute.
Why, I was just as ca'm, a body couldn't be any
ca'mer, and yet, all of a sudden, out it come. I've
often thought of that time, and I can remember just
the way everything looked, same as if it was only last
week. I can see it all: beautiful rolling country with
woods and fields and lakes for hundreds and hundreds
of miles all around, and towns and villages scattered
everywheres under us, here and there and yonder; and
the professor mooning over a chart on his little table,
and Tom's cap flopping in the rigging where it was
hung up to dry. And one thing in particular was a
bird right alongside, not ten foot off, going our way
and trying to keep up, but losing ground all the time;
and a railroad train doing the same thing down there,
sliding among the trees and farms, and pouring out a

3

"Tom Sawyer, you don't mean it!"

"Yes, I do, and it's dead sure. We've covered about fifteen degrees of longitude since we left St. Louis yesterday afternoon, and them clocks are *right*. We've come close on to eight hundred miles."

I didn't believe it, but it made the cold streaks trickle down my back just the same. In my experience I knowed it wouldn't take much short of two weeks to do it down the Mississippi on a raft.

Jim was working his mind and studying. Pretty soon he says:

"'Mars Tom, did you say dem clocks uz right?"

"Yes, they're right."

"Ain't yo' watch right, too?"

"She's right for St. Louis, but she's an hour wrong for here."

"Mars Tom, is you tryin' to let on dat de time ain't de *same* everywheres?"

"No, it ain't the same everywheres, by a long shot."

Jim looked distressed, and says:

"It grieves me to hear you talk like dat, Mars Tom; I's right down ashamed to hear you talk like dat, arter de way you's been raised. Yassir, it'd break yo' Aunt Polly's heart to hear you."

Tom was astonished. He looked Jim over wondering, and didn't say nothing, and Jim went on:

"Mars Tom, who put de people out yonder in St. Louis? De Lord done it. Who put de people here whar we is? De Lord done it. Ain' dey bofe his children? 'Cose dey is. *Well*, den! is he gwine to *scriminate* 'twixt 'em?''

"Scriminate! I never heard such ignorance. There ain't no discriminating about it. When he makes you and some more of his children black, and makes the rest of us white, what do you call that?''

Jim see the p'int. He was stuck. He couldn't answer. Tom says:

"He does discriminate, you see, when he wants to; but this case *here* ain't no discrimination of his, it's man's. The Lord made the day, and he made the night; but he didn't invent the hours, and he didn't distribute them around. Man did that.''

"Mars Tom, is dat so? Man done it?''

"Certainly.''

"Who tole him he could?''

"Nobody. He never asked.''

Jim studied a minute, and says:

"Well, dat do beat me. I wouldn't 'a' tuck no sich resk. But some people ain't scared o' nothin'. Dey bangs right ahead; *dey* don't care what happens. So den dey's allays an hour's diff'unce everywhah, Mars Tom?''

"An hour? No! It's four minutes difference for every degree of longitude, you know. Fifteen of 'em's an hour, thirty of 'em's two hours, and so on. When it's one clock Tuesday morning in England, it's eight o'clock the night before in New York.''

Jim moved a little way along the locker, and you could see he was insulted. He kept shaking his head and muttering, and so I slid along to him and patted him on the leg, and petted him up, and got him over the worst of his feelings, and then he says:

"Mars Tom talkin' sich talk as dat! Choosday in one place en Monday in t'other, bofe in the same day! Huck, dis ain't no place to joke — up here whah we is. Two days in one day! How you gwine to get two days inter one day? Can't git two hours inter one hour, kin you? Can't git two niggers inter one nigger skin, kin you? Can't git two gallons of whisky inter a one-gallon jug, kin you? No, sir, 'twould strain de jug. Yes, en even den you couldn't, *I* don't believe. Why, looky here, Huck, s'posen de Choosday was New Year's — now den! is you gwine to tell me it's dis year in one place en las' year in t'other, bofe in de identical same minute? It's de beatenest rubbage! I can't stan' it — I can't stan' to hear tell 'bout it." Then he begun to shiver and turn gray, and Tom says:

"*Now* what's the matter? What's the trouble?"

Jim could hardly speak, but he says:

"Mars Tom, you ain't jokin', en it's *so*?"

"No, I'm not, and it *is* so."

Jim shivered again, and says:

"Den dat Monday could be de las' day, en dey wouldn't be no las' day in England, en de dead wouldn't be called. We mustn't go over dah, Mars Tom. Please git him to turn back; I wants to be whah —"

All of a sudden we see something, and all jumped

up, and forgot everything and begun to gaze. Tom
says:

"Ain't that the—" He catched his breath, then
says: "It *is*, sure as you live! It's the ocean!"

That made me and Jim catch our breath, too. Then
we all stood petrified but happy, for none of us had
ever seen an ocean, or ever expected to. Tom kept
muttering:

"Atlantic Ocean—Atlantic. Land, don't it sound
great! And that's *it* — and *we* are looking at it — we!
Why, it's just too splendid to believe!"

Then we see a big bank of black smoke; and when
we got nearer, it was a city — and a monster she was,
too, with a thick fringe of ships around one edge; and
we wondered if it was New York, and begun to jaw
and dispute about it, and, first we knowed, it slid from
under us and went flying behind, and here we was, out
over the very ocean itself, and going like a cyclone.
Then we woke up, I tell you!

We made a break aft and raised a wail, and begun to
beg the professor to turn back and land us, but
he jerked out his pistol and motioned us back,
and we went, but nobody will ever know how bad we
felt.

The land was gone, all but a little streak, like a
snake, away off on the edge of the water, and down
under us was just ocean, ocean, ocean — millions of
miles of it, heaving and pitching and squirming, and
white sprays blowing from the wave-tops, and only a
few ships in sight, wallowing around and laying over,

first on one side and then on t'other, and sticking their bows under and then their sterns; and before long there warn't no ships at all, and we had the sky and the whole ocean all to ourselves, and the roomiest place I ever see and the lonesomest.

CHAPTER IV.

AND it got lonesomer and lonesomer. There was the big sky up there, empty and awful deep; and the ocean down there without a thing on it but just the waves. All around us was a ring, where the sky and the water come together; yes, a monstrous big ring it was, and we right in the dead center of it — plumb in the center. We was racing along like a prairie fire, but it never made any difference, we couldn't seem to git past that center no way. I couldn't see that we ever gained an inch on that ring. It made a body feel creepy, it was so curious and unaccountable.

Well, everything was so awful still that we got to talking in a very low voice, and kept on getting creepier and lonesomer and less and less talky, till at last the talk ran dry altogether, and we just set there and "thunk," as Jim calls it, and never said a word the longest time.

The professor never stirred till the sun was overhead, then he stood up and put a kind of triangle to his eye, and Tom said it was a sextant and he was taking the sun to see whereabouts the balloon was. Then he ciphered a little and looked in a book, and then he

(39)

begun to carry on again. He said lots of wild things, and, among others, he said he would keep up this hundred-mile gait till the middle of to-morrow after-noon, and then he'd land in London.

We said we would be humbly thankful.

He was turning away, but he whirled around when we said that, and give us a long look of his blackest kind — one of the maliciousest and suspiciousest looks I ever see. Then he says:

"You want to leave me. Don't try to deny it."

We didn't know what to say, so we held in and didn't say nothing at all.

He went aft and set down, but he couldn't seem to git that thing out of his mind. Every now and then he would rip out something about it, and try to make us answer him, but we dasn't.

It got lonesomer and lonesomer right along, and it did seem to me I couldn't stand it. It was still worse when night begun to come on. By and by Tom pinched me and whispers:

"Look!"

I took a glance aft, and see the professor taking a whet out of a bottle. I didn't like the looks of that. By and by he took another drink, and pretty soon he begun to sing. It was dark now, and getting black and stormy. He went on singing, wilder and wilder, and the thunder begun to mutter, and the wind to wheeze and moan among the ropes, and altogether it was awful. It got so black we couldn't see him any more, and wished we couldn't hear him, but we could.

Then he got still; but he warn't still ten minutes till we got suspicious, and wished he would start up his noise again, so we could tell where he was. By and by there was a flash of lightning, and we see him start to get up, but he staggered and fell down. We heard him scream out in the dark:

"They don't want to go to England. All right, I'll change the course. They want to leave me. I know they do. Well, they shall — and now!"

I 'most died when he said that. Then he was still again — still so long I couldn't bear it, and it did seem to me the lightning wouldn't ever come again. But at last there was a blessed flash, and there he was, on his hands and knees crawling, and not four feet from us. My, but his eyes was terrible! He made a lunge for Tom, and says, "Overboard you go!" but it was already pitch-dark again, and I couldn't see whether he got him or not, and Tom didn't make a sound.

There was another long, horrible wait; then there was a flash, and I see Tom's head sink down outside the boat and disappear. He was on the rope-ladder that dangled down in the air from the gunnel. The professor let off a shout and jumped for him, and straight off it was pitch-dark again, and Jim groaned out, "Po' Mars Tom, he's a goner!" and made a jump for the professor, but the professor warn't there.

Then we heard a couple of terrible screams, and then another not so loud, and then another that was 'way below, and you could only just hear it; and I heard Jim say, "Po' Mars Tom!"

Then it was awful still, and I reckon a person could 'a' counted four thousand before the next flash come. When it come I see Jim on his knees, with his arms on the locker and his face buried in them, and he was crying. Before I could look over the edge it was all dark again, and I was glad, because I didn't want to see. But when the next flash come, I was watching, and down there I see somebody a-swinging in the wind on the ladder, and it was Tom!

"Come up!" I shouts; "come up, Tom!"

His voice was so weak, and the wind roared so, I couldn't make out what he said, but I thought he asked was the professor up there. I shouts:

"No, he's down in the ocean! Come up! Can we help you?"

Of course, all this in the dark.

"Huck, who is you hollerin' at?"

"I'm hollerin' at Tom."

"Oh, Huck, how kin you act so, when you know po' Mars Tom —" Then he let off an awful scream, and flung his head and his arms back and let off another one, because there was a white glare just then, and he had raised up his face just in time to see Tom's, as white as snow, rise above the gunnel and look him right in the eye. He thought it was Tom's ghost, you see.

Tom clumb aboard, and when Jim found it *was* him, and not his ghost, he hugged him, and called him all sorts of loving names, and carried on like he was gone crazy, he was so glad. Says I:

"What did you wait for, Tom? Why didn't you come up at first?"

"I dasn't, Huck. I knowed somebody plunged down past me, but I didn't know who it was in the dark. It could 'a' been you, it could 'a' been Jim."

That was the way with Tom Sawyer — always sound. He warn't coming up till he knowed where the professor was.

The storm let go about this time with all its might; and it was dreadful the way the thunder boomed and tore, and the lightning glared out, and the wind sung and screamed in the rigging, and the rain come down. One second you couldn't see your hand before you, and the next you could count the threads in your coat-sleeve, and see a whole wide desert of waves pitching and tossing through a kind of veil of rain. A storm like that is the loveliest thing there is, but it ain't at its best when you are up in the sky and lost, and it's wet and lonesome, and there's just been a death in the family.

We set there huddled up in the bow, and talked low about the poor professor; and everybody was sorry for him, and sorry the world had made fun of him and treated him so harsh, when he was doing the best he could, and hadn't a friend nor nobody to encourage him and keep him from brooding his mind away and going deranged. There was plenty of clothes and blankets and everything at the other end, but we thought we'd ruther take the rain than go meddling back there.

4 **

CHAPTER V.

LAND

WE tried to make some plans, but we couldn't come to no agreement. Me and Jim was for turning around and going back home, but Tom allowed that by the time daylight come, so we could see our way, we would be so far toward England that we might as well go there, and come back in a ship, and have the glory of saying we done it.

About midnight the storm quit and the moon come out and lit up the ocean, and we begun to feel comfortable and drowsy; so we stretched out on the lockers and went to sleep, and never woke up again till sun-up. The sea was sparkling like di'monds, and it was nice weather, and pretty soon our things was all dry again.

We went aft to find some breakfast, and the first thing we noticed was that there was a dim light burning in a compass back there under a hood. Then Tom was disturbed. He says:

"You know what that means, easy enough. It means that somebody has got to stay on watch and steer this thing the same as he would a ship, or she'll wander around and go wherever the wind wants her to."

"Well," I says, "what's she been doing since — er — since we had the accident?"

"Wandering," he says, kinder troubled —" wandering, without any doubt. She's in a wind now that's blowing her south of east. We don't know how long that's been going on, either."

So then he p'inted her east, and said he would hold her there till we rousted out the breakfast. The professor had laid in everything a body could want; he couldn't 'a' been better fixed. There wasn't no milk for the coffee, but there was water, and everything else you could want, and a charcoal stove and the fixings for it, and pipes and cigars and matches; and wine and liquor, which warn't in our line; and books, and maps, and charts, and an accordion; and furs, and blankets, and no end of rubbish, like brass beads and brass jewelry, which Tom said was a sure sign that he had an idea of visiting among savages. There was money, too. Yes, the professor was well enough fixed.

After breakfast Tom learned me and Jim how to steer, and divided us all up into four-hour watches, turn and turn about; and when his watch was out I took his place, and he got out the professor's papers and pens and wrote a letter home to his aunt Polly, telling her everything that had happened to us, and dated it "*In the Welkin, approaching England*," and folded it together and stuck it fast with a red wafer, and directed it, and wrote above the direction, in big writing," *From Tom Sawyer, the Erronort,*" and said it would stump old Nat Parsons, the postmaster, when it come along in the mail. I says:

"Tom Sawyer, this ain't no welkin; it's a balloon."

"Well, now, who *said* it was a welkin, smarty?"

"You've wrote it on the letter, anyway."

"What of it? That don't mean that the balloon's the welkin."

"Oh, I thought it did. Well, then, what is a welkin?"

I see in a minute he was stuck. He raked and scraped around in his mind, but he couldn't find nothing, so he had to say:

"*I* don't know, and nobody don't know. It's just a word, and it's a mighty good word, too. There ain't many that lays over it. I don't believe there's *any* that does."

"Shucks!" I says. "But what does it *mean?* — that's the p'int."

"*I* don't know what it means, I tell you. It's a word that people uses for — for — well, it's ornamental. They don't put ruffles on a shirt to keep a person warm, do they?"

"Course they don't."

"But they put them *on*, don't they?"

"Yes."

"All right, then; that letter I wrote is a shirt, and the welkin's the ruffle on it."

I judged that that would gravel Jim, and it did.

"Now, Mars Tom, it ain't no use to talk like dat,

en, moreover, it's sinful.   You knows a letter ain't no
shirt, en dey ain't no ruffles on it, nuther.   Dey ain't
no place to put 'em on; you can't put 'em on, and
dey wouldn't stay ef you did."

"Oh, *do* shut up, and wait till something's started
that you know something about."

"Why, Mars Tom, sholy you can't mean to say I
don't know about shirts, when, goodness knows, I's
toted home de washin' ever sence —"

"I tell you, this hasn't got anything to *do* with
shirts.   I only —"

"Why, Mars Tom, you said yo'self dat a letter —"

"Do you want to drive me crazy? Keep still. I
only used it as a metaphor."

That word kinder bricked us up for a minute.   Then
Jim says — rather timid, because he see Tom was getting pretty tetchy:

"Mars Tom, what is a metaphor?"

"A metaphor's a — weil, it's a — a — a metaphor's
an illustration."   He see *that* didn't git home, so he
tried again.   "When I say birds of a feather flocks
together, it's a metaphorical way of saying —"

"But dey *don't*, Mars Tom.   No, sir, 'deed dey
don't.   Dey ain't no feathers dat's more alike den a
bluebird en a jaybird, but ef you waits till you catches
dem birds together, you'll —"

"Oh, give us a rest! You can't get the simplest
little thing through your thick skull.   Now don't bother
me any more."

Jim was satisfied to stop.   He was dreadful pleased
4

sure enough — land all around, as far as you could see, and perfectly level and yaller. We didn't know how long we'd been over it. There warn't no trees, nor hills, nor rocks, nor towns, and Tom and Jim had took it for the sea. They took it for the sea in a dead ca'm; but we was so high up, anyway, that if it had been the sea and rough, it would 'a' looked smooth, all the same, in the night, that way.

We was all in a powerful excitement now, and grabbed the glasses and hunted everywheres for London, but couldn't find hair nor hide of it, nor any other settlement — nor any sign of a lake or a river, either. Tom was clean beat. He said it warn't his notion of England; he thought England looked like America, and always had that idea. So he said we better have breakfast, and then drop down and inquire the quickest way to London. We cut the breakfast pretty short, we was so impatient. As we slanted along down, the weather began to moderate, and pretty soon we shed our furs. But it kept *on* moderating, and in a precious little while it was 'most too moderate. We was close down now, and just blistering!

We settled down to within thirty foot of the land — that is, it was land if sand is land; for this wasn't anything but pure sand. Tom and me clumb down the ladder and took a run to stretch our legs, and it felt amazing good — that is, the stretching did, but the sand scorched our feet like hot embers. Next, we see somebody coming, and started to meet him; but we heard Jim shout, and looked around and he was fairly dancing, and making signs, and yelling. We couldn't make out what he said, but we was scared anyway, and begun to heel it back to the balloon. When we got close enough, we understood the words, and they made me sick:

"Run! Run fo' yo' life! Hit's a lion; I kin see him thoo de glass! Run, boys; do please heel it de bes' you kin. He's bu'sted outen de menagerie, en dey ain't nobody to stop him!"

It made Tom fly, but it took the stiffening all out of my legs. I could only just gasp along the way you do in a dream when there's a ghost gaining on you.

Tom got to the ladder and shinned up it a piece and waited for me; and as soon as I got a foothold on it he shouted to Jim to soar away. But Jim had clean lost his head, and said he had forgot how. So Tom shinned along up and told me to follow; but the lion was arriving, fetching a most ghastly roar with every lope, and my legs shook so I dasn't try to take one of them out of the rounds for fear the other one would give way under me.

But Tom was aboard by this time, and he started the balloon up a little, and stopped it again as soon as the end of the ladder was ten or twelve feet above ground. And there was the lion, a-ripping around under me, and roaring and springing up in the air at the ladder, and only missing it about a quarter of an inch, it seemed to me. It was delicious to be out of his reach, perfectly delicious, and made me feel good and thankful all up one side; but I was hanging there helpless

D**

and couldn't climb, and that made me feel perfectly wretched and miserable all down the other. It is most seldom that a person feels so mixed like that; and it is not to be recommended, either.

Tom asked me what he'd better do, but I didn't know. He asked me if I could hold on whilst he sailed away to a safe place and left the lion behind. I said I could if he didn't go no higher than he was now; but if he went higher I would lose my head and fall, sure. So he said, "Take a good grip," and he started.

"Don't go so fast," I shouted. "It makes my head swim."

He had started like a lightning express. He slowed down, and we glided over the sand slower, but still in a kind of sickening way; for it *is* uncomfortable to see things sliding and gliding under you like that, and not a sound.

But pretty soon there was plenty of sound, for the lion was catching up. His noise fetched others. You could see them coming on the lope from every direction, and pretty soon there was a couple of dozen of them under me, jumping up at the ladder and snarling and snapping at each other; and so we went skimming along over the sand, and these fellers doing what they could to help us to not forgit the occasion; and then some other beasts come, without an invite, and they started a regular riot down there.

We see this plan was a mistake. We couldn't ever git away from them at this gait, and I couldn't hold on forever. So Tom took a think, and struck another

idea. That was, to kill a lion with the pepper-box
revolver, and then sail away while the others stopped
to fight over the carcass. So he stopped the balloon
still, and done it, and then we sailed off while the fuss
was going on, and come down a quarter of a mile off,
and they helped me aboard; but by the time we was
out of reach again, that gang was on hand once more.
And when they see we was really gone and they
couldn't get us, they sat down on their hams and
looked up at us so kind of disappointed that it was as
much as a person could do not to see *their* side of the
matter.

CHAPTER VI.

IT'S A CARAVAN

I WAS so weak that the only thing I wanted was a chance to lay down, so I made straight for my locker-bunk, and stretched myself out there. But a body couldn't get back his strength in no such oven as that, so Tom give the command to soar, and Jim started her aloft.

We had to go up a mile before we struck comfortable weather where it was breezy and pleasant and just right, and pretty soon I was all straight again. Tom had been setting quiet and thinking; but now he jumps up and says:

"I bet you a thousand to one *I* know where we are. We're in the Great Sahara, as sure as guns!"

He was so excited he couldn't hold still; but I wasn't. I says:

"Well, then, where's the Great Sahara? In England or in Scotland?"

" 'Tain't in either; it's in Africa."

Jim's eyes bugged out, and he begun to stare down with no end of interest, because that was where his originals come from; but I didn't more than half be-

lieve it. I couldn't, you know; it seemed too awful
far away for us to have traveled.

But Tom was full of his discovery, as he called it,
and said the lions and the sand meant the Great Desert,
sure. He said he could 'a' found out, before we
sighted land, that we was crowding the land somewheres, if he had thought of one thing; and when we
asked him what, he said:

"These clocks. They're chronometers. You always read about them in sea voyages. One of them
is keeping Grinnage time, and the other is keeping St.
Louis time, like my watch. When we left St. Louis it
was four in the afternoon by my watch and this clock,
and it was ten at night by this Grinnage clock. Well,
at this time of the year the sun sets at about seven
o'clock. Now I noticed the time yesterday evening
when the sun went down, and it was half-past five
o'clock by the Grinnage clock, and half past 11 A. M.
by my watch and the other clock. You see, the sun
rose and set by my watch in St. Louis, and the Grinnage clock was six hours fast; but we've come so far
east that it comes within less than half an hour of setting by the Grinnage clock now, and I'm away out —
more than four hours and a half out. You see, that
meant that we was closing up on the longitude of
Ireland, and would strike it before long if we was
p'inted right — which we wasn't. No, sir, we've been
a-wandering — wandering 'way down south of east, and
it's my opinion we are in Africa. Look at this map.
You see how the shoulder of Africa sticks out to the

west. Think how fast we've traveled; if we had gone straight east we would be long past England by this time. You watch for noon, all of you, and we'll stand up, and when we can't cast a shadow we'll find that this Grinnage clock is coming mighty close to marking twelve. Yes, sir, *I* think we're in Africa; and it's just bully."

Jim was gazing down with the glass. He shook his head and says:

"Mars Tom, I reckon dey's a mistake som'er's. I hain't seen no niggers yit."

"That's nothing; they don't live in the desert. What is that, 'way off yonder? Gimme a glass."

He took a long look, and said it was like a black string stretched across the sand, but he couldn't guess what it was.

"Well," I says, "I reckon maybe you've got a chance now to find out whereabouts this balloon is, because as like as not that is one of these lines here, that's on the map, that you call meridians of longitude, and we can drop down and look at its number, and—"

"Oh, shucks, Huck Finn, I never see such a lunkhead as you. Did you s'pose there's meridians of longitude on the *earth* ?"

"Tom Sawyer, they're set down on the map, and you know it perfectly well, and here they are, and you can see for yourself."

"Of course they're on the map, but that's nothing; there ain't any on the *ground.*'

"Tom, do you know that to be so?"

"Certainly I do."

"Well, then, that map's a liar again. I never see such a liar as that map."

He fired up at that, and I was ready for him, and Jim was warming his opinion, too, and next minute we'd 'a' broke loose on another argument, if Tom hadn't dropped the glass and begun to clap his hands like a maniac and sing out:

"Camels! — Camels!"

So I grabbed a glass and Jim, too, and took a look, but I was disappointed, and says:

"Camels your granny; they're spiders."

"Spiders in a desert, you shad? Spiders walking in a procession? You don't ever reflect, Huck Finn, and I reckon you really haven't got anything to reflect *with*. Don't you know we're as much as a mile up in the air, and that that string of crawlers is two or three miles away? Spiders, good land! Spiders as big as a cow? Perhaps you'd like to go down and milk one of 'em. But they're camels, just the same. It's a caravan, that's what it is, and it's a mile long."

"Well, then, let's go down and look at it. I don't believe in it, and ain't going to till I see it and know it."

"All right," he says, and give the command: "Lower away."

As we come slanting down into the hot weather, we could see that it was camels, sure enough, plodding

along, an everlasting string of them, with bales strapped
to them, and several hundred men in long white robes,
and a thing like a shawl bound over their heads and
hanging down with tassels and fringes; and some of
the men had long guns and some hadn't, and some
was riding and some was walking. And the weather —
well, it was just roasting. And how slow they did
creep along! We swooped down now, all of a
sudden, and stopped about a hundred yards over their
heads.

The men all set up a yell, and some of them fell flat
on their stomachs, some begun to fire their guns at us,
and the rest broke and scampered every which way,
and so did the camels.

We see that we was making trouble, so we went up
again about a mile, to the cool weather, and watched
them from there. It took them an hour to get together
and form the procession again; then they started along,
but we could see by the glasses that they wasn't paying much attention to anything but us. We poked
along, looking down at them with the glasses, and by
and by we see a big sand mound, and something like
people the other side of it, and there was something
like a man laying on top of the mound that raised his
head up every now and then, and seemed to be watching the caravan or us, we didn't know which. As the
caravan got nearer, he sneaked down on the other side
and rushed to the other men and horses — for that is
what they was — and we see them mount in a hurry;
and next, here they come, like a house afire, some with

lances and some with long guns, and all of them yelling the best they could.

They come a-tearing down on to the caravan, and the next minute both sides crashed together and was all mixed up, and there was such another popping of guns as you never heard, and the air got so full of smoke you could only catch glimpses of them struggling together. There must 'a' been six hundred men in that battle, and it was terrible to see. Then they broke up into gangs and groups, fighting tooth and nail, and scurrying and scampering around, and laying into each other like everything; and whenever the smoke cleared a little you could see dead and wounded people and camels scattered far and wide and all about, and camels racing off in every direction.

At last the robbers see they couldn't win, so their chief sounded a signal, and all that was left of them broke away and went scampering across the plain. The last man to go snatched up a child and carried it off in front of him on his horse, and a woman run screaming and begging after him, and followed him away off across the plain till she was separated a long ways from her people; but it warn't no use, and she had to give it up, and we see her sink down on the sand and cover her face with her hands. Then Tom took the hellum, and started for that yahoo, and we come a-whizzing down and made a swoop, and knocked him out of the saddle, child and all; and he was jarred considerable, but the child wasn't hurt, but laid there working its hands and legs in the air like a tumble-bug that's on its back and can't turn over. The man went staggering off to overtake his horse, and didn't know what had hit him, for we was three or four hundred yards up in the air by this time.

We judged the woman would go and get the child now; but she didn't. We could see her, through the glass, still setting there, with her head bowed down on her knees; so of course she hadn't seen the perform- ance, and thought her child was clean gone with the man. She was nearly a half a mile from her people, so we thought we might go down to the child, which was about a quarter of a mile beyond her, and snake it to her before the caravan people could git to us to do us any harm; and besides, we reckoned they had enough business on their hands for one while, anyway, with the wounded. We thought we'd chance it, and we did. We swooped down and stopped, and Jim shinned down the ladder and fetched up the kid, which was a nice fat little thing, and in a noble good humor, too, considering it was just out of a battle and been tumbled off of a horse; and then we started for the mother, and stopped back of her and tolerable near by, and Jim slipped down and crept up easy, and when he was close back of her the child goo-goo'd, the way a child does, and she heard it, and whirled and fetched a shriek of joy, and made a jump for the kid and snatched it and hugged it, and dropped it and hugged Jim, and then snatched off a gold chain and hung it around Jim's neck, and hugged him again, and jerked up the child again, a-sobbing and glorifying all the time; and Jim he shoved for the ladder and up it, and in a minute we was back up in the sky and the woman was staring up, with the back of her head between her shoulders and the child with its arms locked around her neck. And there she stood, as long as we was in sight a-sailing away in the sky.

CHAPTER VII.

TOM RESPECTS THE FLEA

"NOON!" says Tom, and so it was. His shadder was just a blot around his feet. We looked, and the Grinnage clock was so close to twelve the difference didn't amount to nothing. So Tom said London was right north of us or right south of us, one or t'other, and he reckoned by the weather and the sand and the camels it was north; and a good many miles north, too; as many as from New York to the city of Mexico, he guessed.

Jim said he reckoned a balloon was a good deal the fastest thing in the world, unless it might be some kinds of birds — a wild pigeon, maybe, or a railroad.

But Tom said he had read about railroads in England going nearly a hundred miles an hour for a little ways, and there never was a bird in the world that could do that — except one, and that was a flea.

"A flea? Why, Mars Tom, in de fust place he ain't a bird, strickly speakin'—"

"He ain't a bird, eh? Well, then, what is he?"

"I don't rightly know, Mars Tom, but I speck he's only jist a' animal. No, I reckon dat won't do, nuther, he ain't big enough for a' animal. He mus' be a bug. Yassir, dat's what he is, he's a bug."

"I bet he ain't, but let it go. What's your second place?"

"Well, in de second place, birds is creturs dat goes a long ways, but a flea don't."

"He don't, don't he? Come, now, what *is* a long distance, if you know?"

"Why, it's miles, and lots of 'em — anybody knows dat."

"Can't a man walk miles?"

"Yassir, he kin."

"As many as a railroad?"

"Yassir, if you give him time."

"Can't a flea?"

"Well — I s'pose so — ef you gives him heaps of time."

"Now you begin to see, don't you, that *distance* ain't the thing to judge by, at all; it's the time it takes to go the distance *in* that *counts*, ain't it?"

"Well, hit do look sorter so, but I wouldn't 'a' b'lieved it, Mars Tom."

"It's a matter of *proportion*, that's what it is; and when you come to gauge a thing's speed by its size, where's your bird and your man and your railroad, alongside of a flea? The fastest man can't run more than about ten miles in an hour — not much over ten thousand times his own length. But all the books says any common ordinary third-class flea can jump a hundred and fifty times his own length; yes, and he can

5

make five jumps a second too — seven hundred and fifty times his own length, in one little second — for he don't fool away any time stopping and starting — he does them both at the same time; you'll see, if you try to put your finger on him. Now that's a common, ordinary, third-class flea's gait; but you take an Eye-talian *first*-class, that's been the pet of the nobility all his life, and hasn't ever knowed what want or sickness or exposure was, and he can jump more than three hundred times his own length, and keep it up all day, five such jumps every second, which is fifteen hundred times his own length. Well, suppose a man could go fifteen hundred times his own length in a second — say, a mile and a half. It's ninety miles a minute; it's considerable more than five thousand miles an hour. Where's your man *now ?* — yes, and your bird, and your railroad, and your balloon? Laws, they don't amount to shucks 'longside of a flea. A flea is just a comet b'iled down small."

Jim was a good deal astonished, and so was I. Jim said:

" Is dem figgers jist edjackly true, en no jokin' en no lies, Mars Tom?"

" Yes, they are; they're perfectly true."

" Well, den, honey, a body's got to respec' a flea. I ain't had no respec' for um befo', sca'sely, but dey ain't no gittin' roun' it, dey do deserve it, dat's certain."

" Well, I bet they do. They've got ever so much more sense, and brains, and brightness, in proportion to their size, than any other cretur in the world. A person can learn them 'most anything; and they learn it quicker than any other cretur, too. They've been learnt to haul little carriages in harness, and go this way and that way and t'other way according to their orders; yes, and to march and drill like soldiers, doing it as exact, according to orders, as soldiers does it. They've been learnt to do all sorts of hard and troublesome things. S'pose you could cultivate a flea up to the size of a man, and keep his natural smartness a-growing and a-growing right along up, bigger and bigger, and keener and keener, in the same proportion — where'd the human race be, do you reckon? That flea would be President of the United States, and you couldn't any more prevent it than you can prevent lightning."

" My lan', Mars Tom, I never knowed dey was so much *to* de beas'. No, sir, I never had no idea of it, and dat's de fac'."

" There's more to him, by a long sight, than there is to any other cretur, man or beast, in proportion to size. He's the interestingest of them all. People have so much to say about an ant's strength, and an elephant's, and a locomotive's. Shucks, they don't begin with a flea. He can lift two or three hundred times his own weight. And none of them can come anywhere near it. And, moreover, he has got notions of his own, and is very particular, and you can't fool him; his instinct, or his judgment, or whatever it is, is perfectly sound and clear, and don't ever make a mistake.

5**

People think all humans are alike to a flea. It ain't so. There's folks that he won't go near, hungry or not hungry, and I'm one of them. I've never had one of them on me in my life.''

" Mars Tom !''

" It's so; I ain't joking.''

" Well, sah, I hain't ever heard de likes o' dat befo'.''

Jim couldn't believe it, and I couldn't; so we had to drop down to the sand and git a supply and see. Tom was right. They went for me and Jim by the thousand, but not a one of them lit on Tom. There warn't no explaining it, but there it was and there warn't no getting around it. He said it had always been just so, and he'd just as soon be where there was a million of them as not; they'd never touch him nor bother him.

We went up to the cold weather to freeze 'em out, and stayed a little spell, and then come back to the comfortable weather and went lazying along twenty or twenty-five miles an hour, the way we'd been doing for the last few hours. The reason was, that the longer we was in that solemn, peaceful desert, the more the hurry and fuss got kind of soothed down in us, and the more happier and contented and satisfied we got to feeling, and the more we got to liking the desert, and then loving it. So we had cramped the speed down, as I was saying, and was having a most noble good lazy time, sometimes watching through the glasses, sometimes stretched out on the lockers reading, sometimes taking a nap.

It didn't seem like we was the same lot that was in such a state to find land and git ashore, but it was. But we had got over that — clean over it. We was used to the balloon now and not afraid any more, and didn't want to be anywheres else. Why, it seemed just like home; it 'most seemed as if I had been born and raised in it, and Jim and Tom said the same. And always I had had hateful people around me, a-nagging at me, and pestering of me, and scolding, and finding fault, and fussing and bothering, and sticking to me, and keeping after me, and making me do this, and making me do that and t'other, and always selecting out the things I didn't want to do, and then giving me Sam Hill because I shirked and done something else, and just aggravating the life out of a body all the time; but up here in the sky it was so still and sunshiny and lovely, and plenty to eat, and plenty of sleep, and strange things to see, and no nagging and no pestering, and no good people, and just holiday all the time. Land, I warn't in no hurry to git out and buck at civilization again. Now, one of the worst things about civilization is, that anybody that gits a letter with trouble in it comes and tells you all about it and makes you feel bad, and the newspapers fetches you the troubles of everybody all over the world, and keeps you downhearted and dismal 'most all the time, and it's such a heavy load for a person. I hate them newspapers; and I hate letters; and if I had my way I wouldn't allow nobody to load his troubles on to other folks he ain't acquainted with, on t'other side of the world, that way. Well, up in a balloon there ain't any of that, and it's the darlingest place there is.

We had supper, and that night was one of the prettiest nights I ever see. The moon made it just like daylight, only a heap softer; and once we see a lion standing all alone by himself, just all alone on the earth, it seemed like, and his shadder laid on the sand by him like a puddle of ink. That's the kind of moon-light to have.

Mainly we laid on our backs and talked; we didn't want to go to sleep. Tom said we was right in the midst of the Arabian Nights now. He said it was right along here that one of the cutest things in that book happened; so we looked down and watched while he told about it, because there ain't anything that is so interesting to look at as a place that a book has talked about. It was a tale about a camel-driver that had lost his camel, and he come along in the desert and met a man, and says:

" Have you run across a stray camel to-day?"

And the man says:

" Was he blind in his left eye?"

" Yes."

" Had he lost an upper front tooth?"

" Yes."

" Was his off hind leg lame?"

" Yes."

" Was he loaded with millet-seed on one side and honey on the other?"

" Yes, but you needn't go into no more details—

that's the one, and I'm in a hurry. Where did you see him?''

" I hain't seen him at all,'' the man says.

" Hain't seen him at all? How can you describe him so close, then?''

" Because when a person knows how to use his eyes, everything has got a meaning to it; but most people's eyes ain't any good to them. I knowed a camel had been along, because I seen his track. I knowed he was lame in his off hind leg because he had favored that foot and trod light on it, and his track showed it. I knowed he was blind on his left side because he only nibbled the grass on the right side of the trail. I knowed he had lost an upper front tooth because where he bit into the sod his teeth-print showed it. The millet-seed sifted out on one side — the ants told me that; the honey leaked out on the other — the flies told me that. I know all about your camel, but I hain't seen him.''

Jim says:

" Go on, Mars Tom, hit's a mighty good tale, and powerful interestin'.''

" That's all,'' Tom says.

" *All?*'' says Jim, astonished. " What 'come o' de camel?''

" I don't know.''

" Mars Tom, don't de tale say?''

" No.''

Jim puzzled a minute, then he says:

" Well! Ef dat ain't de beatenes' tale ever *I* struck.

Jist gits to de place whah de intrust is gittin' red-hot, en down she breaks. Why, Mars Tom, dey ain't no *sense* in a tale dat acts like dat. Hain't you got no *idea* whether de man got de camel back er not?''

" No, I haven't.''

I see myself there warn't no sense in the tale, to chop square off that way before it come to anything, but I warn't going to say so, because I could see Tom was souring up pretty fast over the way it flatted out and the way Jim had popped on to the weak place in it, and I don't think it's fair for everybody to pile on to a feller when he's down. But Tom he whirls on me and says:

" What do *you* think of the tale?''

Of course, then, I had to come out and make a clean breast and say it did seem to me, too, same as it did to Jim, that as long as the tale stopped square in the middle and never got to no place, it really warn't worth the trouble of telling.

Tom's chin dropped on his breast, and 'stead of being mad, as I reckoned he'd be, to hear me scoff at his tale that way, he seemed to be only sad; and he says:

" Some people can see, and some can't — just as that man said. Let alone a camel, if a cyclone had gone by, *you* duffers wouldn't 'a' noticed the track.''

I don't know what he meant by that, and he didn't say; it was just one of his irrulevances, I reckon — he was full of them, sometimes, when he was in a close place and couldn't see no other way out — but I didn't mind. We'd spotted the soft place in that tale sharp enough, he couldn't git away from that little fact. It graveled him like the nation, too, I reckon, much as he tried not to let on.

CHAPTER VIII.

THE DISAPPEARING LAKE

WE had an early breakfast in the morning, and set looking down on the desert, and the weather was ever so bammy and lovely, although we warn't high up. You have to come down lower and lower after sundown in the desert, because it cools off so fast; and so, by the time it is getting toward dawn, you are skimming along only a little ways above the sand.

We was watching the shadder of the balloon slide along the ground, and now and then gazing off across the desert to see if anything was stirring, and then down on the shadder again, when all of a sudden almost right under us we see a lot of men and camels laying scattered about, perfectly quiet, like they was asleep.

We shut off the power, and backed up and stood over them, and then we see that they was all dead. It give us the cold shivers. And it made us hush down, too, and talk low, like people at a funeral. We dropped down slow and stopped, and me and Tom clumb down and went among them. There was men,

(72)

and women, and children. They was dried by the sun
and dark and shriveled and leathery, like the pictures
of mummies you see in books. And yet they looked
just as human, you wouldn't 'a' believed it; just like
they was asleep.

Some of the people and animals was partly covered
with sand, but most of them not, for the sand was
thin there, and the bed was gravel and hard. Most
of the clothes had rotted away; and when you took
hold of a rag, it tore with a touch, like spider-
web. Tom reckoned they had been laying there for
years.

Some of the men had rusty guns by them, some had
swords on and had shawl belts with long, silver-
mounted pistols stuck in them. All the camels had
their loads on yet, but the packs had busted or rotted
and spilt the freight out on the ground. We didn't
reckon the swords was any good to the dead people
any more, so we took one apiece, and some pistols.
We took a small box, too, because it was so handsome
and inlaid so fine; and then we wanted to bury the
people; but there warn't no way to do it that we could
think of, and nothing to do it with but sand, and that
would blow away again, of course.

Then we mounted high and sailed away, and pretty
soon that black spot on the sand was out of sight, and
we wouldn't ever see them poor people again in this
world. We wondered, and reasoned, and tried to
guess how they come to be there, and how it all happened to them, but we couldn't make it out. First we

thought maybe they got lost, and wandered around and about till their food and water give out and they starved to death; but Tom said no wild animals nor vultures hadn't meddled with them, and so that guess wouldn't do. So at last we give it up, and judged we wouldn't think about it no more, because it made us low-spirited.

Then we opened the box, and it had gems and jewels in it, quite a pile, and some little veils of the kind the dead women had on, with fringes made out of curious gold money that we warn't acquainted with. We wondered if we better go and try to find them again and give it back; but Tom thought it over and said no, it was a country that was full of robbers, and they would come and steal it; and then the sin would be on us for putting the temptation in their way. So we went on; but I wished we had took all they had, so there wouldn't 'a' been no temptation at all left.

We had had two hours of that blazing weather down there, and was dreadful thirsty when we got aboard again. We went straight for the water, but it was spoiled and bitter, besides being pretty near hot enough to scald your mouth. We couldn't drink it. It was Mississippi river water, the best in the world, and we stirred up the mud in it to see if that would help, but no, the mud wasn't any better than the water.

Well, we hadn't been so very, very thirsty before, while we was interested in the lost people, but we was now, and as soon as we found we couldn't have a drink, we was more than thirty-five times as thirsty as we was a quarter of a minute before. Why, in a little while we wanted to hold our mouths open and pant like a dog.

Tom said to keep a sharp lookout, all around, every-wheres, because we'd got to find an oasis or there warn't no telling what would happen. So we done it. We kept the glasses gliding around all the time, till our arms got so tired we couldn't hold them any more. Two hours — three hours — just gazing and gazing, and nothing but sand, sand, *sand*, and you could see the quivering heat-shimmer playing over it. Dear, dear, a body don't know what real misery is till he is thirsty all the way through and is certain he ain't ever going to come to any water any more. At last I couldn't stand it to look around on them baking plains; I laid down on the locker, and give it up.

But by and by Tom raised a whoop, and there she was! A lake, wide and shiny, with pa'm-trees leaning over it asleep, and their shadders in the water just as soft and delicate as ever you see. I never see anything look so good. It was a long ways off, but that warn't anything to us; we just slapped on a hundred-mile gait, and calculated to be there in seven minutes; but she stayed the same old distance away, all the time; we couldn't seem to gain on her; yes, sir, just as far, and shiny, and like a dream; but we couldn't get no nearer; and at last, all of a sudden, she was gone!

Tom's eyes took a spread, and he says:

"Boys, it was a *my*ridge!" Said it like he was glad. I didn't see nothing to be glad about. I says:

6 **

" Maybe. I don't care nothing about its name, the thing I want to know is, what's become of it?"

Jim was trembling all over, and so scared he couldn't speak, but he wanted to ask that question himself if he could 'a' done it. Tom says:

" What's *become* of it? Why, you see yourself it's gone."

" Yes, I know; but where's it gone *to ?*"

He looked me over and says:

" Well, now, Huck Finn, where *would* it go to! Don't you know what a myridge is?"

" No, I don't. What is it?"

" It ain't anything but imagination. There ain't anything *to* it."

It warmed me up a little to hear him talk like that, and I says:

" What's the use you talking that kind of stuff, Tom Sawyer? Didn't I see the lake?"

" Yes — you think you did."

" I don't think nothing about it, I *did* see it."

" I tell you you *didn't* see it either — because it warn't there to see."

It astonished Jim to hear him talk so, and he broke in and says, kind of pleading and distressed:

" Mars Tom, *please* don't say sich things in sich an awful time as dis. You ain't only reskin' yo' own self, but you's reskin' us — same way like Anna Nias en Siffira. De lake *wuz* dah — I seen it jis' as plain as I sees you en Huck dis minute."

I says:

"Why, he seen it himself! He was the very one that seen it first. *Now*, then!"

"Yes, Mars Tom, hit's so — you can't deny it. We all seen it, en dat *prove* it was dah."

"Proves it! *How* does it prove it?"

"Same way it does in de courts en everywheres, Mars Tom. One pusson might be drunk, or dreamy or suthin', en he could be mistaken; en two might, maybe; but I tell you, sah, when three sees a thing, drunk er sober, it's *so*. Dey ain't no gittin' aroun' dat, en you knows it, Mars Tom."

"I don't know nothing of the kind. There used to be forty thousand million people that seen the sun move from one side of the sky to the other every day. Did that prove that the sun *done* it?"

"Course it did. En besides, dey warn't no 'casion to prove it. A body 'at's got any sense ain't gwine to doubt it. Dah she is now — a sailin' thoo de sky, like she allays done."

Tom turned on me, then, and says:

"What do *you* say — is the sun standing still?"

"Tom Sawyer, what's the use to ask such a jackass question? Anybody that ain't blind can see it don't stand still."

"Well," he says, "I'm lost in the sky with no company but a passel of low-down animals that don't know no more than the head boss of a university did three or four hundred years ago."

It warn't fair play, and I let him know it. I says:

"Throwin' mud ain't arguin', Tom Sawyer."

"Oh, my goodness, oh, my goodness gracious, dah's de lake agi'n!" yelled Jim, just then. "*Now*, Mars Tom, what you gwine to say?"

Yes, sir, there was the lake again, away yonder across the desert, perfectly plain, trees and all, just the same as it was before. I says:

"I reckon you're satisfied now, Tom Sawyer."

But he says, perfectly ca'm:

"Yes, satisfied there ain't no lake there."

Jim says:

"*Don't* talk so, Mars Tom — it sk'yers me to hear you. It's so hot, en you's so thirsty, dat you ain't in yo' right mine, Mars Tom. Oh, but don't she look good! 'clah I doan' know how I's gwine to wait tell we gits dah, I's *so* thirsty."

"Well, you'll have to wait; and it won't do you no good, either, because there ain't no lake there, I tell you."

I says:

"Jim, don't you take your eye off of it, and I won't, either."

"'Deed I won't; en bless you, honey, I couldn't ef I wanted to."

We went a-tearing along toward it, piling the miles behind us like nothing, but never gaining an inch on it — and all of a sudden it was gone again! Jim staggered, and 'most fell down. When he got his breath he says, gasping like a fish:

"Mars Tom, hit's a *ghos'*, dat's what it is, en I

hopes to goodness we ain't gwine to see it no mo'. Dey's *been* a lake, en suthin's happened, en de lake's dead, en we's seen its ghos'; we's seen it twiste, en dat's proof. De desert's ha'nted, it's ha'nted, sho; oh, Mars Tom, le' 's git outen it; I'd ruther die den have de night ketch us in it ag'in en de ghos' er dat lake come a-mournin' aroun' us en we asleep en doan' know de danger we's in.''

"Ghost, you gander! It ain't anything but air and heat and thirstiness pasted together by a person's imagination. If I — gimme the glass!''

He grabbed it and begun to gaze off to the right.

"It's a flock of birds,'' he says. "It's getting toward sundown, and they're making a bee-line across our track for somewheres. They mean business — maybe they're going for food or water, or both. Let her go to starb'oard! — Port your hellum! Hard down! There — ease up — steady, as you go.''

We shut down some of the power, so as not to out-speed them, and took out after them. We went skim-ming along a quarter of a mile behind them, and when we had followed them an hour and a half and was get-ting pretty discouraged, and was thirsty clean to unendurableness, Tom says:

"Take the glass, one of you, and see what that is, away ahead of the birds.''

Jim got the first glimpse, and slumped down on the locker sick. He was most crying, and says:

"She's dah ag'in, Mars Tom, she's dah ag'in, en I knows I's gwine to die, 'case when a body sees a ghos'

6

de third time, dat's what it means. I wisht I'd never come in dis balloon, dat I does."

He wouldn't look no more, and what he said made me afraid, too, because I knowed it was true, for that has always been the way with ghosts; so then I wouldn't look any more, either. Both of us begged Tom to turn off and go some other way, but he wouldn't, and said we was ignorant superstitious blatherskites. Yes, and he'll git come up with, one of these days, I says to myself, insulting ghosts that way. They'll stand it for a while, maybe, but they won't stand it always, for anybody that knows about ghosts knows how easy they are hurt, and how revengeful they are.

So we was all quiet and still, Jim and me being scared, and Tom busy. By and by Tom fetched the balloon to a standstill, and says:

" *Now* get up and look, you sapheads."

We done it, and there was the sure-enough water right under us ! — clear, and blue, and cool, and deep, and wavy with the breeze, the loveliest sight that ever was. And all about it was grassy banks, and flowers, and shady groves of big trees, looped together with vines, and all looking so peaceful and comfortable — enough to make a body cry, it was so beautiful.

Jim *did* cry, and rip and dance and carry on, he was so thankful and out of his mind for joy. It was my watch, so I had to stay by the works, but Tom and Jim clumb down and drunk a barrel apiece, and fetched me up a lot, and I've tasted a many a good thing in my life, but nothing that ever begun with that water.

Then we went down and had a swim, and then Tom came up and spelled me, and me and Jim had a swim, and then Jim spelled Tom, and me and Tom had a foot-race and a boxing-mill, and I don't reckon I ever had such a good time in my life. It warn't so very hot, because it was close on to evening, and we hadn't any clothes on, anyway. Clothes is well enough in school, and in towns, and at balls, too, but there ain't no sense in them when there ain't no civilization nor other kinds of bothers and fussiness around.

"Lions a-comin'! — lions! Quick, Mars Tom! Jump for yo' life, Huck!"

Oh, and didn't we! We never stopped for clothes, but waltzed up the ladder just so. Jim lost his head straight off — he always done it whenever he got excited and scared; and so now, 'stead of just easing the ladder up from the ground a little, so the animals couldn't reach it, he turned on a raft of power, and we went whizzing up and was dangling in the sky before he got his wits together and seen what a foolish thing he was doing. Then he stopped her, but he had clean forgot what to do next; so there we was, so high that the lions looked like pups, and we was drifting off on the wind.

But Tom he shinned up and went for the works and begun to slant her down, and back toward the lake, where the animals was gathering like a camp-meeting, and I judged he had lost *his* head, too; for he knowed

6**

I was too scared to climb, and did he want to dump me among the tigers and things?

But no, his head was level, he knowed what he was about. He swooped down to within thirty or forty feet of the lake, and stopped right over the center, and sung out:

" Leggo, and drop!"

I done it, and shot down, feet first, and seemed to go about a mile toward the bottom; and when I come up, he says:

" Now lay on your back and float till you're rested and got your pluck back, then I'll dip the ladder in the water and you can climb aboard."

I done it. Now that was ever so smart in Tom, because if he had started off somewheres else to drop down on the sand, the menagerie would 'a' come along, too, and might 'a' kept us hunting a safe place till I got tuckered out and fell.

And all this time the lions and tigers was sorting out the clothes, and trying to divide them up so there would be some for all, but there was a misunderstanding about it somewheres, on account of some of them trying to hog more than their share; so there was another insurrection, and you never see anything like it in the world. There must 'a' been fifty of them, all mixed up together, snorting and roaring and snapping and biting and tearing, legs and tails in the air, and you couldn't tell which was which, and the sand and fur a-flying. And when they got done, some was dead, and some was limping off crippled, and the rest was setting around on the battlefield, some of them licking their sore places and the others looking up at us and seemed to be kind of inviting us to come down and have some fun, but which we didn't want any.

As for the clothes, they warn't any, any more. Every last rag of them was inside of the animals; and not agreeing with them very well, I don't reckon, for there was considerable many brass buttons on them, and there was knives in the pockets, too, and smoking tobacco, and nails and chalk and marbles and fish-hooks and things. But I wasn't caring. All that was bothering me was, that all we had now was the pro-fessor's clothes, a big enough assortment, but not suit-able to go into company with, if we came across any, because the britches was as long as tunnels, and the coats and things according. Still, there was everything a tailor needed, and Jim was a kind of jack-legged tailor, and he allowed he could soon trim a suit or two down for us that would answer.

CHAPTER IX.

TOM DISCOURSES ON THE DESERT

STILL, we thought we would drop down there a minute, but on another errand. Most of the professor's cargo of food was put up in cans, in the new way that somebody had just invented; the rest was fresh. When you fetch Missouri beefsteak to the Great Sahara, you want to be particular and stay up in the coolish weather. So we reckoned we would drop down into the lion market and see how we could make out there.

We hauled in the ladder and dropped down till we was just above the reach of the animals, then we let down a rope with a slip-knot in it and hauled up a dead lion, a small tender one, then yanked up a cub tiger. We had to keep the congregation off with the revolver, or they would 'a' took a hand in the proceedings and helped.

We carved off a supply from both, and saved the skins, and hove the rest overboard. Then we baited some of the professor's hooks with the fresh meat and went a-fishing. We stood over the lake just a convenient distance above the water, and catched a lot of

"WE CATCHED FISH'

the nicest fish you ever see. It was a most amazing good supper we had; lion steak, tiger steak, fried fish, and hot corn-pone. I don't want nothing better than that.

We had some fruit to finish off with. We got it out of the top of a monstrous tall tree. It was a very slim tree that hadn't a branch on it from the bottom plumb to the top, and there it bursted out like a feather-duster. It was a pa'm-tree, of course; anybody knows a pa'm-tree the minute he see it, by the pictures. We went for cocoanuts in this one, but there warn't none. There was only big loose bunches of things like over-sized grapes, and Tom allowed they was dates, because he said they answered the description in the Arabian Nights and the other books. Of course they mightn't be, and they might be poison; so we had to wait a spell, and watch and see if the birds et them. They done it; so we done it, too, and they was most amazing good.

By this time monstrous big birds begun to come and settle on the dead animals. They was plucky creturs; they would tackle one end of a lion that was being gnawed at the other end by another lion. If the lion drove the bird away, it didn't do no good; he was back again the minute the lion was busy.

The big birds come out of every part of the sky — you could make them out with the glass while they was still so far away you couldn't see them with your naked eye. Tom said the birds didn't find out the meat was there by the smell; they had to find it out by seeing

it. Oh, but ain't that an eye for you! Tom said at
the distance of five mile a patch of dead lions couldn't
look any bigger than a person's finger-nail, and he
couldn't imagine how the birds could notice such a
little thing so far off.

It was strange and unnatural to see lion eat lion,
and we thought maybe they warn't kin. But Jim said
that didn't make no difference. He said a hog was
fond of her own children, and so was a spider, and he
reckoned maybe a lion was pretty near as unprincipled
though maybe not quite. He thought likely a lion
wouldn't eat his own father, if he knowed which was
him, but reckoned he would eat his brother-in-law if
he was uncommon hungry, and eat his mother-in-law
any time. But *reckoning* don't settle nothing. You
can reckon till the cows come home, but that don't
fetch you to no decision. So we give it up and let it
drop.

Generly it was very still in the Desert nights, but this
time there was music. A lot of other animals come to
dinner; sneaking yelpers that Tom allowed was jackals,
and roached-backed ones that he said was hyenas; and
all the whole biling of them kept up a racket all the
time. They made a picture in the moonlight that was
more different than any picture I ever see. We had a
line out and made fast to the top of a tree, and didn't
stand no watch, but all turned in and slept; but I was
up two or three times to look down at the animals and
hear the music. It was like having a front seat at a
menagerie for nothing, which I hadn't ever had before,

and so it seemed foolish to sleep and not make the most of it; I mightn't ever have such a chance again.

We went a-fishing again in the early dawn, and then lazied around all day in the deep shade on an island, taking turn about to watch and see that none of the animals come a-snooping around there after erronorts for dinner. We was going to leave the next day, but couldn't, it was too lovely.

The day after, when we rose up toward the sky and sailed off eastward, we looked back and watched that place till it warn't nothing but just a speck in the Desert, and I tell you it was like saying good-bye to a friend that you ain't ever going to see any more.

Jim was thinking to himself, and at last he says:

"Mars Tom, we's mos' to de end er de Desert now, I speck."

"Why?"

"Well, hit stan' to reason we is. You knows how long we's been a-skimmin' over it. Mus' be mos' out o' san'. Hit's a wonder to me dat it's hilt out as long as it has."

"Shucks, there's plenty sand, you needn't worry."

"Oh, I ain't a-worryin', Mars Tom, only wonderin', dat's all. De Lord's got plenty san', I ain't doubtin' dat; but nemmine, He ain't gwyne to *was'e* it jist on dat account; en I allows dat dis Desert's plenty big enough now, jist de way she is, en you can't spread her out no mo' 'dout was'in' san'."

"Oh, go 'long! we ain't much more than fairly

started across this Desert yet. The United States is a pretty big country, ain't it? Ain't it, Huck?"

"Yes," I says, "there ain't no bigger one, I don't reckon."

"Well," he says, "this Desert is about the shape of the United States, and if you was to lay it down on top of the United States, it would cover the land of the free out of sight like a blanket. There'd be a little corner sticking out, up at Maine and away up north-west, and Florida sticking out like a turtle's tail, and that's all. We've took California away from the Mexicans two or three years ago, so that part of the Pacific coast is ours now, and if you laid the Great Sahara down with her edge on the Pacific, she would cover the United States and stick out past New York six hundred miles into the Atlantic ocean."

I say:

"Good land! have you got the documents for that, Tom Sawyer?"

"Yes, and they're right here, and I've been study-ing them. You can look for yourself. From New York to the Pacific is 2,600 miles. From one end of the Great Desert to the other is 3,200. The United States contains 3,600,000 square miles, the Desert contains 4,162,000. With the Desert's bulk you could cover up every last inch of the United States, and in under where the edges projected out, you could tuck England, Scotland, Ireland, France, Denmark, and all Germany. Yes, sir, you could hide the home of the brave and all of them countries clean out of sight under the Great Sahara, and you would still have 2,000 square miles of sand left.''

"Well," I says, " it clean beats me. Why, Tom, it shows that the Lord took as much pains makin' this Desert as makin' the United States and all them other countries.''

Jim says: " Huck, dat don' stan' to reason. I reckon dis Desert wa'n't made at all. Now you take en look at it like dis — you look at it, and see ef I's right. What's a desert good for? 'Taint good for nuthin'. Dey ain't no way to make it pay. Hain't dat so, Huck?''

" Yes, I reckon.''

" Hain't it so, Mars Tom?''

" I guess so. Go on.''

" Ef a thing ain't no good, it's made in vain, ain't it?''

" Yes.''

" *Now*, den! Do de Lord make anything in vain? You answer me dat.''

" Well — no, He don't.''

" Den how come He make a desert?''

" Well, go on. How *did* He come to make it?''

" Mars Tom, *I* b'lieve it uz jes like when you's buildin' a house; dey's allays a lot o' truck en rubbish lef' over. What does you do wid it? Doan' you take en k'yart it off en dump it into a ole vacant back lot? 'Course. Now, den, it's my opinion hit was jes like dat — dat de Great Sahara warn't made at all, she jes *happen*'.''

I said it was a real good argument, and I believed it was the best one Jim ever made. Tom he said the same, but said the trouble about arguments is, they ain't nothing but *theories*, after all, and theories don't prove nothing, they only give you a place to rest on, a spell, when you are tuckered out butting around and around trying to find out something there ain't no way *to* find out. And he says:

"There's another trouble about theories: there's always a hole in them somewheres, sure, if you look close enough. It's just so with this one of Jim's. Look what billions and billions of stars there is. How does it come that there was just exactly enough star-stuff, and none left over? How does it come there ain't no sand-pile up there?"

But Jim was fixed for him and says:

"What's de Milky Way?—dat's what *I* want to know. What's de Milky Way? Answer me dat!"

In my opinion it was just a sockdologer. It's only an opinion, it's only *my* opinion and others may think different; but I said it then and I stand to it now—it was a sockdologer. And moreover, besides, it landed Tom Sawyer. He couldn't say a word. He had that stunned look of a person that's been shot in the back with a kag of nails. All he said was, as for people like me and Jim, he'd just as soon have intellectual intercourse with a catfish. But anybody can say that —and I notice they always do, when somebody has fetched them a lifter. Tom Sawyer was tired of that end of the subject.

So we got back to talking about the size of the Desert again, and the more we compared it with this

and that and t'other thing, the more nobier and bigger
and grander it got to look right along.   And so, hunting among the figgers, Tom found, by and by, that it
was just the same size as the Empire of China.   Then
he showed us the spread the Empire of China made on
the map, and the room she took up in the world.
Well, it was wonderful to think of, and I says:

"Why, I've heard talk about this Desert plenty of
times, but *I* never knowed before how important she
was."

Then Tom says:

"Important! Sahara important! That's just the
way with some people. If a thing's big, it's important.
That's all the sense they've got. All they can see is
size. Why, look at England. It's the most important
country in the world; and yet you could put it in
China's vest-pocket; and not only that, but you'd
have the dickens's own time to find it again the next
time you wanted it. And look at Russia. It spreads
all around and everywhere, and yet ain't no more important in this world than Rhode Island is, and hasn't
got half as much in it that's worth saving."

Away off now we see a little hill, a-standing up just
on the edge of the world. Tom broke off his talk, and
reached for a glass very much excited, and took a look,
and says:

"That's it — it's the one I've been looking for,
sure. If I'm right, it's the one the dervish took the
man into and showed him all the treasures."

So we begun to gaze, and he begun to tell about it
out of the Arabian Nights.

7 **

CHAPTER X.

TOM said it happened like this.

A dervish was stumping it along through the Desert, on foot, one blazing hot day, and he had come a thousand miles and was pretty poor, and hungry, and ornery and tired, and along about where we are now he run across a camel-driver with a hundred camels, and asked him for some a'ms. But the camel-driver he asked to be excused. The dervish said:

" Don't you own these camels?"

" Yes, they're mine."

" Are you in debt?"

" Who — me? No."

" Well, a man that owns a hundred camels and ain't in debt is rich — and not only rich, but very rich. Ain't it so?"

The camel-driver owned up that it was so. Then the dervish says:

" God has made you rich, and He has made me poor. He has His reasons, and they are wise, blessed be His name. But He has willed that His rich shall help His poor, and you have turned away from me,

(92)

your brother, in my need, and He will remember this, and you will lose by it."

That made the camel-driver feel shaky, but all the same he was born hoggish after money and didn't like to let go a cent; so he begun to whine and explain, and said times was hard, and although he had took a full freight down to Balsora and got a fat rate for it, he couldn't git no return freight, and so he warn't making no great things out of his trip. So the dervish starts along again, and says:

"All right, if you want to take the risk; but I reckon you've made a mistake this time, and missed a chance."

Of course the camel-driver wanted to know what kind of a chance he had missed, because maybe there was money in it; so he run after the dervish, and begged him so hard and earnest to take pity on him that at last the dervish gave in, and says:

"Do you see that hill yonder? Well, in that hill is all the treasures of the earth, and I was looking around for a man with a particular good kind heart and a noble, generous disposition, because if I could find just that man, I've got a kind of a salve I could put on his eyes and he could see the treasures and get them out."

So then the camel-driver was in a sweat; and he cried, and begged, and took on, and went down on his knees, and said he was just that kind of a man, and said he could fetch a thousand people that would say he wasn't ever described so exact before.

"Well, then," says the dervish, "all right. If we load the hundred camels, can I have half of them?"

The driver was so glad he couldn't hardly hold in, and says:

"Now you're shouting."

So they shook hands on the bargain, and the dervish got out his box and rubbed the salve on the driver's right eye, and the hill opened and he went in, and there, sure enough, was piles and piles of gold and jewels sparkling like all the stars in heaven had fell down.

So him and the dervish laid into it, and they loaded every camel till he couldn't carry no more; then they said good-bye, and each of them started off with his fifty. But pretty soon the camel-driver come a-running and overtook the dervish and says:

"You ain't in society, you know, and you don't really need all you've got. Won't you be good, and let me have ten of your camels?"

"Well," the dervish says, "I don't know but what you say is reasonable enough."

So he done it, and they separated and the dervish started off again with his forty. But pretty soon here comes the camel-driver bawling after him again, and whines and slobbers around and begs another ten off of him, saying thirty camel loads of treasures was enough to see a dervish through, because they live very simple, you know, and don't keep house, but board around and give their note.

But that warn't the end yet. That ornery hound kept coming and coming till he had begged back all the camels and had the whole hundred. Then he was satisfied, and ever so grateful, and said he wouldn't ever forgit the dervish as long as he lived, and nobody hadn't been so good to him before, and liberal. So they shook hands good-bye, and separated and started off again.

But do you know, it warn't ten minutes till the camel-driver was unsatisfied again — he was the low-downest reptyle in seven counties — and he come a-running again. And this time the thing he wanted was to get the dervish to rub some of the salve on his other eye.

" Why?" said the dervish.

" Oh, you know," says the driver.

' Know what?"

" Well, you can't fool me," says the driver. " You're trying to keep back something from me, you know it mighty well. You know, I reckon, that if I had the salve on the other eye I could see a lot more things that's valuable. Come — please put it on."

The dervish says:

' I wasn't keeping anything back from you. I don't mind telling you what would happen if I put it on. You'd never see again. You'd be stone-blind the rest of your days."

But do you know that beat wouldn't believe him. No, he begged and begged, and whined and cried, till at last the dervish opened his box and told him to put it on, if he wanted to. So the man done it, and sure enough he was as blind as a bat in a minute.

7

Then the dervish laughed at him and mocked at him and made fun of him; and says:

"Good-bye — a man that's blind hain't got no use for jewelry."

And he cleared out with the hundred camels, and left that man to wander around poor and miserable and friendless the rest of his days in the Desert.

Jim said he'd bet it was a lesson to him.

"Yes," Tom says, "and like a considerable many lessons a body gets. They ain't no account, because the thing don't ever happen the same way again — and can't. The time Hen Scovil fell down the chimbly and crippled his back for life, everybody said it would be a lesson to him. What kind of a lesson? How was he going to use it? He couldn't climb chimblies no more, and he hadn't no more backs to break."

"All de same, Mars Tom, dey *is* sich a thing as learnin' by expe'ence. De Good Book say de burnt chile shun de fire."

"Well, I ain't denying that a thing's a lesson if it's a thing that can happen twice just the same way. There's lots of such things, and *they* educate a person, that's what Uncle Abner always said; but there's forty *million* lots of the other kind — the kind that don't happen the same way twice — and they ain't no real use, they ain't no more instructive than the small-pox. When you've got it, it ain't no good to find out you ought to been vaccinated, and it ain't no good to git vaccinated afterward, because the small-pox don't come but once. But, on the other hand, Uncle Abner

said that the person that had took a bull by the tail
once had learnt sixty or seventy times as much as a
person that hadn't, and said a person that started in to
carry a cat home by the tail was gitting knowledge that
was always going to be useful to him, and warn't ever
going to grow dim or doubtful. But I can tell you,
Jim, Uncle Abner was down on them people that's all
the time trying to dig a lesson out of everything that
happens, no matter whether —"

But Jim was asleep. Tom looked kind of ashamed,
because you know a person always feels bad when he
is talking uncommon fine and thinks the other person
is admiring, and that other person goes to sleep that
way. Of course he oughtn't to go to sleep, because
it's shabby; but the finer a person talks the certainer
it is to make you sleep, and so when you come to look
at it it ain't nobody's fault in particular; both of
them's to blame.

Jim begun to snore — soft and blubbery at first,
then a long rasp, then a stronger one, then a half a
dozen horrible ones like the last water sucking down
the plug-hole of a bath-tub, then the same with more
power to it, and some big coughs and snorts flung in,
the way a cow does that is choking to death; and
when the person has got to that point he is at his level
best, and can wake up a man that is in the next block
with a dipperful of loddanum in him, but can't wake
himself up although all that awful noise of his'n ain't
but three inches from his own ears. And that is the
curiosest thing in the world, seems to me. But you

7 **

rake a match to light the candle, and that little bit of a noise will fetch him. I wish I knowed what was the reason of that, but there don't seem to be no way to find out. Now there was Jim alarming the whole Desert, and yanking the animals out, for miles and miles around, to see what in the nation was going on up there; there warn't nobody nor nothing that was as close to the noise as *he* was, and yet he was the only cretur that wasn't disturbed by it. We yelled at him and whooped at him, it never done no good; but the first time there come a little wee noise that wasn't of a usual kind it woke him up. No, sir, I've thought it all over, and so has Tom, and there ain't no way to find out why a snorer can't hear himself snore.

Jim said he hadn't been asleep; he just shut his eyes so he could listen better.

Tom said nobody warn't accusing him.

That made him look like he wished he hadn't said anything. And he wanted to git away from the subject, I reckon, because he begun to abuse the camel-driver, just the way a person does when he has got catched in something and wants to take it out of somebody else. He let into the camel-driver the hardest he knowed how, and I had to agree with him; and he praised up the dervish the highest he could, and I had to agree with him there, too. But Tom says:

"I ain't so sure. You call that dervish so dreadful liberal and good and unselfish, but I don't quite see it. He didn't hunt up another poor dervish, did he? No, he didn't. If he was so unselfish, why didn't he go in there himself and take a pocketful of jewels and go along and be satisfied? No, sir, the person he was hunting for was a man with a hundred camels. He wanted to get away with all the treasure he could.''

"Why, Mars Tom, he was willin' to divide, fair and square; he only struck for fifty camels.''

"Because he knowed how he was going to get all of them by and by.''

"Mars Tom, he *tole* de man de truck would make him bline.''

"Yes, because he knowed the man's character. It was just the kind of a man he was hunting for — a man that never believes in anybody's word or anybody's honorableness, because he ain't got none of his own. I reckon there's lots of people like that dervish. They swindle, right and left, but they always make the other person *seem* to swindle himself. They keep inside of the letter of the law all the time, and there ain't no way to git hold of them. *They* don't put the salve on — oh, no, that would be sin; but they know how to fool *you* into putting it on, then it's you that blinds yourself. I reckon the dervish and the camel-driver was just a pair — a fine, smart, brainy rascal, and a dull, coarse, ignorant one, but both of them rascals, just the same.''

"Mars Tom, does you reckon dey's any o' dat kind o' salve in de worl' now?''

"Yes, Uncle Abner says there is. He says they've got it in New York, and they put it on country people's eyes and show them all the railroads in the world, and

G**

they go in and git them, and then when they rub the
salve on the other eye the other man bids them good-
bye and goes off with their railroads. Here's the
treasure-hill now.   Lower away!"

We landed, but it warn't as interesting as I thought
it was going to be, because we couldn't find the place
where they went in to git the treasure.   Still, it was
plenty interesting enough, just to see the mere hill
itself where such a wonderful thing happened.   Jim
said he wouldn't 'a' missed it for three dollars, and I
felt the same way.

And to me and Jim, as wonderful a thing as any was
the way Tom could come into a strange big country
like this and go straight and find a little hump like that
and tell it in a minute from a million other humps that
was almost just like it, and nothing to help him but
only his own learning and his own natural smartness.
We talked and talked it over together, but couldn't
make out how he done it.   He had the best head on
him I ever see; and all he lacked was age, to make a
name for himself equal to Captain Kidd or George
Washington.   I bet you it would 'a' crowded either of
them to find that hill, with all their gifts, but it warn't
nothing to Tom Sawyer; he went across Sahara and
put his finger on it as easy as you could pick a nigger
out of a bunch of angels.

We found a pond of salt water close by and scraped
up a raft of salt around the edges, and loaded up the
lion's skin and the tiger's so as they would keep till Jim
could tan them.

CHAPTER XI.

THE SAND-STORM

WE went a-fooling along for a day or two, and then just as the full moon was touching the ground on the other side of the desert, we see a string of little black figgers moving across its big silver face. You could see them as plain as if they was painted on the moon with ink. It was another caravan. We cooled down our speed and tagged along after it, just to have company, though it warn't going our way. It was a rattler, that caravan, and a most bully sight to look at next morning when the sun come a-streaming across the desert and flung the long shadders of the camels on the gold sand like a thousand grand-daddy-long-legses marching in procession. We never went very near it, because we knowed better now than to act like that and scare people's camels and break up their cara-vans. It was the gayest outfit you ever see, for rich clothes and nobby style. Some of the chiefs rode on dromedaries, the first we ever see, and very tall, and they go plunging along like they was on stilts, and they rock the man that is on them pretty violent and churn up his dinner considerable, I bet you, but they make noble good time, and a camel ain't nowheres with them for speed.

The caravan camped, during the middle part of the day, and then started again about the middle of the afternoon. Before long the sun begun to look very curious. First it kind of turned to brass, and then to copper, and after that it begun to look like a blood-red ball, and the air got hot and close, and pretty soon all the sky in the west darkened up and looked thick and foggy, but fiery and dreadful — like it looks through a piece of red glass, you know. We looked down and see a big confusion going on in the caravan, and a rushing every which way like they was scared; and then they all flopped down flat in the sand and laid there perfectly still.

Pretty soon we see something coming that stood up like an amazing wide wall, and reached from the Desert up into the sky and hid the sun, and it was coming like the nation, too. Then a little faint breeze struck us, and then it come harder, and grains of sand begun to sift against our faces and sting like fire, and Tom sung out:

"It's a sand-storm — turn your backs to it!"

We done it; and in another minute it was blowing a gale, and the sand beat against us by the shovelful, and the air was so thick with it we couldn't see a thing. In five minutes the boat was level full, and we was setting on the lockers buried up to the chin in sand, and only our heads out and could hardly breathe.

Then the storm thinned, and we see that monstrous

wall go a-sailing off across the desert, awful to look at, I tell you. We dug ourselves out and looked down, and where the caravan was before there wasn't anything but just the sand ocean now, and all still and quiet. All them people and camels was smothered and dead and buried — buried under ten foot of sand, we reckoned, and Tom allowed it might be years before the wind uncovered them, and all that time their friends wouldn't ever know what become of that caravan. Tom said:

"*Now* we know what it was that happened to the people we got the swords and pistols from."

Yes, sir, that was just it. It was as plain as day now. They got buried in a sand-storm, and the wild animals couldn't get at them, and the wind never uncovered them again until they was dried to leather and warn't fit to eat. It seemed to me we had felt as sorry for them poor people as a person could for anybody, and as mournful, too, but we was mistaken; this last caravan's death went harder with us, a good deal harder. You see, the others was total strangers, and we never got to feeling acquainted with them at all, except, maybe, a little with the man that was watching the girl, but it was different with this last caravan. We was huvvering around them a whole night and 'most a whole day, and had got to feeling real friendly with them, and acquainted. I have found out that there ain't no surer way to find out whether you like people or hate them than to travel with them. Just so with these. We kind of liked them from the start, and

traveling with them put on the finisher. The longer
we traveled with them, and the more we got used to
their ways, the better and better we liked them, and
the gladder and gladder we was that we run across
them. We had come to know some of them so well
that we called them by name when we was talking
about them, and soon got so familiar and sociable that
we even dropped the Miss and Mister and just used
their plain names without any handle, and it did not
seem unpolite, but just the right thing. Of course, it
wasn't their own names, but names we give them.
There was Mr. Elexander Robinson and Miss Adaline
Robinson, and Colonel Jacob McDougal and Miss
Harryet McDougal, and Judge Jeremiah Butler and
young Bushrod Butler, and these was big chiefs mostly
that wore splendid great turbans and simmeters, and
dressed like the Grand Mogul, and their families. But
as soon as we come to know them good, and like them
very much, it warn't Mister, nor Judge, nor nothing,
any more, but only Elleck, and Addy, and Jake, and
Hattie, and Jerry, and Buck, and so on.

And you know the more you join in with people in
their joys and their sorrows, the more nearer and
dearer they come to be to you. Now we warn't cold
and indifferent, the way most travelers is, we was right
down friendly and sociable, and took a chance in everything that was going, and the caravan could depend on
us to be on hand every time, it didn't make no difference what it was.

When they camped, we camped right over them, ten

or twelve hundred feet up in the air. When they et a meal, we et ourn, and it made it ever so much home-liker to have their company. When they had a wed-ding that night, and Buck and Addy got married, we got ourselves up in the very starchiest of the professor's duds for the blow-out, and when they danced we jined in and shook a foot up there.

But it is sorrow and trouble that brings you the nearest, and it was a funeral that done it with us. It was next morning, just in the still dawn. We didn't know the diseased, and he warn't in our set, but that never made no difference; he belonged to the caravan, and that was enough, and there warn't no more sincerer tears shed over him than the ones we dripped on him from up there eleven hundred foot on high.

Yes, parting with this caravan was much more bitterer than it was to part with them others, which was comparative strangers, and been dead so long, anyway. We had knowed these in their lives, and was fond of them, too, and now to have death snatch them from right before our faces while we was looking, and leave us so lonesome and friendless in the middle of that big desert, it did hurt so, and we wished we mightn't ever make any more friends on that voyage if we was going to lose them again like that.

We couldn't keep from talking about them, and they was all the time coming up in our memory, and looking just the way they looked when we was all alive and happy together. We could see the line marching, and the shiny spearheads a-winking in the sun; we could see the dromedaries lumbering along; we could see the wedding and the funeral; and more oftener than anything else we could see them praying, because they don't allow nothing to prevent that; whenever the call come, several times a day, they would stop right there, and stand up and face to the east, and lift back their heads, and spread out their arms and begin, and four or five times they would go down on their knees, and then fall forward and touch their forehead to the ground.

Well, it warn't good to go on talking about them, lovely as they was in their life, and dear to us in their life and death both, because it didn't do no good, and made us too down-hearted. Jim allowed he was going to live as good a life as he could, so he could see them again in a better world; and Tom kept still and didn't tell him they was only Mohammedans; it warn't no use to disappoint him, he was feeling bad enough just as it was.

When we woke up next morning we was feeling a little cheerfuller, and had had a most powerful good sleep, because sand is the comfortablest bed there is, and I don't see why people that can afford it don't have it more. And it's terrible good ballast, too; I never see the balloon so steady before.

Tom allowed we had twenty tons of it, and wondered what we better do with it; it was good sand, and it didn't seem good sense to throw it away. Jim says:

"Mars Tom, can't we tote it back home en sell it? How long'll it take?"

" Depends on the way we go."

" Well, sah, she's wuth a quarter of a dollar a load at home, en I reckon we's got as much as twenty loads, hain't we?   How much would dat be?"

" Five dollars."

" By jings, Mars Tom, le's shove for home right on de spot!   Hit's more'n a dollar en a half apiece, hain't it?"

" Yes."

" Well, ef dat ain't makin' money de easiest ever I struck!   She jes' rained in — never cos' us a lick o' work.   Le's mosey right along, Mars Tom."

But Tom was thinking and ciphering away so busy and excited he never heard him.   Pretty soon he says:

" Five dollars — sho!   Look here, this sand's worth — worth — why, it's worth no end of money."

" How is dat, Mars Tom?   Go on, honey, go on!"

" Well, the minute people knows it's genuwyne sand from the genuwyne Desert of Sahara, they'll just be in a perfect state of mind to git hold of some of it to keep on the what-not in a vial with a label on it for a curiosity.   All we got to do is to put it up in vials and float around all over the United States and peddle them out at ten cents apiece.   We've got all of ten thousand dollars' worth of sand in this boat."

Me and Jim went all to pieces with joy, and begun to shout whoopjamboreehoo, and Tom says:

" And we can keep on coming back and fetching sand, and coming back and fetching more sand, and just keep it a-going till we've carted this whole Desert over there and sold it out; and there ain't ever going to be any opposition, either, because we'll take out a patent.''

'' My goodness,'' I says, '' we'll be as rich as Creosote, won't we, Tom?''

'' Yes — Creesus, you mean. Why, that dervish was hunting in that little hill for the treasures of the earth, and didn't know he was walking over the real ones for a thousand miles. He was blinder than he made the driver.''

'' Mars Tom, how much is we gwyne to be worth?''

'' Well, I don't know yet. It's got to be ciphered, and it ain't the easiest job to do, either, because it's over four million square miles of sand at ten cents a vial.''

Jim was awful excited, but this faded it out considerable, and he shook his head and says:

'' Mars Tom, we can't 'ford all dem vials — a king couldn't. We better not try to take de whole Desert, Mars Tom, de vials gwyne to bust us, sho'.''

Tom's excitement died out, too, now, and I reckoned it was on account of the vials, but it wasn't. He set there thinking, and got bluer and bluer, and at last he says:

' Boys, it won't work; we got to give it up.''

'' Why, Tom?''

'' On account of the duties.''

I couldn't make nothing out of that, neither could Jim. I says:

'' What *is* our duty, Tom? Because if we can't git

around it, why can't we just *do* it? People often has to."

But he says:

"Oh, it ain't that kind of duty. The kind I mean is a tax. Whenever you strike a frontier — that's the border of a country, you know — you find a custom-house there, and the gov'ment officers comes and rummages among your things and charges a big tax, which they call a duty because it's their duty to bust you if they can, and if you don't pay the duty they'll hog your sand. They call it confiscating, but that don't deceive nobody, it's just hogging, and that's all it is. Now if we try to carry this sand home the way we're pointed now, we got to climb fences till we git tired — just frontier after frontier — Egypt, Arabia, Hindostan, and so on, and they'll all whack on a duty, and so you see, easy enough, we *can't* go *that* road."

"Why, Tom," I says, "we can sail right over their old frontiers; how are *they* going to stop us?"

He looked sorrowful at me, and says, very grave:

"Huck Finn, do you think that would be honest?"

I hate them kind of interruptions. I never said nothing, and he went on:

"Well, we're shut off the other way, too. If we go back the way we've come, there's the New York custom-house, and that is worse than all of them others put together, on account of the kind of cargo we've got."

"Why?"

"Well, they can't raise Sahara sand in America, of

course, and when they can't raise a thing there, the duty is fourteen hundred thousand per cent. on it if you try to fetch it in from where they do raise it."

"There ain't no sense in that, Tom Sawyer."

"Who said there *was*? What do you talk to me like that for, Huck Finn? You wait till I say a thing's got sense in it before you go to accusing me of saying it."

"All right, consider me crying about it, and sorry. Go on."

Jim says:

"Mars Tom, do dey jam dat duty onto everything we can't raise in America, en don't make no 'stinction 'twix' anything?"

"Yes, that's what they do."

"Mars Tom, ain't de blessin' o' de Lord de mos' valuable thing dey is?"

"Yes, it is."

"Don't de preacher stan' up in de pulpit en call it down on de people?"

"Yes."

"Whah do it come from?"

"From heaven."

'Yassir! you's jes' right, 'deed you is, honey — it come from heaven, en dat's a foreign country. *Now*, den! do dey put a tax on dat blessin'?"

"No, they don't."

"Course dey don't; en so it stan' to reason dat you's mistaken, Mars Tom. Dey wouldn't put de tax on po' truck like san', dat everybody ain't 'bleeged to

have, en leave it off'n de bes' thing dey is, which
nobody can't git along widout.''

Tom Sawyer was stumped; he see Jim had got him
where he couldn't budge. He tried to wiggle out by
saying they had *forgot* to put on that tax, but they'd
be sure to remember about it, next session of Congress, and then they'd put it on, but that was a poor
lame come-off, and he knowed it. He said there
warn't nothing foreign that warn't taxed but just that
one, and so they couldn't be consistent without taxing
it, and to be consistent was the first law of politics.
So he stuck to it that they'd left it out unintentional
and would be certain to do their best to fix it before
they got caught and laughed at.

But I didn't feel no more interest in such things, as
long as we couldn't git our sand through, and it made
me low-spirited, and Jim the same. Tom he tried to
cheer us up by saying he would think up another
speculation for us that would be just as good as this
one and better, but it didn't do no good, we didn't
believe there was any as big as this. It was mighty
hard; such a little while ago we was so rich, and could
'a' bought a country and started a kingdom and been
celebrated and happy, and now we was so poor and
ornery again, and had our sand left on our hands.
The sand was looking so lovely before, just like gold
and di'monds, and the feel of it was so soft and so
silky and nice, but now I couldn't bear the sight of it,
it made me sick to look at it, and I knowed I wouldn't
ever feel comfortable again till we got shut of it, and I

8

didn't have it there no more to remind us of what we had been and what we had got degraded down to. The others was feeling the same way about it that I was. I knowed it, because they cheered up so, the minute I says le's throw this truck overboard.

Well, it was going to be work, you know, and pretty solid work, too; so Tom he divided it up according to fairness and strength. He said me and him would clear out a fifth apiece of the sand, and Jim three-fifths. Jim he didn't quite like that arrangement. He says:

"Course I's de stronges', en I's willin' to do a share accordin', but by jings you's kinder pilin' it onto ole Jim, Mars Tom, hain't you?"

"Well, I didn't think so, Jim, but you try your hand at fixing it, and let's see."

So Jim reckoned it wouldn't be no more than fair if me and Tom done a *tenth* apiece. Tom he turned his back to git room and be private, and then he smole a smile that spread around and covered the whole Sahara to the westward, back to the Atlantic edge of it where we come from. Then he turned around again and said it was a good enough arrangement, and we was satisfied if Jim was. Jim said he was.

So then Tom measured off our two-tenths in the bow and left the rest for Jim, and it surprised Jim a good deal to see how much difference there was and what a raging lot of sand his share come to, and said he was powerful glad now that he had spoke up in time and got the first arrangement altered, for he said that even the way it was now, there was more sand than enjoyment in his end of the contract, he believed.

Then we laid into it. It was mighty hot work, and tough; so hot we had to move up into cooler weather or we couldn't 'a' stood it. Me and Tom took turn about, and one worked while t'other rested, but there warn't nobody to spell poor old Jim, and he made all that part of Africa damp, he sweated so. We couldn't work good, we was so full of laugh, and Jim he kept fretting and wanting to know what tickled us so, and we had to keep making up things to account for it, and they was pretty poor inventions, but they done well enough, Jim didn't see through them. At last when we got done we was 'most dead, but not with work but with laughing. By and by Jim was 'most dead, too, but it was with work; then we took turns and spelled him, and he was as thankful as he could be, and would set on the gunnel and swab the sweat, and heave and pant, and say how good we was to a poor old nigger, and he wouldn't ever forgit us. He was always the gratefulest nigger I ever see, for any little thing you done for him. He was only nigger outside; inside he was as white as you be.

CHAPTER XII.

THE next few meals was pretty sandy, but that don't make no difference when you are hungry; and when you ain't it ain't no satisfaction to eat, anyway, and so a little grit in the meat ain't no particular drawback, as far as I can see.

Then we struck the east end of the Desert at last, sailing on a northeast course. Away off on the edge of the sand, in a soft pinky light, we see three little sharp roofs like tents, and Tom says:

"It's the pyramids of Egypt."

It made my heart fairly jump. You see, I had seen a many and a many a picture of them, and heard tell about them a hundred times, and yet to come on them all of a sudden, that way, and find they was *real*, 'stead of imaginations, 'most knocked the breath out of me with surprise. It's a curious thing, that the more you hear about a grand and big and bully thing or person, the more it kind of dreamies out, as you may say, and gets to be a big dim wavery figger made out of moonshine and nothing solid to it. It's just so with George Washington, and the same with them pyramids.

(114)

And moreover, besides, the thing they always said about them seemed to me to be stretchers. There was a feller come to the Sunday-school once, and had a picture of them, and made a speech, and said the biggest pyramid covered thirteen acres, and was most five hundred foot high, just a steep mountain, all built out of hunks of stone as big as a bureau, and laid up in perfectly regular layers, like stair-steps. Thirteen acres, you see, for just one building; it's a farm. If it hadn't been in Sunday-school, I would 'a' judged it was a lie; and outside I was certain of it. And he said there was a hole in the pyramid, and you could go in there with candles, and go ever so far up a long slanting tunnel, and come to a large room in the stomach of that stone mountain, and there you would find a big stone chest with a king in it, four thousand years old. I said to myself, then, if that ain't a lie I will eat that king if they will fetch him, for even Methusalem warn't that old, and nobody claims it.

As we come a little nearer we see the yaller sand come to an end in a long straight edge like a blanket, and on to it was joined, edge to edge, a wide country of bright green, with a snaky stripe crooking through it, and Tom said it was the Nile. It made my heart jump again, for the Nile was another thing that wasn't real to me. Now I can tell you one thing which is dead certain: if you will fool along over three thousand miles of yaller sand, all glimmering with heat so that it makes your eyes water to look at it, and you've been a considerable part of a week doing it, the green

H**

country will look so like home and heaven to you that it will make your eyes water *again*.

It was just so with me, and the same with Jim.

And when Jim got so he could believe it *was* the land of Egypt he was looking at, he wouldn't enter it standing up, but got down on his knees and took off his hat, because he said it wasn't fitten' for a humble poor nigger to come any other way where such men had been as Moses and Joseph and Pharaoh and the other prophets. He was a Presbyterian, and had a most deep respect for Moses which was a Presbyterian, too, he said. He was all stirred up, and says:

"Hit's de lan' of Egypt, de lan' of Egypt, en I's 'lowed to look at it wid my own eyes! En dah's de river dat was turn' to blood, en I's looking at de very same groun' whah de plagues was, en de lice, en de frogs, en de locus', en de hail, en whah dey marked de door-pos', en de angel o' de Lord come by in de darkness o' de night en slew de fust-born in all de lan' o' Egypt. Ole Jim ain't worthy to see dis day!"

And then he just broke down and cried, he was so thankful. So between him and Tom there was talk enough, Jim being excited because the land was so full of history — Joseph and his brethren, Moses in the bulrushers, Jacob coming down into Egypt to buy corn, the silver cup in the sack, and all them interesting things; and Tom just as excited too, because the land was so full of history that was in *his* line, about Noureddin, and Bedreddin, and such like monstrous giants, that made Jim's wool rise, and a raft of other

Arabian Nights folks, which the half of them never done the things they let on they done, I don't believe.

Then we struck a disappointment, for one of them early morning fogs started up, and it warn't no use to sail over the top of it, because we would go by Egypt, sure, so we judged it was best to set her by compass straight for the place where the pyramids was gitting blurred and blotted out, and then drop low and skin along pretty close to the ground and keep a sharp lookout. Tom took the hellum, I stood by to let go the anchor, and Jim he straddled the bow to dig through the fog with his eyes and watch out for danger ahead. We went along a steady gait, but not very fast, and the fog got solider and solider, so solid that Jim looked dim and ragged and smoky through it. It was awful still, and we talked low and was anxious. Now and then Jim would say:

"Highst her a p'int, Mars Tom, highst her!" and up she would skip, a foot or two, and we would slide right over a flat-roofed mud cabin, with people that had been asleep on it just beginning to turn out and gap and stretch; and once when a feller was clear up on his hind legs so he could gap and stretch better, we took him a blip in the back and knocked him off. By and by, after about an hour, and everything dead still and we a-straining our ears for sounds and holding our breath, the fog thinned a little, very sudden, and Jim sung out in an awful scare:

"Oh, for de lan's sake, set her back, Mars Tom, here's de biggest giant outen de 'Rabian Nights a-comin' for us!" and he went over backwards in the boat.

Tom slammed on the back-action, and as we slowed to a standstill a man's face as big as our house at home looked in over the gunnel, same as a house looks out of its windows, and I laid down and died. I must 'a' been clear dead and gone for as much as a minute or more; then I come to, and Tom had hitched a boat-hook on to the lower lip of the giant and was holding the balloon steady with it whilst he canted his head back and got a good long look up at that awful face.

Jim was on his knees with his hands clasped, gazing up at the thing in a begging way, and working his lips, but not getting anything out. I took only just a glimpse, and was fading out again, but Tom says:

" He ain't alive, you fools; it's the Sphinx!"

I never see Tom look so little and like a fly; but that was because the giant's head was so big and awful. Awful, yes, so it was, but not dreadful any more, because you could see it was a noble face, and kind of sad, and not thinking about you, but about other things and larger. It was stone, reddish stone, and its nose and ears battered, and that give it an abused look, and you felt sorrier for it for that.

We stood off a piece, and sailed around it and over it, and it was just grand. It was a man's head, or maybe a woman's, on a tiger's body a hundred and twenty-five foot long, and there was a dear little temple between its front paws. All but the head used to be under the sand, for hundreds of years, maybe thousands, but they had just lately dug the sand away and found that little temple. It took a power of sand to bury that cretur; most as much as it would to bury a steamboat, I reckon.

We landed Jim on top of the head, with an American flag to protect him, it being a foreign land; then we sailed off to this and that and t'other distance, to git what Tom called effects and perspectives and proportions, and Jim he done the best he could, striking all the different kinds of attitudes and positions he could study up, but standing on his head and working his legs the way a frog does was the best. The further we got away, the littler Jim got, and the grander the Sphinx got, till at last it was only a clothespin on a dome, as you might say. That's the way perspective brings out the correct proportions, Tom said; he said Julus Cesar's niggers didn't know how big he was, they was too close to him.

Then we sailed off further and further, till we couldn't see Jim at all any more, and then that great figger was at its noblest, a-gazing out over the Nile Valley so still and solemn and lonesome, and all the little shabby huts and things that was scattered about it clean disappeared and gone, and nothing around it now but a soft wide spread of yaller velvet, which was the sand.

That was the right place to stop, and we done it. We set there a-looking and a-thinking for a half an hour, nobody a-saying anything, for it made us feel quiet and kind of solemn to remember it had been

looking over that valley just that same way, and thinking its awful thoughts all to itself for thousands of
years, and nobody can't find out what they are to this
day.

At last I took up the glass and see some little black
things a-capering around on that velvet carpet, and
some more a-climbing up the cretur's back, and then I
see two or three wee puffs of white smoke, and told
Tom to look. He done it, and says:

" They're bugs. No — hold on; they — why, I believe they're men. Yes, it's men — men and horses
both. They're hauling a long ladder up onto the
Sphinx's back — now ain't that odd? And now they're
trying to lean it up a — there's some more puffs of
smoke — it's guns! Huck, they're after Jim."

We clapped on the power, and went for them a-
biling. We was there in no time, and come a-whizzing
down amongst them, and they broke and scattered every
which way, and some that was climbing the ladder after
Jim let go all holts and fell. We soared up and found
him laying on top of the head panting and most
tuckered out, partly from howling for help and partly
from scare. He had been standing a siege a long time
— a week, *he* said, but it warn't so, it only just seemed
so to him because they was crowding him so. They
had shot at him, and rained the bullets all around him,
but he warn't hit, and when they found he wouldn't
stand up and the bullets couldn't git at him when he
was laying down, they went for the ladder, and then
he knowed it was all up with him if we didn't come

pretty quick. Tom was very indignant, and asked him why he didn't show the flag and command them to *git*, in the name of the United States. Jim said he done it, but they never paid no attention. Tom said he would have this thing looked into at Washington, and says:

"You'll see that they'll have to apologize for insulting the flag, and pay an indemnity, too, on top of it, even if they git off *that* easy."

Jim says:

"What's an indemnity, Mars Tom?"

"It's cash, that's what it is."

"Who gits it, Mars Tom?"

"Why, *we* do."

"En who gits de apology?"

"The United States. Or, we can take whichever we please. We can take the apology, if we want to, and let the gov'ment take the money."

"How much money will it be, Mars Tom?"

"Well, in an aggravated case like this one, it will be at least three dollars apiece, and I don't know but more."

"Well, den, we'll take de money, Mars Tom, blame de 'pology. Hain't dat yo' notion, too? En hain't it yourn, Huck?"

We talked it over a little and allowed that that was as good a way as any, so we agreed to take the money. It was a new business to me, and I asked Tom if countries always apologized when they had done wrong, and he says:

" Yes ; the little ones does."

We was sailing around examining the pyramids, you know, and now we soared up and roosted on the flat top of the biggest one, and found it was just like what the man said in the Sunday-school. It was like four pairs of stairs that starts broad at the bottom and slants up and comes together in a point at the top, only these stair-steps couldn't be clumb the way you climb other stairs; no, for each step was as high as your chin, and you have to be boosted up from behind. The two other pyramids warn't far away, and the people moving about on the sand between looked like bugs crawling, we was so high above them.

Tom he couldn't hold himself he was so worked up with gladness and astonishment to be in such a celebrated place, and he just dripped history from every pore, seemed to me. He said he couldn't scarcely believe he was standing on the very identical spot the prince flew from on the Bronze Horse. It was in the Arabian Night times, he said. Somebody give the prince a bronze horse with a peg in its shoulder, and he could git on him and fly through the air like a bird, and go all over the world, and steer it by turning the peg, and fly high or low and land wherever he wanted to.

When he got done telling it there was one of them uncomfortable silences that comes, you know, when a person has been telling a whopper and you feel sorry for him and wish you could think of some way to change the subject and let him down easy, but git stuck

and don't see no way, and before you can pull your
mind together and *do* something, that silence has got in
and spread itself and done the business.   I was embarrassed, Jim he was embarrassed, and neither of us
couldn't say a word.   Well, Tom he glowered at me a
minute, and says:

"Come, out with it.   What do you think?"

I says:

"Tom Sawyer, *you* don't believe that, yourself."

"What's the reason I don't?   What's to hendei
me?"

"There's one thing to hender you: it couldn't
happen, that's all."

"What's the reason it couldn't happen?"

"You tell me the reason it *could* happen."

"This balloon is a good enough reason it could
happen, I should reckon."

"*Why* is it?"

"*Why* is it?   I never saw such an idiot.   Ain't this
balloon and the bronze horse the same thing under
different names?"

"No, they're not.   One is a balloon and the other's
a horse.   It's very different.   Next you'll be saying a
house and a cow is the same thing."

"By Jackson, Huck's got him ag'in!   Dey ain't no
wigglin' outer dat!"

"Shut your head, Jim; you don't know what you're
talking about.   And Huck don't.   Look here, Huck,
I'll make it plain to you, so you can understand.   You
see, it ain't the mere *form* that's got anything to do

9 **

with their being similar or unsimilar, it's the *principle* involved; and the principle is the same in both. Don't you see, now?"

I turned it over in my mind, and says:

"Tom, it ain't no use. Principles is all very well, but they don't git around that one big fact, that the thing that a balloon can do ain't no sort of proof of what a horse can do."

"Shucks, Huck, you don't get the idea at all. Now look here a minute — it's perfectly plain. Don't we fly through the air?"

"Yes."

"Very well. Don't we fly high or fly low, just as we please?"

"Yes."

"Don't we steer whichever way we want to?"

"Yes."

"And don't we land when and where we please?"

"Yes."

"How do we move the balloon and steer it?"

"By touching the buttons."

"*Now* I reckon the thing is clear to you at last. In the other case the moving and steering was done by turning a peg. We touch a button, the prince turned a peg. There ain't an atom of difference, you see. I knowed I could git it through your head if I stuck to it long enough."

He felt so happy he begun to whistle. But me and Jim was silent, so he broke off surprised, and says:

"Looky here, Huck Finn, don't you see it *yet?*"

I says:

"Tom Sawyer, I want to ask you some questions."

"Go ahead," he says, and I see Jim chirk up to listen.

"As I understand it, the whole thing is in the buttons and the peg — the rest ain't of no consequence. A button is one shape, a peg is another shape, but that ain't any matter?"

"No, that ain't any matter, as long as they've both got the same power."

"All right, then. What is the power that's in a candle and in a match?"

"It's the fire."

"It's the same in both, then?"

"Yes, just the same in both."

"All right. Suppose I set fire to a carpenter shop with a match, what will happen to that carpenter shop?"

"She'll burn up."

"And suppose I set fire to this pyramid with a candle — will she burn up?"

"Of course she won't."

"All right. Now the fire's the same, both times. *Why* does the shop burn, and the pyramid don't?"

"Because the pyramid *can't* burn."

"Aha! and *a horse can't fly!*"

"My lan', ef Huck ain't got him ag'in! Huck's landed him high en dry dis time, *I* tell you! Hit's de smartes' trap I ever see a body walk inter — en ef I —"

But Jim was so full of laugh he got to strangling and couldn't go on, and Tom was that mad to see how neat I had floored him, and turned his own argument ag'in him and knocked him all to rags and flinders with it, that all he could manage to say was that whenever he heard me and Jim try to argue it made him ashamed of the human race. I never said nothing; I was feeling pretty well satisfied. When I have got the best of a person that way, it ain't my way to go around crowing about it the way some people does, for I consider that if I was in his place I wouldn't wish him to crow over me. It's better to be generous, that's what I think.

CHAPTER XIII.

GOING FOR TOM'S PIPE

B<small>Y</small> AND BY we left Jim to float around up there in the neighborhood of the pyramids, and we clumb down to the hole where you go into the tunnel, and went in with some Arabs and candles, and away in there in the middle of the pyramid we found a room and a big stone box in it where they used to keep that king, just as the man in the Sunday-school said; but he was gone, now; somebody had got him. But I didn't take no interest in the place, because there could be ghosts there, of course; not fresh ones, but I don't like no kind.

So then we come out and got some little donkeys and rode a piece, and then went in a boat another piece, and then more donkeys, and got to Cairo; and all the way the road was as smooth and beautiful a road as ever I see, and had tall date-pa'ms on both sides, and naked children everywhere, and the men was as red as copper, and fine and strong and handsome. And the city was a curiosity. Such narrow streets — why, they were just lanes, and crowded with people with turbans, and women with veils, and everybody rigged out in blazing bright clothes and all sorts of colors, and you wondered how the camels and the people got by each other in such narrow little cracks, but they done it — a perfect jam, you see, and everybody noisy. The stores warn't big enough to turn around in, but you didn't have to go in; the storekeeper sat tailor fashion on his counter, smoking his snaky long pipe, and had his things where he could reach them to sell, and he was just as good as in the street, for the camel-loads brushed him as they went by.

Now and then a grand person flew by in a carriage with fancy dressed men running and yelling in front of it and whacking anybody with a long rod that didn't get out of the way. And by and by along comes the Sultan riding horseback at the head of a procession, and fairly took your breath away his clothes was so splendid; and everybody fell flat and laid on his stomach while he went by. I forgot, but a feller helped me to remember. He was one that had a rod and run in front.

There was churches, but they don't know enough to keep Sunday; they keep Friday and break the Sabbath. You have to take off your shoes when you go in. There was crowds of men and boys in the church, setting in groups on the stone floor and making no end of noise — getting their lessons by heart, Tom said, out of the Koran, which they think is a Bible, and people that knows better knows enough to not let on. I never see such a big church in my life before. and most awful high, it was; it made you dizzy to look up; our village church at home ain't a circumstance to it; if you was to put it in there, people would think it was a drygoods box.

What I wanted to see was a dervish, because I was interested in dervishes on accounts of the one that played the trick on the camel-driver. So we found a lot in a kind of a church, and they called themselves Whirling Dervishes; and they did whirl, too. I never see anything like it. They had tall sugar-loaf hats on, and linen petticoats; and they spun and spun and spun, round and round like tops, and the petticoats stood out on a slant, and it was the prettiest thing I ever see, and made me drunk to look at it. They was all Moslems, Tom said, and when I asked him what a Moslem was, he said it was a person that wasn't a Presbyterian. So there is plenty of them in Missouri, though I didn't know it before.

We didn't see half there was to see in Cairo, because Tom was in such a sweat to hunt out places that was celebrated in history. We had a most tiresome time to find the granary where Joseph stored up the grain before the famine, and when we found it it warn't worth much to look at, being such an old tumble-down wreck; but Tom was satisfied, and made more fuss over it than I would make if I stuck a nail in my foot. How he ever found that place was too many for me. We passed as much as forty just like it before we come to it, and any of them would 'a' done for me, but none but just the right one would suit him; I never see anybody so particular as Tom Sawyer. The minute he

9**

struck the right one he reconnized it as easy as I would reconnize my other shirt if I had one, but how he done it he couldn't any more tell than he could fly; he said so himself.

Then we hunted a long time for the house where the boy lived that learned the cadi how to try the case of the old olives and the new ones, and said it was out of the Arabian Nights, and he would tell me and Jim about it when he got time. Well, we hunted and hunted till I was ready to drop, and I wanted Tom to give it up and come next day and git somebody that knowed the town and could talk Missourian and could go straight to the place; but no, he wanted to find it himself, and nothing else would answer. So on we went. Then at last the remarkablest thing happened I ever see. The house was gone — gone hundreds of years ago — every last rag of it gone but just one mud brick. Now a person wouldn't ever believe that a backwoods Missouri boy that hadn't ever been in that town before could go and hunt that place over and find that brick, but Tom Sawyer done it. I know he done it, because I see him do it. I was right by his very side at the time, and see him see the brick and see him reconnize it. Well, I says to myself, how *does* he do it? Is it knowledge, or is it instink?

Now there's the facts, just as they happened: let everybody explain it their own way. I've ciphered over it a good deal, and it's my opinion that some of it is knowledge but the main bulk of it is instink. The reason is this: Tom put the brick in his pocket to give

to a museum with his name on it and the facts when he
went home, and I slipped it out and put another brick
considerable like it in its place, and he didn't know the
difference — but there was a difference, you see. I
think that settles it — it's mostly instink, not knowledge.
Instink tells him where the exact *place* is for the brick to
be in, and so he reconnizes it by the place it's in, not
by the look of the brick. If it was knowledge, not
instink, he would know the brick again by the look of
it the next time he seen it — which he didn't. So it
shows that for all the brag you hear about knowledge
being such a wonderful thing, instink is worth forty of
it for real unerringness. Jim says the same.

When we got back Jim dropped down and took us
in, and there was a young man there with a red skull-
cap and tassel on and a beautiful silk jacket and baggy
trousers with a shawl around his waist and pistols in it
that could talk English and wanted to hire to us as
guide and take us to Mecca and Medina and Central
Africa and everywheres for a half a dollar a day and his
keep, and we hired him and left, and piled on the
power, and by the time we was through dinner we was
over the place where the Israelites crossed the Red Sea
when Pharaoh tried to overtake them and was caught
by the waters. We stopped, then, and had a good
look at the place, and it done Jim good to see it. He
said he could see it all, now, just the way it happened;
he could see the Israelites walking along between the
walls of water, and the Egyptians coming, from away
off yonder, hurrying all they could, and see them start

I**

in as the Israelites went out, and then when they was
all in, see the walls tumble together and drown the last
man of them. Then we piled on the power again and
rushed away and huvvered over Mount Sinai, and saw
the place where Moses broke the tables of stone, and
where the children of Israel camped in the plain and
worshiped the golden calf, and it was all just as
interesting as could be, and the guide knowed every
place as well as I knowed the village at home.

But we had an accident, now, and it fetched all the
plans to a standstill. Tom's old ornery corn-cob pipe
had got so old and swelled and warped that she couldn't
hold together any longer, notwithstanding the strings
and bandages, but caved in and went to pieces. Tom
he didn't know *what* to do. The professor's pipe
wouldn't answer; it warn't anything but a mershum,
and a person that's got used to a cob pipe knows it
lays a long ways over all the other pipes in this world,
and you can't git him to smoke any other. He
wouldn't take mine, I couldn't persuade him. So
there he was.

He thought it over, and said we must scour around
and see if we could roust out one in Egypt or Arabia or
around in some of these countries, but the guide said no,
it warn't no use, they didn't have them. So Tom was
pretty glum for a little while, then he chirked up and said
he'd got the idea and knowed what to do. He says:

"I've got another corn-cob pipe, and it's a prime
one, too, and nearly new. It's laying on the rafter
that's right over the kitchen stove at home in the

village. Jim, you and the guide will go and get it, and me and Huck will camp here on Mount Sinai till you come back.''

"But, Mars Tom, we couldn't ever find de village. I could find de pipe, 'case I knows de kitchen, but my lan', *we* can't ever find de village, nur Sent Louis, nur none o' dem places. We don't know de way, Mars Tom.''

That was a fact, and it stumped Tom for a minute. Then he said:

"Looky here, it can be done, sure; and I'll tell you how. You set your compass and sail west as straight as a dart, till you find the United States. It ain't any trouble, because it's the first land you'll strike the other side of the Atlantic. If it's daytime when you strike it, bulge right on, straight west from the upper part of the Florida coast, and in an hour and three quarters you'll hit the mouth of the Mississippi — at the speed that I'm going to send you. You'll be so high up in the air that the earth will be curved considerable — sorter like a washbowl turned upside down — and you'll see a raft of rivers crawling around every which way, long before you get there, and you can pick out the Mississippi without any trouble. Then you can follow the river north nearly, an hour and three quarters, till you see the Ohio come in; then you want to look sharp, because you're getting near. Away up to your left you'll see another thread coming in — that's the Missouri and is a little above St. Louis. You'll come down low then, so as you can examine the villages as you spin along. You'll pass about twenty-five in the next fifteen minutes, and you'll recognize ours when you see it — and if you don't, you can yell down and ask."

" Ef it's dat easy, Mars Tom, I reckon we kin do it — yassir, I knows we kin."

The guide was sure of it, too, and thought that he could learn to stand his watch in a little while.

" Jim can learn you the whole thing in a half an hour," Tom said. " This balloon's as easy to manage as a canoe."

Tom got out the chart and marked out the course and measured it, and says:

" To go back west is the shortest way, you see. It's only about seven thousand miles. If you went east, and so on around, it's over twice as far." Then he says to the guide, " I want you both to watch the tell-tale all through the watches, and whenever it don't mark three hundred miles an hour, you go higher or drop lower till you find a storm-current that's going your way. There's a hundred miles an hour in this old thing without any wind to help. There's two-hundred-mile gales to be found, any time you want to hunt for them."

" We'll hunt for them, sir."

" See that you do. Sometimes you may have to go up a couple of miles, and it'll be p'ison cold, but most of the time you'll find your storm a good deal lower. If you can only strike a cyclone — that's the ticket for you! You'll see by the professor's books

MAP
OF
THE TRIP
made by
Tom Sawyer
Erronotly

that they travel west in these latitudes; and they travel low, too.''

Then he ciphered on the time, and says —

''Seven thousand miles, three hundred miles an hour — you can make the trip in a day — twenty-four hours. This is Thursday; you'll be back here Saturday afternoon. Come, now, hustle out some blankets and food and books and things for me and Huck, and you can start right along. There ain't no occasion to fool around — I want a smoke, and the quicker you fetch that pipe the better.''

All hands jumped for the things, and in eight minutes our things was out and the balloon was ready for America. So we shook hands good-bye, and Tom gave his last orders:

''It's 10 minutes to 2 P.M. now, Mount Sinai time. In 24 hours you'll be home, and it 'll be 6 to-morrow morning, village time. When you strike the village, land a little back of the top of the hill, in the woods, out of sight; then you rush down, Jim, and shove these letters in the post-office, and if you see anybody stirring, pull your slouch down over your face so they won't know you. Then you go and slip in the back way to the kitchen and git the pipe, and lay this piece of paper on the kitchen table, and put something on it to hold it, and then slide out and git away, and don't let Aunt Polly catch a sight of you, nor nobody else. Then you jump for the balloon and shove for Mount Sinai three hundred miles an hour. You won't have lost more than an hour. You'll start back at 7 or

8 A.M., village time, and be here in 24 hours, arriving at 2 or 3 P.M., Mount Sinai time.''

Tom he read the piece of paper to us. He had wrote on it:

     "THURSDAY AFTERNOON. *Tom Sawyer the Erronort sends his love to Aunt Polly from Mount Sinai where the Ark was, and so does Huck Finn, and she will get it to-morrow morning half-past six.*
                       "TOM SAWYER THE ERRONORT.''

"That'll make her eyes bulge out and the tears come,'' he says. Then he says:

"Stand by! One — two — three — away you go!''

And away she *did* go! Why, she seemed to whiz out of sight in a second.

Then we found a most comfortable cave that looked out over the whole big plain, and there we camped to wait for the pipe.

The balloon come back all right, and brung the pipe; but Aunt Polly had catched Jim when he was getting it, and anybody can guess what happened: she sent for Tom. So Jim he says:

"Mars Tom, she's out on de porch wid her eye sot on de sky a-layin' for you, en she say she ain't gwyne to budge from dah tell she gits hold of you. Dey's gwyne to be trouble, Mars Tom, 'deed dey is.''

So then we shoved for home, and not feeling very gay, neither.

---

     * This misplacing of the Ark is probably Huck's error, not Tom's. — M. T.

TOM SAWYER, DETECTIVE*

CHAPTER I.

AN INVITATION FOR TOM AND HUCK

WELL, it was the next spring after me and Tom
Sawyer set our old nigger Jim free, the time he
was chained up for a runaway slave down there on
Tom's uncle Silas's farm in Arkansaw. The frost was
working out of the ground, and out of the air, too, and
it was getting closer and closer onto barefoot time every
day; and next it would be marble time, and next
mumbletypeg, and next tops and hoops, and next
kites, and then right away it would be summer and going in a-swimming. It just makes a boy homesick to
look ahead like that and see how far off summer is.
Yes, and it sets him to sighing and saddening around,
and there's something the matter with him, he don't
know what. But anyway, he gets out by himself and

---

* Strange as the incidents of this story are, they are not inventions, but
facts — even to the public confession of the accused. I take them from an
old-time Swedish criminal trial, change the actors, and transfer the scenes
to America. I have added some details, but only a couple of them are
important ones. — M. T.

mopes and thinks; and mostly he hunts for a lonesome place high up on the hill in the edge of the woods, and sets there and looks away off on the big Mississippi down there a-reaching miles and miles around the points where the timber looks smoky and dim it's so far off and still, and everything's so solemn it seems like everybody you've loved is dead and gone, and you 'most wish you was dead and gone too, and done with it all.

Don't you know what that is? It's spring fever. That is what the name of it is. And when you've got it, you want — oh, you don't quite know what it is you *do* want, but it just fairly makes your heart ache, you want it so! It seems to you that mainly what you want is to get away; get away from the same old tedious things you're so used to seeing and so tired of, and see something new. That is the idea; you want to go and be a wanderer; you want to go wandering far away to strange countries where everything is mysterious and wonderful and romantic. And if you can't do that, you'll put up with considerable less; you'll go anywhere you *can* go, just so as to get away, and be thankful of the chance, too.

Well, me and Tom Sawyer had the spring fever, and had it bad, too; but it warn't any use to think about Tom trying to get away, because, as he said, his Aunt Polly wouldn't let him quit school and go traipsing off somers wasting time; so we was pretty blue. We was setting on the front steps one day about sundown talking this way, when out comes his aunt Polly with a letter in her hand and says:

"'I RECKON I GOT TO BE EXCUSED'

" Tom, I reckon you've got to pack up and go down to Arkansaw — your aunt Sally wants you."

I 'most jumped out of my skin for joy. I reckoned Tom would fly at his aunt and hug her head off; but if you believe me he set there like a rock, and never said a word. It made me fit to cry to see him act so foolish, with such a noble chance as this opening up. Why, we might lose it if he didn't speak up and show he was thankful and grateful. But he set there and studied and studied till I was that distressed I didn't know what to do; then he says, very ca'm, and I could a shot him for it:

"Well," he says, "I'm right down sorry, Aunt Polly, but I reckon I got to be excused — for the present."

His aunt Polly was knocked so stupid and so mad at the cold impudence of it that she couldn't say a word for as much as a half a minute, and this gave me a chance to nudge Tom and whisper:

"Ain't you got any sense? Sp'iling such a noble chance as this and throwing it away?"

But he warn't disturbed. He mumbled back:

" Huck Finn, do you want me to let her *see* how bad I want to go? Why, she'd begin to doubt, right away, and imagine a lot of sicknesses and dangers and objections, and first you know she'd take it all back. You lemme alone; I reckon I know how to work her."

Now I never would 'a' thought of that. But he was right. Tom Sawyer was always right — the levelest head I ever see, and always *at* himself and ready for

10 **

anything you might spring on him. By this time his aunt Polly was all straight again, and she let fly. She says:

"You'll be excused! *You* will! Well, I never heard the like of it in all my days! The idea of you talking like that to *me!* Now take yourself off and pack your traps; and if I hear another word out of you about what you'll be excused from and what you won't, I lay *I'll* excuse you — with a hickory!"

She hit his head a thump with her thimble as we dodged by, and he let on to be whimpering as we struck for the stairs. Up in his room he hugged me, he was so out of his head for gladness because he was going traveling. And he says:

"Before we get away she'll wish she hadn't let me go, but she won't know any way to get around it now. After what she's said, her pride won't let her take it back."

Tom was packed in ten minutes, all except what his aunt and Mary would finish up for him; then we waited ten more for her to get cooled down and sweet and gentle again; for Tom said it took her ten minutes to unruffle in times when half of her feathers was up, but twenty when they was all up, and this was one of the times when they was all up. Then we went down, being in a sweat to know what the letter said.

She was setting there in a brown study, with it laying in her lap. We set down, and she says:

"They're in considerable trouble down there, and they think you and Huck 'll be a kind of diversion for

them — 'comfort,' they say.   Much of that they'll get
out of you and Huck Finn, I reckon.   There's a neighbor named Brace Dunlap that's been wanting to marry
their Benny for three months, and at last they told him
pint blank and once for all, he *couldn't;* so he has soured
on them, and they're worried about it.   I reckon he's
somebody they think they better be on the good side
of, for they've tried to please him by hiring his no-
account brother to help on the farm when they can't
hardly afford it, and don't want him around anyhow.
Who are the Dunlaps?''

"They live about a mile from Uncle Silas's place,
Aunt Polly — all the farmers live about a mile apart
down there — and Brace Dunlap is a long sight richer
than any of the others, and owns a whole grist of niggers.   He's a widower, thirty-six years old, without
any children, and is proud of his money and overbear-
ing, and everybody is a little afraid of him.   I judge he
thought he could have any girl he wanted, just for the
asking, and it must have set him back a good deal when
he found he couldn't get Benny.   Why, Benny's only
half as old as he is, and just as sweet and lovely as —
well, you've seen her.   Poor old Uncle Silas — why,
it's pitiful, him trying to curry favor that way — so hard
pushed and poor, and yet hiring that useless Jubiter
Dunlap to please his ornery brother.''

"What a name — Jubiter!   Where'd he get it?''

"It's only just a nickname.   I reckon they've forgot
his real name long before this.   He's twenty-seven,
now, and has had it ever since the first time he ever

went in swimming. The school teacher seen a round brown mole the size of a dime on his left leg above his knee, and four little bits of moles around it, when he was naked, and he said it minded him of Jubiter and his moons; and the children thought it was funny, and so they got to calling him Jubiter, and he's Jubiter yet. He's tall, and lazy, and sly, and sneaky, and ruther cowardly, too, but kind of good-natured, and wears long brown hair and no beard, and hasn't got a cent, and Brace boards him for nothing, and gives him his old clothes to wear, and despises him. Jubiter is a twin.''

" What's t'other twin like?''

" Just exactly like Jubiter — so they say; used to was, anyway, but he hain't been seen for seven years. He got to robbing when he was nineteen or twenty, and they jailed him; but he broke jail and got away — up North here, somers. They used to hear about him robbing and burglaring now and then, but that was years ago. He's dead, now. At least that's what they say. They don't hear about him any more.''

" What was his name?''

" Jake.''

There wasn't anything more said for a considerable while; the old lady was thinking. At last she says:

" The thing that is mostly worrying your aunt Sally is the tempers that that man Jubiter gets your uncle into.''

Tom was astonished, and so was I. Tom says:

'Tempers? Uncle Silas? Land, you must be joking! I didn't know he *had* any temper.''

"Works him up into perfect rages, your aunt Sally says; says he acts as if he would really hit the man, sometimes."

"Aunt Polly, it beats anything I ever heard of. Why, he's just as gentle as mush."

"Well, she's worried, anyway.   Says your uncle Silas is like a changed man, on account of all this quarreling.   And the neighbors talk about it, and lay all the blame on your uncle, of course, because he's a preacher and hain't got any business to quarrel.   Your aunt Sally says he hates to go into the pulpit he's so ashamed; and the people have begun to cool toward him, and he ain't as popular now as he used to was."

"Well, ain't it strange?   Why, Aunt Polly, he was always so good and kind and moony and absent-minded and chuckle-headed and lovable — why, he was just an angel!   What *can* be the matter of him, do you reckon?"

10

CHAPTER II.

JAKE DUNLAP

WE had powerful good luck; because we got a chance in a stern-wheeler from away North which was bound for one of them bayous or one-horse rivers away down Louisiana way, and so we could go all the way down the Upper Mississippi and all the way down the Lower Mississippi to that farm in Arkansaw without having to change steamboats at St. Louis; not so very much short of a thousand miles at one pull.

A pretty lonesome boat; there warn't but few passengers, and all old folks, that set around, wide apart, dozing, and was very quiet. We was four days getting out of the "upper river," because we got aground so much. But it warn't dull — couldn't be for boys that was traveling, of course.

From the very start me and Tom allowed that there was somebody sick in the stateroom next to ourn, because the meals was always toted in there by the waiters. By and by we asked about it — Tom did — and the waiter said it was a man, but he didn't look sick.

"Well, but *ain't* he sick?"

"I don't know; maybe he is, but 'pears to me he's just letting on."

"What makes you think that?"

"Because if he was sick he would pull his clothes off *some* time or other — don't you reckon he would? Well, this one don't. At least he don't ever pull off his boots, anyway."

"The mischief he don't! Not even when he goes to bed?"

"No."

It was always nuts for Tom Sawyer — a mystery was. If you'd lay out a mystery and a pie before me and him, you wouldn't have to say take your choice; it was a thing that would regulate itself. Because in my nature I have always run to pie, whilst in his nature he has always run to mystery. People are made different. And it is the best way. Tom says to the waiter:

"What's the man's name?"

"Phillips."

"Where'd he come aboard?"

"I think he got aboard at Elexandria, up on the Iowa line."

"What do you reckon he's a-playing?"

"I hain't any notion — I never thought of it."

I says to myself, here's another one that runs to pie.

"Anything peculiar about him?— the way he acts or talks?"

"No — nothing, except he seems so scary, and keeps his doors locked night and day both, and when you knock he won't let you in till he opens the door a crack and sees who it is."

"By jimminy, it's int' resting! I'd like to get a
10**

look at him. Say — the next time you're going in there, don't you reckon you could spread the door and —"

"No, indeedy! He's always behind it. He would block that game."

Tom studied over it, and then he says:

"Looky here. You lend me your apern and let me take him his breakfast in the morning. I'll give you a quarter."

The boy was plenty willing enough, if the head steward wouldn't mind. Tom says that's all right, he reckoned he could fix it with the head steward; and he done it. He fixed it so as we could both go in with aperns on and toting vittles.

He didn't sleep much, he was in such a sweat to get in there and find out the mystery about Phillips; and moreover he done a lot of guessing about it all night, which warn't no use, for if you are going to find out the facts of a thing, what's the sense in guessing out what ain't the facts and wasting ammunition? I didn't lose no sleep. I wouldn't give a dern to know what's the matter of Phillips, I says to myself.

Well, in the morning we put on the aperns and got a couple of trays of truck, and Tom he knocked on the door. The man opened it a crack, and then he let us in and shut it quick. By Jackson, when we got a sight of him, we 'most dropped the trays! and Tom says:

"Why, Jubiter Dunlap, where'd *you* come from?"

Well, the man was astonished, of course; and first off he looked like he didn't know whether to be scared, or glad, or both, or which, but finally he settled down to being glad; and then his color come back, though at first his face had turned pretty white. So we got to talking together while he et his breakfast. And he says:

"But I aint Jubiter Dunlap. I'd just as soon tell you who I am, though, if you'll swear to keep mum, for I ain't no Phillips, either."

Tom says:

"We'll keep mum, but there ain't any need to tell who you are if you ain't Jubiter Dunlap."

"Why?"

"Because if you ain't him you're t'other twin, Jake. You're the spit'n image of Jubiter."

"Well, I *am* Jake. But looky here, how do you come to know us Dunlaps?"

Tom told about the adventures we'd had down there at his uncle Silas's last summer, and when he see that there warn't anything about his folks — or him either, for that matter — that we didn't know, he opened out and talked perfectly free and candid. He never made any bones about his own case; said he'd been a hard lot, was a hard lot yet, and reckoned he'd *be* a hard lot plumb to the end. He said of course it was a dangerous life, and —

He give a kind of gasp, and set his head like a person that's listening. We didn't say anything, and so it was very still for a second or so, and there warn't no sounds but the screaking of the woodwork and the chug-chugging of the machinery down below

Then we got him comfortable again, telling him about his people, and how Brace's wife had been dead three years, and Brace wanted to marry Benny and she shook him, and Jubiter was working for Uncle Silas, and him and Uncle Silas quarreling all the time — and then he let go and laughed.

"Land!" he says, "it's like old times to hear all this tittle-tattle, and does me good. It's been seven years and more since I heard any. How do they talk about me these days?"

"Who?"

"The farmers — and the family."

"Why, they don't talk about you at all — at least only just a mention, once in a long time."

"The nation!" he says, surprised; "why is that?"

"Because they think you are dead long ago."

"No! Are you speaking true? — honor bright, now." He jumped up, excited.

"Honor bright. There ain't anybody thinks you are alive."

"Then I'm saved, I'm saved, sure! I'll go home. They'll hide me and save my life. You keep mum. Swear you'll keep mum — swear you'll never, never tell on me. Oh, boys, be good to a poor devil that's being hunted day and night, and dasn't show his face! I've never done you any harm; I'll never do you any, as God is in the heavens; swear you'll be good to me and help me save my life."

We'd a swore it if he'd been a dog; and so we done it. Well, he couldn't love us enough for it or be grateful enough, poor cuss; it was all he could do to keep from hugging us.

We talked along, and he got out a little hand-bag and begun to open it, and told us to turn our backs. We done it, and when he told us to turn again he was perfectly different to what he was before. He had on blue goggles and the naturalest-looking long brown whiskers and mustashes you ever see. His own mother wouldn't 'a' knowed him. He asked us if he looked like his brother Jubiter, now.

"No," Tom said; "there ain't anything left that's like him except the long hair."

"All right, I'll get that cropped close to my head before I get there; then him and Brace will keep my secret, and I'll live with them as being a stranger, and the neighbors won't ever guess me out. What do you think?"

Tom he studied awhile, then he says:

"Well, of course me and Huck are going to keep mum there, but if you don't keep mum yourself there's going to be a little bit of a risk — it ain't much, maybe, but it's a little. I mean, if you talk, won't people notice that your voice is just like Jubiter's; and mightn't it make them think of the twin they reckoned was dead, but maybe after all was hid all this time under another name?"

"By George," he says, "you're a sharp one! You're perfectly right. I've got to play deef and dumb when there's a neighbor around. If I'd a struck for home and forgot that little detail — However, I wasn't striking for home. I was breaking for any place where I could get away from these fellows that are after me; then I was going to put on this disguise and get some different clothes, and —"

He jumped for the outside door and laid his ear against it and listened, pale and kind of panting. Presently he whispers:

"Sounded like cocking a gun! Lord, what a life to lead!"

Then he sunk down in a chair all limp and sick like, and wiped the sweat off of his face.

CHAPTER III.

A DIAMOND ROBBERY

FROM that time out, we was with him 'most all the time, and one or t'other of us slept in his upper berth. He said he had been so lonesome, and it was such a comfort to him to have company, and somebody to talk to in his troubles. We was in a sweat to find out what his secret was, but Tom said the best way was not to seem anxious, then likely he would drop into it himself in one of his talks, but if we got to asking questions he would get suspicious and shet up his shell. It turned out just so. It warn't no trouble to see that he *wanted* to talk about it, but always along at first he would scare away from it when he got on the very edge of it, and go to talking about something else. The way it come about was this: He got to asking us, kind of indifferent like, about the passengers down on deck. We told him about them. But he warn't satisfied; we warn't particular enough. He told us to describe them better. Tom done it. At last, when Tom was describing one of the roughest and raggedest ones, he gave a shiver and a gasp and says:

"Oh, lordy, that's one of them! They're aboard

sure — I just knowed it. I sort of hoped I had got away, but I never believed it. Go on.''

Presently when Tom was describing another mangy, rough deck passenger, he give that shiver again and says:

'' That's him!— that's the other one. If it would only come a good black stormy night and I could get ashore. You see, they've got spies on me. They've got a right to come up and buy drinks at the bar yonder forrard, and they take that chance to bribe somebody to keep watch on me — porter or boots or somebody. If I was to slip ashore without anybody seeing me, they would know it inside of an hour.''

So then he got to wandering along, and pretty soon, sure enough, he was telling! He was poking along through his ups and downs, and when he come to that place he went right along. He says:

'' It was a confidence game. We played it on a julery-shop in St. Louis. What we was after was a couple of noble big di'monds as big as hazel-nuts, which every-body was running to see. We was dressed up fine, and we played it on them in broad daylight. We ordered the di'monds sent to the hotel for us to see if we wanted to buy, and when we was examining them we had paste counterfeits all ready, and *them* was the things that went back to the shop when we said the water wasn't quite fine enough for twelve thousand dollars.''

'' Twelve — thousand — dollars!'' Tom says. '' Was they really worth all that money, do you reckon?''

'' Every cent of it.''

"And you fellows got away with them?"

"As easy as nothing. I don't reckon the julery people know they've been robbed yet. But it wouldn't be good sense to stay around St. Louis, of course, so we considered where we'd go. One was for going one way, one another, so we throwed up, heads or tails, and the Upper Mississippi won. We done up the di'monds in a paper and put our names on it and put it in the keep of the hotel clerk, and told him not to ever let either of us have it again without the others was on hand to see it done; then we went down town, each by his own self — because I reckon maybe we all had the same notion. I don't know for certain, but I reckon maybe we had."

" What notion?" Tom says.

" To rob the others."

" What — one take everything, after all of you had helped to get it?"

" Cert'nly."

It disgusted Tom Sawyer, and he said it was the orneriest, low-downest thing he ever heard of. But Jake Dunlap said it warn't unusual in the profession. Said when a person was in that line of business he'd got to look out for his own intrust, there warn't nobody else going to do it for him. And then he went on. He says:

" You see, the trouble was, you couldn't divide up two di'monds amongst three. If there'd been three — But never mind about that, there *warn't* three. I loafed along the back streets studying and studying.

And I says to myself, I'll hog them di'monds the first chance I get, and I'll have a disguise all ready, and I'll give the boys the slip, and when I'm safe away I'll put it on, and then let them find me if they can. So I got the false whiskers and the goggles and this countrified suit of clothes, and fetched them along back in a handbag; and when I was passing a shop where they sell all sorts of things, I got a glimpse of one of my pals through the window. It was Bud Dixon. I was glad, you bet. I says to myself, I'll see what he buys. So I kept shady, and watched. Now what do you reckon it was he bought?"

" Whiskers?" said I.

" No."

" Goggles?"

" No."

" Oh, keep still, Huck Finn, can't you, you're only just hendering all you can. What *was* it he bought, Jake?"

" You'd never guess in the world. It was only just a screwdriver — just a wee little bit of a screwdriver."

" Well, I declare ! What did he want with that?"

" That's what *I* thought. It was curious. It clean stumped me. I says to myself, what can he want with that thing? Well, when he come out I stood back out of sight, and then tracked him to a second-hand slop-shop and see him buy a red flannel shirt and some old ragged clothes — just the ones he's got on now, as you've described. Then I went down to the wharf and hid my things aboard the up-river boat that we had picked out, and then started back and had another streak of luck. I seen our other pal lay in *his* stock of old rusty second-handers. We got the di'monds and went aboard the boat.

"But now we was up a stump, for we couldn't go to bed. We had to set up and watch one another. Pity, that was; pity to put that kind of a strain on us, because there was bad blood between us from a couple of weeks back, and we was only friends in the way of business. Bad anyway, seeing there was only two di'monds betwixt three men. First we had supper, and then tramped up and down the deck together smoking till most midnight; then we went and set down in my stateroom and locked the doors and looked in the piece of paper to see if the di'monds was all right, then laid it on the lower berth right in full sight; and there we set, and set, and by-and-by it got to be dreadful hard to keep awake. At last Bud Dixon he dropped off. As soon as he was snoring a good regular gait that was likely to last, and had his chin on his breast and looked permanent, Hal Clayton nodded towards the di'monds and then towards the outside door, and I understood. I reached and got the paper, and then we stood up and waited perfectly still; Bud never stirred; I turned the key of the outside door very soft and slow, then turned the knob the same way, and we went tiptoeing out onto the guard, and shut the door very soft and gentle.

"There warn't nobody stirring anywhere, and the boat was slipping along, swift and steady, through the

big water in the smoky moonlight. We never said a
word, but went straight up onto the hurricane-deck and
plumb back aft, and set down on the end of the sky-
light. Both of us knowed what that meant, without
having to explain to one another. Bud Dixon would
wake up and miss the swag, and would come straight
for us, for he ain't afeard of anything or anybody, that
man ain't. He would come, and we would heave him
overboard, or get killed trying. It made me shiver,
because I ain't as brave as some people, but if I
showed the white feather — well, I knowed better than
do that. I kind of hoped the boat would land somers,
and we could skip ashore and not have to run the risk
of this row, I was so scared of Bud Dixon, but she
was an upper-river tub and there warn't no real chance
of that.

"Well, the time strung along and along, and that
fellow never come! Why, it strung along till dawn
begun to break, and still he never come. 'Thunder,' I
says, 'what do you make out of this?— ain't it suspicious?' 'Land!' Hal says, 'do you reckon he's
playing us?— open the paper!' I done it, and by
gracious there warn't anything in it but a couple of
little pieces of loaf-sugar! *That's* the reason he could
set there and snooze all night so comfortable. Smart?
Well, I reckon! He had had them two papers all fixed
and ready, and he had put one of them in place of
t'other right under our noses.

"We felt pretty cheap. But the thing to do, straight
off, was to make a plan; and we done it. We would

do up the paper again, just as it was, and slip in, very
elaborate and soft, and lay it on the bunk again, and
let on *we* didn't know about any trick, and hadn't any
idea he was a-laughing at us behind them bogus snores
of his'n; and we would stick by him, and the first
night we was ashore we would get him drunk and
search him, and get the di'monds; and *do* for him,
too, if it warn't too risky. If we got the swag, we'd
got to do for him, or he would hunt us down and do for
us, sure. But I didn't have no real hope. I knowed
we could get him drunk — he was always ready for
that — but what's the good of it? You might search
him a year and never find —

"Well, right there I catched my breath and broke
off my thought! For an idea went ripping through my
head that tore my brains to rags — and land, but I felt
gay and good! You see, I had had my boots off, to
unswell my feet, and just then I took up one of them
to put it on, and I catched a glimpse of the heel-
bottom, and it just took my breath away. You re
member about that puzzlesome little screwdriver?"

"You bet I do," says Tom, all excited.

"Well, when I catched that glimpse of that boot
heel, the idea that went smashing through my head
was, *I* know where he's hid the di'monds! You look
at this boot heel, now. See, it's bottomed with a steel
plate, and the plate is fastened on with little screws.
Now there wasn't a screw about that feller anywhere
but in his boot heels; so, if he needed a screwdriver,
I reckoned I knowed why."

" Huck, ain't it bully!'' says Tom.

" Well, I got my boots on, and we went down and slipped in and laid the paper of sugar on the berth, and sat down soft and sheepish and went to listening to Bud Dixon snore. Hal Clayton dropped off pretty soon, but I didn't; I wasn't ever so wide awake in my life. I was spying out from under the shade of my hat brim, searching the floor for leather. It took me a long time, and I begun to think maybe my guess was wrong, but at last I struck it. It laid over by the bulkhead, and was nearly the color of the carpet. It was a little round plug about as thick as the end of your little finger, and I says to myself there's a di'mond in the nest you've come from. Before long I spied out the plug's mate.

" Think of the smartness and coolness of that blatherskite! He put up that scheme on us and reasoned out what we would do, and we went ahead and done it perfectly exact, like a couple of pudd'n-heads. He set there and took his own time to un-screw his heelplates and cut out his plugs and stick in the di'monds and screw on his plates again. He allowed we would steal the bogus swag and wait all night for him to come up and get drownded, and by George it's just what we done! *I* think it was power-ful smart.''

" You bet your life it was!'' says Tom, just full of admiration.

CHAPTER IV.

THE THREE SLEEPERS

"WELL, all day we went through the humbug of watching one another, and it was pretty sickly business for two of us and hard to act out, I can tell you. About night we landed at one of them little Missouri towns high up toward Iowa, and had supper at the tavern, and got a room upstairs with a cot and a double bed in it, but I dumped my bag under a deal table in the dark hall while we was moving along it to bed, single file, me last, and the landlord in the lead with a tallow candle. We had up a lot of whisky, and went to playing high-low-jack for dimes, and as soon as the whisky begun to take hold of Bud we stopped drinking, but we didn't let him stop. We loaded him till he fell out of his chair and laid there snoring.

" We was ready for business now. I said we better pull our boots off, and his'n too, and not make any noise, then we could pull him and haul him around and ransack him without any trouble. So we done it. I set my boots and Bud's side by side, where they'd be handy. Then we stripped him and searched his seams and his pockets and his socks and the inside of his boots, and everything, and searched his bundle. Never

found any di'monds. We found the screwdriver, and
Hal says, 'What do you reckon he wanted with that?'
I said I didn't know; but when he wasn't looking I
hooked it. At last Hal he looked beat and discour-
aged, and said we'd got to give it up. That was what
I was waiting for. I says:

"'There's one place we hain't searched.'

"'What place is that?' he says.

"'His stomach.'

"'By gracious, I never thought of that! *Now* we're
on the homestretch, to a dead moral certainty. How'll
we manage?'

"'Well,' I says, 'just stay by him till I turn out and
hunt up a drug store, and I reckon I'll fetch something
that'll make them di'monds tired of the company
they're keeping.'

"He said that's the ticket, and with him looking
straight at me I slid myself into Bud's boots instead of
my own, and he never noticed. They was just a shade
large for me, but that was considerable better than being too small. I got my bag as I went a-groping
through the hall, and in about a minute I was out the
back way and stretching up the river road at a five-mile
gait.

"And not feeling so very bad, neither — walking on
di'monds don't have no such effect. When I had gone
fifteen minutes I says to myself, there's more'n a mile
behind me, and everything quiet. Another five minutes
and I says there's considerable more land behind me
now, and there's a man back there that's begun to

wonder what's the trouble.   Another five and I says to myself he's getting real uneasy — he's walking the floor now.   Another five, and I says to myself, there's two mile and a half behind me, and he's *awful* uneasy — beginning to cuss, I reckon.   Pretty soon I says to myself, forty minutes gone — he *knows* there's something up!   Fifty minutes — the truth's a-busting on him now! he is reckoning I found the di'monds whilst we was searching, and shoved them in my pocket and never let on — yes, and he's starting out to hunt for me. He'll hunt for new tracks in the dust, and they'll as likely send him down the river as up.

"Just then I see a man coming down on a mule, and before I thought I jumped into the bush.   It was stupid!   When he got abreast he stopped and waited a little for me to come out; then he rode on again. But I didn't feel gay any more.   I says to myself I've botched my chances by that; I surely have, if he meets up with Hal Clayton.

"Well, about three in the morning I fetched Elexandria and see this stern-wheeler laying there, and was very glad, because I felt perfectly safe, now, you know. It was just daybreak.   I went aboard and got this stateroom and put on these clothes and went up in the pilothouse — to watch, though I didn't reckon there was any need of it.   I set there and played with my di'monds and waited and waited for the boat to start, but she didn't.   You see, they was mending her machinery, but I didn't know anything about it, not being very much used to steamboats.

11**

" Well, to cut the tale short, we never left there till plumb noon; and long before that I was hid in this stateroom; for before breakfast I see a man coming, away off, that had a gait like Hal Clayton's, and it made me just sick. I says to myself, if he finds out I'm aboard this boat, he's got me like a rat in a trap. All he's got to do is to have me watched, and wait — wait till I slip ashore, thinking he is a thousand miles away, then slip after me and dog me to a good place and make me give up the di'monds, and then he'll — oh, *I* know what he'll do! Ain't it awful — awful! And now to think the *other* one's aboard, too! Oh, ain't it hard luck, boys — ain't it hard! But you'll help save me, *won't* you? — oh, boys, be good to a poor devil that's being hunted to death, and save me — I'll worship the very ground you walk on!"

We turned in and soothed him down and told him we would plan for him and help him, and he needn't be so afeard; and so by and by he got to feeling kind of comfortable again, and unscrewed his heelplates and held up his di'monds this way and that, admiring them and loving them; and when the light struck into them they *was* beautiful, sure; why, they seemed to kind of bust, and snap fire out all around. But all the same I judged he was a fool. If I had been him I would a handed the di'monds to them pals and got them to go ashore and leave me alone. But he was made different. He said it was a whole fortune and he couldn't bear the idea.

Twice we stopped to fix the machinery and laid a

good while, once in the night; but it wasn't dark enough, and he was afeard to skip. But the third time we had to fix it there was a better chance. We laid up at a country woodyard about forty mile above Uncle Silas's place a little after one at night, and it was thickening up and going to storm. So Jake he laid for a chance to slide. We begun to take in wood. Pretty soon the rain come a-drenching down, and the wind blowed hard. Of course every boat-hand fixed a gunny sack and put it on like a bonnet, the way they do when they are toting wood, and we got one for Jake, and he slipped down aft with his hand-bag and come tramping forrard just like the rest, and walked ashore with them, and when we see him pass out of the light of the torch-basket and get swallowed up in the dark, we got our breath again and just felt grateful and splendid. But it wasn't for long. Somebody told, I reckon; for in about eight or ten minutes them two pals come tearing forrard as tight as they could jump and darted ashore and was gone. We waited plumb till dawn for them to come back, and kept hoping they would, but they never did. We was awful sorry and low-spirited. All the hope we had was that Jake had got such a start that they couldn't get on his track, and he would get to his brother's and hide there and be safe.

He was going to take the river road, and told us to find out if Brace and Jubiter was to home and no strangers there, and then slip out about sundown and tell him. Said he would wait for us in a little bunch of

K**

sycamores right back of Tom's uncle Silas's tobacker field on the river road, a lonesome place.

We set and talked a long time about his chances, and Tom said he was all right if the pals struck up the river instead of down, but it wasn't likely, because maybe they knowed where he was from; more likely they would go right, and dog him all day, him not suspecting, and kill him when it come dark, and take the boots. So we was pretty sorrowful.

CHAPTER V.

A TRAGEDY IN THE WOODS

WE didn't get done tinkering the machinery till away late in the afternoon, and so it was so close to sundown when we got home that we never stopped on our road, but made a break for the sycamores as tight as we could go, to tell Jake what the delay was, and have him wait till we could go to Brace's and find out how things was there. It was getting pretty dim by the time we turned the corner of the woods, sweating and panting with that long run, and see the sycamores thirty yards ahead of us; and just then we see a couple of men run into the bunch and heard two or three terrible screams for help. "Poor Jake is killed, sure," we says. We was scared through and through, and broke for the tobacker field and hid there, trembling so our clothes would hardly stay on; and just as we skipped in there, a couple of men went tearing by, and into the bunch they went, and in a second out jumps four men and took out up the road as tight as they could go, two chasing two.

We laid down, kind of weak and sick, and listened for more sounds, but didn't hear none for a good while but just our hearts. We was thinking of that awful thing laying yonder in the sycamores, and it seemed like being that close to a ghost, and it give me the cold shudders. The moon come a-swelling up out of the ground, now, powerful big and round and bright, behind a comb of trees, like a face looking through prison bars, and the black shadders and white places begun to creep around, and it was miserable quiet and still and night-breezy and graveyardy and scary. All of a sudden Tom whispers:

"Look!— what's that?"

"Don't!" I says. "Don't take a person by surprise that way. I'm 'most ready to die, anyway, without you doing that."

"Look, I tell you. It's something coming out of the sycamores."

"Don't, Tom!"

"It's terrible tall!"

"Oh, lordy-lordy! let's —"

"Keep still — it's a-coming this way."

He was so excited he could hardly get breath enough to whisper. I had to look. I couldn't help it. So now we was both on our knees with our chins on a fence rail and gazing — yes, and gasping, too. It was coming down the road — coming in the shadder of the trees, and you couldn't see it good; not till it was pretty close to us; then it stepped into a bright splotch of moonlight and we sunk right down in our tracks — it was Jake Dunlap's ghost! That was what we said to ourselves.

We couldn't stir for a minute or two; then it was gone. We talked about it in low voices. Tom says:

"They're mostly dim and smoky, or like they're made out of fog, but this one wasn't."

"No," I says; "I seen the goggles and the whiskers perfectly plain."

"Yes, and the very colors in them loud countrified Sunday clothes — plaid breeches, green and black —"

"Cotton-velvet westcot, fire-red and yaller squares—"

"Leather straps to the bottoms of the breeches legs and one of them hanging unbuttoned —"

"Yes, and that hat —"

"What a hat for a ghost to wear!"

You see it was the first season anybody wore that kind — a black stiff-brim stove-pipe, very high, and not smooth, with a round top — just like a sugar-loaf.

"Did you notice if its hair was the same, Huck?"

"No — seems to me I did, then again it seems to me I didn't."

"I didn't either; but it had its bag along, I noticed that."

"So did I. How can there be a ghost-bag, Tom?"

"Sho! I wouldn't be as ignorant as that if I was you, Huck Finn. Whatever a ghost has, turns to ghost-stuff. They've got to have their things, like anybody else. You see, yourself, that its clothes was turned to ghost-stuff. Well, then, what's to hender its bag from turning, too? Of course it done it."

That was reasonable. I couldn't find no fault with

it. Bill Withers and his brother Jack come along by, talking, and Jack says:

"What do you reckon he was toting?"

"I dunno; but it was pretty heavy."

"Yes, all he could lug. Nigger stealing corn from old Parson Silas, I judged."

"So did I. And so I allowed I wouldn't let on to see him."

"That's me, too."

Then they both laughed, and went on out of hearing. It showed how unpopular old Uncle Silas had got to be now. They wouldn't 'a' let a nigger steal anybody else's corn and never done anything to him.

We heard some more voices mumbling along towards us and getting louder, and sometimes a cackle of a laugh. It was Lem Beebe and Jim Lane. Jim Lane says:

"Who?— Jubiter Dunlap?"

"Yes."

"Oh, I don't know. I reckon so. I seen him spading up some ground along about an hour ago, just before sundown — him and the parson. Said he guessed he wouldn't go to-night, but we could have his dog if we wanted him."

"Too tired, I reckon."

"Yes — works so hard!"

"Oh, you bet!"

They cackled at that, and went on by. Tom said we better jump out and tag along after them, because they was going our way and it wouldn't be comfortable to run across the ghost all by ourselves. So we done it, and got home all right.

That night was the second of September — a Saturday. I sha'n't ever forget it. You'll see why, pretty soon.

CHAPTER VI.

PLANS TO SECURE THE DIAMONDS

WE tramped along behind Jim and Lem till we come to the back stile where old Jim's cabin was that he was captivated in, the time we set him free, and here come the dogs piling around us to say howdy, and there was the lights of the house, too; so we warn't afeard any more, and was going to climb over, but Tom says:

"Hold on; set down here a minute. By George!"

"What's the matter?" says I.

"Matter enough!" he says. "Wasn't you expecting we would be the first to tell the family who it is that's been killed yonder in the sycamores, and all about them rapscallions that done it, and about the di'monds they've smouched off of the corpse, and paint it up fine, and have the glory of being the ones that knows a lot more about it than anybody else?"

"Why, of course. It wouldn't be you, Tom Sawyer, if you was to let such a chance go by. I reckon it ain't going to suffer none for lack of paint," I says, "when you start in to scollop the facts."

"Well, now," he says, perfectly ca'm, "what would

you say if I was to tell you I ain't going to start in at all?"

I was astonished to hear him talk so. I says:

" I'd say it's a lie. You ain't in earnest, Tom Sawyer?"

" You'll soon see. Was the ghost barefooted?"

" No, it wasn't. What of it?"

" You wait — I'll show you what. Did it have its boots on?"

" Yes. I seen them plain."

' Swear it?"

" Yes, I swear it."

" So do I. Now do you know what that means?"

" No. What does it mean?"

" Means that them thieves *didn't get the di'monds.*"

" Jimminy! What makes you think that?"

" I don't only think it, I know it. Didn't the breeches and goggles and whiskers and hand-bag and every blessed thing turn to ghost-stuff? Everything it had on turned, didn't it? It shows that the reason its boots turned too was because it still had them on after it started to go ha'nting around, and if that ain't proof that them blatherskites didn't get the boots, I'd like to know what you'd *call* proof."

Think of that now. I never see such a head as that boy had. Why, *I* had eyes and I could see things, but they never meant nothing to me. But Tom Sawyer was different. When Tom Sawyer seen a thing it just got up on its hind legs and *talked* to him — told him everything it knowed. *I* never see such a head.

"Tom Sawyer," I says, "I'll say it again as I've said it a many a time before: I ain't fitten to black your boots. But that's all right—that's neither here nor there. God Almighty made us all, and some He gives eyes that's blind, and some He gives eyes that can see, and I reckon it ain't none of our lookout what He done it for; it's all right, or He'd 'a' fixed it some other way. Go on—I see plenty plain enough, now, that them thieves didn't get way with the di'monds. Why didn't they, do you reckon?"

"Because they got chased away by them other two men before they could pull the boots off of the corpse."

"That's so! I see it now. But looky here, Tom, why ain't we to go and tell about it?"

"Oh, shucks, Huck Finn, can't you see? Look at it. What's a-going to happen? There's going to be an inquest in the morning. Them two men will tell how they heard the yells and rushed there just in time to not save the stranger. Then the jury 'll twaddle and twaddle and twaddle, and finally they'll fetch in a verdict that he got shot or stuck or busted over the head with something, and come to his death by the inspiration of God. And after they've buried him they'll auction off his things for to pay the expenses, and then's *our* chance."

"How, Tom?"

"Buy the boots for two dollars!"

Well, it 'most took my breath.

"My land! Why, Tom, *we'll* get the di'monds!"

"You bet. Some day there'll be a big reward

offered for them — a thousand dollars, sure. That's our money! Now we'll trot in and see the folks. And mind you we don't know anything about any murder, or any di'monds, or any thieves — don't you forget that."

I had to sigh a little over the way he had got it fixed. *I'd 'a' sold* them di'monds — yes, sir — for twelve thousand dollars; but I didn't say anything. It wouldn't done any good. I says:

"But what are we going to tell your aunt Sally has made us so long getting down here from the village, Tom?"

"Oh, I'll leave that to you," he says. "I reckon you can explain it somehow."

He was always just that strict and delicate. He never would tell a lie himself.

We struck across the big yard, noticing this, that, and t'other thing that was so familiar, and we so glad to see it again, and when we got to the roofed big passageway betwixt the double log house and the kitchen part, there was everything hanging on the wall just as it used to was, even to Uncle Silas's old faded green baize working-gown with the hood to it, and raggedy white patch between the shoulders that always looked like somebody had hit him with a snowball; and then we lifted the latch and walked in. Aunt Sally she was just a-ripping and a-tearing around, and the children was huddled in one corner, and the old man he was huddled in the other and praying for help in time of need. She jumped for us with joy and tears

running down her face and give us a whacking box on
the ear, and then hugged us and kissed us and boxed
us again, and just couldn't seem to get enough of it,
she was so glad to see us; and she says:

"Where *have* you been a-loafing to, you good-for-
nothing trash! I've been that worried about you I
didn't know what to do. Your traps has been here
ever so long, and I've had supper cooked fresh about
four times so as to have it hot and good when you
come, till at last my patience is just plumb wore out,
and I declare I — I — why I could skin you alive! You
must be starving, poor things! — set down, set down,
everybody; don't lose no more time."

It was good to be there again behind all that noble
corn-pone and spareribs, and everything that you could
ever want in this world. Old Uncle Silas he peeled off
one of his bulliest old-time blessings, with as many
layers to it as an onion, and whilst the angels was hauling in the slack of it I was trying to study up what to
say about what kept us so long. When our plates was
all loadened and we'd got a-going, she asked me, and
I says:

"Well, you see, — er — Mizzes —"

"Huck Finn! Since when am I Mizzes to you?
Have I ever been stingy of cuffs or kisses for you since
the day you stood in this room and I took you for Tom
Sawyer and blessed God for sending you to me, though
you told me four thousand lies and I believed every
one of them like a simpleton? Call me Aunt Saliy —
like you always done."

So I done it.   And I says:

"Well, me and Tom allowed we would come along afoot and take a smell of the woods, and we run across Lem Beebe and Jim Lane, and they asked us to go with them blackberrying to-night, and said they could borrow Jubiter Dunlap's dog, because he had told them just that minute—"

"Where did they see him?" says the old man; and when I looked up to see how *he* come to take an intrust in a little thing like that, his eyes was just burning into me, he was that eager.   It surprised me so it kind of throwed me off, but I pulled myself together again and says:

"It was when he was spading up some ground along with you, towards sundown or along there."

He only said, "Um," in a kind of a disappointed way, and didn't take no more intrust.   So I went on. I says:

"Well, then, as I was a-saying—"

"That'll do, you needn't go no furder."   It was Aunt Sally.   She was boring right into me with her eyes, and very indignant.   "Huck Finn," she says, "how'd them men come to talk about going a-blackberrying in September—in *this* region?"

I see I had slipped up, and I couldn't say a word. She waited, still a-gazing at me, then she says:

"And how'd they come to strike that idiot idea of going a-blackberrying in the night?"

"Well, m'm, they—er—they told us they had a lantern, and—"

"Oh, *shet* up — do! Looky here; what was they going to do with a dog? — hunt blackberries with it?"

"I think, m'm, they —"

"Now, Tom Sawyer, what kind of a lie are you fixing *your* mouth to contribit to this mess of rubbage? Speak out — and I warn you before you begin, that I don't believe a word of it. You and Huck's been up to something you no business to — *I* know it perfectly well; *I* know you, *both* of you. Now you explain that dog, and them blackberries, and the lantern, and the rest of that rot — and mind you talk as straight as a string — do you hear?"

Tom he looked considerable hurt, and says, very dignified:

"It is a pity if Huck is to be talked to that way, just for making a little bit of a mistake that anybody could make."

"What mistake has he made?"

"Why, only the mistake of saying blackberries when of course he meant strawberries."

"Tom Sawyer, I lay if you aggravate me a little more, I'll —"

"Aunt Sally, without knowing it — and of course without intending it — you are in the wrong. If you'd 'a' studied natural history the way you ought, you would know that all over the world except just here in Arkansaw they *always* hunt strawberries with a dog — and a lantern —"

But she busted in on him there and just piled into him and snowed him under. She was so mad she couldn't get the words out fast enough, and she gushed them out in one everlasting freshet. That was what Tom Sawyer was after. He allowed to work her up and get her started and then leave her alone and let her burn herself out. Then she would be so aggravated with that subject that she wouldn't say another word about it, nor let anybody else. Well, it happened just so. When she was tuckered out and had to hold up, he says, quite ca'm:

"And yet, all the same, Aunt Sally —"

"Shet up!" she says, "I don't want to hear another word out of you."

So we was perfectly safe, then, and didn't have no more trouble about that delay. Tom done it elegant.

CHAPTER VII.

BENNY she was looking pretty sober, and she sighed some, now and then; but pretty soon she got to asking about Mary, and Sid, and Tom's aunt Polly, and then Aunt Sally's clouds cleared off and she got in a good humor and joined in on the questions and was her lovingest best self, and so the rest of the supper went along gay and pleasant. But the old man he didn't take any hand hardly, and was absent-minded and restless, and done a considerable amount of sighing; and it was kind of heart-breaking to see him so sad and troubled and worried.

By and by, a spell after supper, come a nigger and knocked on the door and put his head in with his old straw hat in his hand bowing and scraping, and said his Marse Brace was out at the stile and wanted his brother, and was getting tired waiting supper for him, and would Marse Silas please tell him where he was? I never see Uncle Silas speak up so sharp and fractious before. He says:

"Am *I* his brother's keeper?" And then he kind of wilted together, and looked like he wished he hadn't spoken so, and then he says, very gentle: "But you

(178)

needn't say that, Billy; I was took sudden and irritable, and I ain't very well these days, and not hardly responsible. Tell him he ain't here.''

And when the nigger was gone he got up and walked the floor, backwards and forwards, mumbling and muttering to himself and plowing his hands through his hair. It was real pitiful to see him. Aunt Sally she whispered to us and told us not to take notice of him, it embarrassed him. She said he was always thinking and thinking, since these troubles come on, and she allowed he didn't more'n about half know what he was about when the thinking spells was on him; and she said he walked in his sleep considerable more now than he used to, and sometimes wandered around over the house and even outdoors in his sleep, and if we catched him at it we must let him alone and not disturb him. She said she reckoned it didn't do him no harm, and may be it done him good. She said Benny was the only one that was much help to him these days. Said Benny appeared to know just when to try to soothe him and when to leave him alone.

So he kept on tramping up and down the floor and muttering, till by and by he begun to look pretty tired; then Benny she went and snuggled up to his side and put one hand in his and one arm around his waist and walked with him; and he smiled down on her, and reached down and kissed her; and so, little by little the trouble went out of his face and she persuaded him off to his room. They had very petting ways together, and it was uncommon pretty to see.

L**

Aunt Sally she was busy getting the children ready
for bed; so by and by it got dull and tedious, and me
and Tom took a turn in the moonlight, and fetched up
in the watermelon-patch and et one, and had a good
deal of talk. And Tom said he'd bet the quarreling
was all Jubiter's fault, and he was going to be on hand
the first time he got a chance, and see; and if it was
so, he was going to do his level best to get Uncle Silas
to turn him off.

And so we talked and smoked and stuffed water-
melons much as two hours, and then it was pretty late,
and when we got back the house was quiet and dark,
and everybody gone to bed.

Tom he always seen everything, and now he see that
the old green baize work-gown was gone, and said it
wasn't gone when he went out; so he allowed it was
curious, and then we went up to bed.

We could hear Benny stirring around in her room,
which was next to ourn, and judged she was worried a
good deal about her father and couldn't sleep. We
found we couldn't, neither. So we set up a long time,
and smoked and talked in a low voice, and felt pretty
dull and down-hearted. We talked the murder and the
ghost over and over again, and got so creepy and
crawly we couldn't get sleepy nohow and noway.

By and by, when it was away late in the night and all
the sounds was late sounds and solemn, Tom nudged
me and whispers to me to look, and I done it, and there
we see a man poking around in the yard like he didn't
know just what he wanted to do, but it was pretty dim

and we couldn't see him good. Then he started for the stile, and as he went over it the moon came out strong, and he had a long-handled shovel over his shoulder, and we see the white patch on the old work-gown. So Tom says:

"He's a-walking in his sleep. I wish we was allowed to follow him and see where he's going to. There, he's turned down by the tobacker-field. Out of sight now. It's a dreadful pity he can't rest no better."

We waited a long time, but he didn't come back any more, or if he did he come around the other way; so at last we was tuckered out and went to sleep and had nightmares, a million of them. But before dawn we was awake again, because meantime a storm had come up and been raging, and the thunder and lightning was awful, and the wind was a-thrashing the trees around, and the rain was driving down in slanting sheets, and the gullies was running rivers. Tom says:

"Looky here, Huck, I'll tell you one thing that's mighty curious. Up to the time we went out last night the family hadn't heard about Jake Dunlap being murdered. Now the men that chased Hal Clayton and Bud Dixon away would spread the thing around in a half an hour, and every neighbor that heard it would shin out and fly around from one farm to t'other and try to be the first to tell the news. Land, they don't have such a big thing as that to tell twice in thirty year! Huck, it's mighty strange; I don't understand it."

So then he was in a fidget for the rain to let up, so

we could turn out and run across some of the people
and see if they would say anything about it to us.
And he said if they did we must be horribly surprised
and shocked.

We was out and gone the minute the rain stopped.
It was just broad day then. We loafed along up the
road, and now and then met a person and stopped and
said howdy, and told them when we come, and how we
left the folks at home, and how long we was going to
stay, and all that, but none of them said a word about
that thing; which was just astonishing, and no mistake.
Tom said he believed if we went to the sycamores we
would find that body laying there solitary and alone,
and not a soul around. Said he believed the men
chased the thieves so far into the woods that the thieves
prob'ly seen a good chance and turned on them at last,
and maybe they all killed each other, and so there
wasn't anybody left to tell.

First we knowed, gabbling along that away, we was
right at the sycamores. The cold chills trickled down
my back and I wouldn't budge another step, for all
Tom's persuading. But he couldn't hold in; he'd *got*
to see if the boots was safe on that body yet. So he
crope in — and the next minute out he come again with
his eyes bulging he was so excited, and says:

" Huck, it's gone !"

I *was* astonished ! I says:

" Tom, you don't mean it."

" It's gone, sure. There ain't a sign of it. The
ground is trampled some, but if there was any blood

it's all washed away by the storm, for it's all puddles and slush in there."

At last I give in, and went and took a look myself; and it was just as Tom said — there wasn't a sign of a corpse.

"Dern it," I says, "the di'monds is gone. Don't you reckon the thieves slunk back and lugged him off, Tom?"

"Looks like it. It just does. Now where'd they hide him, do you reckon?"

"I don't know," I says, disgusted, "and what's more I don't care. They've got the boots, and that's all *I* cared about. He'll lay around these woods a long time before *I* hunt him up."

Tom didn't feel no more intrust in him neither, only curiosity to know what come of him; but he said we'd lay low and keep dark and it wouldn't be long till the dogs or somebody rousted him out.

We went back home to breakfast ever so bothered and put out and disappointed and swindled. I warn't ever so down on a corpse before.

CHAPTER VIII.

TALKING WITH THE GHOST

IT warn't very cheerful at breakfast. Aunt Sally she looked old and tired and let the children snarl and fuss at one another and didn't seem to notice it was going on, which wasn't her usual style; me and Tom had a plenty to think about without talking; Benny she looked like she hadn't had much sleep, and whenever she'd lift her head a little and steal a look towards her father you could see there was tears in her eyes; and as for the old man, his things stayed on his plate and got cold without him knowing they was there, I reckon, for he was thinking and thinking all the time, and never said a word and never et a bite.

By and by when it was stillest, that nigger's head was poked in at the door again, and he said his Marse Brace was getting powerful uneasy about Marse Jubiter, which hadn't come home yet, and would Marse Silas please —

He was looking at Uncle Silas, and he stopped there, like the rest of his words was froze; for Uncle Silas he rose up shaky and steadied himself leaning his fingers on the table, and he was panting, and his eyes was set on the nigger, and he kept swallowing, and put his

(184)

other hand up to his throat a couple of times, and at last he got his words started, and says:

"Does he — does he — think — *what* does he think! Tell him — tell him —" Then he sunk down in his chair limp and weak, and says, so as you could hardly hear him: "Go away — go away!"

The nigger looked scared and cleared out, and we all felt — well, I don't know how we felt, but it was awful, with the old man panting there, and his eyes set and looking like a person that was dying. None of us could budge; but Benny she slid around soft, with her tears running down, and stood by his side, and nestled his old gray head up against her and begun to stroke it and pet it with her hands, and nodded to us to go away, and we done it, going out very quiet, like the dead was there.

Me and Tom struck out for the woods mighty solemn, and saying how different it was now to what it was last summer when we was here and everything was so peaceful and happy and everybody thought so much of Uncle Silas, and he was so cheerful and simple-hearted and pudd'n-headed and good — and now look at him. If he hadn't lost his mind he wasn't much short of it. That was what we allowed.

It was a most lovely day now, and bright and sun-shiny; and the further and further we went over the hills towards the prairie the lovelier and lovelier the trees and flowers got to be and the more it seemed strange and somehow wrong that there had to be trouble in such a world as this. And then all of a sudden I catched my breath and grabbed Tom's arm, and all my livers and lungs and things fell down into my legs.

"There it is!" I says. We jumped back behind a bush shivering, and Tom says:

"'Sh!—don't make a noise."

It was setting on a log right in the edge of a little prairie, thinking. I tried to get Tom to come away, but he wouldn't, and I dasn't budge by myself. He said we mightn't ever get another chance to see one, and he was going to look his fill at this one if he died for it. So I looked too, though it give me the fantods to do it. Tom he *had* to talk, but he talked low. He says:

"Poor Jakey, it's got all its things on, just as he said he would. *Now* you see what we wasn't certain about—its hair. It's not long now the way it was: it's got it cropped close to its head, the way he said he would. Huck, I never see anything look any more naturaler than what It does."

"Nor I neither," I says; "I'd recognize it anywheres."

"So would I. It looks perfectly solid and genuwyne, just the way it done before it died."

So we kept a-gazing. Pretty soon Tom says:

"Huck, there's something mighty curious about this one, don't you know? *It* oughtn't to be going around in the daytime."

"That's so, Tom—I never heard the like of it before."

"No, sir, they don't ever come out only at night—

and then not till after twelve. There's something wrong about this one, now you mark my words. I don't believe it's got any right to be around in the daytime. But don't it look natural! Jake was going to play deef and dumb here, so the neighbors wouldn't know his voice. Do you reckon it would do that if we was to holler at it?"

"Lordy, Tom, don't talk so! If you was to holler at it I'd die in my tracks."

"Don't you worry, I ain't going to holler at it. Look, Huck, it's a-scratching its head — don't you see?"

"Well, what of it?"

"Why, this. What's the sense of it scratching its head? There ain't anything there to itch; its head is made out of fog or something like that, and *can't* itch. A fog can't itch; any fool knows that."

"Well, then, if it don't itch and can't itch, what in the nation is it scratching it for? Ain't it just habit, don't you reckon?"

"No, sir, I don't. I ain't a bit satisfied about the way this one acts. I've a blame good notion it's a bogus one — I have, as sure as I'm a-sitting here. Because, if it — Huck!"

"Well, what's the matter now?"

"*You can't see the bushes through it!*"

"Why, Tom, it's so, sure! It's as solid as a cow. I sort of begin to think —"

"Huck, it's biting off a chaw of tobacker! By George, *they* don't chaw — they hain't got anything to chaw *with*. Huck!"

13**

" I'm a-listening."

" It ain't a ghost at all. It's Jake Dunlap his own self !"

" Oh your granny !" I says.

" Huck Finn, did we find any corpse in the sycamores?"

" No."

" Or any sign of one?"

" No."

" Mighty good reason. Hadn't ever been any corpse there."

" Why, Tom, you know we heard —"

" Yes, we did — heard a howl or two. Does that prove anybody was killed? Course it don't. And we seen four men run, then this one come walking out and we took it for a ghost. No more ghost than you are. It was Jake Dunlap his own self, and it's Jake Dunlap now. He's been and got his hair cropped, the way he said he would, and he's playing himself for a stranger, just the same as he said he would. Ghost? Hum !— he's as sound as a nut."

Then I see it all, and how we had took too much for granted. I was powerful glad he didn't get killed, and so was Tom, and we wondered which he would like the best — for us to never let on to know him, or how? Tom reckoned the best way would be to go and ask him. So he started; but I kept a little behind, because I didn't know but it might be a ghost, after all. When Tom got to where he was, he says:

" Me and Huck's mighty glad to see you again,

and you needn't be afeared we'll tell. And if you think it'll be safer for you if we don't let on to know you when we run across you, say the word and you'll see you can depend on us, and would ruther cut our hands off than get you into the least little bit of danger."

First off he looked surprised to see us, and not very glad, either; but as Tom went on he looked pleasanter, and when he was done he smiled, and nodded his head several times, and made signs with his hands, and says:

" Goo-goo — goo-goo," the way deef and dummies does.

Just then we see some of Steve Nickerson's people coming that lived t'other side of the prairie, so Tom says:

" You do it elegant; I never see anybody do it better. You're right; play it on us, too; play it on us same as the others; it'll keep you in practice and prevent you making blunders. We'll keep away from you and let on we don't know you, but any time we can be any help, you just let us know."

Then we loafed along past the Nickersons, and of course they asked if that was the new stranger yonder, and where'd he come from, and what was his name, and which communion was he, Babtis' or Methodis', and which politics, Whig or Democrat, and how long is he staying, and all them other questions that humans always asks when a stranger comes, and animals does, too. But Tom said he warn't able to make anything out of deef and dumb signs, and the same with goo-

gooing. Then we watched them go and bullyrag Jake;
because we was pretty uneasy for him. Tom said it
would take him days to get so he wouldn't forget he
was a deef and dummy sometimes, and speak out before he thought. When we had watched long enough
to see that Jake was getting along all right and working
his signs very good, we loafed along again, allowing to
strike the schoolhouse about recess time, which was a
three-mile tramp.

I was so disappointed not to hear Jake tell about the
row in the sycamores, and how near he come to getting killed, that I couldn't seem to get over it, and
Tom he felt the same, but said if we was in Jake's fix
we would want to go careful and keep still and not take
any chances.

The boys and girls was all glad to see us again, and
we had a real good time all through recess. Coming
to school the Henderson boys had come across the new
deef and dummy and told the rest; so all the scholars
was chuck full of him and couldn't talk about anything
else, and was in a sweat to get a sight of him because
they hadn't ever seen a deef and dummy in their lives,
and it made a powerful excitement.

Tom said it was tough to have to keep mum now;
said we would be heroes if we could come out and tell
all we knowed; but after all, it was still more heroic to
keep mum, there warn't two boys in a million could do
it. That was Tom Sawyer's idea about it, and I
reckoned there warn't anybody could better it.

CHAPTER IX.

FINDING OF JUBITER DUNLAP

IN the next two or three days Dummy he got to be
powerful popular. He went associating around with
the neighbors, and they made much of him, and was
proud to have such a rattling curiosity among them.
They had him to breakfast, they had him to dinner,
they had him to supper; they kept him loaded up
with hog and hominy, and warn't ever tired staring at
him and wondering over him, and wishing they knowed
more about him, he was so uncommon and romantic.
His signs warn't no good; people couldn't understand them and he prob'ly couldn't himself, but he
done a sight of goo-gooing, and so everybody was satisfied, and admired to hear him go it. He toted a
piece of slate around, and a pencil; and people wrote
questions on it and he wrote answers; but there warn't
anybody could read his writing but Brace Dunlap.
Brace said he couldn't read it very good, but he could
manage to dig out the meaning most of the time. He
said Dummy said he belonged away off somers and
used to be well off, but got busted by swindlers which
he had trusted, and was poor now, and hadn't any way
to make a living.

That graveled him, and he says:

"Huck Finn, I never see such a person as you to want to spoil everything. As long as *you* can't see anything hopeful in a thing, you won't let anybody else. What good can it do you to throw cold water on that corpse and get up that selfish theory that there ain't been any murder? None in the world. I don't see how you can act so. I wouldn't treat you like that, and you know it. Here we've got a noble good opportunity to make a ruputation, and —"

"Oh, go ahead," I says. "I'm sorry, and I take it all back. I didn't mean nothing. Fix it any way you want it. *He* ain't any consequence to me. If he's killed, I'm as glad of it as you are; and if he —"

"I never said anything about being glad; I only —"

"Well, then, I'm as *sorry* as you are. Any way you druther have it, that is the way *I* druther have it. He —"

"There ain't any druthers *about* it, Huck Finn; nobody said anything about druthers. And as for —"

He forgot he was talking, and went tramping along, studying. He begun to get excited again, and pretty soon he says:

"Huck, it 'll be the bulliest thing that ever happened if we find the body after everybody else has quit looking, and then go ahead and hunt up the murderer. It won't only be an honor to us, but it 'll be an honor to Uncle Silas because it was us that done it. It 'll set him up again, you see if it don't."

But Old Jeff Hooker he throwed cold water on the

whole business when we got to his blacksmith shop and
told him what we come for.

" You can take the dog," he says, " but you ain't
a-going to find any corpse, because there ain't any
corpse to find.   Everybody's quit looking, and they're
right.   Soon as they come to think, they knowed there
warn't no corpse.   And I'll tell you for why.   What
does a person kill another person *for*, Tom Sawyer?—
answer me that."

" Why, he — er —"

"Answer up !   You ain't no fool.   What does he kill
him *for ?* "

" Well, sometimes it's for revenge, and —"

" Wait.   One thing at a time.   Revenge, says you ;
and right you are.   Now who ever had anything agin
that poor trifling no-account?   Who do you reckon
would want to kill *him ?*— that rabbit !"

Tom was stuck.   I reckon he hadn't thought of a
person having to have a *reason* for killing a person before, and now he sees it warn't likely anybody would
have that much of a grudge against a lamb like Jubiter
Dunlap.   The blacksmith says, by and by :

" The revenge idea won't work, you see.   Well,
then, what's next?   Robbery?   B'gosh, that must 'a'
been it, Tom !   Yes, sirree, I reckon we've struck it
this time.   Some feller wanted his gallus-buckles, and
so he —"

But it was so funny he busted out laughing, and just
went *on* laughing and laughing and laughing till he was
'most dead, and Tom looked so put out and cheap that

M**

I knowed he was ashamed he had come, and he wished
he hadn't. But old Hooker never let up on him. He
raked up everything a person ever could want to kill
another person about, and any fool could see they
didn't any of them fit this case, and he just made no
end of fun of the whole business and of the people
that had been hunting the body; and he said:

" If they'd had any sense they'd 'a' knowed the lazy
cuss slid out because he wanted a loafing spell after all
this work. He'll come pottering back in a couple of
weeks, and then how 'll you fellers feel? But, laws
bless you, take the dog, and go and hunt his re-
mainders. Do, Tom."

Then he busted out, and had another of them forty-
rod laughs of hisn. Tom couldn't back down after all
this, so he said, "All right, unchain him;" and the
blacksmith done it, and we started home and left that
old man laughing yet.

It was a lovely dog. There ain't any dog that's got
a lovelier disposition than a bloodhound, and this one
knowed us and liked us. He capered and raced
around ever so friendly, and powerful glad to be free
and have a holiday; but Tom was so cut up he couldn't
take any intrust in him, and said he wished he'd stopped
and thought a minute before he ever started on such a
fool errand. He said old Jeff Hooker would tell everybody, and we'd never hear the last of it.

So we loafed along home down the back lanes, feeling pretty glum and not talking. When we was passing the far corner of our tobacker field we heard the

dog set up a long howl in there, and we went to the place and he was scratching the ground with all his might, and every now and then canting up his head sideways and fetching another howl.

It was a long square, the shape of a grave; the rain had made it sink down and show the shape. The minute we come and stood there we looked at one another and never said a word. When the dog had dug down only a few inches he grabbed something and pulled it up, and it was an arm and a sleeve. Tom kind of gasped out, and says:

"Come away, Huck — it's found."

I just felt awful. We struck for the road and fetched the first men that come along. They got a spade at the crib and dug out the body, and you never see such an excitement. You couldn't make anything out of the face, but you didn't need to. Everybody said:

"Poor Jubiter; it's his clothes, to the last rag!"

Some rushed off to spread the news and tell the justice of the peace and have an inquest, and me and Tom lit out for the house. Tom was all afire and 'most out of breath when we come tearing in where Uncle Silas and Aunt Sally and Benny was. Tom sung out:

"Me and Huck's found Jubiter Dunlap's corpse all by ourselves with a bloodhound, after everybody else had quit hunting and given it up; and if it hadn't a been for us it never *would* 'a' been found; and he *was* murdered too — they done it with a club or something like that; and I'm going to start in and find the murderer, next, and I bet I'll do it!''

Aunt Sally and Benny sprung up pale and astonished, but Uncle Silas fell right forward out of his chair on to the floor and groans out:

" Oh, my God, you've found him *now!* "

CHAPTER X.

THE ARREST OF UNCLE SILAS

THEM awful words froze us solid. We couldn't move hand or foot for as much as half a minute. Then we kind of come to, and lifted the old man up and got him into his chair, and Benny petted him and kissed him and tried to comfort him, and poor old Aunt Sally she done the same; but, poor things, they was so broke up and scared and knocked out of their right minds that they didn't hardly know what they was about. With Tom it was awful; it 'most petrified him to think maybe he had got his uncle into a thousand times more trouble than ever, and maybe it wouldn't ever happened if he hadn't been so ambitious to get celebrated, and let the corpse alone the way the others done. But pretty soon he sort of come to himself again and says:

"Uncle Silas, don't you say another word like that. It's dangerous, and there ain't a shadder of truth in it."

Aunt Sally and Benny was thankful to hear him say that, and they said the same; but the old man he wagged his head sorrowful and hopeless, and the tears run down his face, and he says:

" No — I done it; poor Jubiter, I done it ! "

It was dreadful to hear him say it. Then he went on and told about it, and said it happened the day me and Tom come — along about sundown. He said Jubiter pestered him and aggravated him till he was so mad he just sort of lost his mind and grabbed up a stick and hit him over the head with all his might, and Jubiter dropped in his tracks. Then he was scared and sorry, and got down on his knees and lifted his head up, and begged him to speak and say he wasn't dead; and before long he come to, and when he see who it was holding his head, he jumped like he was 'most scared to death, and cleared the fence and tore into the woods, and was gone. So he hoped he wasn't hurt bad.

" But laws," he says, " it was only just fear that gave him that last little spurt of strength, and of course it soon played out and he laid down in the bush, and there wasn't anybody to help him, and he died."

Then the old man cried and grieved, and said he was a murderer and the mark of Cain was on him, and he had disgraced his family and was going to be found out and hung. But Tom said:

" No, you ain't going to be found out. You *didn't* kill him. *One* lick wouldn't kill him. Somebody else done it."

" Oh, yes," he says, " I done it — nobody else. Who else had anything against him ? Who else *could* have anything against him ? "

He looked up kind of like he hoped some of us could

mention somebody that could have a grudge against
that harmless no-account, but of course it warn't no
use — he *had* us; we couldn't say a word.   He
noticed that, and he saddened down again, and I never
see a face so miserable and so pitiful to see. Tom
had a sudden idea, and says:

"But hold on! — somebody *buried* him. Now
who —"

He shut off sudden. I knowed the reason. It give
me the cold shudders when he said them words, because
right away I remembered about us seeing Uncle Silas
prowling around with a long-handled shovel away in
the night that night. And I knowed Benny seen him,
too, because she was talking about it one day. The
minute Tom shut off he changed the subject and went
to begging Uncle Silas to keep mum, and the rest of us
done the same, and said he *must*, and said it wasn't his
business to tell on himself, and if he kept mum nobody
would ever know; but if it was found out and any
harm come to him it would break the family's hearts
and kill them, and yet never do anybody any good.
So at last he promised. We was all of us more comfortable, then, and went to work to cheer up the old
man. We told him all he'd got to do was to keep still,
and it wouldn't be long till the whole thing would blow
over and be forgot. We all said there wouldn't anybody ever suspect Uncle Silas, nor ever dream of such
a thing, he being so good and kind, and having such a
good character; and Tom says, cordial and hearty, he
says:

"Why, just look at it a minute; just consider. Here is Uncle Silas, all these years a preacher — at his own expense; all these years doing good with all his might and every way he can think of — at his own expense, all the time; always been loved by everybody, and respected; always been peaceable and minding his own business, the very last man in this whole deestrict to touch a person, and everybody knows it. Suspect *him ?* Why, it ain't any more possible than —"

"By authority of the State of Arkansaw, I arrest you for the murder of Jubiter Dunlap!" shouts the sheriff at the door.

It was awful. Aunt Sally and Benny flung themselves at Uncle Silas, screaming and crying, and hugged him and hung to him, and Aunt Sally said go away, she wouldn't ever give him up, they shouldn't have him, and the niggers they come crowding and crying to the door and — well, I couldn't stand it; it was enough to break a person's heart; so I got out.

They took him up to the little one-horse jail in the village, and we all went along to tell him good-bye; and Tom was feeling elegant, and says to me, "We'll have a most noble good time and heaps of danger some dark night getting him out of there, Huck, and it 'll be talked about everywheres and we will be celebrated;" but the old man busted that scheme up the minute he whispered to him about it. He said no, it was his duty to stand whatever the law done to him, and he would stick to the jail plumb through to the end, even if there warn't no door to it. It disappointed Tom and graveled him a good deal, but he had to put up with it.

But he felt responsible and bound to get his uncle Silas free; and he told Aunt Sally, the last thing, not to worry, because he was going to turn in and work night and day and beat this game and fetch Uncle Silas out innocent; and she was very loving to him and thanked him and said she knowed he would do his very best. And she told us to help Benny take care of the house and the children, and then we had a good-bye cry all around and went back to the farm, and left her there to live with the jailer's wife a month till the trial in October.

14**

CHAPTER XI.

TOM SAWYER DISCOVERS THE MURDERERS

WELL, that was a hard month on us all. Poor Benny, she kept up the best she could, and me and Tom tried to keep things cheerful there at the house, but it kind of went for nothing, as you may say. It was the same up at the jail. We went up every day to see the old people, but it was awful dreary, because the old man warn't sleeping much, and was walking in his sleep considerable, and so he got to looking fagged and miserable, and his mind got shaky, and we all got afraid his troubles would break him down and kill him. And whenever we tried to persuade him to feel cheerfuler, he only shook his head and said if we only knowed what it was to carry around a murderer's load on your heart we wouldn't talk that way. Tom and all of us kept telling him it *wasn't* murder, but just accidental killing, but it never made any difference — it was murder, and he wouldn't have it any other way. He actu'ly begun to come out plain and square towards trial time and acknowledge that he *tried* to kill the man. Why, that was awful, you know. It made things seem fifty times as dreadful, and there warn't no more com-

fort for Aunt Sally and Benny. But he promised he
wouldn't say a word about his murder when others
was around, and we was glad of that.

Tom Sawyer racked the head off of himself all that
month trying to plan some way out for Uncle Silas, and
many's the night he kept me up 'most all night with
this kind of tiresome work, but he couldn't seem to get
on the right track no way. As for me, I reckoned a
body might as well give it up, it all looked so blue and
I was so downhearted; but he wouldn't. He stuck to
the business right along, and went on planning and
thinking and ransacking his head.

So at last the trial come on, towards the middle of
October, and we was all in the court. The place was
jammed, of course. Poor old Uncle Silas, he looked
more like a dead person than a live one, his eyes was so
hollow and he looked so thin and so mournful. Benny
she set on one side of him and Aunt Sally on the other,
and they had veils on, and was full of trouble. But
Tom he set by our lawyer, and had his finger in everywheres, of course. The lawyer let him, and the judge
let him. He 'most took the business out of the lawyer's hands sometimes; which was well enough, because that was only a mud-turtle of a back-settlement
lawyer and didn't know enough to come in when it
rains, as the saying is.

They swore in the jury, and then the lawyer for the
prostitution got up and begun. He made a terrible
speech against the old man, that made him moan and
groan, and made Benny and Aunt Sally cry. The way

he told about the murder kind of knocked us all stupid it was so different from the old man's tale. He said he was going to prove that Uncle Silas was *seen* to kill Jubiter Dunlap by two good witnesses, and done it deliberate, and *said* he was going to kill him the very minute he hit him with the club; and they seen him hide Jubiter in the bushes, and they seen that Jubiter was stone-dead. And said Uncle Silas come later and lugged Jubiter down into the tobacker field, and two men seen him do it. And said Uncle Silas turned out, away in the night, and buried Jubiter, and a man seen him at it.

I says to myself, poor old Uncle Silas has been lying about it because he reckoned nobody seen him and he couldn't bear to break Aunt Sally's heart and Benny's; and right he was: as for me, I would 'a' lied the same way, and so would anybody that had any feeling, to save them such misery and sorrow which *they* warn't no ways responsible for. Well, it made our lawyer look pretty sick; and it knocked Tom silly, too, for a little spell, but then he braced up and let on that he warn't worried — but I knowed he *was*, all the same. And the people — my, but it made a stir amongst them!

And when that lawyer was done telling the jury what he was going to prove, he set down and begun to work his witnesses.

First, he called a lot of them to show that there was bad blood betwixt Uncle Silas and the diseased; and they told how they had heard Uncle Silas threaten the

diseased, at one time and another, and how it got
worse and worse and everybody was talking about it,
and how diseased got afraid of his life, and told two or
three of them he was certain Uncle Silas would up and
kill him some time or another.

Tom and our lawyer asked them some questions;
but it warn't no use, they stuck to what they said.

Next, they called up Lem Beebe, and he took the
stand. It come into my mind, then, how Lem and Jim
Lane had come along talking, that time, about borrow-
ing a dog or something from Jubiter Dunlap; and that
brought up the blackberries and the lantern; and that
brought up Bill and Jack Withers, and how *they* passed
by, talking about a nigger stealing Uncle Silas's corn;
and that fetched up our old ghost that come along
about the same time and scared us so — and here *he*
was too, and a privileged character, on accounts of his
being deef and dumb and a stranger, and they had fixed
him a chair inside the railing, where he could cross his
legs and be comfortable, whilst the other people was all
in a jam so they couldn't hardly breathe. So it all
come back to me just the way it was that day; and it
made me mournful to think how pleasant it was up to
then, and how miserable ever since.

Lem Beebe, sworn, said: "I was a-coming along, that day, second of
September, and Jim Lane was with me, and it was towards sundown, and
we heard loud talk, like quarrelling, and we was very close, only the hazel
bushes between (that's along the fence); and we heard a voice say, ' I've
told you more'n once I'd kill you,' and knowed it was this prisoner's voice;
and then we see a club come up above the bushes and down out of sight
again, and heard a smashing thump and then a groan or two; and then we

14

crope soft to where we could see, and there laid Jupiter Dunlap dead, and
this prisoner standing over him with the club; and the next he hauled the
dead man into a clump of bushes and hid him, and then we stooped low,
to be cut of sight, and got away."

Well, it was awful. It kind of froze everybody's
blood to hear it, and the house was 'most as still whilst
he was telling it as if there warn't nobody in it. And
when he was done, you could hear them gasp and sigh,
all over the house, and look at one another the same
as to say, "Ain't it perfectly terrible — ain't it awful!"

Now happened a thing that astonished me. All the
time the first witnesses was proving the bad blood and
the threats and all that, Tom Sawyer was alive and laying for them; and the minute they was through, he
went for them, and done his level best to catch them in
lies and spile their testimony. But now, how different.
When Lem first begun to talk, and never said anything
about speaking to Jubiter or trying to borrow a dog
off of him, he was all alive and laying for Lem, and you
could see he was getting ready to cross-question him to
death pretty soon, and then I judged him and me would
go on the stand by and by and tell what we heard him
and Jim Lane say. But the next time I looked at Tom
I got the cold shivers. Why, he was in the brownest
study you ever see — miles and miles away. He warn't
hearing a word Lem Beebe was saying; and when he
got through he was still in that brown-study, just the
same. Our lawyer joggled him, and then he looked up
startled, and says, "Take the witness if you want him.
Lemme alone — I want to think."

Well, that beat me. I couldn't understand it. And
Benny and her mother — oh, they looked sick, they
was so troubled. They shoved their veils to one side
and tried to get his eye, but it warn't any use, and I
couldn't get his eye either. So the mud-turtle he
tackled the witness, but it didn't amount to nothing;
and he made a mess of it.

Then they called up Jim Lane, and he told the very
same story over again, exact. Tom never listened to
this one at all, but set there thinking and thinking, miles
and miles away. So the mud-turtle went in alone
again and come out just as flat as he done before. The
lawyer for the prostitution looked very comfortable,
but the judge looked disgusted. You see, Tom was
just the same as a regular lawyer, nearly, because it
was Arkansaw law for a prisoner to choose anybody he
wanted to help his lawyer, and Tom had had Uncle
Silas shove him into the case, and now he was botching
it and you could see the judge didn't like it much.

All that the mud-turtle got out of Lem and Jim was
this: he asked them:

"Why didn't you go and tell what you saw?"

"We was afraid we would get mixed up in it ourselves. And we was just starting down the river
a-hunting for all the week besides; but as soon as we
come back we found out they'd been searching for the
body, so then we went and told Brace Dunlap all
about it."

"When was that?"

"Saturday night, September 9th."

14**

The judge he spoke up and says:

"Mr. Sheriff, arrest these two witnesses on suspicions of being accessionary after the fact to the murder."

The lawyer for the prostitution jumps up all excited, and says:

"Your honor! I protest against this extraordi —"

"Set down!" says the judge, pulling his bowie and laying it on his pulpit. "I beg you to respect the Court."

So he done it. Then he called Bill Withers.

Bill Withers, sworn, said: "I was coming along about sundown, Saturday, September 2d, by the prisoner's field, and my brother Jack was with me, and we seen a man toting off something heavy on his back and allowed it was a nigger stealing corn; we couldn't see distinct; next we made out that it was one man carrying another; and the way it hung, so kind of limp, we judged it was somebody that was drunk; and by the man's walk we said it was Parson Silas, and we judged he had found Sam Cooper drunk in the road, which he was always trying to reform him, and was toting him out of danger."

It made the people shiver to think of poor old Uncle Silas toting off the diseased down to the place in his tobacker field where the dog dug up the body, but there warn't much sympathy around amongst the faces, and I heard one cuss say, "'Tis the coldest blooded work I ever struck, lugging a murdered man around like that, and going to bury him like a animal, and him a preacher at that."

Tom he went on thinking, and never took no notice; so our lawyer took the witness and done the best he could, and it was plenty poor enough.

Then Jack Withers he come on the stand and told the same tale, just like Bill done.

And after him comes Brace Dunlap, and he was looking very mournful, and most crying; and there was a rustle and a stir all around, and everybody got ready to listen, and lots of the women folks said, "Poor cretur, poor cretur," and you could see a many of them wiping their eyes.

Brace Dunlap, sworn, said: "I was in considerable trouble a long time about my poor brother, but I reckoned things warn't near so bad as he made out, and I couldn't make myself believe anybody would have the heart to hurt a poor harmless cretur like that"—[by jings, I was sure I seen Tom give a kind of a faint little start, and then look disappointed again]—"and you know I *couldn't* think a preacher would hurt him — it warn't natural to think such an onlikely thing — so I never paid much attention, and now I sha'n't ever, ever forgive myself; for if I had a done different, my poor brother would be with me this day, and not laying yonder murdered, and him so harmless." He kind of broke down there and choked up, and waited to get his voice; and people all around said the most pitiful things, and women cried; and it was very still in there, and solemn, and old Uncle Silas, poor thing, he give a groan right out so everybody heard him. Then Brace he went on, "Saturday, September 2d, he didn't come home to supper. By-and-by I got a little uneasy, and one of my niggers went over to this prisoner's place, but come back and said he warn't there. So I got uneasier and uneasier, and couldn't rest. I went to bed, but I couldn't sleep; and turned out, away late in the night, and went wandering over to this prisoner's place and all around about there a good while, hoping I would run across my poor brother, and never knowing he was out of his troubles and gone to a better shore—" So he broke down and choked up again, and most all the women was crying now. Pretty soon he got another start and says: "But it warn't no use; so at last I went home and tried to get some sleep, but couldn't. Well, in a day or two everybody was uneasy, and they got to talking about this prisoner's threats, and took to the idea, which I didn't take no stock in, that my brother was murdered; so they hunted around and tried to find his body, but couldn't and give it

N **

up. And so I reckoned he was gone off somers to have a little peace, and would come back to us when his troubles was kind of healed. But late Saturday night, the 9th, Lem Beebe and Jim Lane come to my house and told me all — told me the whole awful 'sassination, and my heart was broke. And *then* I remembered something that hadn't took no hold of me at the time, because reports said this prisoner had took to walking in his sleep and doing all kind of things of no consequence, not knowing what he was about. I will tell you what that thing was that come back into my memory. Away late that awful Saturday night when I was wandering around about this prisoner's place, grieving and troubled, I was down by the corner of the tobacker-field and I heard a sound like digging in a gritty soil; and I crope nearer and peeped through the vines that hung on the rail fence and seen this prisoner *shoveling* — shoveling with a long-handled shovel — heaving earth into a big hole that was most filled up; his back was to me, but it was bright moonlight and I knowed him by his old green baize work-gown with a splattery white patch in the middle of the back like somebody had hit him with a snowball. *He was burying the man he'd murdered!*"

And he slumped down in his chair crying and sobbing, and 'most everybody in the house busted out wailing, and crying, and saying, " Oh, it's awful — awful — horrible ! and there was a most tremendous excitement, and you couldn't hear yourself think; and right in the midst of it up jumps old Uncle Silas, white as a sheet, and sings out:

"*It's true, every word — I murdered him in cold blood !*"

By Jackson, it petrified them ! People rose up wild all over the house, straining and staring for a better look at him, and the judge was hammering with his mallet and the sheriff yelling " Order — order in the court — order !"

And all the while the old man stood there a-quaking and his eyes a-burning, and not looking at his wife and daughter, which was clinging to him and begging him to keep still, but pawing them off with his hands and saying he *would* clear his black soul from crime, he *would* heave off this load that was more than he could bear, and he *wouldn't* bear it another hour! And then he raged right along with his awful tale, everybody a-staring and gasping, judge, jury, lawyers, and everybody, and Benny and Aunt Sally crying their hearts out. And by George, Tom Sawyer never looked at him once! Never once — just set there gazing with all his eyes at something else, I couldn't tell what. And so the old man raged right along, pouring his words out like a stream of fire:

"I killed him! I am guilty! But I never had the notion in my life to hurt him or harm him, spite of all them lies about my threatening him, till the very minute I raised the club — then my heart went cold! — then the pity all went out of it, and I struck to kill! In that one moment all my wrongs come into my mind; all the insults that that man and the scoundrel his brother, there, had put upon me, and how they laid in together to ruin me with the people, and take away my good name, and *drive* me to some deed that would destroy me and my family that hadn't ever done *them* no harm, so help me God! And they done it in a mean revenge — for why? Because my innocent pure girl here at my side wouldn't marry that rich, insolent, ignorant coward, Brace Dunlap, who's been sniveling here over a brother he never cared a brass farthing for "—[I see Tom give a jump and look glad *this* time, to a dead certainty]—"and in that moment I've told you about, I forgot my God and remembered only my heart's bitterness, God forgive me, and I struck to kill. In one second I was miserably sorry — oh, filled with remorse; but I thought of my poor family, and I *must* hide what I'd done for their sakes; and I did hide that corpse in the bushes; and presently I carried it to the tobacker field; and in the deep night I went with my shovel and buried it where —"

Up jumps Tom and shouts:

"*Now*, I've got it!" and waves his hand, oh, ever so fine and starchy, towards the old man, and says:

"Set down! A murder *was* done, but you never had no hand in it!"

Well, sir, you could a heard a pin drop. And the old man he sunk down kind of bewildered in his seat and Aunt Sally and Benny didn't know it, because they was so astonished and staring at Tom with their mouths open and not knowing what they was about. And the whole house the same. *I* never seen people look so helpless and tangled up, and I hain't ever seen eyes bug out and gaze without a blink the way theirn did. Tom says, perfectly ca'm:

"Your honor, may I speak?"

"For God's sake, yes — go on!" says the judge, so astonished and mixed up he didn't know what he was about hardly.

Then Tom he stood there and waited a second or two — that was for to work up an "effect," as he calls it — then he started in just as ca'm as ever, and says:

"For about two weeks now there's been a little bill sticking on the front of this courthouse offering two thousand dollars reward for a couple of big di'monds — stole at St. Louis. Them di'monds is worth twelve thousand dollars. But never mind about that till I get to it. Now about this murder. I will tell you all about it — how it happened — who done it — every *de*tail."

You could see everybody nestle now, and begin to listen for all they was worth.

"This man here, Brace Dunlap, that's been sniveling so about his dead brother that *you* know he never cared a straw for, wanted to marry that young girl there, and she wouldn't have him. So he told Uncle Silas he would make him sorry. Uncle Silas knowed how powerful he was, and how little chance he had against such a man, and he was scared and worried, and done everything he could think of to smooth him over and get him to be good to him: he even took his no-account brother Jubiter on the farm and give him wages and stinted his own family to pay them; and Jubiter done everything his brother could contrive to insult Uncle Silas, and fret and worry him, and try to drive Uncle Silas into doing him a hurt, so as to injure Uncle Silas with the people. And it done it. Everybody turned against him and said the meanest kind of things about him, and it gradully broke his heart — yes, and he was so worried and distressed that often he warn't hardly in his right mind.

"Well, on that Saturday that we've had so much

trouble about, two of these witnesses here, Lem Beebe and Jim Lane, come along by where Uncle Silas and Jubiter Dunlap was at work — and that much of what they've said is true, the rest is lies. They didn't hear Uncle Silas say he would kill Jubiter; they didn't hear no blow struck; they didn't see no dead man, and they didn't see Uncle Silas hide anything in the bushes. Look at them now — how they set there, wishing they hadn't been so handy with their tongues; anyway, they'll wish it before I get done.

"That same Saturday evening Bill and Jack Withers *did* see one man lugging off another one. That much of what they said is true, and the rest is lies. First off they thought it was a nigger stealing Uncle Silas's corn — you notice it makes them look silly, now, to find out somebody overheard them say that. That's because they found out by and by who it was that was doing the lugging, and *they* know best why they swore here that they took it for Uncle Silas by the gait — which it *wasn't*, and they knowed it when they swore to that lie.

"A man out in the moonlight *did* see a murdered person put under ground in the tobacker field — but it wasn't Uncle Silas that done the burying. He was in his bed at that very time.

"Now, then, before I go on, I want to ask you if you've ever noticed this: that people, when they're thinking deep, or when they're worried, are most always doing something with their hands, and they don't know it, and don't notice what it is their hands are doing. Some stroke their chins; some stroke their noses; some

stroke up *under* their chin with their hand; some twirl
a chain, some fumble a button, then there's some that
draws a figure or a letter with their finger on their
cheek, or under their chin or on their under lip. That's
my way. When I'm restless, or worried, or thinking
hard, I draw capital V's on my cheek or on my under
lip or under my chin, and never anything *but* capital
V's — and half the time I don't notice it and don't
know I'm doing it."

That was odd. That is just what I do; only I make
an O. And I could see people nodding to one another,
same as they do when they mean " *That's* so."

" Now, then, I'll go on. That same Saturday — no,
it was the night before — there was a steamboat laying
at Flagler's Landing, forty miles above here, and it
was raining and storming like the nation. And there
was a thief aboard, and he had them two big di'monds
that's advertised out here on this courthouse door;
and he slipped ashore with his hand-bag and struck
out into the dark and the storm, and he was a-hoping
he could get to this town all right and be safe. But he
had two pals aboard the boat, hiding, and he knowed
they was going to kill him the first chance they got and
take the di'monds; because all three stole them, and
then this fellow he got hold of them and skipped.

" Well, he hadn't been gone more'n ten minutes before his pals found it out, and they jumped ashore and
lit out after him. Prob'ly they burnt matches and
found his tracks. Anyway, they dogged along after
him all day Saturday and kept out of his sight; and

towards sundown he come to the bunch of sycamores down by Uncle Silas's field, and he went in there to get a disguise out of his hand-bag and put it on before he showed himself here in the town — and mind you he done that just a little after the time that Uncle Silas was hitting Jubiter Dunlap over the head with a club — for he *did* hit him.

" But the minute the pals see that thief slide into the bunch of sycamores, they jumped out of the bushes and slid in after him.

" They fell on him and clubbed him to death.

" Yes, for all he screamed and howled so, they never had no mercy on him, but clubbed him to death. And two men that was running along the road heard him yelling that way, and they made a rush into the sycamore bunch — which was where they was bound for, anyway — and when the pals saw them they lit out and the two new men after them a-chasing them as tight as they could go. But only a minute or two — then these two new men slipped back very quiet into the sycamores.

"*Then* what did they do? I will tell you what they done. They found where the thief had got his disguise out of his carpet-sack to put on; so one of them strips and puts on that disguise."

Tom waited a little here, for some more " effect "— then he says, very deliberate :

" The man that put on that dead man's disguise was — *Jubiter Dunlap* ! ''

" Great Scott!" everybody shouted, all over the

house, and old Uncle Silas he looked perfectly
astonished.

"Yes, it was Jubiter Dunlap. Not dead, you see.
Then they pulled off the dead man's boots and put
Jubiter Dunlap's old ragged shoes on the corpse and put
the corpse's boots on Jubiter Dunlap. Then Jubiter
Dunlap stayed where he was, and the other man lugged
the dead body off in the twilight ; and after midnight
he went to Uncle Silas's house, and took his old green
work-robe off of the peg where it always hangs in the
passage betwixt the house and the kitchen and put it on,
and stole the long-handled shovel and went off down
into the tobacker field and buried the murdered man."

He stopped, and stood half a minute. Then —

"And who do you reckon the murdered man *was ?*
It was — *Jake* Dunlap, the long-lost burglar!"

"Great Scott!"

"And the man that buried him was — *Brace* Dunlap,
his brother!"

"Great Scott!"

"And who do you reckon is this mowing idiot here
that's letting on all these weeks to be a deef and dumb
stranger? It's — *Jubiter* Dunlap!"

My land, they all busted out in a howl, and you
never see the like of that excitement since the day you
was born. And Tom he made a jump for Jubiter and
snaked off his goggles and his false whiskers, and there
was the murdered man, sure enough, just as alive as
anybody! And Aunt Sally and Benny they went to
hugging and crying and kissing and smothering old
15**

Uncle Silas to that degree he was more muddled and confused and mushed up in his mind than he ever was before, and that is saying considerable. And next, people begun to yell:

"Tom Sawyer! Tom Sawyer! Shut up everybody, and let him go on! Go on, Tom Sawyer!"

Which made him feel uncommon bully, for it was nuts for Tom Sawyer to be a public character thataway, and a hero, as he calls it. So when it was all quiet, he says:

"There ain't much left, only this. When that man there, Bruce Dunlap, had most worried the life and sense out of Uncle Silas till at last he plumb lost his mind and hit this other blatherskite, his brother, with a club, I reckon he seen his chance. Jubiter broke for the woods to hide, and I reckon the game was for him to slide out, in the night, and leave the country. Then Brace would make everybody believe Uncle Silas killed him and hid his body somers; and that would ruin Uncle Silas and drive *him* out of the country — hang him, maybe; I dunno. But when they found their dead brother in the sycamores without knowing him, because he was so battered up, they see they had a better thing; disguise *both* and bury Jake and dig him up presently all dressed up in Jubiter's clothes, and hire Jim Lane and Bill Withers and the others to swear to some handy lies — which they done. And there they set, now, and I told them they would be looking sick before I got done, and that is the way they're looking now.

"Well, me and Huck Finn here, we come down on the boat with the thieves, and the dead one told us all about the di'monds, and said the others would murder him if they got the chance; and we was going to help him all we could. We was bound for the sycamores when we heard them killing him in there; but we was in there in the early morning after the storm and allowed nobody hadn't been killed, after all. And when we see Jubiter Dunlap here spreading around in the very same disguise Jake told us *he* was going to wear, we thought it was Jake his own self — and he was goo-gooing deef and dumb, and *that* was according to agreement.

"Well, me and Huck went on hunting for the corpse after the others quit, and we found it.   And was proud, too; but Uncle Silas he knocked us crazy by telling us *he* killed the man.   So we was mighty sorry we found the body, and was bound to save Uncle Silas's neck if we could; and it was going to be tough work, too, because he wouldn't let us break him out of prison the way we done with our old nigger Jim.

"I done everything I could the whole month to think up some way to save Uncle Silas, but I couldn't strike a thing.   So when we come into court to-day I come empty, and couldn't see no chance anywheres.   But by and by I had a glimpse of something that set me thinking — just a little wee glimpse — only that, and not enough to make sure; but it set me thinking hard — and *watching*, when I was only letting on to think; and by and by, sure enough, when Uncle Silas was piling out that stuff about *him* killing Jubiter Dunlap, I catched that glimpse again, and this time I jumped up and shut down the proceedings, because I *knowed* Jubiter Dunlap was a-setting here before me. I knowed him by a thing which I seen him do — and I remembered it. I'd seen him do it when I was here a year ago.''

He stopped then, and studied a minute — laying for an '' effect ''— I knowed it perfectly well. Then he turned off like he was going to leave the platform, and says, kind of lazy and indifferent:

'' Well, I believe that is all.''

Why, you never heard such a howl!— and it come from the whole house:

'' What *was* it you seen him do? Stay where you are, you little devil! You think you are going to work a body up till his mouth's a-watering and stop there? What *was* it he done?''

That was it, you see — he just done it to get an '' effect ''; you couldn't 'a' pulled him off of that platform with a yoke of oxen.

'' Oh, it wasn't anything much,'' he says. '' I seen him looking a little excited when he found Uncle Silas was actuly fixing to hang himself for a murder that warn't ever done; and he got more and more nervous and worried, I a-watching him sharp but not seeming to look at him — and all of a sudden his hands begun to work and fidget, and pretty soon his left crept up and *his finger drawed a cross on his cheek*, and then I *had* him!''

Well, then they ripped and howled and stomped and clapped their hands till Tom Sawyer was that proud and happy he didn't know what to do with himself.

And then the judge he looked down over his pulpit and says:

"My boy, did you *see* all the various details of this strange conspiracy and tragedy that you've been describing?"

"No, your honor, I didn't see any of them."

"Didn't see any of them! Why, you've told the whole history straight through, just the same as if you'd seen it with your eyes. How did you manage that?"

Tom says, kind of easy and comfortable:

"Oh, just noticing the evidence and piecing this and that together, your honor; just an ordinary little bit of detective work; anybody could 'a' done it."

"Nothing of the kind! Not two in a million could 'a' done it. You are a very remarkable boy."

Then they let go and give Tom another smashing round, and he — well, he wouldn't 'a' sold out for a silver mine. Then the judge says:

"But are you certain you've got this curious history straight?"

"Perfectly, your honor. Here is Brace Dunlap — let him deny his share of it if he wants to take the chance; I'll engage to make him wish he hadn't said anything. . . . . . Well, you see *he's* pretty quiet. And his brother's pretty quiet, and them four witnesses that

15

lied so and got paid for it, they're pretty quiet. And as for Uncle Silas, it ain't any use for him to put in his oar, I wouldn't believe him under oath!''

Well, sir, that fairly made them shout; and even the judge he let go and laughed. Tom he was just feeling like a rainbow. When they was done laughing he looks up at the judge and says:

'' Your honor, there's a thief in this house.''

"A thief?''

'' Yes, sir. And he's got them twelve-thousand-dollar di'monds on him.''

By gracious, but it made a stir! Everybody went shouting:

'' Which is him? which is him? p'int him out!''

And the judge says:

'' Point him out, my lad. Sheriff, you will arrest him. Which one is it?''

Tom says:

'' This late dead man here — Jubiter Dunlap.''

Then there was another thundering let-go of astonishment and excitement; but Jubiter, which was astonished enough before, was just fairly putrified with astonishment this time. And he spoke up, about half crying, and says:

'' Now *that's* a lie. Your honor, it ain't fair; I'm plenty bad enough without that. I done the other things — Brace he put me up to it, and persuaded me, and promised he'd make me rich, some day, and I done it, and I'm sorry I done it, and I wisht I hadn't; but I hain't stole no di'monds, and I hain't *got* no di'monds;

I wisht I may never stir if it ain't so. The sheriff can search me and see."

Tom says:

"Your honor, it wasn't right to call him a thief, and I'll let up on that a little. He did steal the di'monds, but he didn't know it. He stole them from his brother Jake when he was laying dead, after Jake had stole them from the other thieves; but Jubiter didn't know he was stealing them; and he's been swelling around here with them a month; yes, sir, twelve thousand dollars' worth of di'monds on him — all that riches, and going around here every day just like a poor man. Yes, your honor, he's got them on him now."

The judge spoke up and says:

"Search him, sheriff."

Well, sir, the sheriff he ransacked him high and low, and everywhere: searched his hat, socks, seams, boots, everything — and Tom he stood there quiet, laying for another of them effects of hisn. Finally the sheriff he give it up, and everybody looked disappointed, and Jubiter says:

"There, now! what'd I tell you?"

And the judge says:

"It appears you were mistaken this time, my boy."

Then Tom took an attitude and let on to be studying with all his might, and scratching his head. Then all of a sudden he glanced up chipper, and says:

"Oh, now I've got it! I'd forgot."

Which was a lie, and I knowed it. Then he says:

15**

" Will somebody be good enough to lend me a little small screwdriver? There was one in your brother's hand-bag that you smouched, Jubiter, but I reckon you didn't fetch it with you."

" No, I didn't. I didn't want it, and I give it away."

" That was because you didn't know what it was for."

Jubiter had his boots on again, by now, and when the thing Tom wanted was passed over the people's heads till it got to him, he says to Jubiter:

" Put up your foot on this chair." And he kneeled down and begun to unscrew the heel-plate, everybody watching; and when he got that big di'mond out of that boot-heel and held it up and let it flash and blaze and squirt sunlight everwhichaway, it just took everybody's breath; and Jubiter he looked so sick and sorry you never see the like of it. And when Tom held up the other di'mond he looked sorrier than ever. Land! he was thinking how he would 'a' skipped out and been rich and independent in a foreign land if he'd only had the luck to guess what the screwdriver was in the carpet-bag for.

Well, it was a most exciting time, take it all around, and Tom got cords of glory. The judge took the di'monds, and stood up in his pulpit, and cleared his throat, and shoved his spectacles back on his head, and says:

" I'll keep them and notify the owners; and when they send for them it will be a real pleasure to me to hand you the two thousand dollars, for you've earned the money—yes, and you've earned the deepest and most sincerest thanks of this community besides, for lifting a wronged and innocent family out of ruin and shame, and saving a good and honorable man from a felon's death, and for exposing to infamy and the punishment of the law a cruel and odious scoundrel and his miserable creatures!''

Well, sir, if there'd been a brass band to bust out some music, then, it would 'a' been just the perfectest thing I ever see, and Tom Sawyer he said the same.

Then the sheriff he nabbed Brace Dunlap and his crowd, and by and by next month the judge had them up for trial and jailed the whole lot. And everybody crowded back to Uncle Silas's little old church, and was ever so loving and kind to him and the family and couldn't do enough for them; and Uncle Silas he preached them the blamedest jumbledest idiotic sermons you ever struck, and would tangle you up so you couldn't find your way home in daylight; but the people never let on but what they thought it was the clearest and brightest and elegantest sermons that ever was; and they would set there and cry, for love and pity; but, by George, they give me the jim-jams and the fantods and caked up what brains I had, and turned them solid; but by and by they loved the old man's intellects back into him again, and he was as sound in his skull as ever he was, which ain't no flattery, I reckon. And so the whole family was as happy as birds, and nobody could be gratefuler and lovinger than what they was to

Q**

Tom Sawyer; and the same to me, though I hadn't done nothing. And when the two thousand dollars come, Tom give half of it to me, and never told anybody so, which didn't surprise me, because I knowed him.

THE STOLEN WHITE ELEPHANT*

I

THE following curious history was related to me by
a chance railway acquaintance. He was a gentleman more than seventy years of age, and his thoroughly
good and gentle face and earnest and sincere manner
imprinted the unmistakable stamp of truth upon every
statement which fell from his lips. He said:

You know in what reverence the royal white elephant
of Siam is held by the people of that country. You
know it is sacred to kings, only kings may possess it,
and that it is, indeed, in a measure even superior to
kings, since it receives not merely honor but worship.
Very well; five years ago, when the troubles concerning the frontier line arose between Great Britain and
Siam, it was presently manifest that Siam had been in
the wrong. Therefore every reparation was quickly
made, and the British representative stated that he
was satisfied and the past should be forgotten. This

---

* Left out of "A Tramp Abroad," because it was feared that some of
the particulars had been exaggerated, and that others were not true. Before
these suspicions had been proven groundless, the book had gone to press.
— M. T.

greatly relieved the King of Siam, and partly as a token of gratitude, but partly also, perhaps, to wipe out any little remaining vestige of unpleasantness which England might feel toward him, he wished to send the Queen a present — the sole sure way of propitiating an enemy, according to Oriental ideas. This present ought not only to be a royal one, but transcendently royal. Wherefore, what offering could be so meet as that of a white elephant? My position in the Indian civil service was such that I was deemed peculiarly worthy of the honor of conveying the present to her Majesty. A ship was fitted out for me and my servants and the officers and attendants of the elephant, and in due time I arrived in New York harbor and placed my royal charge in admirable quarters in Jersey City. It was necessary to remain awhile in order to recruit the animal's health before resuming the voyage.

All went well during a fortnight — then my calamities began. The white elephant was stolen! I was called up at dead of night and informed of this fearful misfortune. For some moments I was beside myself with terror and anxiety; I was helpless. Then I grew calmer and collected my faculties. I soon saw my course — for, indeed, there was but the one course for an intelligent man to pursue. Late as it was, I flew to New York and got a policeman to conduct me to the headquarters of the detective force. Fortunately I arrived in time, though the chief of the force, the celebrated Inspector Blunt, was just on the point of leaving for his home. He was a man of middle size and compact frame, and when he was thinking deeply he had a way of knitting his brows and tapping his forehead reflectively with his finger, which impressed you at once with the conviction that you stood in the presence of a person of no common order. The very sight of him gave me confidence and made me hopeful. I stated my errand. It did not flurry him in the least; it had no more visible effect upon his iron self-possession that if I had told him somebody had stolen my dog. He motioned me to a seat, and said, calmly:

"Allow me to think a moment, please."

So saying, he sat down at his office table and leaned his head upon his hand. Several clerks were at work at the other end of the room; the scratching of their pens was all the sound I heard during the next six or seven minutes. Meantime the inspector sat there, buried in thought. Finally he raised his head, and there was that in the firm lines of his face which showed me that his brain had done its work and his plan was made. Said he — and his voice was low and impressive:

"This is no ordinary case. Every step must be warily taken; each step must be made sure before the next is ventured. And secrecy must be observed — secrecy profound and absolute. Speak to no one about the matter, not even the reporters. I will take care of *them ;* I will see that they get only what it may suit my ends to let them know." He touched a bell; a youth appeared. "Alaric, tell the reporters to remain for the present." The boy retired. "Now let us proceed to business — and systematically. Nothing can be accomplished in this trade of mine without strict and minute method."

He took a pen and some paper. "Now — name of the elephant?"

"Hassan Ben Ali Ben Selim Abdallah Mohammed Moisé Alhammal Jamsetjejeebhoy Dhuleep Sultan Ebu Bhudpoor."

"Very well. Given name?"

"Jumbo."

"Very well. Place of birth?"

"The capital city of Siam."

" Parents living?"

" No — dead."

" Had they any other issue beside this one?"

" None. He was an only child."

" Very well. These matters are sufficient under that head. Now please describe the elephant, and leave out no particular, however insignificant — that is, insignificant from *your* point of view. To men in my profession there *are* no insignificant particulars; they do not exist."

I described — he wrote. When I was done, he said:

" Now listen. If I have made any mistakes, correct me."

He read as follows:

" Height, 19 feet; length from apex of forehead to insertion of tail, 26 feet; length of trunk, 16 feet; length of tail, 6 feet; total length, including trunk and tail, 48 feet; length of tusks, 9½ feet; ears in keeping with these dimensions; footprint resembles the mark left when one up-ends a barrel in the snow; color of the elephant, a dull white; has a hole the size of a plate in each ear for the insertion of jewelry, and possesses the habit in a remarkable degree of squirting water upon spectators and of maltreating with his trunk not only such persons as he is acquainted with, but even entire strangers; limps slightly with his right hind leg, and has a small scar in his left armpit caused by a former boil; had on, when stolen, a castle containing seats for fifteen persons, and a gold-cloth saddle-blanket the size of an ordinary carpet."

There were no mistakes. The inspector touched the bell, handed the description to Alaric, and said:

" Have fifty thousand copies of this printed at once and mailed to every detective office and pawnbroker's shop on the continent." Alaric retired. " There —

so far, so good.   Next, I must have a photograph of the property.''

I gave him one.   He examined it critically, and said:

"It must do, since we can do no better; but he has his trunk curled up and tucked into his mouth.   That is unfortunate, and is calculated to mislead, for of course he does not usually have it in that position.'' He touched his bell.

"Alaric, have fifty thousand copies of this photograph made the first thing in the morning, and mail them with the descriptive circulars.''

Alaric retired to execute his orders.   The inspector said:

"It will be necessary to offer a reward, of course. Now as to the amount?''

"What sum would you suggest?''

"To *begin* with, I should say — well, twenty-five thousand dollars.   It is an intricate and difficult business; there are a thousand avenues of escape and opportunities of concealment.   These thieves have friends and pals everywhere —''

"Bless me, do you know who they are?''

The wary face, practiced in concealing the thoughts and feelings within, gave me no token, nor yet the replying words, so quietly uttered:

"Never mind about that.   I may, and I may not We generally gather a pretty shrewd inkling of who our man is by the manner of his work and the size of the game he goes after.   We are not dealing with a pickpocket or a hall thief now, make up your mind to that.   This property was not 'lifted' by a novice. But, as I was saying, considering the amount of travel which will have to be done, and the diligence with which the thieves will cover up their traces as they move along, twenty-five thousand may be too small a sum to offer, yet I think it worth while to start with that.''

So we determined upon that figure as a beginning.
Then this man, whom nothing escaped which could by
any possibility be made to serve as a clew, said:

"There are cases in detective history to show that
criminals have been detected through peculiarities in
their appetites. Now, what does this elephant eat, and
how much?"

"Well, as to *what* he eats — he will eat *anything*.
He will eat a man, he will eat a Bible — he will eat
anything *between* a man and a Bible."

"Good — very good, indeed, but too general. Details are necessary — details are the only valuable things
in our trade. Very well — as to men. At one meal —
or, if you prefer, during one day — how many men
will he eat, if fresh?"

"He would not care whether they were fresh or
not; at a single meal he would eat five ordinary men."

"Very good; five men; we will put that down.
What nationalities would he prefer?"

"He is indifferent about nationalities. He prefers
acquaintances, but is not prejudiced against strangers."

"Very good. Now, as to Bibles. How many Bibles
would he eat at a meal?"

"He would eat an entire edition."

"It is hardly succinct enough. Do you mean the
ordinary octavo, or the family illustrated?"

"I think he would be indifferent to illustrations;
that is, I think he would not value illustrations above
simple letter-press."

"No, you do not get my idea. I refer to bulk.
The ordinary octavo Bible weighs about two pounds
and a half, while the great quarto with the illustrations
weighs ten or twelve. How many Doré Bibles would
he eat at a meal?"

"If you knew this elephant, you could not ask. He
would take what they had."

"Well, put it in dollars and cents, then. We must get at it somehow. The Doré costs a hundred dollars a copy, Russia leather, beveled."

"He would require about fifty thousand dollars' worth — say an edition of five hundred copies."

"Now that is more exact. I will put that down. Very well; he likes men and Bibles; so far, so good. What else will he eat? I want particulars."

"He will leave Bibles to eat bricks, he will leave bricks to eat bottles, he will leave bottles to eat clothing, he will leave clothing to eat cats, he will leave cats to eat oysters, he will leave oysters to eat ham, he will leave ham to eat sugar, he will leave sugar to eat pie, he will leave pie to eat potatoes, he will leave potatoes to eat bran, he will leave bran to eat hay, he will leave hay to eat oats, he will leave oats to eat rice, for he was mainly raised on it. There is nothing whatever that he will not eat but European butter, and he would eat that if he could taste it."

"Very good. General quantity at a meal — say about —"

"Well, anywhere from a quarter to half a ton."

"And he drinks —"

"Everything that is fluid. Milk, water, whisky, molasses, castor oil, camphene, carbolic acid — it is no use to go into particulars; whatever fluid occurs to you set it down. He will drink anything that is fluid, except European coffee."

"Very good. As to quantity?"

"Put it down five to fifteen barrels — his thirst varies; his other appetites do not."

"These things are unusual. They ought to furnish quite good clews toward tracing him."

He touched the bell.

"Alaric, summon Captain Burns."

Burns appeared. Inspector Blunt unfolded the whole
16 **

matter to him, detail by detail. Then he said in the clear, decisive tones of a man whose plans are clearly defined in his head, and who is accustomed to command:

"Captain Burns, detail Detectives Jones, Davis, Halsey, Bates, and Hackett to shadow the elephant."

"Yes, sir."

"Detail Detectives Moses, Dakin, Murphy, Rogers, Tupper, Higgins, and Bartholomew to shadow the thieves."

"Yes, sir."

"Place a strong guard — a guard of thirty picked men, with a relief of thirty — over the place from whence the elephant was stolen, to keep strict watch there night and day, and allow none to approach — except reporters — without written authority from me."

"Yes, sir."

"Place detectives in plain c.othes in the railway, steamship, and ferry depots, and upon all roadways leading out of Jersey City, with orders to search all suspicious persons."

"Yes, sir."

"Furnish all these men with photograph and accompanying description of the elephant, and instruct them to search all trains and outgoing ferry-boats and other vessels."

"Yes, sir."

"If the elephant should be found, let him be seized, and the information forwarded to me by telegraph."

"Yes, sir."

"Let me be informed at once if any clews should be found — footprints of the animal, or anything of that kind."

"Yes, sir."

"Get an order commanding the harbor police to patrol the frontages vigilantly."

"Yes, sir."

"Despatch detectives in plain clothes over all the railways, north as far as Canada, west as far as Ohio, south as far as Washington."

"Yes, sir."

"Place experts in all the telegraph offices to listen to all messages; and let them require that all cipher dispatches be interpreted to them."

"Yes, sir."

"Let all these things be done with the utmost secrecy — mind, the most impenetrable secrecy."

"Yes, sir."

"Report to me promptly at the usual hour."

"Yes, sir."

"Go!"

"Yes, sir."

He was gone.

Inspector Blunt was silent and thoughtful a moment, while the fire in his eye cooled down and faded out. Then he turned to me and said in a placid voice:

"I am not given to boasting, it is not my habit; but — we shall find the elephant."

I shook him warmly by the hand and thanked him; and I *felt* my thanks, too. The more I had seen of the man the more I liked him and the more I admired him and marveled over the mysterious wonders of his profession. Then we parted for the night, and I went home with a far happier heart than I had carried with me to his office.

II.

NEXT morning it was all in the newspapers, in the minutest detail. It even had additions — consisting of Detective This, Detective That, and Detective The Other's "Theory" as to how the robbery was done, who the robbers were, and whither they had flown with their booty. There were eleven of these theories, and they covered all the possibilities; and this single fact shows what independent thinkers detectives are. No two theories were alike, or even much resembled each other, save in one striking particular, and in that one all the other eleven theories were absolutely agreed. That was, that although the rear of my building was torn out and the only door remained locked, the elephant had not been removed through the rent, but by some other (undiscovered) outlet. All agreed that the robbers had made that rent only to mislead the detectives. That never would have occurred to me or to any other layman, perhaps, but it had not deceived the detectives for a moment. Thus, what I had supposed was the only thing that had no mystery about it was in fact the very thing I had gone furthest astray in. The eleven theories all named the supposed robbers, but no two named the same robbers; the total number of suspected persons was thirty-seven. The various newspaper accounts all closed with the most important opinion of all — that of Chief Inspector Blunt. A portion of this statement read as follows:

"The chief knows who the two principals are, namely, 'Brick' Duffy and 'Red' McFadden. Ten days before the robbery was achieved he was already aware that it was to be attempted, and had quietly proceeded to shadow these two noted villains; but unfortunately on the night in ques-

tion their track was lost, and before it could be found again the
bird was flown—that is, the elephant.

"Duffy and McFadden are the boldest scoundrels in the profession; the chief has reasons for believing that they are the men
who stole the stove out of the detective headquarters on a bitter
night last winter—in consequence of which the chief and every
detective present were in the hands of the physicians before morning, some with frozen feet, others with frozen fingers, ears, and
other members."

When I read the first half of that I was more astonished than ever at the wonderful sagacity of this strange
man. He not only saw everything in the present with
a clear eye, but even the future could not be hidden
from him. I was soon at his office, and said I could
not help wishing he had had those men arrested, and
so prevented the trouble and loss; but his reply was
simple and unanswerable:

"It is not our province to prevent crime, but to
punish it. We cannot punish it until it is committed."

I remarked that the secrecy with which we had begun
had been marred by the newspapers; not only all our
facts but all our plans and purposes had been revealed;
even all the suspected persons had been named; these
would doubtless disguise themselves now, or go into
hiding.

"Let them. They will find that when I am ready
for them my hand will descend upon them, in their
secret places, as unerringly as the hand of fate. As to
the newspapers, we *must* keep in with them. Fame,
reputation, constant public mention—these are the
detective's bread and butter. He must publish his
facts, else he will be supposed to have none; he must
publish his theory, for nothing is so strange or striking
as a detective's theory, or brings him so much wondering respect; we must publish our plans, for these the
journals insist upon having, and we could not deny
16

them without offending. We must constantly show the public what we are doing, or they will believe we are doing nothing. It is much pleasanter to have a newspaper say, ' Inspector Blunt's ingenious and extraordinary theory is as follows,' than to have it say some harsh thing, or, worse still, some sarcastic one.''

" I see the force of what you say. But I noticed that in one part of your remarks in the papers this morning you refused to reveal your opinion upon a certain minor point.''

"Yes, we always do that; it has a good effect. Besides, I had not formed any opinion on that point, anyway.''

I deposited a considerable sum of money with the inspector, to meet current expenses, and sat down to wait for news. We were expecting the telegrams to begin to arrive at any moment now. Meantime I reread the newspapers and also our descriptive circular, and observed that our $25,000 reward seemed to be offered only to detectives. I said I thought it ought to be offered to anybody who would catch the elephant. The inspector said:

" It is the detectives who will find the elephant, hence the reward will go to the right place. If other people found the animal, it would only be by watching the detectives and taking advantage of clews and indications stolen from them, and that would entitle the detectives to the reward, after all. The proper office of a reward is to stimulate the men who deliver up their time and their trained sagacities to this sort of work, and not to confer benefits upon chance citizens who stumble upon a capture without having earned the benefits by their own merits and labors.''

This was reasonable enough, certainly. Now the telegraphic machine in the corner began to click, and the following dispatch was the result:

FLOWER STATION, N. Y., 7.30 A.M.

Have got a clew. Found a succession of deep tracks across a farm near here. Followed them two miles east without result; think elephant went west. Shall now shadow him in that direction.

DARLEY, *Detective.*

"Darley's one of the best men on the force," said the inspector. "We shall hear from him again before long."

Telegram No. 2 came:

BARKER'S, N. J., 7.40 A.M.

Just arrived. Glass factory broken open here during night, and eight hundred bottles taken. Only water in large quantity near here is five miles distant. Shall strike for there. Elephant will be thirsty. Bottles were empty.

BAKER, *Detective.*

"That promises well, too," said the inspector. "I told you the creature's appetites would not be bad clews."

Telegram No. 3:

TAYLORVILLE, L. I., 8.15 A.M.

A haystack near here disappeared during night. Probably eaten. Have got a clue, and am off.

HUBBARD, *Detective.*

"How he does move around!" said the inspector. "I knew we had a difficult job on hand, but we shall catch him yet."

FLOWER STATION, N. Y., 9 A.M.

Shadowed the tracks three miles westward. Large, deep, and ragged. Have just met a farmer who says they are not elephant tracks. Says they are holes where he dug up saplings for shade-trees when ground was frozen last winter. Give me orders how to proceed.

DARLEY, *Detective.*

"Aha! a confederate of the thieves! The thing grows warm," said the inspector.

16**

He dictated the following telegram to Darley:

Arrest the man and force him to name his pals. Continue to follow the tracks — to the Pacific, if necessary.

                       Chief BLUNT.

Next telegram:

                      CONEY POINT, PA., 8.45 A.M.

Gas office broken open here during night and three months' unpaid gas bills taken. Have got a clue and am away.

                  MURPHY, *Detective.*

" Heavens !" said the inspector; " would he eat gas bills ?"

" Through ignorance — yes; but they cannot support life. At least, unassisted."

Now came this exciting telegram:

                    IRONVILLE, N. Y., 9.30 A.M.

Just arrived. This village in consternation. Elephant passed through here at five this morning. Some say he went east, some say west, some north, some south — but all say they did not wait to notice particularly. He killed a horse; have secured a piece of it for a clew. Killed it with his trunk; from style of blow, think he struck it left-handed. From position in which horse lies, think elephant traveled northward along line of Berkley railway. Has four and a half hours' start, but I move on his track at once.

                  HAWES, *Detective.*

I uttered exclamations of joy. The inspector was as self-contained as a graven image. He calmly touched his bell.

" Alaric, send Captain Burns here."

Burns appeared.

" How many men are ready for instant orders?"

" Ninety-six, sir."

" Send them north at once. Let them concentrate along the line of the Berkley road north of Ironville."

" Yes, sir."

"Let them conduct their movements with the utmost secrecy. As fast as others are at liberty, hold them for orders."

"Yes, sir."

"Go!"

"Yes, sir."

Presently came another telegram:

SAGE CORNERS, N. Y., 10.30.

Just arrived. Elephant passed through here at 8.15. All escaped from the town but a policeman. Apparently elephant did not strike at policeman, but at the lamp-post. Got both. I have secured a portion of the policeman as clew.

STUMM, *Detective.*

"So the elephant has turned westward," said the inspector. "However, he will not escape, for my men are scattered all over that region."

The next telegram said:

GLOVER'S, 11.15.

Just arrived. Village deserted, except sick and aged. Elephant passed through three-quarters of an hour ago. The anti-temperance mass-meeting was in session; he put his trunk in at a window and washed it out with water from cistern. Some swallowed it — since dead; several drowned. Detectives Cross and O'Shaughnessy were passing through town, but going south — so missed elephant. Whole region for many miles around in terror — people flying from their homes. Wherever they turn they meet elephant, and many are killed.

BRANT, *Detective.*

I could have shed tears, this havoc so distressed me. But the inspector only said:

"You see — we are closing in on him. He feels our presence; he has turned eastward again."

Yet further troublous news was in store for us. The telegraph brought this:

HOGANSPORT, 12.19.

Just arrived. Elephant passed through half an hour ago, creating wild-

P **

est fright and excitement. Elephant raged around streets; two plumbers going by, killed one — other escaped. Regret general.

O'FLAHERTY, Detective.

"Now he is right in the midst of my men," said the inspector. "Nothing can save him."

A succession of telegrams came from detectives who were scattered through New Jersey and Pennsylvania, and who were following clews consisting of ravaged barns, factories, and Sunday-school libraries, with high hopes — hopes amounting to certainties, indeed. The inspector said:

"I wish I could communicate with them and order them north, but that is impossible. A detective only visits a telegraph office to send his report; then he is off again, and you don't know where to put your hand on him."

Now came this dispatch:

BRIDGEPORT, CT., 12.15.

Barnum offers rate of $4,000 a year for exclusive privilege of using elephant as traveling advertising medium from now till detectives find him. Wants to paste circus-posters on him. Desires immediate answer.

BOGGS, Detective.

"That is perfectly absurd!" I exclaimed.

"Of course it is," said the inspector. "Evidently Mr. Barnum, who thinks he is so sharp, does not know me — but I know him."

Then he dictated this answer to the dispatch:

Mr. Barnum's offer declined. Make it $7,000 or nothing.

Chief BLUNT.

"There. We shall not have to wait long for an answer. Mr. Barnum is not at home; he is in the telegraph office — it is his way when he has business on hand. Inside of three —"

Done.— P. T. Barnum.

So interrupted the clicking telegraphic instrument. Before I could make a comment upon this extraordinary episode, the following dispatch carried my thoughts into another and very distressing channel:

Bolivia, N. Y., 12.50.

Elephant arrived here from the south and passed through toward the forest at 11.50, dispersing a funeral on the way, and diminishing the mourners by two. Citizens fired some small cannon-balls into him, and then fled. Detective Burke and I arrived ten minutes later, from the north, but mistook some excavations for footprints, and so lost a good deal of time; but at last we struck the right trail and followed it to the woods. We then got down on our hands and knees and continued to keep a sharp eye on the track, and so shadowed it into the brush. Burke was in advance. Unfortunately the animal had stopped to rest; therefore, Burke having his head down, intent upon the track, butted up against the elephant's hind legs before he was aware of his vicinity. Burke instantly arose to his feet, seized the tail, and exclaimed joyfully, "I claim the re—" but got no further, for a single blow of the huge trunk laid the brave fellow's fragments low in death. I fled rearward, and the elephant turned and shadowed me to the edge of the wood, making tremendous speed, and I should inevitably have been lost, but that the remains of the funeral providentially intervened again and diverted his attention. I have just learned that nothing of that funeral is now left; but this is no loss, for there is abundance of material for another. Meantime, the elephant has disappeared again.

Mulrooney, *Detective*.

We heard no news except from the diligent and confident detectives scattered about New Jersey, Pennsylvania, Delaware, and Virginia — who were all following fresh and encouraging clews — until shortly after 2 P. M., when this telegram came:

Baxter Center, 2.15.

Elephant been here, plastered over with circus-bills, and broke up a revival, striking down and damaging many who were on the point of entering upon a better life. Citizens penned him up and established a guard.

When Detective Brown and I arrived, some time after, we entered enclosure and proceeded to identify elephant by photograph and description. All marks tallied exactly except one, which we could not see — the boil-scar under armpit. To make sure, Brown crept under to look, and was immediately brained — that is, head crushed and destroyed, though nothing issued from debris. All fled; so did elephant, striking right and left with much effect. Has escaped, but left bold blood-track from cannon-wounds. Rediscovery certain. He broke southward, through a dense forest.

BRENT, *Detective*.

That was the last telegram. At nightfall a fog shut down which was so dense that objects but three feet away could not be discerned. This lasted all night. The ferry-boats and even the omnibuses had to stop running.

III.

NEXT morning the papers were as full of detective theories as before; they had all our tragic facts in detail also, and a great many more which they had received from their telegraphic correspondents. Column after column was occupied, a third of its way down, with glaring head-lines, which it made my heart sick to read. Their general tone was like this:

"THE WHITE ELEPHANT AT LARGE! HE MOVES UPON HIS FATAL MARCH! WHOLE VILLAGES DESERTED BY THEIR FRIGHT-STRICKEN OCCUPANTS! PALE TERROR GOES BEFORE HIM, DEATH AND DEVASTATION FOLLOW AFTER! AFTER THESE, THE DETECTIVES! BARNS DESTROYED, FACTORIES GUTTED, HARVESTS DEVOURED, PUBLIC ASSEMBLAGES DISPERSED, ACCOMPANIED BY SCENES OF CARNAGE IMPOSSIBLE TO DESCRIBE! THEORIES OF THIRTY-FOUR OF THE MOST DISTINGUISHED DETECTIVES ON THE FORCE! THEORY OF CHIEF BLUNT!"

"There!" said Inspector Blunt, almost betrayed into excitement, "this is magnificent! This is the

greatest windfall that any detective organization ever
had. The fame of it will travel to the ends of the
earth, and endure to the end of time, and my name
with it.''

But there was no joy for me. I felt as if I had committed all those red crimes, and that the elephant was
only my irresponsible agent. And how the list had
grown! In one place he had "interfered with an
election and killed five repeaters.'' He had followed
this act with the destruction of two poor fellows,
named O'Donohue and McFlannigan, who had "found
a refuge in the home of the oppressed of all lands only
the day before, and were in the act of exercising for
the first time the noble right of American citizens at
the polls, when stricken down by the relentless hand of
the Scourge of Siam.'' In another, he had "found a
crazy sensation-preacher preparing his next season's
heroic attacks on the dance, the theater, and other
things which can't strike back, and had stepped on
him.'' And in still another place he had "killed a
lightning-rod agent.'' And so the list went on, growing redder and redder, and more and more heart-
breaking. Sixty persons had been killed, and two
hundred and forty wounded. All the accounts bore
just testimony to the activity and devotion of the detectives, and all closed with the remark that "three
hundred thousand citizens and four detectives saw the
dread creature, and two of the latter he destroyed.''

I dreaded to hear the telegraphic instrument begin
to click again. By and by the messages began to pour
in, but I was happily disappointed in their nature. It
was soon apparent that all trace of the elephant was
lost. The fog had enabled him to search out a good
hiding-place unobserved. Telegrams from the most
absurdly distant points reported that a dim vast mass
had been glimpsed there through the fog at such and

such an hour, and was "undoubtedly the elephant."
This dim vast mass had been glimpsed in New Haven,
in New Jersey, in Pennsylvania, in interior New York,
in Brooklyn, and even in the city of New York itself!
But in all cases the dim vast mass had vanished quickly
and left no trace. Every detective of the large force
scattered over this huge extent of country sent his
hourly report, and each and every one of them had a
clew, and was shadowing something, and was hot upon
the heels of it.

But the day passed without other result.

The next day the same.

The next just the same.

The newspaper reports began to grow monotonous
with facts that amounted to nothing, clews which led
to nothing, and theories which had nearly exhausted
the elements which surprise and delight and dazzle.

By advice of the inspector I doubled the reward.

Four more dull days followed. Then came a bitter
blow to the poor, hardworking detectives — the jour-
nalists declined to print their theories, and coldly said,
"Give us a rest."

Two weeks after the elephant's disappearance I
raised the reward to $75,000 by the inspector's ad-
vice. It was a great sum, but I felt that I would rather
sacrifice my whole private fortune than lose my credit
with my government. Now that the detectives were in
adversity, the newspapers turned upon them, and began
to fling the most stinging sarcasms at them. This gave
the minstrels an idea, and they dressed themselves as
detectives and hunted the elephant on the stage in the
most extravagant way. The caricaturists made pictures
of detectives scanning the country with spy glasses,
while the elephant, at their backs, stole apples out of
their pockets. And they made all sorts of ridiculous
pictures of the detective badge — you have seen that

badge printed in gold on the back of detective novels,
no doubt — it is a wide-staring eye, with the legend,
"WE NEVER SLEEP." When detectives called for a
drink, the would-be facetious barkeeper resurrected an
obsolete form of expression and said, "Will you have
an eye-opener?" All the air was thick with sarcasms.

But there was one man who moved calm, untouched,
unaffected, through it all. It was that heart of oak,
the chief inspector. His brave eye never drooped, his
serene confidence never wavered. He always said:

"Let them rail on; he laughs best who laughs
last."

My admiration for the man grew into a species of
worship. I was at his side always. His office had become an unpleasant place to me, and now became daily
more and more so. Yet if he could endure it I meant
to do so also — at least, as long as I could. So I
came regularly, and stayed — the only outsider who
seemed to be capable of it. Everybody wondered how
I could; and often it seemed to me that I must desert,
but at such times I looked into that calm and apparently
unconscious face, and held my ground.

About three weeks after the elephant's disappearance
I was about to say, one morning, that I should *have* to
strike my colors and retire, when the great detective
arrested the thought by proposing one more superb
and masterly move.

This was to compromise with the robbers. The
fertility of this man's invention exceeded anything I
have ever seen, and I have had a wide intercourse with
the world's finest minds. He said he was confident he
could compromise for $100,000 and recover the ele-
phant. I said I believed I could scrape the amount
together, but what would become of the poor detectives who had worked so faithfully? He said:

" In compromises they always get half."

This removed my only objection.   So the inspector wrote two notes, in this form:

DEAR MADAM,— Your husband can make a large sum of money (and be entirely protected from the law) by making an immediate appointment with me.

Chief BLUNT.

He sent one of these by his confidential messenger to the " reputed wife " of Brick Duffy, and the other to the reputed wife of Red McFadden.

Within the hour these offensive answers came:

YE OWLD FOOL: brick McDuffys bin ded 2 yere.

BRIDGET MAHONEY.

CHIEF BAT,— Red McFadden is hung and in heving 18 month.   Any Ass but a detective knose that.

MARY O'HOOLIGAN.

" I had long suspected these facts," said the in-spector; " this testimony proves the unerring accuracy of my instinct."

The moment one resource failed him he was ready with another.   He immediately wrote an advertisement for the morning papers, and I kept a copy of it:

A.—xwblv. 242 N. Tjnd—fz328wmlg.   Ozpo,—; 2 m! ogw.   Mum.

He said that if the thief was alive this would bring him to the usual rendezvous.   He further explained that the usual rendezvous was a place where all busi-ness affairs between detectives and criminals were con-ducted.   This meeting would take place at twelve the next night.

We could do nothing till then, and I lost no time in getting out of the office, and was grateful indeed for the privilege.

At 11 the next night I brought $100,000 in bank

notes and put them into the chief's hands, and shortly
afterward he took his leave, with the brave old undimmed confidence in his eye. An almost intolerable
hour dragged to a close; then I heard his welcome
tread, and rose gasping and tottered to meet him.
How his fine eyes flamed with triumph! He said:

"We've compromised! The jokers will sing a different tune to-morrow! Follow me!"

He took a lighted candle and strode down into the
vast vaulted basement where sixty detectives always
slept, and where a score were now playing cards to
while the time. I followed close after him. He
walked swiftly down to the dim and remote end of the
place, and just as I succumbed to the pangs of suffoca-
tion and was swooning away he stumbled and fell over
the outlying members of a mighty object, and I heard
him exclaim as he went down:

"Our noble profession is vindicated. Here is your
elephant!"

I was carried to the office above and restored with
carbolic acid. The whole detective force swarmed in,
and such another season of triumphant rejoicing ensued
as I had never witnessed before. The reporters were
called, baskets of champagne were opened, toasts were
drunk, the handshakings and congratulations were con-
tinuous and enthusiastic. Naturally the chief was the
hero of the hour, and his happiness was so complete
and had been so patiently and worthily and bravely
won that it made me happy to see it, though I stood
there a homeless beggar, my priceless charge dead,
and my position in my country's service lost to me
through what would always seem my fatally careless
execution of a great trust. Many an eloquent eye
testified its deep admiration for the chief, and many a
detective's voice murmured, "Look at him — just the
king of the profession; only give him a clew, it's all

17**

he wants, and there ain't anything hid that he can't find." The dividing of the $50,000 made great pleasure; when it was finished the chief made a little speech while he put his share in his pocket, in which he said, "Enjoy it, boys, for you've earned it; and more than that you've earned for the detective profession undying fame."

A telegram arrived, which read:

MONROE, MICH., 10 P.M.

First time I've struck a telegraph office in over three weeks. Have followed those footprints, horseback, through the woods, a thousand miles to here, and they get stronger and bigger and fresher every day. Don't worry—inside of another week I'll have the elephant. This is dead sure.

DARLEY, *Detective.*

The chief ordered three cheers for "Darley, one of the finest minds on the force," and then commanded that he be telegraphed to come home and receive his share of the reward.

So ended that marvelous episode of the stolen elephant. The newspapers were pleasant with praises once more, the next day, with one contemptible exception. This sheet said, "Great is the detective! He may be a little slow in finding a little thing like a mislaid elephant — he may hunt him all day and sleep with his rotting carcass all night for three weeks, but he will find him at last — if he can get the man who mislaid him to show him the place!"

Poor Hassan was lost to me forever. The cannon-shots had wounded him fatally, he had crept to that unfriendly place in the fog, and there, surrounded by his enemies and in constant danger of detection, he had wasted away with hunger and suffering till death gave him peace.

The compromise cost me $100,000; my detective expenses were $42,000 more; I never applied for a

place again under my government; I am a ruined man
and a wanderer in the earth — but my admiration for
that man, whom I believe to be the greatest detective
the world has ever produced, remains undimmed to this
day, and will so remain unto the end.

SOME RAMBLING NOTES OF AN IDLE EXCURSION

I.

ALL the journeyings I had ever done had been purely in the way of business. The pleasant May weather suggested a novelty — namely, a trip for pure recreation, the bread-and-butter element left out. The Reverend said he would go, too; a good man, one of the best of men, although a clergyman. By eleven at night we were in New Haven and on board the New York boat. We bought our tickets, and then went wandering around here and there, in the solid comfort of being free and idle, and of putting distance between ourselves and the mails and telegraphs.

After a while I went to my stateroom and undressed, but the night was too enticing for bed. We were moving down the bay now, and it was pleasant to stand at the window and take the cool night breeze and watch the gliding lights on shore. Presently, two elderly men sat down under that window and began a conversation. Their talk was properly no business of mine, yet I was feeling friendly toward the world and willing to be entertained. I soon gathered that they were brothers, that they were from a small Connecticut village, and that the matter in hand concerned the cemetery. Said one:

" Now, John, we talked it all over amongst ourselves, and this is what we've done.   You see, everybody was a-movin' from the old buryin' ground, and our folks was 'most about left to theirselves, as you may say. They was crowded, too, as you know; lot wa'n't big enough in the first place; and last year, when Seth's wife died, we couldn't hardly tuck her in.   She sort o' overlaid Deacon Shorb's lot, and he soured on her, so to speak, and on the rest of us, too.   So we talked it over, and I was for a lay-out in the new simitery on the hill.   They wa'n't unwilling, if it was cheap. Well, the two best and biggest plots was No. 8 and No. 9 — both of a size; nice comfortable room for twenty-six — twenty-six full-growns, that is; but you reckon in children and other shorts, and strike an everage, and I should say you might lay in thirty, or may be thirty-two or three, pretty genteel — no crowdin' to signify."

" That's a plenty, William.   Which one did you buy?"

" Well, I'm a-comin' to that, John.   You see, No. 8 was thirteen dollars, No. 9 fourteen —"

" I see.   So's't you took No. 8."

" You wait.   I took No. 9.   And I'll tell you for why.   In the first place, Deacon Shorb wanted it. Well, after the way he'd gone on about Seth's wife overlappin' his prem'ses, I'd 'a' beat him out of that No. 9 if I'd 'a' had to stand two dollars extra, let alone one.   That's the way I felt about it.   Says I, what's a dollar, anyway?   Life's on'y a pilgrimage, says I; we ain't here for good, and we can't take it with us, says I.   So I just dumped it down, knowin' the Lord don't suffer a good deed to go for nothin', and cal'latin' to take it out o' somebody in the course o' trade.   Then there was another reason, John.   No. 9's a long way the handiest lot in the simitery, and the

17

likeliest for situation. It lays right on top of a knoll in the dead center of the buryin' ground; and you can see Millport from there, and Tracy's, and Hopper Mount, and a raft o' farms, and so on. There ain't no better outlook from a buryin' plot in the State. Si Higgins says so, and I reckon he ought to know. Well, and that ain't all. 'Course Shorb had to take No. 8; wa'n't no help for 't. Now, No. 8 jines on to No. 9, but it's on the slope of the hill, and every time it rains it'll soak right down on to the Shorbs. Si Higgins says 't when the deacon's time comes, he better take out fire and marine insurance both on his remains.''

Here there was the sound of a low, placid, duplicate chuckle of appreciation and satisfaction.

"Now, John, here's a little rough draught of the ground that I've made on a piece of paper. Up here in the left-hand corner we've bunched the departed; took them from the old graveyard and stowed them one along side o' t'other, on a first-come-first-served plan, no partialities, with Gran'ther Jones for a starter, on'y because it happened so, and windin' up indiscriminate with Seth's twins. A little crowded towards the end of the lay-out, may be, but we reckoned 'twa'n't best to scatter the twins. Well, next comes the livin'. Here, where it's marked A, we're goin' to put Mariar and her family, when they're called; B, that's for Brother Hosea and hisn; C, Calvin and tribe. What's left is these two lots here — just the gem of the whole patch for general style and outlook; they're for me and my folks, and you and yourn. Which of them would you ruther be buried in?''

"I swan, you've took me mighty unexpected, William! It sort of started the shivers. Fact is, I was thinkin' so busy about makin' things comfortable for the others, I hadn't thought about being buried myself.''

" Life's on'y a fleetin' show, John, as the sayin' is.
We've all got to go, sooner or later. To go with a
clean record's the main thing. Fact is, it's the on'y
thing worth strivin' for, John."

" Yes, that's so, William, that's so; there ain't no
getting around it. Which of these lots would you
recommend?"

" Well, it depends, John. Are you particular about
outlook?"

" I don't say I am, William, I don't say I ain't.
Reely, I don't know. But mainly, I reckon, I'd set
store by a south exposure."

" That's easy fixed, John. They're both south exposure. They take the sun, and the Shorbs get the
shade."

" How about sile, William?"

" D's a sandy sile, E's mostly loom."

" You may gimme E, then, William; a sandy sile
caves in, more or less, and costs for repairs."

" All right, set your name down here, John, under
E. Now, if you don't mind payin' me your share of
the fourteen dollars, John, while we're on the business,
everything's fixed."

After some higgling and sharp bargaining the money
was paid, and John bade his brother good night and
took his leave. There was silence for some moments;
then a soft chuckle welled up from the lonely William,
and he muttered: " I declare for 't, if I haven't made
a mistake! It's D that's mostly loom, not E. And
John's booked for a sandy sile, after all."

There was another soft chuckle, and William departed to his rest also.

The next day, in New York, was a hot one. Still we
managed to get more or less entertainment out of it.
Toward the middle of the afternoon we arrived on
board the stanch steamship *Bermuda*, with bag and bag-

17**

gage, and hunted for a shady place. It was blazing summer weather, until we were half way down the harbor. Then I buttoned my coat closely; half an hour later I put on a spring overcoat and buttoned that. As we passed the lightship I added an ulster and tied a handkerchief around the collar to hold it snug to my neck. So rapidly had the summer gone and winter come again!

By nightfall we were far out at sea, with no land in sight. No telegrams could come here, no letters, no news. This was an uplifting thought. It was still more uplifting to reflect that the millions of harassed people on shore behind us were suffering just as usual.

The next day brought us into the midst of the Atlantic solitudes — out of smoke-colored soundings into fathomless deep blue; no ships visible anywhere over the wide ocean; no company but Mother Cary's chickens wheeling, darting, skimming the waves in the sun. There were some seafaring men among the passengers, and conversation drifted into matters concerning ships and sailors. One said that "true as the needle to the pole" was a bad figure, since the needle seldom pointed to the pole. He said a ship's compass was not faithful to any particular point, but was the most fickle and treacherous of the servants of man. It was forever changing. It changed every day in the year; consequently the amount of the daily variation had to be ciphered out and allowance made for it, else the mariner would go utterly astray. Another said there was a vast fortune waiting for the genius who should invent a compass that would not be affected by the local influences of an iron ship. He said there was only one creature more fickle than a wooden ship's compass, and that was the compass of an iron ship. Then came reference to the well-known fact that an experienced mariner can look at the compass of a new iron vessel, thousands of miles from her birthplace, and tell which way her head was pointing when she was in process of building.

Now an ancient whale-ship master fell to talking about the sort of crews they used to have in his early days. Said he:

"Sometimes we'd have a batch of college students. Queer lot. Ignorant? Why, they didn't know the catheads from the main brace. But if you took them for fools you'd get bit, sure. They'd learn more in a month than another man would in a year. We had one, once, in the *Mary Ann*, that came aboard with gold spectacles on. And besides, he was rigged out from main truck to keelson in the nobbiest clothes that ever saw a fo'castle. He had a chest full, too; cloaks, and broadcloth coats, and velvet vests; everything swell, you know; and didn't the salt water fix them out for him? I guess not! Well, going to sea, the mate told him to go aloft and help shake out the fore-to'gallants'l. Up he shins to the foretop, with his spectacles on, and in a minute down he comes again, looking insulted. Says the mate, 'What did you come down for?' Says the chap, 'P'r'aps you didn't notice that there ain't any ladders above there.' You see we hadn't any shrouds above the foretop. The men bursted out in a laugh such as I guess you never heard the like of. Next night, which was dark and rainy, the mate ordered this chap to go aloft about something, and I'm dummed if he didn't start up with an umbrella and a lantern! But no matter; he made a mighty good sailor before the voyage was done, and we had to hunt up something else to laugh at. Years afterwards, when I had forgot all about him, I comes into Boston, mate of a ship, and was loafing around town with the second mate, and it so happened that we stepped into the Revere House, thinking maybe we

Q**

would chance the salt-horse in that big dining-room
for a flyer, as the boys say. Some fellows were talking just at our elbow, and one says, ' Yonder's the new
governor of Massachusetts — at that table over there
with the ladies.' We took a good look, my mate and
I, for we hadn't either of us ever seen a governor before. I looked and looked at that face, and then all
of a sudden it popped on me! But I didn't give any
sign. Says I, ' Mate, I've a notion to go over and
shake hands with him.' Says he, ' I think I see you
doing it, Tom.' Says I, ' Mate, I'm a-going to do it.'
Says he, ' Oh, yes, I guess so! May be you don't
want to bet you will, Tom?' Says I, ' I don't mind
going a V on it, mate.' Says he, ' Put it up.' ' Up
she goes,' says I, planking the cash. This surprised
him. But he covered it, and says, pretty sarcastic,
' Hadn't you better take your grub with the governor
and the ladies, Tom?' Says I, ' Upon second thoughts,
I will.' Says he, ' Well, Tom, you *are* a dum fool.'
Says I, ' Maybe I am, maybe I ain't; but the main
question is, do you want to risk two and a half that I
won't do it?' ' Make it a V,' says he. ' Done,' says
I. I started, him a-giggling and slapping his hand on
his thigh, he felt so good. I went over there and
leaned my knuckles on the table a minute and looked
the governor in the face, and says I, ' Mr. Gardner,
don't you know me?' He stared, and I stared, and
he stared. Then all of a sudden he sings out, ' Tom
Bowling, by the holy poker! Ladies, it's old Tom
Bowling, that you've heard me talk about — shipmate
of mine in the *Mary Ann*.' He rose up and shook
hands with me ever so hearty — I sort of glanced
around and took a realizing sense of my mate's saucer
eyes — and then says the governor, ' Plant yourself,
Tom, plant yourself; you can't cat your anchor again
till you've had a feed with me and the ladies!' I

planted myself alongside the governor, and canted my
eye around toward my mate. Well, sir, his dead-
lights were bugged out like tompions; and his mouth
stood that wide open that you could have laid a ham in
it without him noticing it.''

There was great applause at the conclusion of the
old captain's story; then, after a moment's silence, a
grave, pale young man said:

" Had you ever met the governor before?"

The old captain looked steadily at this inquirer
awhile, and then got up and walked aft without making
any reply. One passenger after another stole a furtive
glance at the inquirer, but failed to make him out, and
so gave him up. It took some little work to get the
talk-machinery to running smoothly again after this
derangement; but at length a conversation sprang up
about that important and jealously guarded instrument,
a ship's timekeeper, its exceeding delicate accuracy,
and the wreck and destruction that have sometimes
resulted from its varying a few seemingly trifling moments from the true time; then, in due course, my
comrade, the Reverend, got off on a yarn, with a fair
wind and everything drawing. It was a true story,
too — about Captain Rounceville's shipwreck — true in
every detail. It was to this effect:

Captain Rounceville's vessel was lost in mid-Atlantic,
and likewise his wife and his two little children. Captain Rounceville and seven seamen escaped with life,
but with little else. A small, rudely constructed raft
was to be their home for eight days. They had neither
provisions nor water. They had scarcely any clothing;
no one had a coat but the captain. This coat was
changing hands all the time, for the weather was very
cold. Whenever a man became exhausted with the
cold, they put the coat on him and laid him down between two shipmates until the garment and their bodies

had warmed life into him again. Among the sailors
was a Portuguese who knew no English.   He seemed to
have no thought of his own calamity, but was concerned
only about the captain's bitter loss of wife and children.
By day he would look his dumb compassion in the
captain's face; and by night, in the darkness and the
driving spray and rain, he would seek out the captain
and try to comfort him with caressing pats on the
shoulder.   One day, when hunger and thirst were
making their sure inroads upon the men's strength and
spirits, a floating barrel was seen at a distance.   It
seemed a great find, for doubtless it contained food of
some sort.   A brave fellow swam to it, and after long
and exhausting effort got it to the raft.   It was eagerly
opened.   It was a barrel of magnesia!   On the fifth
day an onion was spied.   A sailor swam off and got it.
Although perishing with hunger, he brought it in its
integrity and put it into the captain's hand.   The
history of the sea teaches that among starving, ship-
wrecked men selfishness is rare, and a wonder-
compelling magnanimity the rule.   The onion was
equally divided into eight parts, and eaten with deep
thanksgivings.   On the eighth day a distant ship was
sighted.   Attempts were made to hoist an oar, with
Captain Rounceville's coat on it for a signal.   There
were many failures, for the men were but skeletons
now, and strengthless.   At last success was achieved,
but the signal brought no help.   The ship faded out of
sight and left despair behind her.   By and by another
ship appeared, and passed so near that the castaways,
every eye eloquent with gratitude, made ready to welcome the boat that would be sent to save them.   But
this ship also drove on, and left these men staring their
unutterable surprise and dismay into each other's ashen
faces.   Late in the day, still another ship came up out
of the distance, but the men noted with a pang that

her course was one which would not bring her nearer.
Their remnant of life was nearly spent; their lips and
tongues were swollen, parched, cracked with eight
days' thirst; their bodies starved; and here was their
last chance gliding relentlessly from them; they would
not be alive when the next sun rose. For a day or two
past the men had lost their voices, but now Captain
Rounceville whispered, "Let us pray." The Portuguese patted him on the shoulder in sign of deep approval. All knelt at the base of the oar that was
waving the signal-coat aloft, and bowed their heads.
The sea was tossing; the sun rested, a red, rayless
disk, on the sea-line in the west. When the men presently raised their heads they would have roared a halle-
lujah if they had had a voice; the ship's sails lay
wrinkled and flapping against her masts — she was
going about! Here was rescue at last, and in the very
last instant of time that was left for it. No, not rescue
yet — only the imminent prospect of it. The red disk
sank under the sea, and darkness blotted out the ship.
By and by came a pleasant sound — oars moving in a
boat's rowlocks. Nearer it came, and nearer — within
thirty steps, but nothing visible. Then a deep voice:
"Hol-*lo* !" The castaways could not answer; their
swollen tongues refused voice. The boat skirted round
and round the raft, started away — the agony of it ! —
returned, rested the oars, close at hand, listening, no
doubt. The deep voice again: "Hol-*lo* ! Where are
ye, shipmates?" Captain Rounceville whispered to
his men, saying: "Whisper your best, boys! now —
all at once!" So they sent out an eightfold whisper
in hoarse concert: "Here!" There was life in it if it
succeeded; death if it failed. After that supreme moment Captain Rounceville was conscious of nothing
until he came to himself on board the saving ship.
Said the Reverend, concluding:

"There was one little moment of time in which that raft could be visible from that ship, and only one. If that one little fleeting moment had passed unfruitful, those men's doom was sealed. As close as that does God shave events foreordained from the beginning of the world. When the sun reached the water's edge that day, the captain of that ship was sitting on deck reading his prayer-book. The book fell; he stooped to pick it up, and happened to glance at the sun. In that instant that far-off raft appeared for a second against the red disk, its needle-like oar and diminutive signal cut sharp and black against the bright surface, and in the next instant was thrust away into the dusk again. But that ship, that captain, and that pregnant instant had had their work appointed for them in the dawn of time and could not fail of the performance. The chronometer of God never errs!"

There was deep, thoughtful silence for some moments. Then the grave, pale young man said:

"What is the chronometer of God?"

II.

AT dinner, six o'clock, the same people assembled whom we had talked with on deck and seen at luncheon and breakfast this second day out, and at dinner the evening before. That is to say, three journeying shipmasters, a Boston merchant, and a returning Bermudian who had been absent from his Bermuda thirteen years; these sat on the starboard side. On the port side sat the Reverend in the seat of honor; the pale young man next to him; I next; next to me an aged Bermudian, returning to his sunny islands after an absence of twenty-seven years. Of course, our captain was at the head of the table, the purser at the foot of it. A small company, but small companies are pleasantest.

No racks upon the table; the sky cloudless, the sun brilliant, the blue sea scarcely ruffled; then what had become of the four married couples, the three bachelors, and the active and obliging doctor from the rural districts of Pennsylvania? — for all these were on deck when we sailed down New York harbor. This is the explanation. I quote from my note-book:

Thursday, 3.30 P.M. Under way, passing the Battery. The large party, of four married couples, three bachelors, and a cheery, exhilarating doctor from the wilds of Pennsylvania, are evidently traveling together. All but the doctor grouped in camp-chairs on deck.

Passing principal fort. The doctor is one of those people who has an infallible preventive of sea-sickness; is flitting from friend to friend administering it and saying, "Don't you be afraid; I *know* this medicine; absolutely infallible; prepared under my own supervision." Takes a dose himself, intrepidly.

4.15 P.M. Two of those ladies have struck their colors, notwithstanding the "infallible." They have gone below. The other two begin to show distress.

5 P.M. Exit one husband and one bachelor. These still had their infallible in cargo when they started, but arrived at the companionway without it.

5.10. Lady No. 3, two bachelors, and one married man have gone below with their own opinion of the infallible.

5.20. Passing Quarantine Hulk. The infallible has done the business for all the party except the Scotchman's wife and the author of that formidable remedy.

Nearing the Light-Ship. Exit the Scotchman's wife, head drooped on stewardess's shoulder.

Entering the open sea. Exit doctor!

The rout seems permanent; hence the smallness of the company at table since the voyage began. Our captain is a grave, handsome Hercules of thirty-five, with a brown hand of such majestic size that one cannot eat for admiring it and wondering if a single kid or calf could furnish material for gloving it.

Conversation not general; drones along between couples. One catches a sentence here and there. Like this, from Bermudian of thirteen years' absence: "It is the nature of women to ask trivial, irrelevant, and pursuing questions — questions that pursue you from a beginning in nothing to a run-to-cover in nowhere." Reply of Bermudian of twenty-seven years' absence: "Yes; and to think they have logical, analytical minds and argumentative ability. You see 'em begin to whet up whenever they smell argument in the air." Plainly these be philosophers.

Twice since we left port our engines have stopped for a couple of minutes at a time. Now they stop again. Says the pale young man, meditatively, "There! — that engineer is sitting down to rest again."

Grave stare from the captain, whose mighty jaws cease to work, and whose harpooned potato stops in mid-air on its way to his open, paralyzed mouth. Presently he says in measured tones, "Is it your idea that the engineer of this ship propels her by a crank turned by his own hands?"

The pale young man studies over this a moment, then lifts up his guileless eyes, and says, "Don't he?"

Thus gently falls the death-blow to further conversation, and the dinner drags to its close in a reflective silence, disturbed by no sounds but the murmurous wash of the sea and the subdued clash of teeth.

After a smoke and a promenade on deck, where is no motion to discompose our steps, we think of a game of whist. We ask the brisk and capable stewardess from Ireland if there are any cards in the ship.

"Bless your soul, dear, indeed there is. Not a whole pack, true for ye, but not enough missing to signify."

However, I happened by accident to bethink me of a

new pack in a morocco case, in my trunk, which I had placed there by mistake, thinking it to be a flask of something. So a party of us conquered the tedium of the evening with a few games and were ready for bed at six bells, mariner's time, the signal for putting out the lights.

There was much chat in the smoking-cabin on the upper deck after luncheon to-day, mostly whaler yarns from those old sea captains. Captain Tom Bowling was garrulous. He had that garrulous attention to minor detail which is born of secluded farm life or life at sea on long voyages, where there is little to do and time no object. He would sail along till he was right in the most exciting part of a yarn, and then say, "Well, as I was saying, the rudder was fouled, ship driving before the gale, head-on, straight for the iceberg, all hands holding their breath, turned to stone, top-hamper giving 'way, sails blown to ribbons, first one stick going, then another, boom! smash! crash! duck your head and stand from under! when up comes Johnny Rogers, capstan bar in hand, eyes a-blazing, hair a-flying......no, 'twa'n't Johnny Rogers...... lemme see......seems to me Johnny Rogers wa'n't along that voyage; he was along *one* voyage, I know that mighty well, but somehow it seems to me that he signed the articles for this voyage, but — but — whether he come along or not, or got left, or something happened —"

And so on and so on till the excitement all cooled down and nobody cared whether the ship struck the iceberg or not.

In the course of his talk he rambled into a criticism upon New England degrees of merit in shipbuilding. Said he "You get a vessel built away down Maine-way; Bath, for instance; what's the result? First thing you do, you want to heave her down for repairs

18**

— *that's* the result! Well, sir, she hain't been hove down a week till you can heave a dog through her seams. You send that vessel to sea, and what's the result? She wets her oakum the first trip! Leave it to any man if 'tain't so. Well, you let *our* folks build you a vessel — down New Bedford-way. What's the result? Well, sir, you might take that ship and heave her down, and keep her hove down six months, and she'll never shed a tear!''

Everybody, landsmen and all, recognized the descriptive neatness of that figure, and applauded, which greatly pleased the old man. A moment later, the meek eyes of the pale young fellow heretofore mentioned came up slowly, rested upon the old man's face a moment, and the meek mouth began to open.

'' Shet your head!'' shouted the old mariner.

It was a rather startling surprise to everybody, but it was effective in the matter of its purpose. So the conversation flowed on instead of perishing.

There was some talk about the perils of the sea, and a landsman delivered himself of the customary nonsense about the poor mariner wandering in far oceans, tempest-tossed, pursued by dangers, every storm-blast and thunder-bolt in the home skies moving the friends by snug firesides to compassion for that poor mariner, and prayers for his succor. Captain Bowling put up with this for a while, and then burst out with a new view of the matter.

'' Come, belay there! I have read this kind of rot all my life in poetry and tales and such like rubbage. Pity for the poor mariner! sympathy for the poor mariner! All right enough, but not in the way the poetry puts it. Pity for the mariner's wife! all right again, but not in the way the poetry puts it. Look-a-here! whose life's the safest in the whole world? The poor mariner's. You look at the statistics, you'll see.

So don't you fool away any sympathy on the poor mariner's dangers and privations and sufferings. Leave that to the poetry muffs. Now you look at the other side a minute. Here is Captain Brace, forty years old, been at sea thirty. On his way now to take command of his ship and sail south from Bermuda. Next week he'll be under way; easy times; comfortable quarters; passengers, sociable company; just enough to do to keep his mind healthy and not tire him; king over his ship, boss of everything and everybody; thirty years' safety to learn him that his profession ain't a dangerous one. Now you look back at his home. His wife's a feeble woman; she's a stranger in New York; shut up in blazing hot or freezing cold lodgings, according to the season; don't know anybody hardly; no company but her lonesomeness and her thoughts; husband gone six months at a time. She has borne eight children; five of them she has buried without her husband ever setting eyes on them. She watched them all the long nights till they died — he comfortable on the sea; she followed them to the grave, she heard the clods fall that broke her heart — he comfortable on the sea; she mourned at home, weeks and weeks, missing them every day and every hour — he cheerful at sea, knowing nothing about it. Now look at it a minute — turn it over in your mind and size it: five children born, she among strangers, and him not by to hearten her; buried, and him not by to comfort her; think of that! Sympathy for the poor mariner's perils is rot; give it to his wife's hard lines, where it belongs! Poetry makes out that all the wife worries about is the dangers her husband's running. She's got substantialer things to worry over, I tell you. Poetry's always pitying the poor mariner on account of his perils at sea; better a blamed sight pity him for the nights he can't sleep for thinking of how he had to leave his wife in her very birth pains, lonesome and friendless, in the thick of disease and trouble and death. If there's one thing that can make me madder than another, it's this sappy, damned maritime poetry!"

Captain Brace was a patient, gentle, seldom-speaking man, with a pathetic something in his bronzed face that had been a mystery up to this time, but stood interpreted now since we had heard his story. He had voyaged eighteen times to the Mediterranean, seven times to India, once to the arctic pole in a discovery-ship, and "between times" had visited all the remote seas and ocean corners of the globe. But he said that twelve years go, on account of his family, he "settled down," and ever since then had ceased to roam. And what do you suppose was this simple-hearted, lifelong wanderer's idea of settling down and ceasing to roam? Why, the making of two five-month voyages a year between Surinam and Boston for sugar and molasses!

Among other talk to-day, it came out that whale-ships carry no doctor. The captain adds the doctor-ship to his own duties. He not only gives medicines, but sets broken limbs after notions of his own, or saws them off and sears the stump when amputation seems best. The captain is provided with a medicine-chest, with the medicines numbered instead of named. A book of directions goes with this. It describes diseases and symptoms, and says, "Give a teaspoonful of No. 9 once an hour," or "Give ten grains of No. 12 every half hour," etc. One of our sea captains came across a skipper in the North Pacific who was in a state of great surprise and perplexity. Said he:

"There's something rotten about this medicine-chest business. One of my men was sick — nothing much the matter. I looked in the book: it said, give him a teaspoonful of No. 15. I went to the medicine-chest, and I see I was out of No. 15. I judged I'd got to

get up a combination somehow that would fill the bill;
so I hove into the fellow half a teaspoonful of No. 8
and half a teaspoonful of No. 7, and I'll be hanged if
it didn't kill him in fifteen minutes! There's something about this medicine-chest system that's too many
for me!''

There was a good deal of pleasant gossip about old
Captain '' Hurricane '' Jones, of the Pacific ocean —
peace to his ashes! Two or three of us present had
known him; I particularly well, for I had made four sea-
voyages with him. He was a very remarkable man.
He was born in a ship; he picked up what little educa-
tion he had among his shipmates; he began life in the
forecastle, and climbed grade by grade to the cap-
taincy. More than fifty years of his sixty-five were
spent at sea. He had sailed all oceans, seen all lands,
and borrowed a tint from all climates. When a man
has been fifty years at sea he necessarily knows nothing
of men, nothing of the world but its surface, nothing
of the world's thought, nothing of the world's learning
but its A B C, and that blurred and distorted by the
unfocused lenses of an untrained mind. Such a man
is only a gray and bearded child. That is what old
Hurricane Jones was — simply an innocent, lovable old
infant. When his spirit was in repose he was as sweet
and gentle as a girl; when his wrath was up he was a
hurricane that made his nickname seem tamely descriptive. He was formidable in a fight, for he was of
powerful build and dauntless courage. He was fres-
coed from head to heel with pictures and mottoes
tattooed in red and blue India ink. I was with him
one voyage when he got his last vacant space tattooed;
this vacant space was around his left ankle. During
three days he stumped about the ship with his ankle
bare and swollen, and this legend gleaming red and
angry out from a clouding of India ink: '' Virtue is its

18

own R'd.'' (There was a lack of room.) He was deeply and sincerely pious, and swore like a fish-woman. He considered swearing blameless, because sailors would not understand an order unillumined by it. He was a profound biblical scholar — that is, he thought he was. He believed everything in the Bible but he had his own methods of arriving at his beliefs. He was of the "advanced" school of thinkers, and applied natural laws to the interpretation of all miracles, somewhat on the plan of the people who make the six days of creation six geological epochs, and so forth. Without being aware of it, he was a rather severe satire on modern scientific religionists. Such a man as I have been describing is rabidly fond of disquisition and argument; one knows that without being told it.

One trip the captain had a clergyman on board, but did not know he was a clergyman, since the passenger list did not betray the fact. He took a great liking to this Reverend Mr. Peters, and talked with him a great deal; told him yarns, gave him toothsome scraps of personal history, and wove a glittering streak of pro-fanity through his garrulous fabric that was refreshing to a spirit weary of the dull neutralities of undecorated speech. One day the captain said, " Peters, do you ever read the Bible?"

" Well — yes."

" I judge it ain't often, by the way you say it. Now, you tackle it in dead earnest once, and you'll find it'll pay. Don't you get discouraged, but hang right on. First, you won't understand it; but by and by things will begin to clear up, and then you wouldn't lay it down to eat."

" Yes, I have heard that said."

" And it's so, too. There ain't a book that begins with it. It lays over'm all, Peters. There's some pretty tough things in it — there ain't any getting around that — but you stick to them and think them out, and when once you get on the inside everything's plain as day."

"The miracles, too, captain?"

"Yes, sir! the miracles, too. Every one of them. Now, there's that business with the prophets of Baal; like enough that stumped you?"

"Well, I don't know but —"

"Own up now; it stumped you. Well, I don't wonder. You hadn't had any experience in raveling such things out, and naturally it was too many for you. Would you like to have me explain that thing to you, and show you how to get at the meat of these matters?"

"Indeed, I would, captain, if you don't mind."

Then the captain proceeded as follows: "I'll do it with pleasure. First, you see, I read and read, and thought and thought, till I got to understand what sort of people they were in the old Bible times, and then after that it was all clear and easy. Now this was the way I put it up, concerning Isaac* and the prophets of Baal. There was some mighty sharp men among the public characters of that old ancient day, and Isaac was one of them. Isaac had his failings — plenty of them, too; it ain't for me to apologize for Isaac; he played it on the prophets of Baal, and like enough he was justifiable, considering the odds that was against him. No, all I say is, 'twa'n't any miracle, and that I'll show you so's't you can see it yourself.

"Well, times had been getting rougher and rougher for prophets — that is, prophets of Isaac's denomination. There was four hundred and fifty prophets of Baal in the community, and only one Presbyterian; that is, if Isaac *was* a Presbyterian, which I reckon he was, but it don't say. Naturally, the prophets of Baal

---

* This is the captain's own mistake.

18**

took all the trade. Isaac was pretty low-spirited, I
reckon, but he was a good deal of a man, and no doubt
he went a-prophesying around, letting on to be doing a
land-office business, but 'twa'n't any use; he couldn't
run any opposition to amount to anything. By and by
things got desperate with him; he sets his head to
work and thinks it all out, and then what does he do?
Why, he begins to throw out hints that the other
parties are this and that and t'other — nothing very
definite, maybe, but just kind of undermining their
reputation in a quiet way. This made talk, of course,
and finally got to the king. The king asked Isaac
what he meant by his talk. Says Isaac, ' Oh, nothing
particular; only, can they pray down fire from heaven
on an altar? It ain't much, maybe, your majesty,
only can they *do* it? That's the idea.' So the king
was a good deal disturbed, and he went to the prophets
of Baal, and they said, pretty airy, that if he had an
altar ready, *they* were ready; and they intimated he
better get it insured, too.

" So next morning all the children of Israel and their
parents and the other people gathered themselves together. Well, here was that great crowd of prophets
of Baal packed together on one side, and Isaac walking
up and down all alone on the other, putting up his job.
When time was called, Isaac let on to be comfortable
and indifferent; told the other team to take the first
innings. So they went at it, the whole four hundred
and fifty, praying around the altar, very hopeful, and
doing their level best. They prayed an hour — two
hours — three hours — and so on, plumb till noon. It
wa'n't any use; they hadn't took a trick. Of course
they felt kind of ashamed before all those people, and
well they might. Now, what would a magnanimous
man do? Keep still, wouldn't he? Of course. What
did Isaac do? He graveled the prophets of Baal every

way he could think of. Says he, 'You don't speak up loud enough; your god's asleep, like enough, or maybe he's taking a walk; you want to holler, you know'— or words to that effect; I don't recollect the exact language. Mind, I don't apologize for Isaac; he had his faults.

"Well, the prophets of Baal prayed along the best they knew how all the afternoon, and never raised a spark. At last, about sundown, they were all tuckered out, and they owned up and quit.

"What does Isaac do now? He steps up and says to some friends of his there, 'Pour four barrels of water on the altar!' Everybody was astonished; for the other side had prayed at it dry, you know, and got whitewashed. They poured it on. Says he, 'Heave on four more barrels.' Then he says, 'Heave on four more.' Twelve barrels, you see, altogether. The water ran all over the altar, and all down the sides, and filled up a trench around it that would hold a couple of hogsheads — 'measures,' it says; I reckon it means about a hogshead. Some of the people were going to put on their things and go, for they allowed he was crazy. They didn't know Isaac. Isaac knelt down and began to pray; he strung along, and strung along, about the heathen in distant lands, and about the sister churches, and about the state and the country at large, and about those that's in authority in the government, and all the usual programme, you know, till everybody had got tired and gone to thinking about something else, and then, all of a sudden, when nobody was noticing, he outs with a match and rakes it on the under side of his leg, and pff! up the whole thing blazes like a house afire! Twelve barrels of *water?* *Petroleum*, sir, PETROLEUM! that's what it was!"

"Petroleum, captain?"

"Yes. sir· the country was full of it. Isaac knew

all about that.   You read the Bible.   Don't you worry
about the tough places.   They ain't tough when you
come to think them out and throw light on them.
There ain't a thing in the Bible but what is true; all
you want is to go prayerfully to work and cipher out
how 't was done.''

At eight o'clock on the third morning out from New
York, land was sighted.   Away across the sunny waves
one saw a faint dark stripe stretched along under the
horizon — or pretended to see it, for the credit of his
eyesight.   Even the Reverend said he saw it, a thing
which was manifestly not so.   But I never have seen
any one who was morally strong enough to confess
that he could not see land when others claimed that
they could.

By and by the Bermuda islands were easily visible.
The principal one lay upon the water in the distance,
a long, dull-colored body, scalloped with slight hills
and valleys.   We could not go straight at it, but had
to travel all the way around it, sixteen miles from
shore, because it is fenced with an invisible coral reef.
At last we sighted buoys, bobbing here and there, and
then we glided into a narrow channel among them,
'' raised the reef,'' and came upon shoaling blue water
that soon further shoaled into pale green, with a surface scarcely rippled.   Now came the resurrection
hour; the berths gave up their dead.   Who are these
pale specters in plug hats and silken flounces that file
up the companion-way in melancholy procession and
step upon the deck?   These are they which took the
infallible preventive of seasickness in New York harbor
and then disappeared and were forgotten.   Also there
came two or three faces not seen before until this moment.   One's impulse is to ask, '' Where did *you* come
aboard?''

We followed the narrow channel a long time, with

land on both sides — low hills that might have been green and grassy, but had a faded look instead. However, the land-locked water was lovely, at any rate, with its glittering belts of blue and green where moderate soundings were, and its broad splotches of rich brown where the rocks lay near the surface. Everybody was feeling so well that even the grave, pale young man (who, by a sort of kindly common consent, had come latterly to be referred to as "The Ass") received frequent and friendly notice — which was right enough, for there was no harm in him.

At last we steamed between two island points whose rocky jaws allowed only just enough room for the vessel's body, and now before us loomed Hamilton on her clustered hillsides and summits, the whitest mass of terraced architecture that exists in the world, perhaps.

It was Sunday afternoon, and on the pier were gathered one or two hundred Bermudians, half of them black, half of them white, and all of them nobbily dressed, as the poet says.

Several boats came off to the ship, bringing citizens. One of these citizens was a faded, diminutive old gentleman, who approached our most ancient passenger with a childlike joy in his twinkling eyes, halted before him, folded his arms, and said, smiling with all his might and with all the simple delight that was in him, "You don't know me, John! Come, out with it now; you know you don't!"

The ancient passenger scanned him perplexedly, scanned the napless, threadbare costume of venerable fashion that had done Sunday service no man knows how many years, contemplated the marvelous stovepipe hat of still more ancient and venerable pattern, with its poor pathetic old stiff brim canted up "gallusly" in the wrong places, and said, with a hesitation that indicated strong internal effort to "place" the

gentle old apparition, "Why......let me see......
plague on it......there's *something* about you that
.....er......er......but I've been gone from Bermuda for twenty-seven years, and......hum, hum
......I don't seem to get at it, somehow, but there's
something about you that is just as familiar to me
as —"

"Likely it might be his hat," murmured the Ass,
with innocent, sympathetic interest.

III.

SO the Reverend and I had at last arrived at Hamilton, the principal town in the Bermuda Islands. A
wonderfully white town; white as snow itself. White
as marble; white as flour. Yet looking like none of
these, exactly. Never mind, we said; we shall hit
upon a figure by and by that will describe this peculiar
white.

It was a town that was compacted together upon the
sides and tops of a cluster of small hills. Its outlying
borders fringed off and thinned away among the cedar
forests, and there was no woody distance of curving
coast, or leafy islet sleeping upon the dimpled, painted
sea, but was flecked with shining white points— half-
concealed houses peeping out of the foliage. The
architecture of the town was mainly Spanish, inherited
from the colonists of two hundred and fifty years ago.
Some ragged-topped cocoa-palms, glimpsed here and
there, gave the land a tropical aspect.

There was an ample pier of heavy masonry; upon
this, under shelter, were some thousands of barrels containing that product which has carried the fame of Bermuda to many lands, the potato. With here and there

an onion. That last sentence is facetious; for they grow at least two onions in Bermuda to one potato. The onion is the pride and joy of Bermuda. It is her jewel, her gem of gems. In her conversation, her pulpit, her literature, it is her most frequent and eloquent figure. In Bermuda metaphor it stands for perfection —-perfection absolute.

The Bermudian weeping over the departed exhausts praise when he says, " He was an onion!" The Bermudian extolling the living hero bankrupts applause when he says, " He is an onion!" The Bermudian setting his son upon the stage of life to dare and do for himself climaxes all counsel, supplication, admonition, comprehends all ambition, when he says, " Be an onion!"

When parallel with the pier, and ten or fifteen steps outside it, we anchored. It was Sunday, bright and sunny. The groups upon the pier — men, youths, and boys — were whites and blacks in about equal proportion. All were well and neatly dressed, many of them nattily, a few of them very stylishly. One would have to travel far before he would find another town of twelve thousand inhabitants that could represent itself so respectably, in the matter of clothes, on a freight pier, without premeditation or effort. The women and young girls, black and white, who occasionally passed by, were nicely clad, and many were elegantly and fashionably so. The men did not affect summer clothing much, but the girls and women did, and their white garments were good to look at, after so many months of familiarity with somber colors.

Around one isolated potato barrel stood four young gentlemen, two black, two white, becomingly dressed, each with the head of a slender cane pressed against his teeth, and each with a foot propped up on the barrel. Another young gentleman came up, looked longingly at the barrel, but saw no rest for his foot there, and turned pensively away to seek another barrel. He wandered here and there, but without result. Nobody sat upon a barrel, as is the custom of the idle in other lands, yet all the isolated barrels were humanly occupied. Whosoever had a foot to spare put it on a barrel, if all the places on it were not already taken. The habits of all peoples are determined by their circumstances. The Bermudians lean upon barrels because of the scarcity of lamp-posts.

Many citizens came on board and spoke eagerly to the officers — inquiring about the Turco-Russian war news, I supposed. However, by listening judiciously I found that this was not so. They said, "What is the price of onions?" or, "How's onions?" Naturally enough this was their first interest; but they dropped into the war the moment it was satisfied.

We went ashore and found a novelty of a pleasant nature: there were no hackmen, hacks, or omnibuses on the pier or about it anywhere, and nobody offered his services to us, or molested us in any way. I said it was like being in heaven. The Reverend rebukingly and rather pointedly advised me to make the most of it, then. We knew of a boarding-house, and what we needed now was somebody to pilot us to it. Presently a little barefooted colored boy came along, whose raggedness was conspicuously un-Bermudian. His rear was so marvelously bepatched with colored squares and triangles that one was half persuaded he had got it out of an atlas. When the sun struck him right, he was as good to follow as a lightning-bug. We hired him and dropped into his wake. He piloted us through one picturesque street after another, and in due course deposited us where we belonged. He charged nothing for his map, and but a trifle for his services: so the Reverend doubled it. The little chap received the money with a beaming applause in his eye which plainly said, "This man's an onion!"

We had brought no letters of introduction; our names had been misspelt in the passenger list; nobody knew whether we were honest folk or otherwise. So we were expecting to have a good private time in case there was nothing in our general aspect to close boarding-house doors against us. We had no trouble. Bermuda has had but little experience of rascals, and is not suspicious. We got large, cool, well-lighted rooms on a second floor, overlooking a bloomy display of flowers and flowering shrubs,—calla and annunciation lilies, lantanas, heliotrope, jessamine, roses, pinks, double geraniums, oleanders, pomegranates, blue morning-glories of a great size, and many plants that were unknown to me.

We took a long afternoon walk, and soon found out that that exceedingly white town was built of blocks of white coral. Bermuda is a coral island, with a six-inch crust of soil on top of it, and every man has a quarry on his own premises. Everywhere you go you see square recesses cut into the hillsides, with perpendicular walls unmarred by crack or crevice, and perhaps you fancy that a house grew out of the ground there, and has been removed in a single piece from the mould. If you do, you err. But the material for a house has been quarried there. They cut right down through the coral, to any depth that is convenient — ten to twenty feet — and take it out in great square blocks. This cutting is done with a chisel that has a handle twelve or fifteen feet long, and is used as one uses a crowbar when he is drilling a hole, or a dasher when he is churning. Thus soft is this stone. Then with a common handsaw they saw the great blocks into handsome, huge bricks that are two feet long, a foot wide, and about six inches thick. These stand loosely piled during a month to harden; then the work of building begins.

The house is built of these blocks; it is roofed with broad coral slabs an inch thick, whose edges lap upon each other, so that the roof looks like a succession of shallow steps or terraces; the chimneys are built of the coral blocks, and sawed into graceful and picturesque patterns; the ground-flour veranda is paved with coral blocks; also the walk to the gate; the fence is built of coral blocks — built in massive panels, with broad cap-stones and heavy gateposts, and the whole trimmed into easy lines and comely shape with the saw. Then they put a hard coat of whitewash, as thick as your thumb nail, on the fence and all over the house, roof, chimneys, and all; the sun comes out and shines on this spectacle, and it is time for you to shut your unac-customed eyes, lest they be put out. It is the whitest white you can conceive of, and the blindingest. A Bermuda house does not look like marble; it is a much intenser white than that; and, besides, there is a dainty, indefinable something else about its look that is not marble-like. We put in a great deal of solid talk and reflection over this matter of trying to find a figure that would describe the unique white of a Bermuda house, and we contrived to hit upon it at last. It is exactly the white of the icing of a cake, and has the same un-emphasized and scarcely perceptible polish. The white of marble is modest and retiring compared with it.

After the house is cased in its hard scale of white-wash, not a crack, or sign of a seam, or joining of the blocks is detectable, from base-stone to chimney-top; the building looks as if it had been carved from a single block of stone, and the doors and windows sawed out afterwards. A white marble house has a cold, tomb-like, unsociable look, and takes the conversation out of a body and depresses him. Not so with a Bermuda

house.   There is something exhilarating, even hilarious,
about its vivid whiteness when the sun plays upon it.
If it be of picturesque shape and graceful contour—
and many of the Bermudian dwellings are — it will so
fascinate you that you will keep your eyes on it until
they ache.   One of those clean-cut, fanciful chimneys
— too pure and white for this world — with one side
glowing in the sun and the other touched with a soft
shadow, is an object that will charm one's gaze by the
hour.   I know of no other country that has chimneys
worthy to be gazed at and gloated over.   One of those
snowy houses, half concealed and half glimpsed through
green foliage, is a pretty thing to see; and if it takes
one by surprise and suddenly, as he turns a sharp
corner of a country road, it will wring an exclamation
from him, sure.

Wherever you go, in town or country, you find those
snowy houses, and always with masses of bright-colored
flowers about them, but with no vines climbing their
walls; vines cannot take hold of the smooth, hard
whitewash.   Wherever you go, in the town or along
the country roads, among little potato farms and
patches or expensive country seats, these stainless white
dwellings, gleaming out from flowers and foliage, meet
you at every turn.   The least little bit of a cottage is
as white and blemishless as the stateliest mansion.
Nowhere is there dirt or stench, puddle or hog-wallow,
neglect, disorder, or lack of trimness and neatness.
The roads, the streets, the dwellings, the people, the
clothes,— this neatness extends to everything that falls
under the eye.   It is the tidiest country in the world.
And very much the tidiest, too.

Considering these things, the question came up,
Where do the poor live?   No answer was arrived at.
Therefore, we agreed to leave this conundrum for
future statesmen to wrangle over.

19 *

What a bright and startling spectacle one of those blazing white country palaces, with its brown-tinted window caps and ledges, and green shutters, and its wealth of caressing flowers and foliage, would be in black London! And what a gleaming surprise it would be in nearly any American city one could mention, too!

Bermuda roads are made by cutting down a few inches into the solid white coral — or a good many feet, where a hill intrudes itself — and smoothing off the surface of the roadbed. It is a simple and easy process. The grain of the coral is coarse and porous; the roadbed has the look of being made of coarse white sugar. Its excessive cleanness and whiteness are a trouble in one way: the sun is reflected into your eyes with such energy as you walk along that you want to sneeze all the time. Old Captain Tom Bowling found another difficulty. He joined us in our walk, but kept wandering unrestfully to the roadside. Finally he explained. Said he, " Well, I chew, you know, and the road's so plaguy clean."

We walked several miles that afternoon in the bewildering glare of the sun, the white roads, and the white buildings. Our eyes got to paining us a good deal. By and by a soothing, blessed twilight spread its cool balm around. We looked up in pleased surprise and saw that it proceeded from an intensely black negro who was going by. We answered his military salute in the grateful gloom of his near presence, and then passed on into the pitiless white glare again.

The colored women whom we met usually bowed and spoke; so did the children. The colored men commonly gave the military salute. They borrow this fashion from the soldiers, no doubt; England has kept a garrison here for generations. The younger men's custom of carrying small canes is also borrowed from the soldiers, I suppose, who always carry a cane, in

Bermuda as everywhere else in Britain's broad dominions.

The country roads curve and wind hither and thither in the delightfulest way, unfolding pretty surprises at every turn: billowy masses of oleander that seem to float out from behind distant projections like the pink cloud-banks of sunset; sudden plunges among cottages and gardens, life and activity, followed by as sudden plunges into the somber twilight and stillness of the woods; flitting visions of white fortresses and beacon towers pictured against the sky on remote hilltops; glimpses of shining green sea caught for a moment through opening headlands, then lost again; more woods and solitude; and by and by another turn lays bare, without warning, the full sweep of the inland ocean, enriched with its bars of soft color and graced with its wandering sails.

Take any road you please, you may depend upon it you will not stay in it half a mile. Your road is everything that a road ought to be: it is bordered with trees, and with strange plants and flowers; it is shady and pleasant, or sunny and still pleasant; it carries you by the prettiest and peacefulest and most homelike of homes, and through stretches of forest that lie in a deep hush sometimes, and sometimes are alive with the music of birds; it curves always, which is a continual promise, whereas straight roads reveal everything at a glance and kill interest. Your road is all this, and yet you will not stay in it half a mile, for the reason that little seductive, mysterious roads are always branching out from it on either hand, and as these curve sharply also and hide what is beyond, you cannot resist the temptation to desert your own chosen road and explore them. You are usually paid for your trouble; consequently, your walk inland always turns out to be one of the most crooked, involved, purposeless, and interesting experiences a body can imagine. There is enough of variety. Sometimes you are in the level open, with marshes thick grown with flag-lances that are ten feet high on the one hand, and potato and onion orchards on the other; next, you are on a hilltop, with the ocean and the islands spread around you; presently the road winds through a deep cut, shut in by perpendicular walls thirty or forty feet high, marked with the oddest and abruptest stratum lines, suggestive of sudden and eccentric old upheavals, and garnished with here and there a clinging adventurous flower, and here and there a dangling vine; and by and by your way is along the sea edge, and you may look down a fathom or two through the transparent water and watch the diamond-like flash and play of the light upon the rocks and sands on the bottom until you are tired of it — if you are so constituted as to be able to get tired of it.

You may march the country roads in maiden meditation, fancy free, by field and farm, for no dog will plunge out at you from unsuspected gate, with breath-taking surprise of ferocious bark, notwithstanding it is a Christian land and a civilized. We saw upwards of a million cats in Bermuda, but the people are very abstemious in the matter of dogs. Two or three nights we prowled the country far and wide, and never once were accosted by a dog. It is a great privilege to visit such a land. The cats were no offense when properly distributed, but when piled they obstructed travel.

As we entered the edge of the town that Sunday afternoon, we stopped at a cottage to get a drink of water. The proprietor, a middle-aged man with a good face, asked us to sit down and rest. His dame brought chairs, and we grouped ourselves in the shade of the trees by the door. Mr. Smith — that was not his name, but it will answer — questioned us about ourselves and our country, and we answered him truthfully, as a general thing, and questioned him in return. It was all very simple and pleasant and sociable. Rural, too; for there was a pig and a small donkey and a hen anchored out, close at hand, by cords to their legs, on a spot that purported to be grassy. Presently, a woman passed along, and although she coldly said nothing she changed the drift of our talk. Said Smith:

"She didn't look this way, you noticed? Well, she is our next neighbor on one side, and there's another family that's our next neighbors on the other side; but there's a general coolness all around now, and we don't speak. Yet these three families, one generation and another, have lived here side by side and been as friendly as weavers for a hundred and fifty years, till about a year ago."

"Why, what calamity could have been powerful enough to break up so old a friendship?"

"Well, it was too bad, but it couldn't be helped. It happened like this: About a year or more ago, the rats got to pestering my place a good deal, and I set up a steel trap in my back-yard. Both of these neighbors run considerable to cats, and so I warned them about the trap, because their cats were pretty sociable around here nights, and they might get into trouble without my intending it. Well, they shut up their cats for a while, but you know how it is with people; they got careless, and sure enough one night the trap took Mrs. Jones's principal tomcat into camp and finished him up. In the morning Mrs. Jones comes here with the corpse in her arms, and cries and takes on the same as if it was a child. It was a cat by the name of Yelverton — Hector G. Yelverton — a troublesome old rip, with no more principle than an Injun, though you couldn't make *her* believe it. I said all a man could to comfort her, but no, nothing would do but I must pay for him. Finally, I said I warn't investing in cats now as much as I was, and with that she walked off in a huff, carrying the remains with her. That closed our intercourse with the Joneses. Mrs. Jones joined another church and took her tribe with her. She said she would not hold fellowship with assassins. Well, by and by comes Mrs. Brown's turn — she that went by here a minute ago. She had a disgraceful old yellow cat that she thought as much of as if he was twins, and one night he tried that trap on his neck, and it fitted him so, and was so sort of satisfactory, that he laid down and curled up and stayed with it. Such was the end of Sir John Baldwin."

"Was that the name of the cat?"

"The same. There's cats around here with names that would surprise you. Maria" (to his wife), "what was that cat's name that eat a keg of ratsbane by mistake over at Hooper's, and started home and got struck by lightning and took the blind staggers and fell in the well and was most drowned before they could fish him out?"

"That was that colored Deacon Jackson's cat. I only remember the last end of its name, which was Hold-The-Fort-For-I-Am-Coming Jackson."

"Sho! that ain't the one. That's the one that eat up an entire box of Seidlitz powders, and then hadn't any more judgment than to go and take a drink. He was considered to be a great loss, but I never could see it. Well, no matter about the names. Mrs. Brown wanted to be reasonable, but Mrs. Jones wouldn't let her. She put her up to going to law for damages. So to law she went, and had the face to claim seven shillings and sixpence. It made a great stir. All the neighbors went to court. Everybody took sides. It got hotter and hotter, and broke up all the friendships for three hundred yards around — friendships that had lasted for generations and generations.

"Well, I proved by eleven witnesses that the cat was of a low character and very ornery, and warn't worth a canceled postage-stamp, anyway, taking the average of cats here; but I lost the case. What could I expect? The system is all wrong here, and is bound to make revolution and bloodshed some day. You see, they give the magistrate a poor little starvation salary, and then turn him loose on the public to gouge for fees and costs to live on. What is the natural result? Why, he never looks into the justice of a case — never once. All he looks at is which client has got the money. So this one piled the fees and costs and everything on to me. I could pay specie, don't you see? and he knew mighty well that if he put the verdict on to Mrs. Brown, where it belonged, he'd have to take his swag in currency."

"Currency? Why, has Bermuda a currency?"

"Yes — onions. And they were forty per cent. discount, too, then, because the season had been over as much as three months. So I lost my case. I had to pay for that cat. But the general trouble the case made was the worst thing about it. Broke up so much good feeling. The neighbors don't speak to each other now. Mrs. Brown had named a child after me. But she changed its name right away. She is a Baptist. Well, in the course of baptizing it over again, it got drowned. I was hoping we might get to be friendly again some time or other, but of course this drowning the child knocked that all out of the question. It would have saved a world of heart-break and ill blood if she had named it dry."

I knew by the sigh that this was honest. All this trouble and all this destruction of confidence in the purity of the bench on account of a seven-shilling lawsuit about a cat! Somehow, it seemed to "size" the country.

19**

At this point we observed that an English flag had just been placed at half-mast on a building a hundred yards away. I and my friends were busy in an instant trying to imagine whose death, among the island dignitaries, could command such a mark of respect as this. Then a shudder shook them and me at the same moment, and I knew that we had jumped to one and the same conclusion: "The governor has gone to England; it is for the British admiral!"

At this moment Mr. Smith noticed the flag. He said with emotion:

"That's on a boarding-house. I judge there's a boarder dead."

A dozen other flags within view went to half-mast.

"It's a boarder, sure," said Smith.

"But would they half-mast the flags here for a boarder, Mr. Smith?"

"Why, certainly they would, if he was *dead*."

That seemed to size the country again.

IV.

THE early twilight of a Sunday evening in Hamilton, Bermuda, is an alluring time. There is just enough of whispering breeze, fragrance of flowers, and sense of repose to raise one's thoughts heavenward; and just enough amateur piano music to keep him reminded of the other place. There are many venerable pianos in Hamilton, and they all play at twilight. Age enlarges and enriches the powers of some musical instruments — notably those of the violin — but it seems to set a piano's teeth on edge. Most of the music in vogue there is the same that those pianos prattled in their innocent infancy; and there is something very pathetic about it when they go over it now, in their asthmatic second childhood, dropping a note here and there, where a tooth is gone.

We attended evening service at the stately Episcopal church on the hill, where were five or six hundred people, half of them white and the other half black, according to the usual Bermudian proportions; and all well dressed — a thing which is also usual in Bermuda and to be confidently expected. There was good music, which we heard, and doubtless a good sermon, but there was a wonderful deal of coughing, and so only the high parts of the argument carried over it. As we came out, after service, I overheard one young girl says to another:

"Why, you don't mean to say you pay duty on gloves and laces! I only pay postage; have them done up and sent in the Boston *Advertiser*."

There are those that believe that the most difficult thing to create is a woman who can comprehend that it is wrong to smuggle; and that an impossible thing to create is a woman who will not smuggle, whether or no, when she gets a chance. But these may be errors.

We went wandering off toward the country, and were soon far down in the lonely black depths of a road that was roofed over with the dense foliage of a double rank of great cedars. There was no sound of any kind there, it was perfectly still. And it was so dark that one could detect nothing but somber outlines. We strode farther and farther down this tunnel, cheering the way with chat.

Presently the chat took this shape: "How insensibly the character of the people and of a government makes its impress upon a stranger, and gives him a sense of security or of insecurity without his taking deliberate thought upon the matter or asking anybody a question! We have been in this land half a day; we have seen

8**

none but honest faces; we have noted the British flag
flying, which means efficient government and good
order; so without inquiry we plunge unarmed and with
perfect confidence into this dismal place, which in
almost any other country would swarm with thugs and
garroters—''

"Sh! What was that? Stealthy footsteps! Low
voices! We gasp, we close up together, and wait.
A vague shape glides out of the dusk and confronts us.
A voice speaks—demands money!

"A shilling, gentlemen, if you please, to help build
the new Methodist church.''

Blessed sound! Holy sound! We contribute with
thankful avidity to the new Methodist church, and are
happy to think how lucky it was that those little colored
Sunday-school scholars did not seize upon everything
we had with violence, before we recovered from our
momentary helpless condition. By the light of cigars
we write down the names of weightier philanthropists
than ourselves on the contribution cards, and then pass
on into the farther darkness, saying, What sort of a
government do they call this, where they allow little
black pious children, with contribution cards, to plunge
out upon peaceable strangers in the dark and scare
them to death?

We prowled on several hours, sometimes by the sea
side, sometimes inland, and finally managed to get lost,
which is a feat that requires talent in Bermuda. I had
on new shoes. They were No. 7's when I started, but
were not more than 5's now, and still diminishing. I
walked two hours in those shoes after that, before we
reached home. Doubtless I could have the reader's
sympathy for the asking. Many people have never had
the headache or the toothache, and I am one of those
myself; but everybody has worn tight shoes for two or
three hours, and known the luxury of taking them off

in a retired place and seeing his feet swell up and ob-
scure the firmament.   Once when I was a callow, bash-
ful cub, I took a plain, unsentimental country girl to a
comedy one night.   I had known her a day;   she
seemed divine; I wore my new boots.   At the end of
the first half-hour she said, "Why do you fidget so
with your feet?"   I said, "Did I?"   Then I put my
attention there and kept still.   At the end of another
half-hour she said, "Why do you say, 'Yes, oh yes!'
and 'Ha, ha, oh, certainly! very true!' to everything
I say, when half the time those are entirely irrelevant
answers?"   I blushed, and explained that I had been a
little absent-minded.   At the end of another half-hour
she said, "Please, why do you grin so steadfastly at
vacancy, and yet look so sad?"   I explained that I
always did that when I was reflecting.   An hour passed,
and then she turned and contemplated me with her
earnest eyes and said, "Why do you cry all the time?"
I explained that very funny comedies always made me
cry.   At last human nature surrendered, and I secretly
slipped my boots off.   This was a mistake.   I was not
able to get them on any more.   It was a rainy night;
there were no omnibuses going our way; and as I
walked home, burning up with shame, with the girl on
one arm and my boots under the other, I was an object
worthy of some compassion — especially in those
moments of martyrdom when I had to pass through
the glare that fell upon the pavement from street
lamps.   Finally, this child of the forest said, "Where
are your boots?" and being taken unprepared, I put a
fitting finish to the follies of the evening with the stupid
remark, "The higher classes do not wear them to the
theater."

The Reverend had been an army chaplain during the
war, and while we were hunting for a road that would

lead to Hamilton he told a story about two dying soldiers which interested me in spite of my feet. He said that in the Potomac hospitals rough pine coffins were furnished by government, but that it was not always possible to keep up with the demand; so, when a man died, if there was no coffin at hand he was buried without one. One night, late, two soldiers lay dying in a ward. A man came in with a coffin on his shoulder, and stood trying to make up his mind which of these two poor fellows would be likely to need it first. Both of them begged for it with their fading eyes — they were past talking. Then one of them protruded a wasted hand from his blankets and made a feeble beckoning sign with the fingers, to signify, "Be a good fellow; put it under my bed, please." The man did it, and left. The lucky soldier painfully turned himself in his bed until he faced the other warrior, raised himself partly on his elbow, and began to work up a mysterious expression of some kind in his face. Gradually, irksomely, but surely and steadily, it developed, and at last it took definite form as a pretty successful *wink*. The sufferer fell back exhausted with his labor, but bathed in glory. Now entered a personal friend of No. 2, the despoiled soldier. No. 2 pleaded with him with eloquent eyes, till presently he understood, and removed the coffin from under No. 1's bed and put it under No. 2's. No. 2 indicated his joy, and made some more signs; the friend understood again, and put his arm under No. 2's shoulders and lifted him partly up. Then the dying hero turned the dim exultation of his eye upon No. 1, and began a slow and labored work with his hands; gradually he lifted one hand up toward his face; it grew weak and dropped back again; once more he made the effort, but failed again. He took a rest; he gathered all the remnant of his strength, and this time he slowly but surely carried his thumb to the side of his nose, spread the gaunt fingers wide in triumph, and dropped back dead. That picture sticks by me yet. The " situation " is unique.

The next morning, at what seemed a very early hour, the little white table-waiter appeared suddenly in my room and shot a single word out of himself: " Breakfast!"

This was a remarkable boy in many ways. He was about eleven years old; he had alert, intent black eyes; he was quick of movement; there was no hesitation, no uncertainty about him anywhere; there was a military decision in his lip, his manner, his speech, that was an astonishing thing to see in a little chap like him; he wasted no words; his answers always came so quick and brief that they seemed to be part of the question that had been asked instead of a reply to it. When he stood at table with his fly-brush, rigid, erect, his face set in a cast-iron gravity, he was a statue till he detected a dawning want in somebody's eye; then he pounced down, supplied it, and was instantly a statue again. When he was sent to the kitchen for anything, he marched upright till he got to the door; he turned hand-springs the rest of the way.

" Breakfast!"

I thought I would make one more effort to get some conversation out of this being.

" Have you called the Reverend, or are —"

" Yes s'r!"

" Is it early, or is —"

" Eight-five."

" Do you have to do all the 'chores,' or is there somebody to give you a —"

" Colored girl."

" Is there only one parish in this island, or are there —"

" Eight!"

" Is the big church on the hill a parish church, or is it —"

" Chapel-of-ease !"

" Is taxation here classified into poll, parish, town, and —"

" Don't know !"

Before I could cudgel another question out of my head, he was below, hand-springing across the back-yard. He had slid down the balusters, head-first. I gave up trying to provoke a discussion with him. The essential element of discussion had been left out of him; his answers were so final and exact that they did not leave a doubt to hang conversation on. I suspect that there is the making of a mighty man or a mighty rascal in this boy — according to circumstances — but they are going to apprentice him to a carpenter. It is the way the world uses its opportunities.

During this day and the next we took carriage drives about the island and over to the town of St. George's, fifteen or twenty miles away. Such hard, excellent roads to drive over are not to be found elsewhere out of Europe. An intelligent young colored man drove us, and acted as guide-book. In the edge of the town we saw five or six mountain-cabbage palms (atrocious name!) standing in a straight row, and equidistant from each other. These were not the largest or the tallest trees I have ever seen, but they were the state-liest, the most majestic. That row of them must be the nearest that nature has ever come to counterfeiting a colonnade. These trees are all the same height, say sixty feet; the trunks as gray as granite, with a very gradual and perfect taper; without sign of branch or knot or flaw; the surface not looking like bark, but like granite that has been dressed and not polished. Thus all the way up the diminishing shaft for fifty feet; then it begins to take the appearance of being closely wrapped,

spool-fashion, with gray cord, or of having been turned
in a lathe.   Above this point there is an outward swell,
and thence upwards, for six feet or more, the cylinder
is a bright, fresh green, and is formed of wrappings
like those of an ear of green Indian corn.   Then comes
the great, spraying palm plume, also green.   Other
palm trees always lean out of the perpendicular, or
have a curve in them.   But the plumb-line could not
detect a deflection in any individual of this stately
row; they stand as straight as the colonnade of Baal-
bec; they have its great height, they have its grace-
fulness, they have its dignity; in moonlight or twilight,
and shorn of their plumes, they would duplicate it.

The birds we came across in the country were singularly tame; even that wild creature, the quail, would
pick around in the grass at ease while we inspected it
and talked about it at leisure.   A small bird of the
canary species had to be stirred up with the butt-end
of the whip before it would move, and then it moved
only a couple of feet.   It is said that even the suspicious flea is tame and sociable in Bermuda, and will
allow himself to be caught and caressed without misgivings.   This should be taken with allowance, for doubtless there is more or less brag about it.   In San Francisco they used to claim that their native flea could kick
a child over, as if it were a merit in a flea to be able to
do that; as if the knowledge of it trumpeted abroad
ought to entice immigration.   Such a thing in nine
cases out of ten would be almost sure to deter a thinking man from coming.

We saw no bugs or reptiles to speak of, and so I was
thinking of saying in print, in a general way, that there
were none at all; but one night after I had gone to bed,
the Reverend came into my room carrying something,
and asked, '' Is this your boot?''   I said it was, and
he said he had met a spider going off with it.   Next

morning he stated that just at dawn the same spider raised his window and was coming in to get a shirt, but saw him and fled.

I inquired, " Did he get the shirt?"

" No."

" How did you know it was a shirt he was after?"

" I could see it in his eye."

We inquired around, but could hear of no Bermudian spider capable of doing these things. Citizens said that their largest spiders could not more than spread their legs over an ordinary saucer, and that they had always been considered honest. Here was testimony of a clergyman against the testimony of mere worldings — interested ones, too. On the whole, I judged it best to lock up my things.

Here and there on the country roads we found lemon, papaw, orange, lime, and fig trees; also several sorts of palms, among them the cocoa, the date, and the palmetto. We saw some bamboos forty feet high, with stems as thick as a man's arm. Jungles of the mangrove-tree stood up out of swamps, propped on their interlacing roots as upon a tangle of stilts. In drier places the noble tamarind sent down its grateful cloud of shade. Here and there the blossomy tamarisk adorned the roadside. There was a curious gnarled and twisted black tree, without a single leaf on it. It might have passed itself off for a dead apple tree but for the fact that it had a star-like, red-hot flower sprinkled sparsely over its person. It had the scattery red glow that a constellation might have when glimpsed through smoked glass. It is possible that our constellations have been so constructed as to be invisible through smoked glass; if this is so it is a great mistake.

We saw a tree that bears grapes, and just as calmly and unostentatiously as a vine would do it. We saw an India-rubber-tree, but out of season, possibly, so there were no shoes on it, nor suspenders, nor anything that a person would properly expect to find there. This gave it an impressively fraudulent look. There was exactly one mahogany tree on the island. I know this to be reliable, because I saw a man who said he had counted it many a time and could not be mistaken. He was a man with a harelip and a pure heart, and everybody said he was as true as steel. Such men are all too few.

One's eye caught near and far the pink cloud of the oleander and the red blaze of the pomegranate blossom. In one piece of wild wood the morning-glory vines had wrapped the trees to their very tops, and decorated them all over with couples and clusters of great blue bells — a fine and striking spectacle, at a little distance. But the dull cedar is everywhere, and is the prevailing foliage. One does not appreciate how dull it is until the varnished, bright green attire of the infrequent lemon tree pleasantly intrudes its contrast. In one thing Bermuda is eminently tropical — was in May, at least — the unbrilliant, slightly faded, unrejoicing look of the landscape. For forests arrayed in a blemishless magnificence of glowing green foliage that seems to exult in its own existence and can move the beholder to an enthusiasm that will make him either shout or cry, one must go to countries that have malignant winters.

We saw scores of colored farmers digging their crops of potatoes and onions, their wives and children helping — entirely contented and comfortable, if looks go for anything. We never met a man, or woman, or child anywhere in this sunny island who seemed to be unprosperous, or discontented, or sorry about anything. This sort of monotony became very tiresome presently, and even something worse. The spectacle of an entire nation groveling in contentment is an infuriating thing.

20 ✠✠

We felt the lack of something in this community — a vague, an undefinable, an elusive something, and yet a lack. But after considerable thought we made out what it was — tramps. Let them go there, right now, in a body. It is utterly virgin soil. Passage is cheap. Every true patriot in America will help buy tickets. Whole armies of these excellent beings can be spared from our midst and our polls; they will find a delicious climate and a green, kind-hearted people. There are potatoes and onions for all, and a generous welcome for the first batch that arrives, and elegant graves for the second.

It was the Early Rose potato the people were digging. Later in the year they have another crop, which they call the Garnet. We buy their potatoes (retail) at fifteen dollars a barrel; and those colored farmers buy ours for a song, and live on them. Havana might exchange cigars with Connecticut in the same advantageous way, if she thought of it.

We passed a roadside grocery with a sign up, " Potatoes Wanted." An ignorant stranger, doubtless. He could not have gone thirty steps from his place without finding plenty of them.

In several fields the arrowroot crop was already sprouting. Bermuda used to make a vast annual profit out of this staple before firearms came into such general use.

The island is not large. Somewhere in the interior a man ahead of us had a very slow horse. I suggested that we had better go by him; but the driver said the man had but a little way to go. I waited to see, wondering how he could know. Presently the man did turn down another road. I asked, " How did you know he would?"

" Because I knew the man, and where he lived."

I asked him, satirically, if he knew everybody in the

island; he answered, very simply, that he did. This gives a body's mind a good substantial grip on the dimensions of the place.

At the principal hotel at St. George's, a young girl, with a sweet, serious face, said we could not be furnished with dinner, because we had not been expected, and no preparation had been made. Yet it was still an hour before dinner time. We argued, she yielded not; we supplicated, she was serene. The hotel had not been expecting an inundation of two people, and so it seemed that we should have to go home dinnerless. I said we were not very hungry; a fish would do. My little maid answered, it was not the market day for fish. Things began to look serious; but presently the boarder who sustained the hotel came in, and when the case was laid before him he was cheerfully willing to divide. So we had much pleasant chat at table about St. George's chief industry, the repairing of damaged ships; and in between we had a soup that had something in it that seemed to taste like the hereafter, but it proved to be only pepper of a particularly vivacious kind. And we had an iron-clad chicken that was deliciously cooked, but not in the right way. Baking was not the thing to convince his sort. He ought to have been put through a quartz mill until the " tuck " was taken out of him, and then boiled till we came again. We got a good deal of sport out of him, but not enough sustenance to leave the victory on our side. No matter; we had potatoes and a pie and a sociable good time. Then a ramble through the town, which is a quaint one, with interesting, crooked streets, and narrow, crooked lanes, with here and there a grain of dust. Here, as in Hamilton, the dwellings had Venetian blinds of a very sensible pattern. They were not double shutters, hinged at the sides, but a single broad shutter, hinged at the top; you push it outward, from the bottom, and fasten it at any angle required by the sun or desired by yourself.

All about the island one sees great white scars on the hill-slopes. These are dished spaces where the soil has been scraped off and the coral exposed and glazed with hard whitewash. Some of these are a quarter-acre in size. They catch and carry the rainfall to reservoirs; for the wells are few and poor, and there are no natural springs and no brooks.

They say that the Bermuda climate is mild and equable, with never any snow or ice, and that one may be very comfortable in spring clothing the year round, there. We had delightful and decided summer weather in May, with a flaming sun that permitted the thinnest of raiment, and yet there was a constant breeze; consequently we were never discomforted by heat. At four or five in the afternoon the mercury began to go down, and then it became necessary to change to thick garments. I went to St. George's in the morning clothed in the thinnest of linen, and reached home at five in the afternoon with two overcoats on. The nights are said to be always cool and bracing. We had mosquito nets, and the Reverend said the mosquitoes persecuted him a good deal. I often heard him slapping and banging at these imaginary creatures with as much zeal as if they had been real. There are no mosquitoes in the Bermudas in May.

The poet Thomas Moore spent several months in Bermuda more than seventy years ago. He was sent out to be registrar of the admiralty. I am not quite clear as to the function of a registrar of the admiralty of Bermuda, but I think it is his duty to keep a record of all the admirals born there. I will inquire into this. There was not much doing in admirals, and Moore got tired and went away. A reverently preserved souvenir of him is still one of the treasures of the islands. I gathered the idea, vaguely, that it was a jug, but was persistently thwarted in the twenty-two efforts I made to visit it. However, it was no matter, for I found out afterwards that it was only a chair.

There are several "sights" in the Bermudas, of course, but they are easily avoided. This is a great advantage — one cannot have it in Europe. Bermuda is the right country for a jaded man to "loaf" in. There are no harassments; the deep peace and quiet of the country sink into one's body and bones and give his conscience a rest, and chloroform the legion of invisible small devils that are always trying to whitewash his hair. A good many Americans go there about the first of March and remain until the early spring weeks have finished their villainies at home.

The Bermudians are hoping soon to have telegraphic communication with the world. But even after they shall have acquired this curse it will still be a good country to go to for a vacation, for there are charming little islets scattered about the enclosed sea where one could live secure from interruption. The telegraph boy would have to come in a boat, and one could easily kill him while he was making his landing.

We had spent four days in Bermuda — three bright ones out of doors and one rainy one in the house, we being disappointed about getting a yacht for a sail; and now our furlough was ended, and we entered into the ship again and sailed homeward.

We made the run home to New York quarantine in three days and five hours, and could have gone right along up to the city if we had had a health permit. But health permits are not granted after seven in the evening, partly because a ship cannot be inspected and overhauled with exhaustive thoroughness except in daylight, and partly because health officers are liable to catch cold if they expose themselves to the night air. Still, you can *buy* a permit after hours for five dollars extra, and the officer will do the inspecting next week. Our ship and passengers lay under expense and in humiliating captivity all night, under the very nose of the little official reptile who is supposed to protect New York from pestilence by his vigilant "inspections." This imposing rigor gave everybody a solemn and awful idea of the beneficent watchfulness of our government, and there were some who wondered if anything finer could be found in other countries.

In the morning we were all a-tiptoe to witness the intricate ceremony of inspecting the ship. But it was a disappointing thing. The health officer's tug ranged alongside for a moment, our purser handed the lawful three-dollar permit fee to the health officer's bootblack, who passed us a folded paper in a forked stick, and away we went. The entire "inspection" did not occupy thirteen seconds.

The health officer's place is worth a hundred thousand dollars a year to him. His system of inspection is perfect, and therefore cannot be improved on; but it seems to me that his system of collecting his fees might be amended. For a great ship to lie idle all night is a most costly loss of time; for her passengers to have to do the same thing works to them the same damage, with the addition of an amount of exasperation and bitterness of soul that the spectacle of that health officer's ashes on a shovel could hardly sweeten. Now why would it not be better and simpler to let the ships pass in unmolested, and the fees and permits be exchanged once a year by post?

THE FACTS CONCERNING THE RECENT CARNIVAL OF CRIME IN CONNECTICUT

I WAS feeling blithe, almost jocund. I put a match to my cigar, and just then the morning's mail was handed in. The first superscription I glanced at was in a handwriting that sent a thrill of pleasure through and through me. It was Aunt Mary's; and she was the person I loved and honored most in all the world, outside of my own household. She had been my boyhood's idol; maturity, which is fatal to so many enchantments, had not been able to dislodge her from her pedestal; no, it had only justified her right to be there, and placed her dethronement permanently among the impossibilities. To show how strong her influence over me was, I will observe that long after everybody else's " *do*-stop-smoking" had ceased to affect me in the slightest degree, Aunt Mary could still stir my torpid conscience into faint signs of life when she touched upon the matter. But all things have their limit in this world. A happy day came at last, when even Aunt Mary's words could no longer move me. I was not merely glad to see that day arrive; I was more than glad — I was grateful; for when its sun had set, the one alloy that was able to mar my enjoyment of my aunt's society was gone. The remainder of her

20**

stay with us that winter was in every way a delight. Of course she pleaded with me just as earnestly as ever, after that blessed day, to quit my pernicious habit, but to no purpose whatever; the moment she opened the subject I at once became calmly, peacefully, contentedly indifferent — absolutely, adamantinely indifferent. Consequently the closing weeks of that memorable visit melted away as pleasantly as a dream, they were so freighted for me with tranquil satisfaction. I could not have enjoyed my pet vice more if my gentle tormentor had been a smoker herself, and an advocate of the practice. Well, the sight of her handwriting reminded me that I was getting very hungry to see her again. I easily guessed what I should find in her letter. I opened it. Good! just as I expected; she was coming! Coming this very day, too, and by the morning train; I might expect her any moment.

I said to myself, "I am thoroughly happy and content now. If my most pitiless enemy could appear before me at this moment, I would freely right any wrong I may have done him."

Straightway the door opened, and a shriveled, shabby dwarf entered. He was not more than two feet high. He seemed to be about forty years old. Every feature and every inch of him was a trifle out of shape; and so, while one could not put his finger upon any particular part and say, "This is a conspicuous deformity," the spectator perceived that this little person was a deformity as a whole — a vague, general, evenly blended, nicely adjusted deformity. There was a fox-like cunning in the face and the sharp little eyes, and also alertness and malice. And yet, this vile bit of human rubbish seemed to bear a sort of remote and ill-defined resemblance to me! It was dully perceptible in the mean form, the countenance, and even the clothes, gestures, manner, and attitudes of the creature.

He was a far-fetched, dim suggestion of a burlesque upon me, a caricature of me in little. One thing about him struck me forcibly, and most unpleasantly: he was covered all over with a fuzzy, greenish mould, such as one sometimes sees upon mildewed bread. The sight of it was nauseating.

He stepped along with a chipper air, and flung himself into a doll's chair in a very free-and-easy way, without waiting to be asked. He tossed his hat into the waste-basket. He picked up my old chalk pipe from the floor, gave the stem a wipe or two on his knee, filled the bowl from the tobacco-box at his side, and said to me in a tone of pert command:

"Gimme a match!"

I blushed to the roots of my hair; partly with indignation, but mainly because it somehow seemed to me that this whole performance was very like an exaggeration of conduct which I myself had sometimes been guilty of in my intercourse with familiar friends — but never, never with strangers, I observed to myself. I wanted to kick the pigmy into the fire, but some incomprehensible sense of being legally and legitimately under his authority forced me to obey his order. He applied the match to the pipe, took a contemplative whiff or two, and remarked, in an irritatingly familiar way:

"Seems to me it's devilish odd weather for this time of year."

I flushed again, and in anger and humiliation as before; for the language was hardly an exaggeration of some that I have uttered in my day, and moreover was delivered in a tone of voice and with an exasperating drawl that had the seeming of a deliberate travesty of my style. Now there is nothing I am quite so sensitive about as a mocking imitation of my drawling infirmity of speech. I spoke up sharply and said:

T**

"Look here, you miserable ash-cat! you will have to give a little more attention to your manners, or I will throw you out of the window!"

The manikin smiled a smile of malicious content and security, puffed a whiff of smoke contemptuously toward me, and said, with a still more elaborate drawl:

"Come — go gently now; don't put on *too* many airs with your betters."

This cool snub rasped me all over, but it seemed to subjugate me, too, for a moment. The pigmy contemplated me awhile with his weasel eyes, and then said, in a peculiarly sneering way:

"You turned a tramp away from your door this morning."

I said crustily:

"Perhaps I did, perhaps I didn't. How do *you* know?"

"Well, I know. It isn't any matter *how* I know."

"Very well. Suppose I *did* turn a tramp away from the door — what of it?"

"Oh, nothing; nothing in particular. Only you lied to him."

"I *didn't* ! That is, I —"

"Yes, but you did; you lied to him."

I felt a guilty pang — in truth, I had felt it forty times before that tramp had traveled a block from my door — but still I resolved to make a show of feeling slandered; so I said:

"This is a baseless impertinence. I said to the tramp —"

"There — wait. You were about to lie again. *I* know what you said to him. You said the cook was gone down town and there was nothing left from breakfast. Two lies. You knew the cook was behind the door, and plenty of provisions behind *her*."

This astonishing accuracy silenced me; and it filled

me with wondering speculations, too, as to how this cub could have got his information. Of course he could have culled the conversation from the tramp, but by what sort of magic had he contrived to find out about the concealed cook? Now the dwarf spoke again:

"It was rather pitiful, rather small, in you to refuse to read that poor young woman's manuscript the other day, and give her an opinion as to its literary value; and she had come so far, too, and *so* hopefully. Now *wasn't* it?"

I felt like a cur! And I had felt so every time the thing had recurred to my mind, I may as well confess. I flushed hotly and said:

"Look here, have you nothing better to do than prowl around prying into other people's business? Did that girl tell you that?"

"Never mind whether she did or not. The main thing is, you did that contemptible thing. And you felt ashamed of it afterward. Aha! you feel ashamed of it *now*!"

This was a sort of devilish glee. With fiery earnestness I responded:

"I told that girl, in the kindest, gentlest way, that I could not consent to deliver judgment upon *any* one's manuscript, because an individual's verdict was worthless. It might underrate a work of high merit and lose it to the world, or it might overrate a trashy production and so open the way for its infliction upon the world. I said that the great public was the only tribunal competent to sit in judgment upon a literary effort, and therefore it must be best to lay it before that tribunal in the outset, since in the end it must stand or fall by that mighty court's decision anyway."

"Yes, you said all that. So you did, you juggling, small-souled shuffler! And yet when the happy hope-

fulness faded out of that poor girl's face, when you
saw her furtively slip beneath her shawl the scroll she
had so patiently and honestly scribbled at — so ashamed
of her darling now, so proud of it before — when you
saw the gladness go out of her eyes and the tears come
there, when she crept away so humbly who had come
so —"

"Oh, peace! peace! peace! Blister your merciless
tongue, haven't all these thoughts tortured me enough
without *your* coming here to fetch them back again!"

Remorse! remorse! It seemed to me that it would
eat the very heart out of me! And yet that small
fiend only sat there leering at me with joy and con-
tempt, and placidly chuckling. Presently he began to
speak again. Every sentence was an accusation, and
every accusation a truth. Every clause was freighted
with sarcasm and derision, every slow-dropping word
burned like vitriol. The dwarf reminded me of times
when I had flown at my children in anger and punished
them for faults which a little inquiry would have taught
me that others, and not they, had committed. He reminded me of how I had disloyally allowed old friends
to be traduced in my hearing, and been too craven to
utter a word in their defense. He reminded me of
many dishonest things which I had done; of many
which I had procured to be done by children and other
irresponsible persons; of some which I had planned,
thought upon, and longed to do, and been kept from
the performance by fear of consequences only. With
exquisite cruelty he recalled to my mind, item by item,
wrongs and unkindnesses I had inflicted and humilia-
tions I had put upon friends since dead, "who died
thinking of those injuries, maybe, and grieving over
them," he added, by way of poison to the stab.

"For instance," said he, "take the case of your
younger brother, when you two were boys together,

many a long year ago. He always lovingly trusted in you with a fidelity that your manifold treacheries were not able to shake. He followed you about like a dog, content to suffer wrong and abuse if he might only be with you; patient under these injuries so long as it was your hand that inflicted them. The latest picture you have of him in health and strength must be such a comfort to you! You pledged your honor that if he would let you blindfold him no harm should come to him; and then, giggling and choking over the rare fun of the joke, you led him to a brook thinly glazed with ice, and pushed him in; and how you did laugh! Man, you will never forget the gentle, reproachful look he gave you as he struggled shivering out, if you live a thousand years! Oho! you see it now, you see it *now* !"

" Beast, I have seen it a million times, and shall see it a million more! and may you rot away piecemeal, and suffer till doomsday what I suffer now, for bringing it back to me again!"

The dwarf chuckled contentedly, and went on with his accusing history of my career. I dropped into a moody, vengeful state, and suffered in silence under the merciless lash. At last this remark of his gave me a sudden rouse:

"Two months ago, on a Tuesday, you woke up, away in the night, and fell to thinking, with shame, about a peculiarly mean and pitiful act of yours toward a poor ignorant Indian in the wilds of the Rocky Mountains in the winter of eighteen hundred and —"

" Stop a moment, devil! Stop! Do you mean to tell me that even my very *thoughts* are not hidden from you?"

" It seems to look like that. Didn't you think the thoughts I have just mentioned?"

" If I didn't, I wish I may never breathe again!

Look here, friend — look me in the eye. Who *are*
you?"

"Well, who do you think?"

"I think you are Satan himself. I think you are
the devil."

"No."

"No? Then who *can* you be?"

"Would you really like to know?"

"*Indeed* I would."

"Well, I am your *Conscience !*"

In an instant I was in a blaze of joy and exultation
I sprang at the creature, roaring:

"Curse you, I have wished a hundred million times
that you were tangible, and that I could get my hands
on your throat once! Oh, but I will wreak a deadly
vengeance on —"

Folly! Lightning does not move more quickly than
my Conscience did! He darted aloft so suddenly that
in the moment my fingers clutched the empty air he
was already perched on the top of the high bookcase,
with his thumb at his nose in token of derision. I
flung the poker at him, and missed. I fired the boot-
jack. In a blind rage I flew from place to place, and
snatched and hurled any missile that came handy; the
storm of books, inkstands, and chunks of coal gloomed
the air and beat about the manikin's perch relentlessly,
but all to no purpose; the nimble figure dodged every
shot; and not only that, but burst into a cackle of
sarcastic and triumphant laughter as I sat down exhausted. While I puffed and gasped with fatigue and
excitement, my Conscience talked to this effect:

"My good slave, you are curiously witless — no, I
mean characteristically so. In truth, you are always
consistent, always yourself, always an ass. Otherwise
it must have occurred to you that if you attempted this
murder with a sad heart and a heavy conscience, I

would droop under the burdening influence instantly. Fool, I should have weighed a ton, and could not have budged from the floor; but instead, you are so cheerfully anxious to kill me that your conscience is as light as a feather; hence I am away up here out of your reach. I can almost respect a mere ordinary sort of fool; but *you* — pah!"

I would have given anything, then, to be heavy-hearted, so that I could get this person down from there and take his life, but I could no more be heavy-hearted over such a desire than I could have sorrowed over its accomplishment. So I could only look longingly up at my master, and rave at the ill-luck that denied me a heavy conscience the one only time that I had ever wanted such a thing in my life. By and by I got to musing over the hour's strange adventure, and of course my human curiosity began to work. I set myself to framing in my mind some questions for this fiend to answer. Just then one of my boys entered, leaving the door open behind him, and exclaimed:

"My! what *has* been going on here? The bookcase is all one riddle of —"

I sprang up in consternation, and shouted:

"Out of. this! Hurry! Jump! Fly! Shut the door! Quick, or my Conscience will get away!"

The door slammed to, and I locked it. I glanced up and was grateful, to the bottom of my heart, to see that my owner was still my prisoner. I said:

"Hang you, I might have lost you! Children are the heedlessest creatures. But look here, friend, the boy did not seem to notice you at all; how is that?"

"For a very good reason. I am invisible to all but you."

I made a mental note of that piece of information with a good deal of satisfaction. I could kill this miscreant now, if I got a chance, and no one would know it. But this very reflection made me so light-hearted that my Conscience could hardly keep his seat, but was like to float aloft toward the ceiling like a toy balloon. I said, presently:

"Come, my Conscience, let us be friendly. Let us fly a flag of truce for a while. I am suffering to ask you some questions."

"Very well. Begin."

"Well, then, in the first place, why were you never visible to me before?"

"Because you never asked to see me before; that is, you never asked in the right spirit and the proper form before. You were just in the right spirit this time, and when you called for your most pitiless enemy I was that person by a very large majority, though you did not suspect it."

"Well, did that remark of mine turn you into flesh and blood?"

"No. It only made me visible to you. I am unsubstantial, just as other spirits are."

This remark prodded me with a sharp misgiving. If he was unsubstantial, how was I going to kill him? But I dissembled, and said persuasively:

"Conscience, it isn't sociable of you to keep at such a distance. Come down and take another smoke."

This was answered with a look that was full of derision, and with this observation added:

"Come where you can get at me and kill me? The invitation is declined with thanks."

"All right," said I to myself; "so it seems a spirit *can* be killed, after all; there will be one spirit lacking in this world, presently, or I lose my guess." Then I said aloud:

"Friend —"

"There; wait a bit. I am not your friend, I am your enemy; I am not your equal, I am your master.

Call me 'my lord,' if you please. You are too familiar.''

"I don't like such titles. I am willing to call you *sir*. That is as far as —''

"We will have no argument about this. Just obey; that is all. Go on with your chatter.''

"Very well, my lord — since nothing but my lord will suit you — I was going to ask you how long you will be visible to me?''

"Always!''

I broke out with strong indignation: "This is simply an outrage. That is what I think of it. You have dogged, and dogged, and *dogged* me, all the days of my life, invisible. That was misery enough; now to have such a looking thing as you tagging after me like another shadow all the rest of my days is an intolerable prospect. You have my opinion, my lord; make the most of it.''

"My lad, there was never so pleased a conscience in this world as I was when you made me visible. It gives me an inconceivable advantage. *Now* I can look you straight in the eye, and call you names, and leer at you, jeer at you, sneer at you; and *you* know what eloquence there is in visible gesture and expression, more especially when the effect is heightened by audible speech. I shall always address you henceforth in your o-w-n s-n-i-v-e-l-i-n-g d-r-a-w-l — baby!''

I let fly with the coal-hod. No result. My lord said:

"Come, come! Remember the flag of truce!''

"Ah, I forgot that. I will try to be civil; and *you* try it, too, for a novelty. The idea of a *civil* conscience! It is a good joke; an excellent joke. All the consciences *I* have ever heard of were nagging, badgering, fault-finding, execrable savages! Yes; and always in a sweat about some poor little insignificant trifle or other — destruction catch the lot of them, *I* say! I would trade mine for the small-pox and seven kinds of consumption, and be glad of the chance. Now tell me, why *is* it that a conscience can't haul a man over the coals once, for an offense, and then let him alone? Why is it that it wants to keep on pegging at him, day and night and night and day, week in and week out, forever and ever, about the same old thing? There is no sense in that, and no reason in it. I think a conscience that will act like that is meaner than the very dirt itself."

"Well, *we* like it; that suffices."

"Do you do it with the honest intent to improve a man?"

That question produced a sarcastic smile, and this reply:

"No, sir. Excuse me. We do it simply because it is 'business.' It is our trade. The *purpose* of it *is* to improve the man, but *we* are merely disinterested agents. We are appointed by authority, and haven't anything to say in the matter. We obey orders and leave the consequences where they belong. But I am willing to admit this much: we *do* crowd the orders a trifle when we get a chance, which is most of the time. We enjoy it. We are instructed to remind a man a few times of an error; and I don't mind acknowledging that we try to give pretty good measure. And when we get hold of a man of a peculiarly sensitive nature, oh, but we do haze him! I have consciences to come all the way from China and Russia to see a person of that kind put through his paces, on a special occasion. Why, I knew a man of that sort who had accidentally crippled a mulatto baby; the news went abroad, and I wish you may never commit another sin if the consciences didn't flock from all over the earth to enjoy the fun and help his master exercise him. That man walked the floor in torture for forty-eight hours, without eating or sleeping, and then blew his brains out. The child was perfectly well again in three weeks."

"Well, you are a precious crew, not to put it too strong. I think I begin to see now why you have always been a trifle inconsistent with me. In your anxiety to get all the juice you can out of a sin, you make a man repent of it in three or four different ways. For instance, you found fault with me for lying to that tramp, and I suffered over that. But it was only yesterday that I told a tramp the square truth, to wit, that, it being regarded as bad citizenship to encourage vagrancy, I would give him nothing. What did you do *then?* Why, you made me say to myself, 'Ah, it would have been so much kinder and more blameless to ease him off with a little white lie, and send him away feeling that if he could not have bread, the gentle treatment was at least something to be grateful for!' Well, I suffered all day about *that.* Three days before I had fed a tramp, and fed him freely, supposing it a virtuous act. Straight off you said, 'Oh, false citizen, to have fed a tramp!' and I suffered as usual. I gave a tramp work; you objected to it — *after* the contract was made, of course; you never speak up beforehand. Next, I *refused* a tramp work; you objected to *that.* Next, I proposed to kill a tramp; you kept me awake all night, oozing remorse at every pore. Sure I was going to be right *this* time, I sent the next tramp away with my benediction; and I wish you may live as long as I do, if you didn't make me smart all night again because I didn't kill him. Is there *any* way of satisfying that malignant invention which is called a conscience?"

"Ha, ha! this is luxury! Go on!"

"But come, now, answer me that question. *Is* there any way?"

"Well, none that I propose to tell *you*, my son. Ass! I don't care *what* act you may turn your hand to, I can straightway whisper a word in your ear and make you think you have committed a dreadful meanness. It is my *business* — and my joy — to make you repent of *every*thing you do. If I have fooled away any opportunities it was not intentional; I beg to assure you it was not intentional!"

"Don't worry; you haven't missed a trick that *I* know of. I never did a thing in all my life, virtuous or otherwise, that I didn't repent of in twenty-four hours. In church last Sunday I listened to a charity sermon. My first impulse was to give three hundred and fifty dollars; I repented of that and reduced it a hundred; repented of that and reduced it another hundred; repented of that and reduced it another hundred; repented of that and reduced the remaining fifty to twenty-five; repented of that and came down to fifteen; repented of that and dropped to two dollars and a half; when the plate came around at last, I repented once more and contributed ten cents. Well, when I got home, I did wish to goodness I had that ten cents back again! You never *did* let me get through a charity sermon without having something to sweat about."

"Oh, and I never shall, I never shall. You can always depend on me."

"I think so. Many and many's the restless night I've wanted to take you by the neck. If I could only get hold of you now!"

"Yes, no doubt. But I am not an ass; I am only the saddle of an ass. But go on, go on. You entertain me more than I like to confess."

"I am glad of that. (You will not mind my lying a little, to keep in practice.) Look here; not to be too personal, I think you are about the shabbiest and most contemptible little shriveled-up reptile that can be imagined. I am grateful enough that you are invisible to other people, for I should die with shame to be seen with such a mildewed monkey of a conscience as *you* are. Now if you were five or six feet high, and —"

" Oh, come! who is to blame?"

" *I* don't know."

" Why, you are; nobody else."

" Confound you, I wasn't consulted about your personal appearance."

" I don't care, you had a good deal to do with it, nevertheless. When you were eight or nine years old, I was seven feet high, and as pretty as a picture."

" I wish you had died young! So you have grown the wrong way, have you?"

" Some of us grow one way and some the other. You had a large conscience once; if you've a small conscience now I reckon there are reasons for it. However, both of us are to blame, you and I. You see, you used to be conscientious about a great many things; morbidly so, I may say. It was a great many years ago. You probably do not remember it now. Well, I took a great interest in my work, and I so enjoyed the anguish which certain pet sins of yours afflicted you with, that I kept pelting at you until I rather overdid the matter. You began to rebel. Of course I began to lose ground, then, and shrivel a little — diminish in stature, get mouldy, and grow deformed. The more I weakened, the more stubbornly you fastened on to those particular sins; till at last the places on my person that represent those vices became as callous as shark skin. Take smoking, for instance. I played that card a little too long, and I lost. When people plead with you at this late day to quit that vice, that old callous place seems to enlarge and cover me all over like a shirt of mail. It exerts a mysterious, smothering effect; and presently I, your faithful hater,

21

your devoted Conscience, go sound asleep! Sound?
It is no name for it. I couldn't hear it thunder at
such a time. You have some few other vices — perhaps eighty, or maybe ninety — that affect me in much
the same way."

"This is flattering; you must be asleep a good part
of your time."

"Yes, of late years. I should be asleep *all* the
time, but for the help I get."

"Who helps you?"

"Other consciences. Whenever a person whose
conscience I am acquainted with tries to plead with
you about the vices you are callous to, I get my friend
to give his client a pang concerning some villainy of his
own, and that shuts off his meddling and starts him off
to hunt personal consolation. My field of usefulness
is about trimmed down to tramps, budding authoresses,
and that line of goods now; but don't you worry —
I'll harry you on *them* while they last! Just you put
your trust in me."

"I think I can. But if you had only been good
enough to mention these facts some thirty years ago, I
should have turned my particular attention to sin, and
I think that by this time I should not only have had
you pretty permanently asleep on the entire list of
human vices, but reduced to the size of a homœopathic
pill, at that. That is about the style of conscience *I*
am pining for. If I only had you shrunk down to a
homœopathic pill, and could get my hands on you,
would I put you in a glass case for a keepsake? No,
sir. I would give you to a yellow dog! That is where
you ought to be — you and all your tribe. You are
not fit to be in society, in my opinion. Now another
question. Do you know a good many consciences in
this section?"

"Plenty of them."

"I would give anything to see some of them! Could you bring them here? And would they be visible to me?"

"Certainly not."

"I suppose I ought to have known that without asking. But no matter, you can describe them. Tell me about my neighbor Thompson's conscience, please."

"Very well. I know him intimately; have known him many years. I knew him when he was eleven feet high and of a faultless figure. But he is very rusty and tough and misshapen now, and hardly ever interests himself about anything. As to his present size — well, he sleeps in a cigar box."

"Likely enough. There are few smaller, meaner men in this region than Hugh Thompson. Do you know Robinson's conscience?"

"Yes. He is a shade under four and a half feet high; used to be a blonde; is a brunette now, but still shapely and comely."

"Well, Robinson is a good fellow. Do you know Tom Smith's conscience?"

"I have known him from childhood. He was thirteen inches high, and rather sluggish, when he was two years old — as nearly all of us are at that age. He is thirty-seven feet high now, and the stateliest figure in America. His legs are still racked with growing-pains, but he has a good time, nevertheless. Never sleeps. He is the most active and energetic member of the New England Conscience Club; is president of it. Night and day you can find him pegging away at Smith, panting with his labor, sleeves rolled up, countenance all alive with enjoyment. He has got his victim splendidly dragooned now. He can make poor Smith imagine that the most innocent little thing he does is an odious sin; and then he sets to work and almost tortures the soul out of him about it."

21**

"Smith is the noblest man in all this section, and the purest; and yet is always breaking his heart because he cannot be good! Only a conscience *could* find pleasure in heaping agony upon a spirit like that. Do you know my aunt Mary's conscience?"

"I have seen her at a distance, but am not acquainted with her. She lives in the open air altogether, because no door is large enough to admit her."

"I can believe that. Let me see. Do you know the conscience of that publisher who once stole some sketches of mine for a 'series' of his, and then left me to pay the law expenses I had to incur in order to choke him off?"

"Yes. He has a wide fame. He was exhibited, a month ago, with some other antiquities, for the benefit of a recent Member of the Cabinet's conscience that was starving in exile. Tickets and fares were high, but I traveled for nothing by pretending to be the conscience of an editor, and got in for half-price by representing myself to be the conscience of a clergyman. However, the publisher's conscience, which was to have been the main feature of the entertainment, was a failure — as an exhibition. He was there, but what of that? The management had provided a microscope with a magnifying power of only thirty thousand diameters, and so nobody got to see him, after all. There was great and general dissatisfaction, of course, but —"

Just here there was an eager footstep on the stair; I opened the door, and my aunt Mary burst into the room. It was a joyful meeting and a cheery bombardment of questions and answers concerning family matters ensued. By and by my aunt said:

"But I am going to abuse you a little now. You promised me, the day I saw you last, that you would look after the needs of the poor family around the corner as faithfully as I had done it myself. Well, I found out by accident that you failed of your promise. *Was* that right?"

In simple truth, I never had thought of that family a second time! And now such a splintering pang of guilt shot through me! I glanced up at my Conscience. Plainly, my heavy heart was affecting him. His body was drooping forward; he seemed about to fall from the bookcase. My aunt continued:

"And think how you have neglected my poor *protégé* at the almshouse, you dear, hard-hearted promise-breaker!" I blushed scarlet, and my tongue was tied. As the sense of my guilty negligence waxed sharper and stronger, my Conscience began to sway heavily back and forth; and when my aunt, after a little pause, said in a grieved tone, "Since you never once went to see her, maybe it will not distress you now to know that that poor child died, months ago, utterly friendless and forsaken!" my Conscience could no longer bear up under the weight of my sufferings, but tumbled headlong from his high perch and struck the floor with a dull, leaden thump. He lay there writhing with pain and quaking with apprehension, but straining every muscle in frantic efforts to get up. In a fever of expectancy I sprang to the door, locked it, placed my back against it, and bent a watchful gaze upon my struggling master. Already my fingers were itching to begin their murderous work.

"Oh, what *can* be the matter!" exclaimed by aunt, shrinking from me, and following with her frightened eyes the direction of mine. My breath was coming in short, quick gasps now, and my excitement was almost uncontrollable. My aunt cried out:

"Oh, do not look so! You appall me! Oh, what can the matter be? What is it you see? Why do you stare so? Why do you work your fingers like that?"

U**

"Peace, woman!" I said, in a hoarse whisper. "Look elsewhere; pay no attention to me; it is nothing — nothing. I am often this way. It will pass in a moment. It comes from smoking too much."

My injured lord was up, wild-eyed with terror, and trying to hobble toward the door. I could hardly breathe, I was so wrought up. My aunt wrung her hands, and said:

"Oh, I knew how it would be; I knew it would come to this at last! Oh, I implore you to crush out that fatal habit while it may yet be time! You must not, you shall not be deaf to my supplications longer!" My struggling Conscience showed sudden signs of weariness! "Oh, promise me you will throw off this hateful slavery of tobacco!" My Conscience began to reel drowsily, and grope with his hands — enchanting spectacle! "I beg you, I beseech you, I implore you! Your reason is deserting you! There is madness in your eye! It flames with frenzy! Oh, hear me, hear me, and be saved! See, I plead with you on my very knees!" As she sank before me my Conscience reeled again, and then drooped languidly to the floor, blinking toward me a last supplication for mercy, with heavy eyes. "Oh, promise, or you are lost! Promise, and be redeemed! Promise! Promise and live!" With a long-drawn sigh my conquered Conscience closed his eyes and fell fast asleep!

With an exultant shout I sprang past my aunt, and in an instant I had my lifelong foe by the throat. After so many years of waiting and longing, he was mine at last. I tore him to shreds and fragments. I rent the fragments to bits. I cast the bleeding rubbish into the fire, and drew into my nostrils the grateful incense of my burnt-offering. At last, and forever, my Conscience was dead!

I was a free man! I turned upon my poor aunt, who was almost petrified with terror, and shouted:

"Out of this with your paupers, your charities, your reforms, your pestilent morals! You behold before you a man whose life-conflict is done, whose soul is at peace; a man whose heart is dead to sorrow, dead to suffering, dead to remorse; a man WITHOUT A CON-SCIENCE! In my joy I spare you, though I could throttle you and never feel a pang! Fly!"

She fled. Since that day my life is all bliss. Bliss, unalloyed bliss. Nothing in all the world could per-suade me to have a conscience again. I settled all my old outstanding scores, and began the world anew. I killed thirty-eight persons during the first two weeks — all of them on account of ancient grudges. I burned a dwelling that interrupted my view. I swindled a widow and some orphans out of their last cow, which is a very good one, though not thoroughbred, I believe. I have also committed scores of crimes, of various kinds, and have enjoyed my work exceedingly, whereas it would formerly have broken my heart and turned my hair gray, I have no doubt.

In conclusion, I wish to state, by way of advertise-ment, that medical colleges desiring assorted tramps for scientific purposes, either by the gross, by cord measurement, or per ton, will do well to examine the lot in my cellar before purchasing elsewhere, as these were all selected and prepared by myself, and can be had at a low rate, because I wish to clear out my stock and get ready for the spring trade.

ABOUT MAGNANIMOUS-INCIDENT LITERATURE

ALL my life, from boyhood up, I have had the habit of reading a certain set of anecdotes, written in the quaint vein of The World's ingenious Fabulist, for the lesson they taught me and the pleasure they gave me. They lay always convenient to my hand, and whenever I thought meanly of my kind I turned to them, and they banished that sentiment; whenever I felt myself to be selfish, sordid, and ignoble I turned to them, and they told me what to do to win back my self-respect. Many times I wished that the charming anecdotes had not stopped with their happy climaxes, but had continued the pleasing history of the several benefactors and beneficiaries. This wish rose in my breast so persistently that at last I determined to satisfy it by seeking out the sequels of those anecdotes myself. So I set about it, and after great labor and tedious research accomplished my task. I will lay the result before you, giving you each anecdote in its turn, and following it with its sequel as I gathered it through my investigations.

THE GRATEFUL POODLE

One day a benevolent physician (who had read the books) having found a stray poodle suffering from a broken leg, conveyed the poor creature to his home,

and after setting and bandaging the injured limb gave
the little outcast its liberty again, and thought no more
about the matter. But how great was his surprise,
upon opening his door one morning, some days later,
to find the grateful poodle patiently waiting there, and
in its company another stray dog, one of whose legs,
by some accident, had been broken. The kind physician at once relieved the distressed animal, nor did he
forget to admire the inscrutable goodness and mercy of
God, who had been willing to use so humble an instrument as the poor outcast poodle for the inculcating of,
etc., etc., etc.

SEQUEL

The next morning the benevolent physician found
the two dogs, beaming with gratitude, waiting at his
door, and with them two other dogs — cripples. The
cripples were speedily healed, and the four went their
way, leaving the benevolent physician more overcome
by pious wonder than ever. The day passed, the
morning came. There at the door sat now the four
reconstructed dogs, and with them four others requir-
ing reconstruction. This day also passed, and another
morning came; and now sixteen dogs, eight of them
newly crippled, occupied the sidewalk, and the people
were going around. By noon the broken legs were all
set, but the pious wonder in the good physician's
breast was beginning to get mixed with involuntary
profanity. The sun rose once more, and exhibited
thirty-two dogs, sixteen of them with broken legs, oc-
cupying the sidewalk and half of the street; the human
spectators took up the rest of the room. The cries of
the wounded, the songs of the healed brutes, and the
comments of the on-looking citizens made great and in-
spiring cheer, but traffic was interrupted in that street.
The good physician hired a couple of assistant surgeons

and got through his benevolent work before dark, first taking the precaution to cancel his church membership, so that he might express himself with the latitude which the case required.

But some things have their limits. When once more the morning dawned, and the good physician looked out upon a massed and far-reaching multitude of clamorous and beseeching dogs, he said, " I might as well acknowledge it, I have been fooled by the books; they only tell the pretty part of the story, and then stop. Fetch me the shotgun; this thing has gone along far enough."

He issued forth with his weapon, and chanced to step upon the tail of the original poodle, who promptly bit him in the leg. Now the great and good work which this poodle had been engaged in had engendered in him such a mighty and augmenting enthusiasm as to turn his weak head at last and drive him mad. A month later, when the benevolent physician lay in the death throes of hydrophobia, he called his weeping friends about him, and said:

" Beware of the books. They tell but half of the story. Whenever a poor wretch asks you for help, and you feel a doubt as to what result may flow from your benevolence, give yourself the benefit of the doubt and kill the applicant."

And so saying he turned his face to the wall and gave up the ghost.

THE BENEVOLENT AUTHOR

A poor and young literary beginner had tried in vain to get his manuscripts accepted. At last, when the horrors of starvation were staring him in the face, he laid his sad case before a celebrated author, beseeching his counsel and assistance. This generous man immediately put aside his own matters and proceeded to peruse one of the despised manuscripts. Having completed his kindly task, he shook the poor young man cordially by the hand, saying, "I perceive merit in this; come again to me on Monday." At the time specified, the celebrated author, with a sweet smile, but saying nothing, spread open a magazine which was damp from the press. What was the poor young man's astonishment to discover upon the printed page his own article. "How can I ever," said he, falling upon his knees and bursting into tears, "testify my gratitude for this noble conduct!"

The celebrated author was the renowned Snodgrass; the poor young beginner thus rescued from obscurity and starvation was the afterwards equally renowned Snagsby. Let this pleasing incident admonish us to turn a charitable ear to all beginners that need help.

SEQUEL

The next week Snagsby was back with five rejected manuscripts. The celebrated author was a little surprised, because in the books the young struggler had needed but one lift, apparently. However, he plowed through these papers, removing unnecessary flowers and digging up some acres of adjective stumps, and then succeeded in getting two of the articles accepted.

A week or so drifted by, and the grateful Snagsby arrived with another cargo. The celebrated author had felt a mighty glow of satisfaction within himself the first time he had successfully befriended the poor young struggler, and had compared himself with the generous people in the books with high gratification; but he was beginning to suspect now that he had struck upon something fresh in the noble-episode line. His enthusiasm took a chill. Still, he could not bear to repulse this struggling young author, who clung to him with such pretty simplicity and trustfulness.

Well, the upshot of it all was that the celebrated author presently found himself permanently freighted with the poor young beginner. All his mild efforts to unload this cargo went for nothing. He had to give daily counsel, daily encouragement; he had to keep on procuring magazine acceptances, and then revamping the manuscripts to make them presentable. When the young aspirant got a start at last, he rode into sudden fame by describing the celebrated author's private life with such a caustic humor and such minuteness of blistering detail that the book sold a prodigious edition, and broke the celebrated author's heart with mortification. With his latest gasp he said, "Alas, the books deceived me; they do not tell the whole story. Beware of the struggling young author, my friends. Whom God sees fit to starve, let not man presumptuously rescue to his own undoing."

THE GRATEFUL HUSBAND

One day a lady was driving through the principal street of a great city with her little boy, when the horses took fright and dashed madly away, hurling the coachman from his box and leaving the occupants of the carriage paralyzed with terror. But a brave youth who was driving a grocery wagon threw himself before the plunging animals, and succeeded in arresting their flight at the peril of his own.* The grateful lady took his number, and upon arriving at her home she related the heroic act to her husband (who had read the books), who listened with streaming eyes to the moving recital, and who, after returning thanks, in conjunction with his restored loved ones, to Him who suffereth not even a sparrow to fall to the ground unnoticed, sent for the

---

* This is probably a misprint.— M. T.

brave young person, and, placing a check for five
hundred dollars in his hand, said, "Take this as a reward for your noble act, William Ferguson, and if ever
you shall need a friend, remember that Thompson Mc-
Spadden has a grateful heart." Let us learn from this
that a good deed cannot fail to benefit the doer, however humble he may be.

SEQUEL

William Ferguson called the next week and asked
Mr. McSpadden to use his influence to get him a
higher employment, he feeling capable of better things
than driving a grocer's wagon. Mr. McSpadden got
him an underclerkship at a good salary.

Presently William Ferguson's mother fell sick, and
William — Well, to cut the story short, Mr. Mc-
Spadden consented to take her into his house. Before
long she yearned for the society of her younger
children; so Mary and Julia were admitted also, and
little Jimmy, their brother. Jimmy had a pocket-knife,
and he wandered into the drawing-room with it one
day, alone, and reduced ten thousand dollars' worth of
furniture to an indeterminable value in rather less than
three-quarters of an hour. A day or two later he fell
downstairs and broke his neck, and seventeen of his
family's relatives came to the house to attend the
funeral. This made them acquainted, and they kept
the kitchen occupied after that, and likewise kept the
McSpaddens busy hunting up situations of various sorts
for them, and hunting up more when they wore these
out. The old woman drank a good deal and swore a good
deal; but the grateful McSpaddens knew it was their
duty to reform her, considering what her son had done
for them, so they clave nobly to their generous task.
William came often and got decreasing sums of money,
and asked for higher and more lucrative employments

22**

— which the grateful McSpadden more or less promptly procured for him. McSpadden consented also, after some demur, to fit William for college; but when the first vacation came and the hero requested to be sent to Europe for his health, the persecuted McSpadden rose against the tyrant and revolted. He plainly and squarely refused. William Ferguson's mother was so astounded that she let her gin-bottle drop, and her profane lips refused to do their office. When she recovered she said in a half-gasp, '' Is this your gratitude? Where would your wife and boy be now, but for my son?''

William said, '' Is this your gratitude? Did I save your wife's life or not? Tell me that !''

Seven relations swarmed in from the kitchen and each said, ''And this is his gratitude !''

William's sisters stared, bewildered, and said, ''And this is his grat —'' but were interrupted by their mother, who burst into tears and exclaimed, '' To think that my sainted little Jimmy threw away his life in the service of such a reptile !''

Then the pluck of the revolutionary McSpadden rose to the occasion, and he replied with fervor, '' Out of my house, the whole beggarly tribe of you ! I was beguiled by the books, but shall never be beguiled again — once is sufficient for me.'' And turning to William he shouted, '' Yes, you did save my wife's life, and the next man that does it shall die in his tracks !''

Not being a clergyman, I place my text at the end of my sermon instead of at the beginning. Here it is, from Mr. Noah Brooks's Recollections of President Lincoln in *Scribner's Monthly :*

J. H. Hackett, in his part of Falstaff, was an actor who gave Mr. Lincoln great delight. With his usual desire to signify to others his sense of obligation, Mr. Lincoln wrote a genial little note to the actor expressing his pleasure at witnessing his performance. Mr. Hackett, in reply, sent a book of some sort; perhaps it was one of his own authorship. He also wrote several notes to the President. One night, quite late, when the episode had passed out of my mind, I went to the White House in answer to a message. Passing into the President's office, I noticed, to my surprise, Hackett sitting in the anteroom as if waiting for an audience. The President asked me if any one was outside. On being told, he said, half sadly, "Oh, I can't see him, I can't see him; I was in hopes he had gone away." Then he added, "Now this just illustrates the difficulty of having pleasant friends and acquaintances in this place. You know how I liked Hackett as an actor, and how I wrote to tell him so. He sent me that book, and there I thought the matter would end. He is a master of his place in the profession, I suppose, and well fixed in it; but just because we had a little friendly correspondence, such as any two men might have, he wants something. What do you suppose he wants ?" I could not guess, and Mr. Lincoln added, "Well, he wants to be consul to London. Oh, dear!"

I will observe, in conclusion, that the William Ferguson incident occurred, and within my personal knowledge — though I have changed the nature of the details, to keep William from recognizing himself in it.

All the readers of this article have in some sweet and gushing hour of their lives played the role of Magnanimous-Incident hero. I wish I knew how many there are among them who are willing to talk about that episode and like to be reminded of the consequences that flowed from it.

PUNCH, BROTHERS, PUNCH

WiLL the reader please to cast his eye over the following lines, and see if he can discover anything harmful in them?

> Conductor, when you receive a fare,
> Punch in the presence of the passenjare!
> A blue trip slip for an eight-cent fare,
> A buff trip slip for a six-cent fare,
> A pink trip slip for a three-cent fare,
> Punch in the presence of the passenjare!

> CHORUS
> Punch, brothers! punch with care!
> Punch in the presence of the passenjare!

I came across these jingling rhymes in a newspaper, a little while ago, and read them a couple of times. They took instant and entire possession of me. All through breakfast they went waltzing through my brain; and when, at last, I rolled up my napkin, I could not tell whether I had eaten anything or not. I had carefully laid out my day's work the day before — a thrilling tragedy in the novel which I am writing. I went to my den to begin my deed of blood. I took up my pen, but all I could get it to say was, " Punch in the presence of the passenjare." I fought hard for an hour, but it was useless. My head kept humming,

"A blue trip slip for an eight-cent fare, a buff trip slip for a six-cent fare," and so on and so on, without peace or respite. The day's work was ruined — I could see that plainly enough. I gave up and drifted down-town, and presently discovered that my feet were keeping time to that relentless jingle. When I could stand it no longer I altered my step. But it did no good; those rhymes accommodated themselves to the new step and went on harassing me just as before. I returned home, and suffered all the afternoon; suffered all through an unconscious and unrefreshing dinner; suffered, and cried, and jingled all through the evening; went to bed and rolled, tossed, and jingled right along, the same as ever; got up at midnight frantic, and tried to read; but there was nothing visible upon the whirling page except " Punch! punch in the presence of the passenjare." By sunrise I was out of my mind, and everybody marveled and was distressed at the idiotic burden of my ravings — "Punch! oh, punch! punch in the presence of the passenjare!"

Two days later, on Saturday morning, I arose, a tottering wreck, and went forth to fulfill an engagement with a valued friend, the Rev. Mr.———, to walk to the Talcott Tower, ten miles distant. He stared at me, but asked no questions. We started. Mr.——— talked, talked, talked — as is his wont. I said nothing; I heard nothing. At the end of a mile, Mr.——— said:

"Mark, are you sick? I never saw a man look so haggard and worn and absent-minded. Say something, do!"

Drearily, without enthusiasm, I said: "Punch, brothers, punch with care! Punch in the presence of the passenjare!"

My friend eyed me blankly, looked perplexed, then said:

aa

"I do not think I get your drift, Mark. There does not seem to be any relevancy in what you have said, certainly nothing sad; and yet — maybe it was the way you *said* the words — I never heard anything that sounded so pathetic. What is —"

But I heard no more. I was already far away with my pitiless, heart-breaking "blue trip slip for an eight-cent fare, buff trip slip for a six-cent fare, pink trip slip for a three-cent fare; punch in the presence of the passenjare." I do not know what occurred during the other nine miles. However, all of a sudden Mr. —— laid his hand on my shoulder and shouted:

"Oh, wake up! wake up! wake up! Don't sleep all day! Here we are at the Tower, man! I have talked myself deaf and dumb and blind, and never got a response. Just look at this magnificent autumn landscape! Look at it! look at it! Feast your eyes on it! You have traveled; you have seen boasted landscapes elsewhere. Come, now, deliver an honest opinion. What do you say to this?"

I sighed wearily, and murmured:

"A buff trip slip for a six-cent fare, a pink trip slip for a three-cent fare, punch in the presence of the passenjare."

Rev. Mr. —— stood there, very grave, full of concern, apparently, and looked long at me; then he said:

"Mark, there is something about this that I cannot understand. Those are about the same words you said before; there does not seem to be anything in them, and yet they nearly break my heart when you say them. Punch in the — how is it they go?"

I began at the beginning and repeated all the lines. My friend's face lighted with interest. He said:

"Why, what a captivating jingle it is! It is almost music. It flows along so nicely. I have nearly caught the rhymes myself. Say them over just once more, and then I'll have them, sure."

I said them over. Then Mr. —— said them. He made one little mistake, which I corrected. The next time and the next he got them right. Now a great burden seemed to tumble from my shoulders. That torturing jingle departed out of my brain, and a grateful sense of rest and peace descended upon me. I was light-hearted enough to sing; and I did sing for half an hour, straight along, as we went jogging homeward. Then my freed tongue found blessed speech again, and the pent talk of many a weary hour began to gush and flow. It flowed on and on, joyously, jubilantly, until the fountain was empty and dry. As I wrung my friend's hand at parting, I said:

"Haven't we had a royal good time! But now I remember, you haven't said a word for two hours. Come, come, out with something!"

The Rev. Mr. —— turned a lack-lustre eye upon me, drew a deep sigh, and said, without animation, without apparent consciousness:

"Punch, brothers, punch with care! Punch in the presence of the passenjare!"

A pang shot through me as I said to myself, "Poor fellow, poor fellow! *he* has got it, now."

I did not see Mr. —— for two or three days after that. Then, on Tuesday evening, he staggered into my presence and sank dejectedly into a seat. He was pale, worn; he was a wreck. He lifted his faded eyes to my face and said:

"Ah, Mark, it was a ruinous investment that I made in those heartless rhymes. They have ridden me like a nightmare, day and night, hour after hour, to this very moment. Since I saw you I have suffered the torments of the lost. Saturday evening I had a sudden call, by telegraph, and took the night train for Boston.

22**

The occasion was the death of a valued old friend who
had requested that I should preach his funeral sermon.
I took my seat in the cars and set myself to framing
the discourse. But I never got beyond the opening
paragraph; for then the train started and the car-wheels
began their ' clack, clack — clack-clack-clack! clack-
clack — clack-clack-clack!' and right away those odious
rhymes fitted themselves to that accompaniment. For
an hour I sat there and set a syllable of those rhymes
to every separate and distinct clack the car-wheels
made. Why, I was as fagged out, then, as if I had
been chopping wood all day. My skull was splitting
with headache. It seemed to me that I must go mad
if I sat there any longer; so I undressed and went to
bed. I stretched myself out in my berth, and — well,
you know what the result was. The thing went right
along, just the same. ' Clack-clack-clack, a blue trip
slip, clack-clack-clack, for an eight-cent fare; clack-
clack-clack, a buff trip slip, clack-clack-clack, for a six-
cent fare, and so on, and so on, and so on — *punch* in
the presence of the passenjare!' Sleep? Not a single
wink! I was almost a lunatic when I got to Boston.
Don't ask me about the funeral. I did the best I could,
but every solemn individual sentence was meshed and
tangled and woven in and out with ' Punch, brothers,
punch with care, punch in the presence of the passenjare.' And the most distressing thing was that my
delivery dropped into the undulating rhythm of those
pulsing rhymes, and I could actually catch absent-
minded people nodding *time* to the swing of it
with their stupid heads. And, Mark, you may believe it or not, but before I got through, the entire
assemblage were placidly bobbing their heads in solemn
unison, mourners, undertaker, and all. The moment I
had finished, I fled to the anteroom in a state bordering
on frenzy. Of course it would be my luck to find a

sorrowing and aged maiden aunt of the deceased there, who had arrived from Springfield too late to get into the church. She began to sob, and said:

"'Oh, oh, he is gone, he is gone, and I didn't see him before he died!'

"'Yes!' I said, 'he *is* gone, he *is* gone, he *is* gone — oh, *will* this suffering never cease!'

"'*You* loved him, then! Oh, you too loved him!'

"'Loved him! Loved *who?*'

"'Why, my poor George! my poor nephew!'

"'Oh — *him!* Yes — oh, yes, yes. Certainly — certainly. Punch — punch — oh, this misery will kill me!'

"'Bless you! bless you, sir, for these sweet words! *I*, too, suffer in this dear loss. Were you present during his last moments?'

"'Yes. I — *whose* last moments?'

"'*His.* The dear departed's.'

"'Yes! Oh, yes — yes —*yes!* I suppose so, I think so, *I* don't know! Oh, certainly — I was there — *I* was there!'

"'Oh, what a privilege! what a precious privilege! And his last words — oh, tell me, tell me his last words! What did he say?'

"'He said — he said — oh, my head, my head, my head! He said — he said — he never said *any*thing but Punch, punch, *punch* in the presence of the passenjare! Oh, leave me, madam! In the name of all that is generous, leave me to my madness, my misery, my despair! — a buff trip slip for a six-cent fare, a pink trip slip for a three-cent fare — endu-rance *can* no fur-ther go! — PUNCH in the presence of the passenjare!'"

My friend's hopeless eyes rested upon mine a preg-nant minute, and then he said impressively:

"Mark, you do not say anything. You do not offer
v**

me any hope. But, ah me, it is just as well — it is just as well. You could not do me any good. The time has long gone by when words could comfort me. Something tells me that my tongue is doomed to wag forever to the jigger of that remorseless jingle. There — there it is coming on me again: a blue trip slip for an eight-cent fare, a buff trip slip for a —''

Thus murmuring faint and fainter, my friend sank into a peaceful trance and forgot his sufferings in a blessed respite.

How did I finally save him from an asylum? I took him to a neighboring university and made him discharge the burden of his persecuting rhymes into the eager ears of the poor, unthinking students. How is it with *them*, now? The result is too sad to tell. Why did I write this article? It was for a worthy, even a noble, purpose. It was to warn you, reader, if you should come across those merciless rhymes, to avoid them — avoid them as you would a pestilence!

THE GREAT REVOLUTION IN PITCAIRN

LET me refresh the reader's memory a little. Nearly a hundred years ago the crew of the British ship *Bounty* mutinied, set the captain and his officers adrift upon the open sea, took possession of the ship, and sailed southward. They procured wives for themselves among the natives of Tahiti, then proceeded to a lonely little rock in mid-Pacific, called Pitcairn's Island, wrecked the vessel, stripped her of everything that might be useful to a new colony, and established themselves on shore.

Pitcairn's is so far removed from the track of commerce that it was many years before another vessel touched there. It had always been considered an uninhabited island; so when a ship did at last drop its anchor there, in 1808, the captain was greatly surprised to find the place peopled. Although the mutineers had fought among themselves, and gradually killed each other off until only two or three of the original stock remained, these tragedies had not occurred before a number of children had been born; so in 1808 the island had a population of twenty-seven persons. John Adams, the chief mutineer, still survived, and was to live many years yet, as governor and patriarch of the flock. From being mutineer and homicide, he had turned Christian and teacher, and his nation of twenty-seven persons was now the purest and devoutest in Christendom. Adams had long ago hoisted the British flag and constituted his island an appanage of the British crown.

To-day the population numbers ninety persons — sixteen men, nineteen women, twenty-five boys, and thirty girls — all descendants of the mutineers, all bearing the family names of those mutineers, and all speaking English, and English only. The island stands high up out of the sea, and has precipitous walls. It is about three-quarters of a mile long, and in places is as much as half a mile wide. Such arable land as it affords is held by the several families, according to a division made many years ago. There is some live-stock — goats, pigs, chickens, and cats; but no dogs, and no large animals. There is one church building — used also as a capitol, a schoolhouse, and a public library. The title of the governor has been, for a generation or two, "Magistrate and Chief Ruler, in subordination to her Majesty the Queen of Great Britain." It was his province to *make* the laws, as well as execute them. His office was elective; every-body over seventeen years old had a vote — no matter about the sex.

The sole occupations of the people were farming and fishing; their sole recreation, religious services. There has never been a shop in the island, nor any money. The habits and dress of the people have always been primitive, and their laws simple to puerility. They have lived in a deep Sabbath tranquillity, far from the world and its ambitions and vexations, and neither knowing nor caring what was going on in the mighty empires that lie beyond their limitless ocean solitudes. Once in three or four years a ship touched there, moved them with aged news of bloody battles, devas-tating epidemics, fallen thrones, and ruined dynasties, then traded them some soap and flannel for some yams and breadfruit, and sailed away, leaving them to retire into their peaceful dreams and pious dissipations once more.

On the 8th of last September, Admiral de Horsey, commander-in-chief of the British fleet in the Pacific, visited Pitcairn's Island, and speaks as follows in his official report to the admiralty:

They have beans, carrots, turnips, cabbages, and a little maize; pineapples, fig-trees, custard-apples, and oranges; lemons, and cocoa-nuts. Clothing is obtained alone from passing ships, in barter for refreshments. There are no springs on the island, but as it rains generally once a month they have plenty of water, although at times, in former years, they have suffered from drought. No alcoholic liquors, except for medicinal purposes, are used, and a drunkard is unknown. . . .

The necessary articles required by the islanders are best shown by those we furnished in barter for refreshments: namely, flannel, serge, drill, half-boots, combs, tobacco, and soap. They also stand much in need of maps and slates for their school, and tools of any kind are most acceptable. I caused them to be supplied from the public stores with a union-jack for display on the arrival of ships, and a pit-saw, of which they were greatly in need. This, I trust, will meet the approval of their lordships. If the munificent people of England were only aware of the wants of this most deserving little colony, they would not long go unsupplied. . . .

Divine service is held every Sunday at 10.30 A.M. and at 3 P.M., in the house built and used by John Adams for that purpose until he died in 1829. It is conducted strictly in accordance with the liturgy of the Church of England, by Mr. Simon Young, their selected pastor, who is much respected. A Bible class is held every Wednesday, when all who conveniently can attend. There is also a general meeting for prayer on the first Friday in every month. Family prayers are said in every house the first thing in the morning and the last thing in the evening, and no food is partaken of without asking God's blessing before and afterwards. Of these islanders' religious attributes no one can speak without deep respect. A people whose greatest pleasure and privilege is to commune in prayer with their God, and to join in hymns of praise, and who are, moreover, cheerful, diligent, and probably freer from vice than any other community, need no priest among them.

Now I come to a sentence in the admiral's report which he dropped carelessly from his pen, no doubt, and never gave the matter a second thought. He little imagined what a freight of tragic prophecy it bore! This is the sentence:

One stranger, an American, has settled on the island — *a doubtful acquisition*.

A doubtful acquisition, indeed! Captain Ormsby, in the American ship *Hornet*, touched at Pitcairn's nearly four months after the admiral's visit, and from the facts which he gathered there we now know all about that American. Let us put these facts together in historical form. The American's name was Butter-worth Stavely. As soon as he had become well acquainted with all the people — and this took but a few days, of course — he began to ingratiate himself with them by all the arts he could command. He became exceedingly popular, and much looked up to; for one of the first things he did was to forsake his worldly way of life, and throw all his energies into religion. He was always reading his Bible, or praying, or singing hymns, or asking blessings. In prayer, no one had such "liberty" as he, no one could pray so long or so well.

At last, when he considered the time to be ripe, he began secretly to sow the seeds of discontent among the people. It was his deliberate purpose, from the beginning, to subvert the government, but of course he kept that to himself for a time. He used different arts with different individuals. He awakened dissatisfaction in one quarter by calling attention to the shortness of the Sunday services; he argued that there should be three three-hour services on Sunday instead of only two. Many had secretly held this opinion before; they now privately banded themselves into a party to work for it. He showed certain of the women that they were not allowed sufficient voice in the prayer-meetings; thus another party was formed. No weapon was beneath his notice; he even descended to the children, and awoke discontent in their breasts because — as *he* discovered for them — they had not enough Sunday-school. This created a third party.

Now, as the chief of these parties, he found himself the strongest power in the community. So he proceeded to his next move — a no less important one than the impeachment of the chief magistrate, James Russell Nickoy; a man of character and ability, and possessed of great wealth, he being the owner of a house with a parlor to it, three acres and a half of yam land, and the only boat in Pitcairn's, a whale-boat; and, most unfortunately, a pretext for this impeachment offered itself at just the right time. One of the earliest and most precious laws of the island was the law against trespass. It was held in great reverence, and was regarded as the palladium of the people's liberties. About thirty years ago an important case came before the courts under this law, in this wise: a chicken belonging to Elizabeth Young (aged, at that time, fifty-eight, a daughter of John Mills, one of the mutineers of the *Bounty*) trespassed upon the grounds of Thursday October Christian (aged twenty-nine, a grandson of Fletcher Christian, one of the mutineers). Christian killed the chicken. According to the law, Christian could keep the chicken; or, if he preferred, he could restore its remains to the owner, and receive damages in " produce " to an amount equivalent to the waste and injury wrought by the trespasser. The court records set forth that " the said Christian aforesaid did deliver the aforesaid remains to the said Elizabeth Young, and did demand one bushel of yams in satisfaction of the damage done." But Elizabeth Young considered the demand exorbitant; the parties could not agree; therefore Christian brought suit in the courts. He 'ost his case in the justice's court; at least, he was awarded only a half peck of yams, which he considered insufficient, and in the nature of a defeat. He appealed. The case lingered several years in an ascending grade of courts, and always resulted in decrees sustaining the original verdict; and finally the thing got into the supreme court, and there it stuck for twenty years. But last summer, even the supreme court managed to arrive at a decision at last. Once more the original verdict was sustained. Christian then said he was satisfied; but Stavely was present, and whispered to him and to his lawyer, suggesting, "as a mere form," that the original law be exhibited, in order to make sure that it still existed. It seemed an odd idea, but an ingenious one. So the demand was made. A messenger was sent to the magistrate's house; he presently returned with the tidings that it had disappeared from among the state archives.

The court now pronounced its late decision void, since it had been made under a law which had no actual existence.

Great excitement ensued immediately. The news swept abroad over the whole island that the palladium of the public liberties was lost — maybe treasonably destroyed. Within thirty minutes almost the entire nation were in the courtroom — that is to say, the church. The impeachment of the chief magistrate followed, upon Stavely's motion. The accused met his misfortune with the dignity which became his great office. He did not plead, or even argue; he offered the simple defense that he had not meddled with the missing law; that he had kept the state archives in the same candle-box that had been used as their depository from the beginning; and that he was innocent of the removal or destruction of the lost document.

But nothing could save him; he was found guilty of misprision of treason, and degraded from his office, and all his property was confiscated.

The lamest part of the whole shameful matter was the *reason* suggested by his enemies for his destruction of the law, to wit: that he did it to favor Christian, because Christian was his cousin! Whereas Stavely was the only individual in the entire nation who was *not* his cousin. The reader must remember that all these people are the descendants of half a dozen men; that the first children intermarried together and bore grandchildren to the mutineers; that these grandchildren intermarried; after them, great and great-great-grandchildren intermarried; so that to-day everybody is blood kin to everybody. Moreover, the relationships are wonderfully, even astoundingly, mixed up and complicated. A stranger, for instance, says to an islander:

"You speak of that young woman as your cousin; a while ago you called her your aunt."

"Well, she *is* my aunt, and my cousin, too. And also my step-sister, my niece, my fourth cousin, my thirty-third cousin, my forty-second cousin, my great-aunt, my grandmother; my widowed sister-in-law — and next week she will be my wife."

So the charge of nepotism against the chief magistrate was weak. But no matter; weak or strong, it suited Stavely. Stavely was immediately elected to the vacant magistracy, and, oozing reform from every pore, he went vigorously to work. In no long time religious services raged everywhere and unceasingly. By command, the second prayer of the Sunday morning service, which had customarily endured some thirty-five or forty minutes, and had pleaded for the world, first by continent and then by national and tribal detail, was extended to an hour and a half, and made to in-

23 **

clude supplications in behalf of the possible peoples in
the several planets.   Everybody was pleased with this;
everybody said, "Now *this* is something *like*."   By
command, the usual three-hour sermons were doubled
in length.   The nation came in a body to testify their
gratitude to the new magistrate.   The old law for-
bidding cooking on the Sabbath was extended to the
prohibition of eating, also.   By command, Sunday-
school was privileged to spread over into the week.
The joy of all classes was complete.   In one short
month the new magistrate had become the people's
idol!

The time was ripe for this man's next move.   He
began, cautiously at first, to poison the public mind
against England.   He took the chief citizens aside,
one by one, and conversed with them on this topic.
Presently he grew bolder, and spoke out.   He said the
nation owed it to itself, to its honor, to its great tradi-
tions, to rise in its might and throw off "this galling
English yoke."

But the simple islanders answered:

"We had not noticed that it galled.   How does it
gall?   England sends a ship once in three or four years
to give us soap and clothing, and things which we
sorely need and gratefully receive; but she never
troubles us; she lets us go our own way."

"She lets you go your own way!   So slaves have
felt and spoken in all the ages!   This speech shows
how fallen you are, how base, how brutalized you
have become, under this grinding tyranny!   What!
has all manly pride forsaken you?   Is liberty nothing?
Are you content to be a mere appendage to a foreign
and hateful sovereignty, when you might rise up and
take your rightful place in the august family of nations,
great, free, enlightened, independent, the minion of no
sceptered master, but the arbiter of your own destiny,

and a voice and a power in decreeing the destinies of
your sister-sovereignties of the world?''

Speeches like this produced an effect by and by.
Citizens began to feel the English yoke; they did not
know exactly how or whereabouts they felt it, but they
were perfectly certain they did feel it. They got to
grumbling a good deal, and chafing under their chains,
and longing for relief and release. They presently fell
to hating the English flag, that sign and symbol of their
nation's degradation; they ceased to glance up at it as
they passed the capitol, but averted their eyes and
grated their teeth; and one morning, when it was
found trampled into the mud at the foot of the staff,
they left it there, and no man put his hand to it to
hoist it again. A certain thing which was sure to happen sooner or later happened now. Some of the chief
citizens went to the magistrate by night, and said:

'' We can endure this hated tyranny no longer. How
can we cast it off?''

'' By a *coup d'état*.''

'' How?''

'' A coup d'état. It is like this: everything is got
ready, and at the appointed moment I, as the official
head of the nation, publicly and solemnly proclaim its
independence, and absolve it from allegiance to any
and all other powers whatsoever.''

'' That sounds simple and easy. We can do that
right away. Then what will be the next thing to do?''

'' Seize all the defenses and public properties of all
kinds, establish martial law, put the army and navy on
a war footing, and proclaim the empire!''

This fine program dazzled these innocents. They
said:

'' This is grand — this is splendid; but will not England resist?''

'' Let her. This rock is a Gibraltar.''

"True. But about the empire? Do we *need* an empire and an emperor?"

"What you *need*, my friends, is unification. Look at Germany; look at Italy. They are unified. Unification is the thing. It makes living dear. That constitutes progress. We must have a standing army, and a navy. Taxes follow, as a matter of course. All these things summed up make grandeur. With unification and grandeur, what more can you want? Very well — only the empire can confer these boons."

So on the 8th day of December Pitcairn's Island was proclaimed a free and independent nation; and on the same day the solemn coronation of Butterworth I., emperor of Pitcairn's Island, took place, amid great rejoicings and festivities. The entire nation, with the exception of fourteen persons, mainly little children, marched past the throne in single file, with banners and music, the procession being upwards of ninety feet long; and some said it was as much as three-quarters of a minute passing a given point. Nothing like it had ever been seen in the history of the island before. Public enthusiasm was measureless.

Now straightway imperial reforms began. Orders of nobility were instituted. A minister of the navy was appointed, and the whale-boat put in commission. A minister of war was created, and ordered to proceed at once with the formation of a standing army. A first lord of the treasury was named, and commanded to get up a taxation scheme, and also open negotiations for treaties, offensive, defensive, and commercial, with foreign powers. Some generals and admirals were appointed; also some chamberlains, some equerries in waiting, and some lords of the bedchamber.

At this point all the material was used up. The Grand Duke of Galilee, minister of war, complained that all the sixteen grown men in the empire had been given great offices, and consequently would not consent to serve in the ranks; wherefore his standing army was at a standstill. The Marquis of Ararat, minister of the navy, made a similar complaint. He said he was willing to steer the whale-boat himself, but he *must* have somebody to man her.

The emperor did the best he could in the circumstances: he took all the boys above the age of ten years away from their mothers, and pressed them into the army, thus constructing a corps of seventeen privates, officered by one lieutenant-general and two major-generals. This pleased the minister of war, but procured the enmity of all the mothers in the land; for they said their precious ones must now find bloody graves in the fields of war, and he would be answerable for it. Some of the more heartbroken and unappeasable among them lay constantly in wait for the emperor and threw yams at him, unmindful of the bodyguard.

On account of the extreme scarcity of material, it was found necessary to require the Duke of Bethany, postmaster-general, to pull stroke-oar in the navy, and thus sit in the rear of a noble of lower degree, namely, Viscount Canaan, lord justice of the common pleas. This turned the Duke of Bethany into a tolerably open malcontent and a secret conspirator — a thing which the emperor foresaw, but could not help.

Things went from bad to worse. The emperor raised Nancy Peters to the peerage on one day, and married her the next, notwithstanding, for reasons of state, the cabinet had strenuously advised him to marry Emmeline, eldest daughter of the Archbishop of Bethlehem. This caused trouble in a powerful quarter — the church. The new empress secured the support and friendship of two-thirds of the thirty-six grown women in the nation by absorbing them into her court as maids of honor; but this made deadly enemies of the remaining twelve.

23

The families of the maids of honor soon began to rebel,
because there was nobody at home to keep house.
The twelve snubbed women refused to enter the imperial kitchen as servants; so the empress had to require
the Countess of Jericho and other great court dames to
fetch water, sweep the palace, and perform other menial
and equally distasteful services. This made bad blood
in that department.

Everybody fell to complaining that the taxes levied
for the support of the army, the navy, and the rest of
the imperial establishment were intolerably burdensome,
and were reducing the nation to beggary. The emperor's reply —'' Look at Germany; look at Italy. Are
you better than they? and haven't you unification?''—
did not satisfy them. They said, '' People can't *eat*
unification, and we are starving. Agriculture has
ceased. Everybody is in the army, everybody is in the
navy, everybody is in the public service, standing
around in a uniform, with nothing whatever to do,
nothing to eat, and nobody to till the fields —''

'' Look at Germany; look at Italy. It is the same
there. Such is unification, and there's no other way
to get it — no other way to keep it after you've got it,''
said the poor emperor always.

But the grumblers only replied, '' We can't *stand* the
taxes — we can't *stand* them.''

Now right on top of this the cabinet reported a
national debt amounting to upwards of forty-five dollars — half a dollar to every individual in the nation.
And they proposed to fund something. They had
heard that this was always done in such emergencies.
They proposed duties on exports; also on imports.
And they wanted to issue bonds; also paper money,
redeemable in yams and cabbages in fifty years. They
said the pay of the army and of the navy and of the
whole governmental machine was far in arrears, and

unless something was done, and done immediately, national bankruptcy must ensue, and possibly insurrection and revolution. The emperor at once resolved upon a high-handed measure, and one of a nature never before heard of in Pitcairn's Island. He went in state to the church on Sunday morning, with the army at his back, and commanded the minister of the treasury to take up a collection.

That was the feather that broke the camel's back. First one citizen, and then another, rose and refused to submit to this unheard-of outrage — and each refusal was followed by the immediate confiscation of the malcontent's property. This vigor soon stopped the refusals, and the collection proceeded amid a sullen and ominous silence. As the emperor withdrew with the troops, he said, " I will teach you who is master here." Several persons shouted, " Down with unification!" They were at once arrested and torn from the arms of their weeping friends by the soldiery.

But in the meantime, as any prophet might have foreseen, a Social Democrat had been developed. As the emperor stepped into the gilded imperial wheelbarrow at the church door, the social democrat stabbed at him fifteen or sixteen times with a harpoon, but fortunately with such a peculiarly social democratic unprecision of aim as to do no damage.

That very night the convulsion came. The nation rose as one man — though forty-nine of the revolutionists were of the other sex. The infantry threw down their pitchforks; the artillery cast aside their cocoanuts; the navy revolted; the emperor was seized, and bound hand and foot in his palace. He was very much depressed. He said:

" I freed you from a grinding tyranny; I lifted you up out of your degradation, and made you a nation among nations; I gave you a strong, compact, centralized government; and, more than all, I gave you the blessing of blessings,— unification. I have done all this, and my reward is hatred, insult, and these bonds. Take me; do with me as you will. I here resign my crown and all my dignities, and gladly do I release myself from their too heavy burden. For your sake I took them up; for your sake I lay them down. The imperial jewel is no more; now bruise and defile as ye will the useless setting."

By a unanimous voice the people condemned the exemperor and the social democrat to perpetual banishment from church services, or to perpetual labor as galley-slaves in the whale-boat — whichever they might prefer. The next day the nation assembled again, and rehoisted the British flag, reinstated the British tyranny, reduced the nobility to the condition of commoners again, and then straightway turned their diligent attention to the weeding of the ruined and neglected yam patches, and the rehabilitation of the old useful industries and the old healing and solacing pieties. The exemperor restored the lost trespass law, and explained that he had stolen it — not to injure any one, but to further his political projects. Therefore the nation gave the late chief magistrate his office again, and also his alienated property.

Upon reflection, the ex-emperor and the social democrat chose perpetual banishment from religious services in preference to perpetual labor as galley-slaves "*with* perpetual religious services," as they phrased it; wherefore the people believed that the poor fellows' troubles had unseated their reason, and so they judged it best to confine them for the present. Which they did.

Such is the history of Pitcairn's "doubtful acquisition."

ON THE DECAY OF THE ART OF LYING

ESSAY, FOR DISCUSSION, READ AT A MEETING OF THE HIS-
TORICAL AND ANTIQUARIAN CLUB OF HARTFORD, AND OF-
FERED FOR THE THIRTY DOLLAR PRIZE. NOW FIRST
PUBLISHED.*

OBSERVE, I do not mean to suggest that the *custom*
of lying has suffered any decay or interruption —
no, for the Lie, as a Virtue, a Principle, is eternal; the
Lie, as a recreation, a solace, a refuge in time of need,
the fourth Grace, the tenth Muse, man's best and surest
friend, is immortal, and cannot perish from the earth
while this Club remains. My complaint simply con-
cerns the decay of the *art* of lying. No high-minded
man, no man of right feeling, can contemplate the
lumbering and slovenly lying of the present day without grieving to see a noble art so prostituted. In this
veteran presence I naturally enter upon this scheme
with diffidence; it is like an old maid trying to teach
nursery matters to the mothers in Israel. It would not
become me to criticise you, gentlemen, who are nearly
all my elders — and my superiors, in this thing — and
so, if I should here and there *seem* to do it, I trust it
will in most cases be more in a spirit of admiration than

---

* Did not take the prize.

w**

of fault-finding; indeed, if this finest of the fine arts had everywhere received the attention, encouragement, and conscientious practice and development which this Club has devoted to it, I should not need to utter this lament, or shed a single tear. I do not say this to flatter: I say it in a spirit of just and appreciative recognition.

[It had been my intention, at this point, to mention names and give illustrative specimens, but indications observable about me admonished me to beware of particulars and confine myself to generalities.]

No fact is more firmly established than that lying is a necessity of our circumstances — the deduction that it is then a Virtue goes without saying. No virtue can reach its highest usefulness without careful and diligent cultivation — therefore, it goes without saying, that this one ought to be taught in the public schools — at the fireside — even in the newspapers. What chance has the ignorant, uncultivated liar against the educated expert? What chance have I against Mr. Per — against a lawyer? *Judicious* lying is what the world needs. I sometimes think it were even better and safer not to lie at all than to lie injudiciously. An awkward, unscientific lie is often as ineffectual as the truth.

Now let us see what the philosophers say. Note that venerable proverb: Children and fools *always* speak the truth. The deduction is plain — adults and wise persons *never* speak it. Parkman, the historian, says, "The principle of truth may itself be carried into an absurdity." In another place in the same chapter he says, "The saying is old that truth should not be spoken at all times; and those whom a sick conscience worries into habitual violation of the maxim are imbeciles and nuisances." It is strong language, but true. None of us could *live* with an habitual truth-teller; but, thank goodness, none of us has to. An habitual truth-teller is simply an impossible creature; he does not exist; he never has existed. Of course there are people who *think* they never lie, but it is not so — and this ignorance is one of the very things that shame our so-called civilization. Everybody lies — every day; every hour; awake; asleep; in his dreams; in his joy; in his mourning; if he keeps his tongue still, his hands, his feet, his eyes, his attitude, will convey deception — and purposely. Even in sermons — but that is a platitude.

In a far country where I once lived the ladies used to go around paying calls, under the humane and kindly pretense of wanting to see each other; and when they returned home, they would cry out with a glad voice, saying, "We made sixteen calls and found fourteen of them out"— not meaning that they found out anything against the fourteen — no, that was only a colloquial phrase to signify that they were not at home — and their manner of saying it expressed their lively satisfaction in that fact. Now their pretense of wanting to see the fourteen — and the other two whom they had been less lucky with — was that commonest and mildest form of lying which is sufficiently described as a deflection from the truth. Is it justifiable? Most certainly. It is beautiful, it is noble; for its object is, *not* to reap profit, but to convey a pleasure to the sixteen. The iron-souled truth-monger would plainly manifest, or even utter the fact that he didn't want to see those people — and he would be an ass, and inflict a totally unnecessary pain. And next, those ladies in that far country — but never mind, they had a thousand pleasant ways of lying, that grew out of gentle impulses, and were a credit to their intelligence and an honor to their hearts. Let the particulars go.

The men in that far country were liars, every one. Their mere howdy-do was a lie, because *they* didn't care how you did, except they were undertakers. To the ordinary inquirer you lied in return; for you made no conscientious diagnosis of your case, but answered at random, and usually missed it considerably. You lied to the undertaker, and said your health was failing — a wholly commendable lie, since it cost you nothing and pleased the other man. If a stranger called and interrupted you, you said with your hearty tongue, "I'm glad to see you," and said with your heartier soul, "I wish you were with the cannibals and it was dinner-time." When he went, you said regretfully, "*Must* you go?" and followed it with a "Call again;" but you did no harm, for you did not deceive anybody nor inflict any hurt, whereas the truth would have made you both unhappy.

I think that all this courteous lying is a sweet and loving art, and should be cultivated. The highest perfection of politeness is only a beautiful edifice, built, from the base to the dome, of graceful and gilded forms of charitable and unselfish lying.

What I bemoan is the growing prevalence of the brutal truth. Let us do what we can to eradicate it. An injurious truth has no merit over an injurious lie. Neither should ever be uttered. The man who speaks an injurious truth, lest his soul be not saved if he do otherwise, should reflect that that sort of a soul is not strictly worth saving. The man who tells a lie to help a poor devil out of trouble, is one of whom the angels doubtless say, "Lo, here is an heroic soul who casts his own welfare into jeopardy to succor his neighbor's; let us exalt this magnanimous liar."

An injurious lie is an uncommendable thing; and so, also, and in the same degree, is an injurious truth — a fact which is recognized by the law of libel.

Among other common lies, we have the *silent* lie — the deception which one conveys by simply keeping still and concealing the truth. Many obstinate truth-mongers indulge in this dissipation, imagining that if they *speak* no lie, they lie not at all. In that far country where I once lived, there was a lovely spirit, a lady whose impulses were always high and pure, and whose character answered to them. One day I was there at dinner, and remarked, in a general way, that we are all liars. She was amazed, and said, " Not *all ?* " It was before " Pinafore's " time, so I did not make the response which would naturally follow in our day, but frankly said, " Yes, *all* — we are all liars; there are no exceptions." She looked almost offended, and said, " Why, do you include *me ?* " " Certainly," I said, " I think you even rank as an expert." She said, " 'Sh — 'sh ! the children !" So the subject was changed in deference to the children's presence, and we went on talking about other things. But as soon as the young people were out of the way, the lady came warmly back to the matter and said, " I have made it the rule of my life to never tell a lie; and I have never departed from it in a single instance." I said, " I don't mean the least harm or disrespect, but really you have been lying like smoke ever since I've been sitting here. It has caused me a good deal of pain, because I am not used to it." She required of me an instance — just a single instance. So I said:

" Well, here is the unfilled duplicate of the blank which the Oakland hospital people sent to you by the hand of the sick-nurse when she came here to nurse your little nephew through his dangerous illness. This blank asks all manner of questions as to the conduct of that sick-nurse: ' Did she ever sleep on her watch? Did she ever forget to give the medicine?' and so forth and so on. You are warned to be very careful and explicit in your answers, for the welfare of the service requires that the nurses be promptly fined or otherwise punished for derelictions. You told me you were perfectly delighted with that nurse — that she had a thousand perfections and only one fault: you found you never could depend on her wrapping Johnny up half sufficiently while he waited in a chilly chair for her to rearrange the warm bed. You filled up the duplicate of this paper, and sent it back to the hospital by the hand of the nurse. How did you answer this question — ' Was the nurse at any time guilty of a negligence which was likely to result in the patient's taking cold?' Come — everything is decided by a bet here in California: ten dollars to ten cents you lied when you answered that question." She said, " I didn't; *I left it blank !* " " Just so — you have told a *silent* lie; you have left it to be inferred that you had no fault to find in that matter." She said, " Oh, was that a lie? And how *could* I mention her one single fault, and she so good? — it would have been cruel." I said, " One ought always to lie, when one can do good by it; your impulse was right, but your judgment was crude; this comes of unintelligent practice. Now observe the result of this inexpert deflection of yours. You know Mr. Jones's Willie is lying very low with scarlet fever; well, your recommendation was so enthusiastic that that girl is there nursing him, and the worn-out family have all been trustingly sound asleep for the last fourteen hours, leaving their darling with full confidence in those fatal hands, because you, like young George Washington, have a reputa— However, if you are not going to have anything to do, I will come around to-morrow and we'll attend the funeral together, for, of course, you'll naturally feel a peculiar interest in Willie's case — as personal a one, in fact, as the undertaker."

But that was all lost. Before I was half-way through she was in a carriage and making thirty miles an hour

toward the Jones mansion to save what was left of Willie
and tell all she knew about the deadly nurse. All of
which was unnecessary, as Willie wasn't sick; I had
been lying myself. But that same day, all the same,
she sent a line to the hospital which filled up the
neglected blank, and stated the *facts*, too, in the
squarest possible manner.

Now, you see, this lady's fault was *not* in lying, but
only in lying injudiciously. She should have told the
truth, *there*, and made it up to the nurse with a fraudulent compliment further along in the paper. She
could have said, " In one respect the sick-nurse is perfection — when she is on watch, she never snores."
Almost any little pleasant lie would have taken the
sting out of that troublesome but necessary expression
of the truth.

Lying is universal — we *all* do it; we all *must* do it.
Therefore, the wise thing is for us diligently to train
ourselves to lie thoughtfully, judiciously; to lie with
a good object, and not an evil one; to lie for others'
advantage, and not our own; to lie healingly, chari-
tably, humanely, not cruelly, hurtfully, maliciously; to
lie gracefully and graciously, not awkwardly and clum-
sily; to lie firmly, frankly, squarely, with head erect,
not haltingly, tortuously, with pusillanimous mien, as
being ashamed of our high calling. Then shall we be
rid of the rank and pestilent truth that is rotting the
land; then shall we be great and good and beautiful,
and worthy dwellers in a world where even benign
Nature habitually lies, except when she promises execrable weather. Then — But I am but a new and
feeble student in this gracious art; I cannot instruct
this Club.

Joking aside, I think there is much need of wise ex-
amination into what sorts of lies are best and whole-
somest to be indulged, seeing we *must* all lie and *do* all

lie, and what sorts it may be best to avoid — and this is a thing which I feel I can confidently put into the hands of this experienced Club — a ripe body, who may be termed, in this regard, and without undue flattery, Old Masters.

THE CANVASSER'S TALE

POOR, sad-eyed stranger! There was that about his humble mien, his tired look, his decayed-gentility clothes, that almost reached the mustard seed of charity that still remained, remote and lonely, in the empty vastness of my heart, notwithstanding I observed a portfolio under his arm, and said to myself, Behold, Providence hath delivered his servant into the hands of another canvasser.

Well, these people always get one interested. Before I well knew how it came about, this one was telling me his history, and I was all attention and sympathy. He told it something like this:

My parents died, alas, when I was a little, sinless child. My uncle Ithuriel took me to his heart and reared me as his own. He was my only relative in the wide world; but he was good and rich and generous. He reared me in the lap of luxury. I knew no want that money could satisfy.

In the fullness of time I was graduated, and went with two of my servants — my chamberlain and my valet — to travel in foreign countries. During four years I flitted upon careless wing amid the beauteous gardens of the distant strand, if you will permit this form of speech in one whose tongue was ever attuned to poesy; and indeed I so speak with confidence, as one unto his

24 **   (363)

kind, for I perceive by your eyes that you too, sir, are gifted with the divine inflation. In those far lands I reveled in the ambrosial food that fructifies the soul, the mind, the heart. But of all things, that which most appealed to my inborn æsthetic taste was the prevailing custom there, among the rich, of making collections of elegant and costly rarities, dainty *objets de vertu*, and in an evil hour I tried to uplift my uncle Ithuriel to a plane of sympathy with this exquisite employment.

I wrote and told him of one gentlemen's vast collection of shells; another's noble collection of meerschaum pipes; another's elevating and refining collection of undecipherable autographs; another's priceless collection of old china; another's enchanting collection of postage stamps — and so forth and so on. Soon my letters yielded fruit. My uncle began to look about for something to make a collection of. You may know, perhaps, how fleetly a taste like this dilates. His soon became a raging fever, though I knew it not. He began to neglect his great pork business; presently he wholly retired and turned an elegant leisure into a rabid search for curious things. His wealth was vast, and he spared it not. First he tried cow-bells. He made a collection which filled five large *salons*, and comprehended all the different sorts of cow-bells that ever had been contrived, save one. That one — an antique, and the only specimen extant — was possessed by another collector. My uncle offered enormous sums for it, but the gentleman would not sell. Doubtless you know what necessarily resulted. A true collector attaches no value to a collection that is not complete. His great heart breaks, he sells his hoard, he turns his mind to some field that seems unoccupied.

Thus did my uncle. He next tried brickbats. After piling up a vast and intensely interesting collection, the former difficulty supervened; his great heart broke again; he sold out his soul's idol to the retired brewer who possessed the missing brick. Then he tried flint hatchets and other implements of Primeval Man, but by and by discovered that the factory where they were made was supplying other collectors as well as himself. He tried Aztec inscriptions and stuffed whales — another failure, after incredible labor and expense. When his collection seemed at last perfect, a stuffed whale arrived from Greenland and an Aztec inscription from the Cundurango regions of Central America that made all former specimens insignificant. My uncle hastened to secure these noble gems. He got the stuffed whale, but another collector got the inscription. A real Cundurango, as possibly you know, is a possession of such supreme value that, when once a collector gets it, he will rather part with his family than with it. So my uncle sold out, and saw his darlings go forth, never more to return; and his coal-black hair turned white as snow in a single night.

Now he waited, and thought. He knew another disappointment might kill him. He was resolved that he would choose things next time that no other man was collecting. He carefully made up his mind, and once more entered the field — this time to make a collection of echoes.

"Of what?" said I.

Echoes, sir. His first purchase was an echo in Georgia that repeated four times; his next was a six-repeater in Maryland; his next was a thirteen-repeater in Maine; his next was a nine-repeater in Kansas; his next was a twelve-repeater in Tennessee, which he got cheap, so to speak, because it was out of repair, a portion of the crag which reflected it having tumbled down. He believed he could repair it at a cost of a few thousand dollars, and, by increasing the elevation with masonry, treble the repeating capacity; but the archi-

tect who undertook the job had never built an echo before, and so he utterly spoiled this one. Before he
meddled with it, it used to talk back like a mother-in-
law, but now it was only fit for the deaf and dumb
asylum. Well, next he bought a lot of cheap little
double-barreled echoes, scattered around over various
States and Territories; he got them at twenty per cent.
off by taking the lot. Next he bought a perfect Gat-
ling-gun of an echo in Oregon, and it cost a fortune, I
can tell you. You may know, sir, that in the echo
market the scale of prices is cumulative, like the carat-
scale in diamonds; in fact, the same phraseology is
used. A single-carat echo is worth but ten dollars over
and above the value of the land it is on; a two-carat
or double-barreled echo is worth thirty dollars; a five-
carat is worth nine hundred and fifty; a ten-carat is
worth thirteen thousand. My uncle's Oregon echo,
which he called the Great Pitt Echo, was a twenty-two
carat gem, and cost two hundred and sixteen thousand
dollars — they threw the land in, for it was four
hundred miles from a settlement.

Well, in the meantime my path was a path of roses.
I was the accepted suitor of the only and lovely daughter
of an English earl, and was beloved to distraction. In
that dear presence I swam in seas of bliss. The family
were content, for it was known that I was sole heir to
an uncle held to be worth five millions of dollars.
However, none of us knew that my uncle had become
a collector, at least in anything more than a small way,
for æsthetic amusement.

Now gathered the clouds above my unconscious head.
That divine echo, since known throughout the world
as the Great Koh-i-noor, or Mountain of Repetitions,
was discovered. It was a sixty-five-carat gem. You
could utter a word and it would talk back at you for
fifteen minutes, when the day was otherwise quiet.

But behold, another fact came to light at the same time: another echo collector was in the field. The two rushed to make the peerless purchase. The property consisted of a couple of small hills with a shallow swale between, out yonder among the back settlements of New York State. Both men arrived on the ground at the same time, and neither knew the other was there. The echo was not all owned by one man; a person by the name of Williamson Bolivar Jarvis owned the east hill, and a person by the name of Harbison J. Bledso owned the west hill; the swale between was the dividing line. So while my uncle was buying Jarvis's hill for three million two hundred and eighty-five thousand dollars, the other party was buying Bledso's hill for a shade over three million.

Now, do you perceive the natural result? Why, the noblest collection of echoes on earth was forever and ever incomplete, since it possessed but the one-half of the king echo of the universe. Neither man was content with this divided ownership, yet neither would sell to the other. There were jawings, bickerings, heart-burnings. And at last that other collector, with a malignity which only a collector can ever feel toward a man and a brother, proceeded to cut down his hill!

You see, as long as he could not have the echo, he was resolved that nobody should have it. He would remove his hill, and then there would be nothing to reflect my uncle's echo. My uncle remonstrated with him, but the man said, " I own one end of this echo; I choose to kill my end; you must take care of your own end yourself."

Well, my uncle got an injunction put on him. The other man appealed and fought it in a higher court. They carried it on up, clear to the Supreme Court of the United States. It made no end of trouble there. Two of the judges believed that an echo was personal

24

property, because it was impalpable to sight and touch, and yet was purchaseable, salable, and consequently taxable; two others believed that an echo was real estate, because it was manifestly attached to the land, and was not removable from place to place; other of the judges contended that an echo was not property at all.

It was finally decided that the echo was property; that the hills were property; that the two men were separate and independent owners of the two hills, but tenants in common in the echo; therefore defendant was at full liberty to cut down his hill, since it belonged solely to him, but must give bonds in three million dollars as indemnity for damages which might result to my uncle's half of the echo. This decision also debarred my uncle from using defendant's hill to reflect his part of the echo, without defendant's consent; he must use only his own hill; if his part of the echo would not go, under these circumstances, it was sad, of course, but the court could find no remedy. The court also debarred defendant from using my uncle's hill to reflect *his* end of the echo, without consent. You see the grand result! Neither man would give consent, and so that astonishing and most noble echo had to cease from its great powers; and since that day that magnificent property is tied up and unsalable.

A week before my wedding day, while I was still swimming in bliss and the nobility were gathering from far and near to honor our espousals, came news of my uncle's death, and also a copy of his will, making me his sole heir. He was gone; alas, my dear benefactor was no more. The thought surcharges my heart even at this remote day. I handed the will to the earl; I could not read it for the blinding tears. The earl read it; then he sternly said, "Sir, do you call this wealth? — but doubtless you do in your inflated country. Sir,

you are left sole heir to a vast collection of echoes — if
a thing can be called a collection that is scattered far
and wide over the huge length and breadth of the
American continent; sir, this is not all; you are head
and ears in debt; there is not an echo in the lot but
has a mortgage on it; sir, I am not a hard man, but I
must look to my child's interest; if you had but one
echo which you could honestly call your own, if you
had but one echo which was free from incumbrance, so
that you could retire to it with my child, and by humble, painstaking industry, cultivate and improve it, and
thus wrest from it a maintenance, I would not say you
nay; but I cannot marry my child to a beggar. Leave
his side, my darling; go, sir, take your mortgage-
ridden echoes and quit my sight forever."

My noble Celestine clung to me in tears, with loving
arms, and swore she would willingly, nay gladly,
marry me, though I had not an echo in the world.
But it could not be. We were torn asunder, she to
pine and die within the twelve month, I to toil life's
long journey sad and alone, praying daily, hourly, for
that release which shall join us together again in that
dear realm where the wicked cease from troubling and
the weary are at rest. Now, sir, if you will be so kind
as to look at these maps and plans in my portfolio, I
am sure I can sell you an echo for less money than any
man in the trade. Now this one, which cost my uncle
ten dollars, thirty years ago, and is one of the sweetest
things in Texas, I will let you have for —

"Let me interrupt you," I said. "My friend, I
have not had a moment's respite from canvassers this
day. I have bought a sewing-machine which I did not
want; I have bought a map which is mistaken in all
its details; I have bought a clock which will not go; I
have bought a moth poison which the moths prefer to
any other beverage; I have bought no end of useless
24**

inventions, and now I have had enough of this foolish-
ness.   I would not have one of your echoes if you were
even to give it to me.   I would not let it stay on the
place.   I always hate a man that tries to sell me
echoes.   You see this gun?   Now take your collection
and move on; let us not have bloodshed."

But he only smiled a sad, sweet smile, and got out
some more diagrams.   You know the result perfectly
well, because you know that when you have once
opened the door to a canvasser, the trouble is done and
you have got to suffer defeat.

I compromised with this man at the end of an intolerable hour.   I bought two double-barreled echoes in
good condition, and he threw in another, which he said
was not salable because it only spoke German.   He
said, " She was a perfect polyglot once, but somehow'
her palate got down."

AN ENCOUNTER WITH AN INTERVIEWER

THE nervous, dapper, " peart " young man took the chair I offered him, and said he was connected with the *Daily Thunderstorm*, and added:

" Hoping it's no harm, I've come to interview you."

" Come to what?"

"*Interview* you."

"Ah! I see. Yes — yes. Um! Yes — yes."

I was not feeling bright that morning. Indeed, my powers seemed a bit under a cloud. However, I went to the bookcase, and when I had been looking six or seven minutes, I found I was obliged to refer to the young man. I said:

" How do you spell it?"

" Spell what?"

" Interview."

" Oh, my goodness! what do you want to spell it for?"

" I don't want to spell it; I want to see what it means."

" Well, this is astonishing, I must say. *I* can tell you what it means, if you — if you —"

" Oh, all right! That will answer, and much obliged to you, too."

" In, *in*, ter, *ter*, *in*ter —"

" Then you spell it with an *I*?"

x**   (371)

" Why, certainly ! "

" Oh, that is what took me so long."

" Why, my *dear* sir, what did *you* propose to spell it with?"

" Well, I — I — hardly know. I had the Unabridged, and I was ciphering around in the back end, hoping I might tree her among the pictures. But it's a very old edition."

" Why, my friend, they wouldn't have a *picture* of it in even the latest e— My dear sir, I beg your pardon, I mean no harm in the world, but you do not look as — as — intelligent as I had expected you would. No harm — I mean no harm at all."

" Oh, don't mention it! It has often been said, and by people who would not flatter and who could have no inducement to flatter, that I am quite remarkable in that way. Yes — yes; they always speak of it with rapture."

" I can easily imagine it. But about this interview. You know it is the custom, now, to interview any man who has become notorious."

" Indeed, I had not heard of it before. It must be very interesting. What do you do it with?"

"Ah, well — well — well — this is disheartening. It *ought* to be done with a club in some cases; but customarily it consists in the interviewer asking questions and the interviewed answering them. It is all the rage now. Will you let me ask you certain questions calculated to bring out the salient points of your public and private history?"

" Oh, with pleasure — with pleasure. I have a very bad memory, but I hope you will not mind that. That is to say, it is an irregular memory — singularly irregular. Sometimes it goes in a gallop, and then again it will be as much as a fortnight passing a given point. This is a great grief to me."

" Oh, it is no matter, so you will try to do the best you can."

" I will.   I will put my whole mind on it."

" Thanks.   Are you ready to begin?"

" Ready."

Q. How old are you?

A. Nineteen, in June.

Q. Indeed.   I would have taken you to be thirty-five or six.   Where were you born?

A. In Missouri.

Q. When did you begin to write?

A. In 1836.

Q. Why, how could that be, if you are only nineteen now?

A. I don't know.   It does seem curious, somehow.

Q. It does, indeed.   Whom do you consider the most remarkable man you ever met ?

A. Aaron Burr.

Q. But you never could have met Aaron Burr, if you are only nineteen years —

A. Now, if you know more about me than I do, what do you ask me for?

Q. Well, it was only a suggestion; nothing more. How did you happen to meet Burr?

A. Well, I happened to be at his funeral one day, and he asked me to make less noise, and —

Q. But, good heavens! if you were at his funeral, he must have been dead, and if he was dead how could he care whether you made a noise or not?

A. I don't know.   He was always a particular kind of a man that way.

Q. Still, I don't understand it at all.   You say he spoke to you, and that he was dead.

A. I didn't say he was dead.

Q. But wasn't he dead?

A. Well, some said he was, some said he wasn't.

Q. What did you think?

A. Oh, it was none of my business! It wasn't any of my funeral.

Q. Did you — However, we can never get this matter straight. Let me ask about something else. What was the date of your birth?

A. Monday, October 31, 1693.

Q. What! Impossible! That would make you a hundred and eighty years old. How do you account for that?

A. I don't account for it at all.

Q. But you said at first you were only nineteen, and now you make yourself out to be one hundred and eighty. It is an awful discrepancy.

A. Why, have you noticed that? (Shaking hands.) Many a time it has seemed to me like a discrepancy, but somehow I couldn't make up my mind. How quick you notice a thing!

Q. Thank you for the compliment, as far as it goes. Had you, or have you, any brothers or sisters?

A. Eh! I — I — I think so — yes — but I don't remember.

Q. Well, that is the most extraordinary statement I ever heard!

A. Why, what makes you think that?

Q. How could I think otherwise? Why, look here! Who is this a picture of on the wall? Isn't that a brother of yours?

A. Oh, yes, yes, yes! Now you remind me of it; that *was* a brother of mine. That's William — *Bill* we called him. Poor old Bill!

Q. Why? Is he dead, then?

A. Ah! well, I suppose so. We never could tell. There was a great mystery about it.

Q. That is sad, very sad. He disappeared, then?

A. Well, yes, in a sort of general way. We buried him.

Q. Buried him! *Buried* him, without knowing whether he was dead or not?

A. Oh, no! Not that. He was dead enough.

Q. Well, I confess that I can't understand this. If you buried him, and you knew he was dead —

A. No! no! We only thought he was.

Q. Oh, I see! He came to life again?

A. I bet he didn't.

Q. Well, I never heard anything like this. *Somebody* was dead. *Somebody* was buried. Now, where was the mystery?

A. Ah! that's just it! That's it exactly. You see, we were twins — defunct and I — and we got mixed in the bathtub when we were only two weeks old, and one of us was drowned. But we didn't know which. Some think it was Bill. Some think it was me.

Q. Well, that *is* remarkable. What do *you* think?

A. Goodness knows! I would give whole worlds to know. This solemn, this awful mystery has cast a gloom over my whole life. But I will tell you a secret now, which I never have revealed to any creature before. One of us had a peculiar mark — a large mole on the back of his left hand; that was *me. That child was the one that was drowned !*

Q. Very well, then, I don't see that there is any mystery about it, after all.

A. You don't? Well, *I* do. Anyway, I don't see how they could ever have been such a blundering lot as to go and bury the wrong child. But, 'sh! — don't mention it where the family can hear of it. Heaven knows they have heart-breaking troubles enough without adding this.

Q. Well, I believe I have got material enough for the present, and I am very much obliged to you for the pains you have taken.   But I was a good deal interested in that account of Aaron Burr's funeral.   Would you mind telling me what particular circumstance it was that made you think Burr was such a remarkable man?

A. Oh! it was a mere trifle!   Not one man in fifty would have noticed it at all.   When the sermon was over, and the procession all ready to start for the cemetery, and the body all arranged nice in the hearse, he said he wanted to take a last look at the scenery, and so he *got up and rode with the driver.*

Then the young man reverently withdrew.   He was very pleasant company, and I was sorry to see him go.

PARIS NOTES*

THE Parisian travels but little, he knows no language but his own, reads no literature but his own, and consequently he is pretty narrow and pretty self-sufficient. However, let us not be too sweeping; there are Frenchmen who know languages not their own: these are the waiters. Among the rest, they know English; that is, they know it on the European plan — which is to say, they can speak it, but can't understand it. They easily make themselves understood, but it is next to impossible to word an English sentence in such a way as to enable them to comprehend it. They think they comprehend it; they pretend they do; but they don't. Here is a conversation which I had with one of these beings; I wrote it down at the time, in order to have it exactly correct.

I. These are fine oranges. Where are they grown?

He. More? Yes, I will bring them.

I. No, do not bring any more; I only want to know where they are from — where they are raised.

He. Yes? (with imperturbable mien, and rising inflection.)

I. Yes. Can you tell me what country they are from?

He. Yes? (blandly, with rising inflection.)

---

* Crowded out of "A Tramp Abroad" to make room for more vital statistics.— M. T.

I (disheartened). They are very nice.

He. Good night. (Bows, and retires, quite satisfied with himself.)

That young man could have become a good English scholar by taking the right sort of pains, but he was French, and wouldn't do that. How different is the case with our people; they utilize every means that offers. There are some alleged French Protestants in Paris, and they built a nice little church on one of the great avenues that lead away from the Arch of Triumph, and proposed to listen to the correct thing, preached in the correct way, there, in their precious French tongue, and be happy. But their little game does not succeed. Our people are always there ahead of them Sundays, and take up all the room. When the minister gets up to preach, he finds his house full of devout foreigners, each ready and waiting, with his little book in his hand — a morocco-bound Testament, apparently. But only apparently; it is Mr. Bellows's admirable and exhaustive little French-English dictionary, which in look and binding and size is just like a Testament — and those people are there to study French. The building has been nicknamed "The Church of the Gratis French Lesson."

These students probably acquire more language than general information, for I am told that a French sermon is like a French speech — it never names a historical event, but only the date of it; if you are not up in dates, you get left. A French speech is something like this:

Comrades, citizens, brothers, noble parts of the only sublime and perfect nation, let us not forget that the 21st January cast off our chains ; that the 10th August relieved us of the shameful presence of foreign spies; that the 5th September was its own justification before heaven and humanity; that the 18th Brumaire contained the seeds of its own punishment; that the 14th July was the mighty voice of liberty proclaiming the resurrection, the new day, and inviting the oppressed peoples of the earth to look upon the divine face of France and live; and let us here record our everlasting curse against the man of the 2d December, and declare in thunder tones, the native tones of France, that but for him there had been no 17th March in history, no 12th October, no 19th January, no 22d April, no 16th November, no 30th September, no 2d July, no 14th February, no 29th June, no 15th August, no 31st May — that but for him, France the pure, the grand, the peerless, had had a serene and vacant almanac to-day!

I have heard of one French sermon which closed in this odd yet eloquent way:

My hearers, we have sad cause to remember the man of the 13th January. The results of the vast crime of the 13th January have been in just proportion to the magnitude of the act itself. But for it there had been no 30th November — sorrowful spectacle! The grisly deed of the 16th June had not been done but for it, nor had the man of the 16th June known existence; to it alone the 3d September was due, also the fatal 12th October. Shall we, then, be grateful for the 13th January, with its freight of death for you and me and all that breathe? Yes, my friends, for it gave us also that which had never come but for it, and it alone — the blessed 25th December.

It may be well enough to explain, though in the case of many of my readers this will hardly be necessary. The man of the 13th January is Adam; the crime of that date was the eating of the apple; the sorrowful spectacle of the 30th November was the expulsion from Eden; the grisly deed of the 16th June was the murder of Abel; the act of the 3d September was the beginning of the journey to the land of Nod; the 12th day of October, the last mountain-tops disappeared under the flood. When you go to church in France, you want to take your almanac with you — annotated.

25**

LEGEND OF SAGENFELD IN GERMANY*

I.

MORE than a thousand years ago this small district
was a kingdom — a little bit of a kingdom, a
sort of dainty little toy kingdom, as one might say. It
was far removed from the jealousies, strifes, and tur-
moils of that old warlike day, and so its life was a
simple life, its people a gentle and guileless race; it
lay always in a deep dream of peace, a soft Sabbath
tranquillity; there was no malice, there was no envy,
there was no ambition, consequently there were no
heart-burnings, there was no unhappiness in the land.

In the course of time the old king died and his little
son Hubert came to the throne. The people's love for
him grew daily; he was so good and so pure and so
noble, that by and by this love became a passion, almost
a worship. Now at his birth the soothsayers had diligently studied the stars and found something written in
that shining book to this effect:

*In Hubert's fourteenth year a pregnant event will
happen; the animal whose singing shall sound sweetest
in Hubert's ear shall save Hubert's life. So long as the*

---

* Left out of "A Tramp Abroad" because its authenticity seemed
doubtful, and could not at that time be proved.— M. T.

*king and the nation shall honor this animal's race for
this good deed, the ancient dynasty shall not fail of an
heir, nor the nation know war or pestilence or poverty.
But beware an erring choice!*

All through the king's thirteenth year but one thing
was talked of by the soothsayers, the statesmen, the
little parliament, and the general people. That one
thing was this: How is the last sentence of the
prophecy to be understood? What goes before seems
to mean that the saving animal will choose *itself*, at the
proper time; but the closing sentence seems to mean
that the *king* must choose beforehand, and say what
singer among the animals pleases him best, and that if
he choose wisely the chosen animal will save his life,
his dynasty, his people, but that if he should make
" an erring choice "— beware!

By the end of the year there were as many opinions
about this matter as there had been in the beginning;
but a majority of the wise and the simple were agreed
that the safest plan would be for the little king to make
choice beforehand, and the earlier the better. So an
edict was sent forth commanding all persons who
owned singing creatures to bring them to the great hall
of the palace in the morning of the first day of the new
year. This command was obeyed. When everything
was in readiness for the trial, the king made his solemn
entry with the great officers of the crown, all clothed
in their robes of state. The king mounted his golden
throne and prepared to give judgment. But he
presently said:

" These creatures all sing at once; the noise is unen-
durable; no one can choose in such a turmoil. Take
them all away, and bring back one at a time."

This was done. One sweet warbler after another
charmed the young king's ear and was removed to

make way for another candidate. The precious minutes slipped by; among so many bewitching songsters
he found it hard to choose, and all the harder because
the promised penalty for an error was so terrible that it
unsettled his judgment and made him afraid to trust
his own ears. He grew nervous and his face showed
distress. His ministers saw this, for they never took
their eyes from him a moment. Now they began to
say in their hearts:

"He has lost courage — the cool head is gone — he
will err — he and his dynasty and his people are
doomed!"

At the end of an hour the king sat silent awhile, and
then said:

"Bring back the linnet."

The linnet trilled forth her jubilant music. In the
midst of it the king was about to uplift his scepter in
sign of choice, but checked himself and said:

"But let us be sure. Bring back the thrush; let
them sing together."

The thrush was brought, and the two birds poured
out their marvels of song together. The king wavered,
then his inclination began to settle and strengthen —
one could see it in his countenance. Hope budded in
the hearts of the old ministers, their pulses began to
beat quicker, the scepter began to rise slowly, when:

There was a hideous interruption! It was a sound
like this — just at the door:

"Waw. . . . . .*he !* — waw. . . . . .*he !* — waw-he!
waw-he! — waw-he!"

Everybody was sorely startled — and enraged at himself for showing it.

The next instant the dearest, sweetest, prettiest little
peasant maid of nine years came tripping in, her brown
eyes glowing with childish eagerness; but when she
saw that august company and those angry faces she

stopped and hung her head and put her poor coarse
apron to her eyes. Nobody gave her welcome, none
pitied her. Presently she looked up timidly through
her tears, and said:

"My lord the king, I pray you pardon me, for I
meant no wrong. I have no father and no mother,
but I have a goat and a donkey, and they are all in all
to me. My goat gives me the sweetest milk, and when
my dear good donkey brays it seems to me there is no
music like to it. So when my lord the king's jester
said the sweetest singer among all the animals should
save the crown and nation, and moved me to bring him
here —"

All the court burst into a rude laugh, and the child
fled away crying, without trying to finish her speech.
The chief minister gave a private order that she and
her disastrous donkey be flogged beyond the precincts
of the palace and commanded to come within them no
more.

Then the trial of the birds was resumed. The two
birds sang their best, but the scepter lay motionless in
the king's hand. Hope died slowly out in the breasts
of all. An hour went by; two hours; still no decision.
The day waned to its close, and the waiting multitudes
outside the palace grew crazed with anxiety and apprehension. The twilight came on, the shadows fell deeper
and deeper. The king and his court could no longer
see each other's faces. No one spoke — none called
for lights. The great trial had been made; it had
failed; each and all wished to hide their faces from the
light and cover up their deep trouble in their own
hearts.

Finally — hark! A rich, full strain of the divinest
melody streamed forth from a remote part of the hall —
the nightingale's voice!

"Up!" shouted the king, "let all the bells make
25

proclamation to the people, for the choice is made and
we have not erred. King, dynasty, and nation are
saved. From henceforth let the nightingale be honored
throughout the land forever. And publish it among
all the people that whosoever shall insult a nightingale,
or injure it, shall suffer death. The king hath spoken.''

All that little world was drunk with joy. The castle
and the city blazed with bonfires all night long, the
people danced and drank and sang, and the triumphant
clamor of the bells never ceased.

From that day the nightingale was a sacred bird.
Its song was heard in every house; the poets wrote its
praises; the painters painted it; its sculptured image
adorned every arch and turret and fountain and public
building. It was even taken into the king's councils;
and no grave matter of state was decided until the
soothsayers had laid the thing before the state nightingale and translated to the ministry what it was that the
bird had sung about it.

II.

THE young king was very fond of the chase. When
the summer was come he rode forth with hawk and
hound, one day, in a brilliant company of his nobles.
He got separated from them by and by, in a great
forest, and took what he imagined a near cut, to find
them again; but it was a mistake. He rode on and
on, hopefully at first, but with sinking courage finally.
Twilight came on, and still he was plunging through a
lonely and unknown land. Then came a catastrophe.
In the dim light he forced his horse through a tangled
thicket overhanging a steep and rocky declivity. When
horse and rider reached the bottom, the former had a

broken neck and the latter a broken leg. The poor little king lay there suffering agonies of pain, and each hour seemed a long month to him. He kept his ear strained to hear any sound that might promise hope of rescue; but he heard no voice, no sound or horn or bay of hound. So at last he gave up all hope, and said, "Let death come, for come it must."

Just then the deep, sweet song of a nightingale swept across the still wastes of the night.

"Saved!" the king said   Saved! It is the sacred bird, and the prophecy is come true. The gods themselves protected me from error in the choice."

He could hardly contain his joy; he could not word his gratitude. Every few moments now he thought he caught the sound of approaching succor. But each time it was a disappointment; no succor came. The dull hours drifted on. Still no help came — but still the sacred bird sang on. He began to have misgivings about his choice, but he stifled them. Toward dawn the bird ceased. The morning came, and with it thirst and hunger; but no succor. The day waxed and waned. At last the king cursed the nightingale.

Immediately the song of the thrush came from out the wood. The king said in his heart, "This was the true bird — my choice was false — succor will come now."

But it did not come. Then he lay many hours insensible. When he came to himself, a linnet was singing. He listened — with apathy. His faith was gone. "These birds," he said, "can bring no help; I and my house and my people are doomed." He turned him about to die; for he was grown very feeble from hunger and thirst and suffering, and felt that his end was near. In truth, he wanted to die, and be released from pain. For long hours he lay without thought or feeling or motion. Then his senses returned. The

dawn of the third morning was breaking. Ah, the
world seemed very beautiful to those worn eyes. Suddenly a great longing to live rose up in the lad's heart,
and from his soul welled a deep and fervent prayer
that Heaven would have mercy upon him and let him
see his home and his friends once more. In that instant a soft, a faint, a far-off sound, but oh, how
inexpressibly sweet to his waiting ear, came floating
out of the distance:

"Waw......*he!* waw......*he!* waw-he! — waw-
he! — waw-he!"

"*That*, oh, *that* song is sweeter, a thousand times
sweeter than the voice of the nightingale, thrush, or
linnet, for it brings not mere hope, but *certainty* of
succor; and now, indeed, am I saved! The sacred
singer has chosen itself, as the oracle intended; the
prophecy is fulfilled, and my life, my house, and my
people are redeemed. The ass shall be sacred from
this day!"

The divine music grew nearer and nearer, stronger
and stronger — and ever sweeter and sweeter to the
perishing sufferer's ear. Down the declivity the docile
little donkey wandered, cropping herbage and singing
as he went; and when at last he saw the dead horse
and the wounded king, he came and snuffed at them
with simple and marveling curiosity. The king petted
him, and he knelt down as had been his wont when his
little mistress desired to mount. With great labor and
pain the lad drew himself upon the creature's back,
and held himself there by aid of the generous ears.
The ass went singing forth from the place and carried
the king to the little peasant maid's hut. She gave
him her pallet for a bed, refreshed him with goat's milk,
and then flew to tell the great news to the first scouting-
party of searchers she might meet.

The king got well. His first act was to proclaim the

sacredness and inviolability of the ass; his second was
to add this particular ass to his cabinet and make him
chief minister of the crown; his third was to have all
the statues and effigies of nightingales throughout his
kingdom destroyed, and replaced by statues and effigies
of the sacred donkey; and his fourth was to announce
that when the little peasant maid should reach her
fifteenth year he would make her his queen — and he
kept his word.

Such is the legend. This explains why the moulder-
ing image of the ass adorns all these old crumbling
walls and arches; and it explains why, during many
centuries, an ass was always the chief minister in that
royal cabinet, just as is still the case in most cabinets
to this day; and it also explains why, in that little
kingdom, during many centuries, all great poems, all
great speeches, all great books, all public solemnities,
and all royal proclamations, always began with these
stirring words:

" Waw......*he* ! — waw......*he* ! — waw-he ! —
waw-he ! — waw-he !"

SPEECH ON THE BABIES

AT THE BANQUET, IN CHICAGO, GIVEN BY THE ARMY OF THE TENNESSEE TO THEIR FIRST COMMANDER, GENERAL U. S. GRANT, NOVEMBER, 1879.

[The fifteenth regular toast was "The Babies — As they comfort us in our sorrows, let us not forget them in our festivities."]

I LIKE that. We have not all had the good fortune to be ladies. We have not all been generals, or poets, or statesmen; but when the toast works down to the babies, we stand on common ground. It is a shame that for a thousand years the world's banquets have utterly ignored the baby, as if he didn't amount to anything. If you will stop and think a minute — if you will go back fifty or one hundred years to your early married life and recontemplate your first baby — you will remember that he amounted to a good deal, and even something over. You soldiers all know that when that little fellow arrived at family headquarters you had to hand in your resignation. He took entire command. You became his lackey, his mere body-servant, and you had to stand around, too. He was not a commander who made allowances for time, distance, weather, or anything else. You had to execute his order whether it was possible or not. And there

(388)

was only one form of marching in his manual of tactics, and that was the double-quick. He treated you with every sort of insolence and disrespect, and the bravest of you didn't dare to say a word. You could face the death-storm at Donelson and Vicksburg, and give back blow for blow; but when he clawed your whiskers, and pulled your hair, and twisted your nose, you had to take it. When the thunders of war were sounding in your ears you set your faces toward the batteries, and advanced with steady tread; but when he turned on the terrors of his warwhoop you advanced in the other direction, and mighty glad of the chance, too. When he called for soothing-syrup, did you venture to throw out any side remarks about certain services being unbecoming an officer and a gentleman? No. You got up and *got* it. When he ordered his pap bottle and it was not warm, did you talk back? Not you. You went to work and *warmed* it. You even descended so far in your menial office as to take a suck at that warm, insipid stuff yourself, to see if it was right — three parts water to one of milk, a touch of sugar to modify the colic, and a drop of peppermint to kill those immortal hiccoughs. I can taste that stuff yet. And how many things you learned as you went along! Sentimental young folks still take stock in that beautiful old saying that when the baby smiles in his sleep, it is because the angels are whispering to him. Very pretty, but too thin — simply wind on the stomach, my friends. If the baby proposed to take a walk at his usual hour, two o'clock in the morning, didn't you rise up promptly and remark, with a mental addition which would not improve a Sunday-school book *much*, that that was the very thing you were about to propose yourself? Oh! you were under good discipline, and as you went fluttering up and down the room in your undress uniform, you not only prattled undignified baby-talk, but even tuned up your martial voices and tried to *sing !* — " Rock-a-by baby in the tree-top," for instance. What a spectacle for an Army of the Tennessee! And what an affliction for the neighbors, too; for it is not everybody within a mile around that likes military music at three in the morning. And when you had been keeping this sort of thing up two or three hours, and your little velvet-head intimated that nothing suited him like exercise and noise, what did you do? [" *Go on* !"] You simply *went* on until you dropped in the last ditch. The idea that a *baby* doesn't *amount* to anything! Why, *one* baby is just a house and a front yard full by itself. *One* baby can furnish more business than you and your whole Interior Department can attend to. He is enterprising, irrepressible, brimful of lawless activities. Do what you please, you can't make him stay on the reservation. Sufficient unto the day is one baby. As long as you are in your right mind don't you ever pray for twins. Twins amount to a permanent riot. And there ain't any real difference between triplets and an insurrection.

Yes, it was high time for a toast-master to recognize the importance of the babies. Think what is in store for the present crop! Fifty years from now we shall all be dead, I trust, and then this flag, if it still survive (and let us hope it may), will be floating over a Republic numbering 200,000,000 souls, according to the settled laws of our increase. Our present schooner of State will have grown into a political leviathan — a Great Eastern. The cradled babies of to-day will be on deck. Let them be well trained, for we are going to leave a big contract on their hands. Among the three or four million cradles now rocking in the land are some which this nation would preserve for ages as sacred things, if we could know which ones they are.

In one of these cradles the unconscious Farragut of the future is at this moment teething — think of it! — and putting in a world of dead earnest, unarticulated, but perfectly justifiable profanity over it, too. In another the future renowned astronomer is blinking at the shining Milky Way with but a languid interest — poor little chap! — and wondering what has become of that other one they call the wet-nurse. In another the future great historian is lying — and doubtless will continue to lie until his earthly mission is ended. In another the future President is busying himself with no profounder problem of state than what the mischief has become of his hair so early; and in a mighty array of other cradles there are now some 60,000 future office-seekers, getting ready to furnish him occasion to grapple with that same old problem a second time. And in still one more cradle, somewhere under the flag, the future illustrious commander-in-chief of the American armies is so little burdened with his approaching grandeurs and responsibilities as to be giving his whole strategic mind at this moment to trying to find out some way to get his big toe into his mouth — an achievement which, meaning no disrespect, the illustrious guest of this evening turned *his* entire attention to some fifty-six years ago; and if the child is but a prophecy of the man, there are mighty few who will doubt that he *succeeded*.

SPEECH ON THE WEATHER

AT THE NEW ENGLAND SOCIETY'S SEVENTY-FIRST ANNUAL DINNER, NEW YORK CITY.

The next toast was: "The Oldest Inhabitant — The Weather of New England."

> Who can lose it and forget it ?
> Who can have it and regret it ?
>
> " Be interposer 'twixt us Twain."
> *Merchant of Venice.*

To this Samuel L. Clemens (Mark Twain) replied as follows:—

I REVERENTLY believe that the Maker who made us all makes everything in New England but the weather. I don't know who makes that, but I think it must be raw apprentices in the weather-clerk's factory who experiment and learn how, in New England, for board and clothes, and then are promoted to make weather for countries that require a good article, and will take their custom elsewhere if they don't get it. There is a sumptuous variety about the New England weather that compels the stranger's admiration — and regret. The weather is always doing something there; always attending strictly to business; always getting up new designs and trying them on the people to see how they will go. But it gets through more business

in spring than in any other season. In the spring I
have counted one hundred and thirty-six different kinds
of weather inside of four-and-twenty hours. It was I
that made the fame and fortune of that man that had
that marvelous collection of weather on exhibition at
the Centennial, that so astounded the foreigners. He
was going to travel all over the world and get specimens from all the climes. I said, " Don't you do it;
you come to New England on a favorable spring day."
I told him what we could do in the way of style,
variety, and quantity. Well, he came and he made
his collection in four days. As to variety, why, he con-
fessed that he got hundreds of kinds of weather that he
had never heard of before. And as to quantity —
well, after he had picked out and discarded all that
was blemished in any way, he not only had weather
enough, but weather to spare; weather to hire out;
weather to sell; to deposit; weather to invest; weather
to give to the poor. The people of New England are
by nature patient and forbearing, but there are some
things which they will not stand. Every year they kill
a lot of poets for writing about " Beautiful Spring."
These are generally casual visitors, who bring their
notions of spring from somewhere else, and cannot, of
course, know how the natives feel about spring. And
so the first thing they know the opportunity to inquire
how they feel has permanently gone by. Old Proba-
bilities has a mighty reputation for accurate prophecy,
and thoroughly well deserves it. You take up the
paper and observe how crisply and confidently he
checks off what to-day's weather is going to be on the
Pacific, down South, in the Middle States, in the Wis-
consin region. See him sail along in the joy and pride
of his power till he gets to New England, and then see
his tail drop. *He* doesn't know what the weather is
going to be in New England. Well, he mulls over it,

and by and by he gets out something about like this:
Probable northeast to southwest winds, varying to the
southward and westward and eastward, and points between, high and low barometer swapping around from
place to place; probable areas of rain, snow, hail, and
drought, succeeded or preceded by earthquakes, with
thunder and lightning. Then he jots down this post-
script from his wandering mind, to cover accidents:
" But it is possible that the programme may be wholly
changed in the mean time." Yes, one of the brightest
gems in the New England weather is the dazzling uncertainty of it. There is only one thing certain about
it: you are certain there is going to be plenty of it —
a perfect grand review; but you never can tell which
end of the procession is going to move first. You fix
up for the drought; you leave your umbrella in the
house and sally out, and two to one you get drowned.
You make up your mind that the earthquake is due;
you stand from under, and take hold of something to
steady yourself, and the first thing you know you get
struck by lightning. These are great disappointments;
but they can't be helped. The lightning there is peculiar; it is so convincing, that when it strikes a thing it
doesn't leave enough of that thing behind for you to
tell whether — Well, you'd think it was something
valuable, and a Congressman had been there. And the
thunder. When the thunder begins to merely tune up
and scrape and saw, and key up the instruments for the
performance, strangers say, " Why, what awful thunder
you have here!" But when the baton is raised and the
real concert begins, you'll find that stranger down in
the cellar with his head in the ash-barrel. Now as to
the *size* of the weather in New England — lengthways,
I mean. It is utterly disproportioned to the size of
that little country. Half the time, when it is packed
as full as it can stick, you will see that New England

weather sticking out beyond the edges and projecting around hundreds and hundreds of miles over the neighboring States. She can't hold a tenth part of her weather. You can see cracks all about where she has strained herself trying to do it. I could speak volumes about the inhuman perversity of the New England weather, but I will give but a single specimen. I like to hear rain on a tin roof. So I covered part of my roof with tin, with an eye to that luxury. Well, sir, do you think it ever rains on that tin? No, sir; skips it every time. Mind, in this speech I have been trying merely to do honor to the New England weather — no language could do it justice. But, after all, there is at least one or two things about that weather (or, if you please, effects produced by it) which we residents would not like to part with. If we hadn't our bewitching autumn foliage, we should still have to credit the weather with one feature which compensates for all its bullying vagaries — the ice-storm: when a leafless tree is clothed with ice from the bottom to the top — ice that is as bright and clear as crystal; when every bough and twig is strung with ice-beads, frozen dewdrops, and the whole tree sparkles cold and white, like the Shah of Persia's diamond plume. Then the wind waves the branches and the sun comes out and turns all those myriads of beads and drops to prisms that glow and burn and flash with all manner of colored fires, which change and change again with inconceivable rapidity from blue to red, from red to green, and green to gold — the tree becomes a spraying fountain, a very explosion of dazzling jewels; and it stands there the acme, the climax, the supremest possibility in art or nature, of bewildering, intoxicating, intolerable magnificence. One cannot make the words too strong.

26**

CONCERNING THE AMERICAN LAN-
GUAGE *

THERE was an Englishman in our compartment,
and he complimented me on — on what? But
you would never guess. He complimented me on my
English. He said Americans in general did not speak
the English language as correctly as I did. I said I
was obliged to him for his compliment, since I knew he
meant it for one, but that I was not fairly entitled to it,
for I did not speak English at all — I only spoke
American.

He laughed, and said it was a distinction without a
difference. I said no, the difference was not prodigious, but still it was considerable. We fell into a
friendly dispute over the matter. I put my case as
well as I could, and said:

" The languages were identical several generations
ago, but our changed conditions and the spread of our
people far to the south and far to the west have made
many alterations in our pronunciation, and have introduced new words among us and changed the meanings
of many old ones. English people talk through their
noses; we do not. We say *know*, English people say
näo ; we say *cow*, the Briton says *käow ;* we —"

---

* Being part of a chapter which was crowded out of " A Tramp
Abroad."— M. T.

"Oh, come! that is pure Yankee; everybody knows that."

"Yes, it is pure Yankee; that is true. One cannot hear it in America outside of the little corner called New England, which is Yankee land. The English themselves planted it there, two hundred and fifty years ago, and there it remains; it has never spread. But England talks through her nose yet; the Londoner and the backwoods New-Englander pronounce 'know' and 'cow' alike, and then the Briton unconsciously satirizes himself by making fun of the Yankee's pronunciation."

We argued this point at some length; nobody won; but no matter, the fact remains — Englishmen say *näo* and *käow* for "know" and "cow," and that is what the rustic inhabitant of a very small section of America does.

"You conferred your *a* upon New England, too, and there it remains; it has not traveled out of the narrow limits of those six little States in all these two hundred and fifty years. All England uses it, New England's small population — say four millions — use it, but we have forty-five millions who do not use it. You say 'glahs of wawtah,' so does New England; at least, New England says *glahs*. America at large flattens the *a*, and says 'glass of water.' These sounds are pleasanter than yours; you may think they are not right — well, in English they are *not* right, but in 'American' they are. You say *flahsk*, and *bahsket*, and *jackahss;* we say 'flask,' 'basket,' 'jackass' — sounding the *a* as it is in 'tallow,' 'fallow,' and so on. Up to as late as 1847 Mr. Webster's Dictionary had the impudence to still pronounce 'basket' *bahsket*, when he knew that outside of his little New England all America shortened the *a* and paid no attention to his English broadening of it. However, it called itself an

English Dictionary, so it was proper enough that it should stick to English forms, perhaps. It still calls itself an English Dictionary to-day, but it has quietly ceased to pronounce ' basket ' as if it were spelt *bahsket*. In the American language the *h* is respected; the *h* is not dropped or added improperly.''

" The same is the case in England — I mean among the educated classes, of course.''

" Yes, that is true; but a nation's language is a very large matter. It is not simply a manner of speech obtaining among the educated handful; the manner obtaining among the vast uneducated multitude must be considered also. Your uneducated masses speak English, you will not deny that; our uneducated masses speak American — it won't be fair for you to deny that, for you can see, yourself, that when your stable-boy says, ' It isn't the 'unting that 'urts the 'orse, but the 'ammer, 'ammer, 'ammer on the 'ard 'ighway,' and our stable-boy makes the same remark without suffocating a single *h*, these two people are manifestly talking two different languages. But if the signs are to be trusted, even your educated classes used to drop the *h*. They say *humble*, now, and *heroic*, and *historic*, etc., but I judge that they used to drop those *h*'s because your writers still keep up the fashion of putting *an* before those words, instead of *a*. This is what Mr. Darwin might call a ' rudimentary ' sign that an *an* was justifiable once, and useful — when your educated classes used to say '*umble*, and '*eroic*, and '*istorical*. Correct writers of the American language do not put *an* before those words.''

The English gentleman had something to say upon this matter, but never mind what he said — I'm not arguing his case. I have him at a disadvantage, now. I proceeded:

" In England you encourage an orator by exclaiming

' H'yaah! h'yaah!' We pronounce it *heer* in some sections, ' h'*yer*' in others, and so on; but our whites do not say ' h'yaah ', pronouncing the *a*'s like the *a* in *ah*. I have heard English ladies say ' don't you '— making two separate and distinct words of it; your Mr. Burnand has satirized it. But we always say ' dontchu.' This is much better. Your ladies say, ' Oh, it's *o*ful nice !' Ours say, ' Oh, it's *aw*ful nice !' We say, '*Four* hundred,' you say '*For*'— as in the word *or*. Your clergymen speak of ' the Lawd,' ours of ' the Lord,' yours speak of ' the gawds of the heathen,' ours of ' the gods of the heathen.' When you are exhausted, you say you are ' knocked up.' We don't. When you say you will do a thing ' directly,' you mean ' immediately'; in the American language — generally speaking — the word signifies ' after a little.' When you say ' clever,' you mean ' capable'; with us the word used to mean ' accommodating,' but I don't know what it means now. Your word ' stout ' means ' fleshy'; our word ' stout ' usually means ' strong.' Your words ' gentleman ' and ' lady ' have a very restricted meaning; with us they include the barmaid, butcher, burglar, harlot, and horse thief. You say, ' I haven't *got* any stockings on,' ' I haven't *got* any memory,' ' I haven't *got* any money in my purse'; we usually say, ' I haven't any stockings on,' ' I haven't any memory,' ' I haven't any money in my purse.' You say ' out of window'; we always put in a *the*. If one asks ' How old is that man?' the Briton answers, ' He will be about forty;' in the American language, we should say, ' He *is* about forty.' However, I won't tire you, sir; but if I wanted to, I could pile up differences here until I not only convinced you that English and American are separate languages, but that when I speak my native tongue in its utmost purity an Englishman can't understand me at all.''

26

on the table — an ancient extinguisher of the " slouch " pattern, limp and shapeless with age, discolored by vicissitudes of the weather, and banded by an equator of bear's grease that had stewed through.

Another time he examined my coat. I had no terrors, for over my tailor's door was the legend, " By Special Appointment Tailor to H. R. H. the Prince of Wales," etc. I did not know at the time that the most of the tailor shops had the same sign out, and that whereas it takes nine tailors to make an ordinary man, it takes a hundred and fifty to make a prince. He was full of compassion for my coat. Wrote down the address of his tailor for me. Did not tell me to mention my *nom de plume* and the tailor would put his best work on my garment, as complimentary people sometimes do, but said his tailor would hardly trouble himself for an unknown person (unknown person, when I thought I was so celebrated in England!— that was the cruelest cut), but cautioned me to mention *his* name, and it would be all right. Thinking to be facetious, I said :

" But he might sit up all night and injure his health."

" Well, *let* him," said Rogers; " I've done enough for him, for him to show some appreciation of it."

I might as well have tried to disconcert a mummy with my facetiousness. Said Rogers: " I get all my coats there — they're the only coats fit to be seen in."

I made one more attempt. I said, " I wish you had brought one with you — I would like to look at it."

" Bless your heart, haven't I got one on?— *this* article is Morgan's make."

I examined it. The coat had been bought ready-made, of a Chatham Street Jew, without any question — about 1848. It probably cost four dollars when it was new. It was ripped, it was frayed, it was napless and greasy. I could not resist showing him where it was ripped. It so affected him that I was almost sorry I had done it. First he seemed plunged into a bottomless abyss of grief. Then he roused himself, made a feint with his hands as if waving off the pity of a nation, and said — with what seemed to me a manufactured emotion —" No matter; no matter; don't mind me; do not bother about it. I can get another."

When he was thoroughly restored, so that he could examine the rip and command his feelings, he said, ah, *now* he understood it — his servant must have done it while dressing him that morning.

His servant! There was something awe-inspiring in effrontery like this.

Nearly every day he interested himself in some article of my clothing. One would hardly have expected this sort of infatuation in a man who always wore the same suit, and it a suit that seemed coeval with the Conquest.

It was an unworthy ambition, perhaps, but I *did* wish I could make this man admire *something* about me or something I did — you would have felt the same way. I saw my opportunity: I was about to return to London, and had " listed " my soiled linen for the wash. It made quite an imposing mountain in the corner of the room — fifty-four pieces. I hoped he would fancy it was the accumulation of a single week. I took up the wash list, as if to see that it was all right, and then tossed it on the table, with pretended forgetfulness. Sure enough, he took it up and ran his eye along down to the grand total. Then he said, " You get off easy," and laid it down again.

His gloves were the saddest ruin, but he told me where I could get some like them. His shoes would hardly hold walnuts without leaking, but he liked to put his feet up on the mantel-piece and contemplate

z**

page, but can't have any wine or cigars without the butler, and can't dress without my valet.''

I offered to help him dress, but he would not hear of it; and besides, he said he would not feel comfortable unless dressed by a practiced hand. However, he finally concluded that he was such old friends with the Earl that it would not make any difference how he was dressed. So we took a cab, he gave the driver some directions, and we started. By and by we stopped before a large house and got out. I never had seen this man with a collar on. He now stepped under a lamp and got a venerable paper collar out of his coat pocket, along with a hoary cravat, and put them on. He ascended the stoop, and entered. Presently he reappeared, descended rapidly, and said:

'' Come — quick!''

We hurried away, and turned the corner.

'' Now we're safe,'' he said, and took off his collar and cravat and returned them to his pocket.

'' Made a mighty narrow escape,'' said he.

'' How?'' said I.

'' B' George, the Countess was there!''

'' Well, what of that?— don't she know you?''

'' Know me? Absolutely worships me. I just did happen to catch a glimpse of her before she saw me — and out I shot. Haven't seen her for two months — to rush in on her without any warning might have been fatal. She could *not* have stood it. I didn't know *she* was in town — thought she was at the castle. Let me lean on you — just a moment — there; now I am better — thank you; thank you ever so much. Lord bless me, what an escape!''

So I never got to call on the Earl after all. But I marked the house for future reference. It proved to be an ordinary family hotel, with about a thousand plebeians roosting in it.

In most things Rogers was by no means a fool. In some things it was plain enough that he was a fool, but he certainly did not know it. He was in the " deadest" earnest in these matters. He died at sea, last summer, as the " Earl of Ramsgate."

THE LOVES OF ALONZO FITZ CLARENCE AND ROSANNAH ETHELTON

IT was well along in the forenoon of a bitter winter's day. The town of Eastport, in the State of Maine, lay buried under a deep snow that was newly fallen. The customary bustle in the streets was wanting. One could look long distances down them and see nothing but a dead-white emptiness, with silence to match. Of course I do not mean that you could *see* the silence —no, you could only hear it. The sidewalks were merely long, deep ditches, with steep snow walls on either side. Here and there you might hear the faint, far scrape of a wooden shovel, and if you were quick enough you might catch a glimpse of a distant black figure stooping and disappearing in one of those ditches, and reappearing the next moment with a motion which you would know meant the heaving out of a shovelful of snow. But you needed to be quick, for that black figure would not linger, but would soon drop that shovel and scud for the house, thrashing itself with its arms to warm them. Yes, it was too venomously cold for snow shovelers or any body else to stay out long.

Presently the sky darkened; then the wind rose and began to blow in fitful, vigorous gusts, which sent clouds of powdery snow aloft, and straight ahead, and everywhere. Under the impulse of one of these gusts, great white drifts banked themselves like graves across the streets; a moment later, another gust shifted them around the other way, driving a fine spray of snow from their sharp crests, as the gale drives the spume flakes from wave-crests at sea; a third gust swept that place as clean as your hand, if it saw fit. This was fooling, this was play; but each and all of the gusts dumped some snow into the sidewalk ditches, for that was business.

Alonzo Fitz Clarence was sitting in his snug and elegant little parlor, in a lovely blue silk dressing-gown, with cuffs and facings of crimson satin, elaborately quilted. The remains of his breakfast were before him, and the dainty and costly little table service added a harmonious charm to the grace, beauty, and richness of the fixed appointments of the room. A cheery fire was blazing on the hearth.

A furious gust of wind shook the windows, and a great wave of snow washed against them with a drenching sound, so to speak. The handsome young bachelor murmured:

"That means, no going out to-day. Well, I am content. But what to do for company? Mother is well enough, Aunt Susan is well enough; but these, like the poor, I have with me always. On so grim a day as this, one needs a new interest, a fresh element, to whet the dull edge of captivity. That was very neatly said, but it doesn't mean anything. One doesn't *want* the edge of captivity sharpened up, you know, but just the reverse."

He glanced at his pretty French mantel-clock.

"That clock's wrong again. That clock hardly ever knows what time it is; and when it does know, it lies about it — which amounts to the same thing. Alfred!"

There was no answer.

"Alfred! . . . . . . Good servant, but as uncertain as the clock."

Alonzo touc ed an electric bell button in the wall. He waited a moment, then touched it again; waited a few moments more, and said:

" Battery out of order, no doubt. But now that I have started, I *will* find out what time it is." He stepped to a speaking-tube in the wall, blew its whistle, and called, " Mother!" and repeated it twice.

" Well, *that's* no use. Mother's battery is out of order, too. Can't raise anybody downstairs — that is plain."

He sat down at a rosewood desk, leaned his chin on the left-hand edge of it, and spoke, as if to the floor: "Aunt Susan!"

A low, pleasant voice answered, " Is that you, Alonzo?"

" Yes. I'm too lazy and comfortable to go downstairs; I am in extremity, and I can't seem to scare up any help."

" Dear me, what is the matter?"

" Matter enough, I can tell you!"

" Oh, don't keep me in suspense, dear! What *is* it?"

" I want to know what time it is."

" You abominable boy, what a turn you did give me! Is that all?"

"All — on my honor. Calm yourself. Tell me the time, and receive my blessing."

" Just five minutes after nine. No charge — keep your blessing."

" Thanks. It wouldn't have impoverished me, aunty, nor so enriched you that you could live without other means."

He got up, murmuring, " Just five minutes after nine," and faced his clock. "Ah," said he, " you are doing better than usual. You are only thirty-four minutes wrong. Let me see . . . . . . let me see . . . . . . Thirty-three and twenty-one are fifty-four; four times fifty-four are two hundred and thirty-six. One off, leaves two hundred and thirty-five. That's right.''

He turned the hands of his clock forward till they marked twenty-five minutes to one, and said, '' Now see if you can't keep right for a while . . . . . . else I'll raffle you !''

He sat down at the desk again, and said, ''Aunt Susan !''

'' Yes, dear.''

'' Had breakfast?''

'' Yes, indeed, an hour ago.''

'' Busy?''

'' No — except sewing. Why?''

'' Got any company?''

'' No, but I expect some at half-past nine.''

'' I wish *I* did. I'm lonesome. I want to talk to somebody.''

'' Very well, talk to me.''

'' But this is very private.''

'' Don't be afraid — talk right along, there's nobody here but me.''

'' I hardly know whether to venture or not, but —''

'' But what? Oh, don't stop there ! You *know* you can trust me, Alonzo — you know you can.''

'' I feel it, aunt, but this is very serious. It affects me deeply — me, and all the family — even the whole community.''

'' Oh, Alonzo, tell me ! I will never breathe a word of it. What is it?''

''Aunt, if I might dare —''

'' Oh, please go on ! I love you, and feel for you. Tell me all. Confide in me. What *is* it?''

27 **

" The weather!"

" Plague take the weather! I don't see how you can have the heart to serve me so, Lon."

" There, there, aunty dear, I'm sorry; 1 am, on my honor. I won't do it again. Do you forgive me?"

" Yes, since you seem so sincere about it, though I know I oughtn't to. You will fool me again as soon as I have forgotten this time."

" No, I won't, honor bright. But such weather, oh, such weather! You've *got* to keep your spirits up artificially. It is snowy, and blowy, and gusty, and bitter cold! How is the weather with you?"

" Warm and rainy and melancholy. The mourners go about the streets with their umbrellas running streams from the end of every whalebone. There's an elevated double pavement of umbrellas stretching down the sides of the streets as far as I can see. I've got a fire for cheerfulness, and the windows open to keep cool. But it is vain, it is useless: nothing comes in but the balmy breath of December, with its burden of mocking odors from the flowers that possess the realm outside, and rejoice in their lawless profusion whilst the spirit of man is low, and flaunt their gaudy splendors in his face while his soul is clothed in sackcloth and ashes and his heart breaketh."

Alonzo opened his lips to say, " You ought to print that, and get it framed," but checked himself, for he heard his aunt speaking to some one else. He went and stood at the window and looked out upon the wintry prospect. The storm was driving the snow before it more furiously than ever; window-shutters were slamming and banging; a forlorn dog, with bowed head and tail withdrawn from service, was pressing his quaking body against a windward wall for shelter and protection; a young girl was plowing knee-deep through the drifts, with her face turned from the blast,

and the cape of her waterproof blowing straight rearward over her head. Alonzo shuddered, and said with
a sigh, " Better the slop, and the sultry rain, and even
the insolent flowers, than this !"

He turned from the window, moved a step, and
stopped in a listening attitude. The faint, sweet notes
of a familiar song caught his ear. He remained there,
with his head unconsciously bent forward, drinking in
the melody, stirring neither hand nor foot, hardly
breathing. There was a blemish in the execution of
the song, but to Alonzo it seemed an added charm instead of a defect. This blemish consisted of a marked
flatting of the third, fourth, fifth, sixth, and seventh
notes of the refrain or chorus of the piece. When the
music ended, Alonzo drew a deep breath, and said,
"Ah, I never have heard ' In the Sweet By-and-by '
sung like that before !"

He stepped quickly to the desk, listened a moment,
and said in a guarded, confidential voice, "Aunty, who
is this divine singer ?"

" She is the company I was expecting. Stays with
me a month or two. I will introduce you. Miss —"

" For goodness' sake, wait a moment, Aunt Susan !
You never stop to think what you are about !"

He flew to his bedchamber, and returned in a moment
perceptibly changed in his outward appearance, and
remarking, snappishly :

" Hang it, she would have introduced me to this
angel in that sky-blue dressing-gown with red-hot
lapels ! Women never think, when they get a-going."

He hastened and stood by the desk, and said eagerly,
" Now, Aunty, I am ready," and fell to smiling and
bowing with all the persuasiveness and elegance that
were in him.

" Very well. Miss Rosannah Ethelton, let me introduce to you my favorite nephew, Mr. Alonzo Fitz

Clarence. There! You are both good people, and I like you; so I am going to trust you together while I attend to a few household affairs. Sit down, Rosannah; sit down, Alonzo. Good-bye; I sha'n't be gone long."

Alonzo had been bowing and smiling all the while, and motioning imaginary young ladies to sit down in imaginary chairs, but now he took a seat himself, mentally saying, " Oh, this is luck! Let the winds blow now, and the snow drive, and the heavens frown ! Little I care !"

While these young people chat themselves into an acquaintanceship, let us take the liberty of inspecting the sweeter and fairer of the two. She sat alone, at her graceful ease, in a richly furnished apartment which was manifestly the private parlor of a refined and sensible lady, if signs and symbols may go for anything. For instance, by a low, comfortable chair stood a dainty, top-heavy workstand, whose summit was a fancifully embroidered shallow basket, with varicolored crewels, and other strings and odds and ends protruding from under the gaping lid and hanging down in negligent profusion. On the floor lay bright shreds of Turkey red, Prussian blue, and kindred fabrics, bits of ribbon, a spool or two, a pair of scissors, and a roll or so of tinted silken stuffs. On a luxurious sofa, upholstered with some sort of soft Indian goods wrought in black and gold threads interwebbed with other threads not so pronounced in color, lay a great square of coarse white stuff, upon whose surface a rich bouquet of flowers was growing, under the deft cultivation of the crochet-needle. The household cat was asleep on this work of art. In a bay-window stood an easel with an unfinished picture on it, and a palette and brushes on a chair beside it. There were books everywhere: Robertson's Sermons, Tennyson, Moody and

Sanky, Hawthorne, "Rab and his Friends," cook-books, prayer-books, pattern-books — and books about all kinds of odious and exasperating pottery, of course. There was a piano, with a deck-load of music, and more in a tender. There was a great plenty of pictures on the walls, on the shelves of the mantel-piece, and around generally; where coigns of vantage offered were statuettes, and quaint and pretty gimcracks, and rare and costly specimens of peculiarly devilish china. The bay-window gave upon a garden that was ablaze with foreign and domestic flowers and flowering shrubs.

But the sweet young girl was the daintiest thing these premises, within or without, could offer for con-templation: delicately chiseled features, of Grecian cast; her complexion the pure snow of a japonica that is receiving a faint reflected enrichment from some scar-let neighbor of the garden; great, soft blue eyes fringed with long, curving lashes; an expression made up of the trustfulness of a child and the gentleness of a fawn; a beautiful head crowned with its own prodigal gold; a lithe and rounded figure, whose every attitude and movement were instinct with native grace.

Her dress and adornment were marked by that ex-quisite harmony that can come only of a fine natural taste perfected by culture. Her gown was of a simple magenta tulle, cut bias, traversed by three rows of light blue flounces, with the selvage edges turned up with ashes-of-roses chenille; overdress of dark bay tarlatan with scarlet satin lambrequins; corn-colored polonaise, *en panier*, looped with mother-of-pearl buttons and silver cord, and hauled aft and made fast by buff-velvet lashings; basque of lavender reps, picked out with valenciennes; low neck, short sleeves; maroon-velvet necktie edged with delicate pink silk; inside handker-chief of some simple three-ply ingrain fabric of a soft saffron tint; coral bracelets and locket-chain; coiffure

27

of forget-me-nots and lilies of the valley massed around a noble calla.

This was all; yet even in this subdued attire she was divinely beautiful.   Then what must she have been when adorned for the festival or the ball?

All this time she had been busily chatting with Alonzo, unconscious of our inspection.   The minutes still sped, and still she talked.   But by and by she happened to look up, and saw the clock.   A crimson blush sent its rich flood through her cheeks, and she exclaimed:

" There, good-bye, Mr. Fitz Clarence; I must go now!"

She sprang from her chair with such haste that she hardly heard the young man's answering good-bye. She stood radiant, graceful, beautiful, and gazed, wondering, upon the accusing clock.   Presently her pouting lips parted, and she said:

" Five minutes after eleven!   Nearly two hours, and it did not seem twenty minutes!   Oh, dear, what will he think of me!"

At the self-same moment Alonzo was staring at *his* clock.   And presently he said:

" Twenty-five minutes to three!   Nearly two hours, and I didn't believe it was two minutes!   Is it possible that this clock is humbugging again?   Miss Ethelton! Just one moment, please.   Are you there yet?"

" Yes, but be quick; I'm going right away."

" Would you be so kind as to tell me what time it is?"

The girl blushed again, murmured to herself, " It's right down cruel of him to ask me!" and then spoke up and answered with admirably counterfeited uncon- cern, " Five minutes after eleven."

" Oh, thank you!   You have to go, now, have you?"

" Yes."

" I'm sorry."

No reply.

" Miss Ethelton !"

" Well?"

" You — you're there yet, *ain't* you?"

" Yes; but please hurry. What did you want to say?"

" Well, I — well, nothing in particular. It's very lonesome here. It's asking a great deal, I know, but would you mind talking with me again by and by — that is, if it will not trouble you too much?"

" I don't know — but I'll think about it. I'll try."

" Oh, thanks! Miss Ethelton ! . . . . . . Ah, me, she's gone, and here are the black clouds and the whirling snow and the raging winds come again! But she said *good-bye*. She didn't say good-morning, she said good-bye! . . . . . . The clock was right, after all. What a lightning-winged two hours it was!"

He sat down, and gazed dreamily into his fire for awhile, then heaved a sigh and said :

" How wonderful it is! Two little hours ago I was a free man, and now my heart's in San Francisco !"

About that time Rosannah Ethelton, propped in the window-seat of her bed-chamber, book in hand, was gazing vacantly out over the rainy seas that washed the Golden Gate, and whispering to herself, " How different he is from poor Burley, with his empty head and his single little antic talent of mimicry !"

II.

FOUR weeks later Mr. Sidney Algernon Burley was entertaining a gay luncheon company, in a sumptuous drawing-room on Telegraph Hill, with some capital

Imitations of the voices and gestures of certain popular actors and San Franciscan literary people and Bonanza grandees. He was elegantly upholstered, and was a handsome fellow, barring a trifling cast in his eye. He seemed very jovial, but nevertheless he kept his eye on the door with an expectant and uneasy watchfulness. By and by a nobby lackey appeared, and delivered a message to the mistress, who nodded her head under-standingly. That seemed to settle the thing for Mr. Burley; his vivacity decreased little by little, and a de-jected look began to creep into one of his eyes and a sinister one into the other.

The rest of the company departed in due time, leav-ing him with the mistress, to whom he said:

" There is no longer any question about it. She avoids me. She continually excuses herself. If I could see her, if I could speak to her only a moment — but this suspense —''

" Perhaps her seeming avoidance is mere accident, Mr. Burley. Go to the small drawing-room upstairs and amuse yourself a moment. I will despatch a household order that is on my mind, and then I will go to her room. Without doubt she will be persuaded to see you.''

Mr. Burley went upstairs, intending to go to the small drawing-room, but as he was passing "Aunt Susan's '' private parlor, the door of which stood slightly ajar, he heard a joyous laugh which he recog-nized; so without knock or announcement he stepped confidently in. But before he could make his presence known he heard words that harrowed up his soul and chilled his young blood. He heard a voice say:

" Darling, it has come !''

Then he heard Rosannah Ethelton, whose back was toward him, say:

" So has yours, dearest !''

He saw her bowed form bend lower; he heard her
kiss something — not merely once, but again and again!
His soul raged within him. The heart-breaking conversation went on:

" Rosannah, I knew you must be beautiful, but this
is dazzling, this is blinding, this is intoxicating!"

"Alonzo, it is such happiness to hear you say it. I
know it is not true, but I am *so* grateful to have you
think it is, nevertheless! I knew you must have a
noble face, but the grace and majesty of the reality
beggar the poor creation of my fancy."

Burley heard that rattling shower of kisses again.

" Thank you, my Rosannah! The photograph flat-
ters me, but you must not allow yourself to think of
that. Sweetheart?"

" Yes, Alonzo."

" I am so happy, Rosannah."

" Oh, Alonzo, none that have gone before me knew
what love was, none that come after me will ever know
what happiness is. I float in a gorgeous cloudland, a
boundless firmament of enchanted and bewildering
ecstasy!"

" Oh, my Rosannah!— for you are mine, are you
not?"

" Wholly, oh, wholly yours, Alonzo, now and forever! All the day long, and all through my nightly
dreams, one song sings itself, and its sweet burden is,
'Alonzo Fitz Clarence, Alonzo Fitz Clarence, Eastport,
State of Maine! '"

" Curse him, I've got his address, anyway!" roared
Burley, inwardly, and rushed from the place.

Just behind the unconscious Alonzo stood his mother,
a picture of astonishment. She was so muffled from
head to heel in furs that nothing of herself was visible
but her eyes and nose. She was a good allegory of
winter, for she was powdered all over with snow.

Behind the unconscious Rosannah stood "Aunt Susan," another picture of astonishment. She was a good allegory of summer, for she was lightly clad, and was vigorously cooling the perspiration on her face with a fan.

Both of these women had tears of joy in their eyes.

"So ho!" exclaimed Mrs. Fitz Clarence, "this explains why nobody has been able to drag you out of your room for six weeks, Alonzo!"

"So ho!" exclaimed Aunt Susan, "this explains why you have been a hermit for the past six weeks, Rosannah!"

The young couple were on their feet in an instant, abashed, and standing like detected dealers in stolen goods awaiting Judge Lynch's doom.

"Bless you, my son! I am happy in your happiness. Come to your mother's arms, Alonzo!"

"Bless you, Rosannah, for my dear nephew's sake! Come to my arms!"

Then was there a mingling of hearts and of tears of rejoicing on Telegraph Hill and in Eastport Square.

Servants were called by the elders, in both places. Unto one was given the order, "Pile this fire high with hickory wood, and bring me a roasting-hot lemonade."

Unto the other was given the order, "Put out this fire, and bring me two palmleaf fans and a pitcher of ice-water."

Then the young people were dismissed, and the elders sat down to talk the sweet surprise over and make the wedding plans.

Some minutes before this Mr. Burley rushed from the mansion on Telegraph Hill without meeting or taking formal leave of anybody. He hissed through his teeth, in unconscious imitation of a popular favorite in

melodrama, " Him shall she never wed! I have sworn
it! Ere great Nature shall have doffed her winter's
ermine to don the emerald gauds of spring, she shall
be mine!"

III.

Two weeks later. Every few hours, during some
three or four days, a very prim and devout-looking
Episcopal clergyman, with a cast in his eye, had visited
Alonzo. According to his card, he was the Rev.
Melton Hargrave, of Cincinnati. He said he had retired from the ministry on account of his health. If he
had said on account of ill-health, he would probably
have erred, to judge by his wholesome looks and firm
build. He was the inventor of an improvement in tele-
phones, and hoped to make his bread by selling the
privilege of using it. "At present," he continued,
" a man may go and tap a telegraph wire which is
conveying a song or a concert from one State to another,
and he can attach his private telephone and steal a
hearing of that music as it passes along. My invention will stop all that."

" Well, answered Alonzo, " if the owner of the
music could not miss what was stolen, why should he
care?"

" He shouldn't care," said the Reverend.

" Well?" said Alonzo, inquiringly.

" Suppose," replied the Reverend, " suppose that,
instead of music that was passing along and being
stolen, the burden of the wire was loving endearments
of the most private and sacred nature?"

Alonzo shuddered from head to heel. " Sir, it is a
priceless invention," said he; " I must have it at any
cost."

But the invention was delayed somewhere on the road from Cincinnati, most unaccountably. The impatient Alonzo could hardly wait. The thought of Rosannah's sweet words being shared with him by some ribald thief was galling to him. The Reverend came frequently and lamented the delay, and told of measures he had taken to hurry things up. This was some little comfort to Alonzo.

One forenoon the Reverend ascended the stairs and knocked at Alonzo's door. There was no response. He entered, glanced eagerly around, closed the door softly, then ran to the telephone. The exquisitely soft and remote strains of the " Sweet By-and-by " came floating through the instrument. The singer was flatting, as usual, the five notes that follow the first two in the chorus, when the Reverend interrupted her with this word, in a voice which was an exact imitation of Alonzo's, with just the faintest flavor of impatience added :

" Sweetheart ? "

" Yes, Alonzo ? "

" Please don't sing that any more this week — try something modern."

The agile step that goes with a happy heart was heard on the stairs, and the Reverend, smiling diabolically, sought sudden refuge behind the heavy folds of the velvet window-curtains. Alonzo entered and flew to the telephone. Said he :

" Rosannah, dear, shall we sing something together ? "

" Something *modern ?* " asked she, with sarcastic bitterness.

" Yes, if you prefer."

" Sing it yourself, if you like ! "

This snappishness amazed and wounded the young man. He said :

" Rosannah, that was not like you."

" I suppose it becomes me as much as your very polite speech became you, Mr. Fitz Clarence."

"*Mister* Fitz Clarence! Rosannah, there was nothing impolite about my speech."

" Oh, indeed! Of course, then, I misunderstood you, and I most humbly beg your pardon, ha-ha-ha! No doubt you said, ' Don't sing it any more *to-day*.' "

" Sing *what* any more to-day?"

" The song you mentioned, of course. How very obtuse we are, all of a sudden!"

" I never mentioned any song."

" Oh, you *didn't* ? "

" No, I *didn't !* "

" I am compelled to remark that you *did*."

"And I am obliged to reiterate that I *didn't*."

"A second rudeness! That is sufficient, sir. I will never forgive you. All is over between us."

Then came a muffled sound of crying. Alonzo hastened to say:

' Oh, Rosannah, unsay those words! There is some dreadful mystery here, some hideous mistake. I am utterly earnest and sincere when I say I never said anything about any song. I would not hurt you for the whole world . . . . . Rosannah, dear! . . . . . . Oh, speak to me, won't you?"

There was a pause; then Alonzo heard the girl's sobbings retreating, and knew she had gone from the telephone. He rose with a heavy sigh, and hastened from the room, saying to himself, " I will ransack the charity missions and the haunts of the poor for my mother. She will persuade her that I never meant to wound her."

A minute later, the Reverend was crouching over the telephone like a cat that knoweth the ways of the prey. He had not very many minutes to wait. A soft, repentant voice, tremulous with tears, said:

there an hour, with his ear at a little box, then come sighing down, and wander wearily away. Sometimes they shot at him, as peasants do at aeronauts, thinking him mad and dangerous. Thus his clothes were much shredded by bullets and his person grievously lacerated. But he bore it all patiently.

In the beginning of his pilgrimage he used often to say, " Ah, if I could but hear the ' Sweet By and By ' !" But toward the end of it he used to shed tears of anguish and say, " Ah, if I could but hear something else!"

Thus a month and three weeks drifted by, and at last some humane people seized him and confined him in a private mad-house in New York. He made no moan, for his strength was all gone, and with it all heart and all hope. The superintendent, in pity, gave up his own comfortable parlor and bedchamber to him and nursed him with affectionate devotion.

At the end of a week the patient was able to leave his bed for the first time. He was lying, comfortably pillowed, on a sofa, listening to the plaintive Miserere of the bleak March winds, and the muffled sound of tramping feet in the street below — for it was about six in the evening, and New York was going home from work. He had a bright fire and the added cheer of a couple of student lamps. So it was warm and snug within, though bleak and raw without; it was light and bright within, though outside it was as dark and dreary as if the world had been lit with Hartford gas. Alonzo smiled feebly to think how his loving vagaries had made him a maniac in the eyes of the world, and was proceeding to pursue his line of thought further, when a faint, sweet strain, the very ghost of sound, so remote and attenuated it seemed, struck upon his ear. His pulses stood still; he listened with parted lips and bated breath. The song flowed

on — he waiting, listening, rising slowly and unconsciously from his recumbent position.   At last he exclaimed:

" It is! it is she!   Oh, the divine flatted notes!"

He dragged himself eagerly to the corner whence the
sounds proceeded, tore aside a curtain, and discovered
a telephone.   He bent over, and as the last note died
away he burst forth with the exclamation:

" Oh, thank Heavens, found at last!   Speak to me,
Rosannah, dearest!   The cruel mystery has been un-
raveled; it was the villain Burley who mimicked my
voice and wounded you with insolent speech!"

There was a breathless pause, a waiting age to
Alonzo; then a faint sound came, framing itself into
language:

" Oh, say those precious words again, Alonzo!"

" They are the truth, the veritable truth, my Rosannah, and you shall have the proof, ample and abundant
proof!"

" Oh, Alonzo, stay by me!   Leave me not for a
moment!   Let me feel that you are near me!   Tell
me we shall never be parted more!   Oh, this happy
hour, this blessed hour, this memorable hour!"

" We will make record of it, my Rosannah; every
year, as this dear hour chimes from the clock, we will
celebrate it with thanksgivings, all the years of our
life."

" We will, we will, Alonzo!"

" Four minutes after six, in the evening, my Rosannah, shall henceforth —"

" Twenty-three minutes after twelve, afternoon,
shall —"

" Why, Rosannah, darling, where are you?"

" In Honolulu, Sandwich Islands.   And where are
you?   Stay by me; do not leave me for a moment.   I
cannot bear it.   Are you at home?"

28 **

" No, dear, I am in New York — a patient in the doctor's hands."

An agonizing shriek came buzzing to Alonzo's ear, like the sharp buzzing of a hurt gnat; it lost power in traveling five thousand miles. Alonzo hastened to say:

" Calm yourself, my child. It is nothing. Already I am getting well under the sweet healing of your presence. Rosannah?"

" Yes, Alonzo? Oh, how you terrified me! Say on."

" Name the happy day, Rosannah!"

There was a little pause. Then a diffident small voice replied, " I blush — but it is with pleasure, it is with happiness. Would — would you like to have it soon?"

" This very night, Rosannah! Oh, let us risk no more delays. Let it be now! — this very night, this very moment!"

" Oh, you impatient creature! I have nobody here but my good old uncle, a missionary for a generation, and now retired from service — nobody but him and his wife. I would so dearly like it if your mother and your Aunt Susan —"

" *Our* mother and *our* Aunt Susan, my Rosannah."

" Yes, *our* mother and *our* Aunt Susan — I am content to word it so if it pleases you; I would so like to have them present."

" So would I. Suppose you telegraph Aunt Susan. How long would it take her to come?"

" The steamer leaves San Francisco day after to-morrow. The passage is eight days. She would be here the 31st of March."

" Then name the 1st of April; do, Rosannah, dear."

" Mercy, it would make us April fools, Alonzo!"

" So we be the happiest ones that that day's sun looks down upon in the whole broad expanse of the globe, why need we care? Call it the 1st of April, dear."

" Then the 1st of April it shall be, with all my heart!"

" Oh, happiness! Name the hour, too, Rosannah."

" I like the morning, it is so blithe. Will eight in the morning do, Alonzo?"

" The loveliest hour in the day — since it will make you mine."

There was a feeble but frantic sound for some little time, as if wool-lipped, disembodied spirits were exchanging kisses; then Rosannah said, " Excuse me just a moment, dear; I have an appointment, and am called to meet it."

The young girl sought a large parlor and took her place at a window which looked out upon a beautiful scene. To the left one could view the charming Nuuana Valley, fringed with its ruddy flush of tropical flowers and its plumed and graceful cocoa palms; its rising foot-hills clothed in the shining green of lemon, citron, and orange groves; its storied precipice beyond, where the first Kamehameha drove his defeated foes over to their destruction — a spot that had forgotten its grim history, no doubt, for now it was smiling, as almost always at noonday, under the glowing arches of a succession of rainbows. In front of the window one could see the quaint town, and here and there a picturesque group of dusky natives, enjoying the blistering weather; and far to the right lay the restless ocean, tossing its white mane in the sunshine.

Rosannah stood there, in her filmy white raiment, fanning her flushed and heated face, waiting. A Kanaka boy, clothed in a damaged blue necktie and part of a silk hat, thrust his head in at the door, and announced, " 'Frisco *haole* !"

" Show him in," said the girl, straightening herself

piece of river with the " High Bridge " over it got left out to one side by reason of a slip of the graving-tool, which rendered it necessary to change the entire course of the River Rhine, or else spoil the map. After having spent two days in digging and gouging at the map, I would have changed the course of the Atlantic Ocean before I would lose so much work.

I never had so much trouble with anything in my life as I had with this map. I had heaps of little fortifications scattered all around Paris at first, but every now and then my instruments would slip and fetch away whole miles of batteries, and leave the vicinity as clean as if the Prussians had been there.

The reader will find it well to frame this map for future reference, so that it may aid in extending popular intelligence, and in dispelling the widespread ignorance of the day.   MARK TWAIN.

OFFICIAL COMMENDATIONS.

It is the only map of the kind I ever saw.

         U. S. GRANT.

_____

It places the situation in an entirely new light.

         BISMARCK.

_____

I cannot look upon it without shedding tears.

         BRIGHAM YOUNG.

_____

It is very nice large print.

         NAPOLEON.

_____

My wife was for years afflicted with freckles, and, though everything was done for her relief that could be done, all was in vain. But, sir, since her first glance at your map, they have entirely left her. She has nothing but convulsions now.

         J. SMITH.

MAP OF PARIS

BB**

If I had had this map, I could have got out of Metz without any trouble.

BAZAINE.

I have seen a great many maps in my time, but none that this one reminds me of.

TROCHU.

It is but fair to say that in some respects it is a truly remarkable map.

W. T. SHERMAN.

I said to my son Frederick William, "If you could only make a map like that. I should be perfectly willing to see you die — even anxious."

WILLIAM III.

LETTER READ AT A DINNER

OF THE KNIGHTS OF ST. PATRICK

HARTFORD, CONN., March 16, 1876.

TO THE CHAIRMAN:

DEAR SIR,— I am very sorry that I cannot be with the Knights of St. Patrick to-morrow evening. In this centennial year we ought to find a peculiar pleasure in doing honor to the memory of a man whose good name has endured through fourteen centuries. We ought to find pleasure in it for the reason that at this time we naturally have a fellow-feeling for such a man. He wrought a great work in his day. He found Ireland a prosperous republic, and looked about him to see if he might find some useful thing to turn his hand to. He observed that the president of that republic was in the habit of sheltering his great officials from deserved punishment, so he lifted up his staff and smote him, and he died. He found that the secretary of war had been so unbecomingly economical as to have laid up $12,000 a year out of a salary of $8,000; and he killed him. He found that the secretary of the interior always prayed over every separate and distinct barrel of salt beef that was intended for the unconverted savage, and then kept that beef himself, so he killed him also. He found that the secretary of the navy knew more about handling suspicious claims than he did

(437)

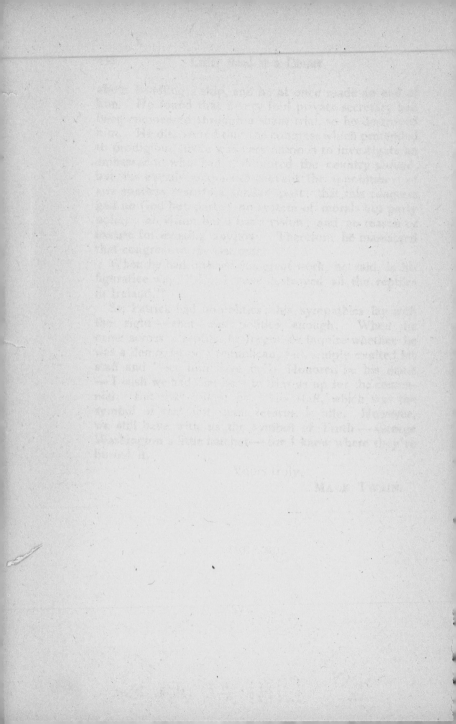

about founding a club, and he at once made us one of them. He found that every last private secretary had been engaged through a single firm, so he dismissed him. He discovered that the congress which prevented its founding, appointed a committee to investigate an implement which had wellnigh cost the country untold loss and expense, suspected that the operations of our machine would be exactly such; that this congress had no fixed legislation, no system of members, no party policy, on whom but I have relied, and no manner of excuse for existing anyhow. Therefore he reasoned that congress would be useless.

"When he had done his wonderful work, he said, in his figurative way, ... he destroyed all the reptiles in Ireland."

So I think that no orator, his sympathies lay with the right—that was probably enough. When he came across a republican I began to inquire whether he was a Democrat or a republican, but simply realized his zeal and . . . his case. . . . Heaven be his mind. —I wish we could see him be flung up for his country. . . . . . which was the symbol of that our own country, ... However, we still have with us the symbol of Truth—George Washington's little hatchet— for I know where they've buried it.

                        Yours truly,
                                MARK TWAIN.